Zero Degree Murder

David A. Thyfault

ISBN 978-1-950647-18-7

Published by BookCrafters, Parker, Colorado.
www.bookcrafters.net

This book may be ordered from online bookstores.

DEDICATION

To my readers.

Without you, this retired writer might have to keep all his goofy ideas to himself and instead spend his time watching daytime game shows on TV. That could drive a person insane.

Thank you all for inspiring me, encouraging me and indulging me as I hide my thoughts inside the minds of the characters who reside in the pages of my books.

ACKNOWLEDGEMENTS

George Andrews, for federal police information
Ricky Fitzsimmons, volunteer editor
Liz Netzel, professional editor
Dan Rhode, for boating terms
Chris Tracy, banking expert
BookCrafters Publishing

Extra-special thanks goes out to my long-time friend, the real Allen, who was indeed an undercover officer for the LAPD. We had sit-down meetings, phone calls, recorded conversations and plenty of email exchanges. This is not his biography, but a large portion of the plot is based on his real-life experiences. On the other hand, this is a fiction book, and writers are allowed a few liberties.

1

1978 - NORTH HOLLYWOOD, CALIFORNIA

"Have you ever killed a nigger?"

Of course, I hadn't. I hated that word and the people who used it, but I couldn't tell the KKK's premier interrogator and his shiny-headed partner that because I'd told them otherwise when I first went undercover and infiltrated their group, or den, as they called it.

Furthermore, there was no telling what the 16 assholes down the hall would do if they discovered I had duped them all. Despite the fact that I was hooked up to their lie detector, I had to stick with my original story, vulgarities and all. "Hell, yes," I lied, "and that black bastard deserved it."

The needle danced.

"We know," the polygrapher said without lifting his head. "Just gimme a simple yes or no."

Yeah, right. Easy for them to say. Contrary to my surface-level confidence, I was caught completely off-guard because my handler, Lieutenant Jack Aladar, had fucked up big time. He should have warned me that there might come a day when some of my new sheet-headed affiliates would drag me into a back room for this purpose. I had to think fast.

I knew full well that they asked that particular question

because of the sham newspaper article I'd slipped them months earlier when I made my initial contact.

In that article, an African American father of three in Mississippi had been intentionally run over multiple times and died as a result. The article speculated that the perps of that bogus crime were either Klan members carrying out one of the Grand Wizard's death orders or a like-minded lone wolf.

Like I said, that article was as phony as a three-dollar bill, but the department could get away with printing shit like that in the pre-tech era of the late '70s.

Anyway, since the faux murder was supposed to have taken place clear across the country, it would be nearly impossible for any outsider, even a Klan member from another den, to verify who killed the fictitious victim; therefore, the door was wide open for my scam and these knuckleheads fell for it.

Prior to that day, if somebody were to have asked me what I'd expect the Klan's super quizzer to look like, I would have defined a diminutive brainiac with glasses, a white shirt and a skinny necktie, but this fella looked more like a former interior lineman for the NFL. Balding, with big muscular hands, the dude was a pharmaceuticals salesman by day and usually hid his tats beneath long sleeves.

Ironically, everybody around there called him Tiny, but his real name was Samuel Goode. That night he was on loan from one of the other nearby dens.

"Are you in law enforcement?" he asked.

Of course, I was—in an undercover role for the LAPD's Public Disorder Intelligence Division, or PDID, but I couldn't admit that to these two.

"No," I lied.

This time the needle yawned. How the hell could that be? I'd lied both times but got two completely different responses. Apparently, polys were like people; you could fool all of them some of the time. As he had done several times before, Tiny penciled in his notebook.

Skinhead's real name was Earl Someda. He'd retired after spending a couple decades working on offshore oilrigs. He too was pudgy. He also happened to be my greatest cheerleader. At that moment, he had a hell of lot more confidence in me than I had.

I later learned that the regulars brought their new guys, like me, along slowly to make 'em comfortable; then, when the leaders thought they had the best chance to catch us off-guard, an impromptu quiz like this sprang from their bowels. This particular reaming was in Skinhead's basement. Like it or not, I was the equivalent of a fat man's suppository; wedged right in the middle of a couple king-sized butt cheeks.

I had no idea how this little game of three-man chess would play out, but I did know that I had to act cocky, like a legit Klansman would. I pointed my chin at Tiny as if I welcomed his next question.

"Have you ever worked for the government?"

They'd already asked a few questions along those lines, so I was beginning to figure out their goals and tactics. "Just the Marines," I said, knowing they'd correct me and I'd have a little more time to gather my wits.

Tiny sighed. "Just say yes or no."

"Sorry, but I didn't know if the Marines qualified as a government job."

"Forget it. I'll ask you something else."

Of course, I knew plenty about lying, both from my personal life and from all the people I'd pulled over as an LA police officer when I patrolled in a black and white.

In those situations, the liars tended to look around and blink their eyes quite a bit, as opposed to the truth tellers. They usually looked right at me. Obviously, none of that shit mattered to the tattletale machine because it couldn't read my eyes.

Even though I knew plenty about lying, I only had a little experience with polys. It occurred to me that if I played by their rules, I'd likely fail their exam and things could get very ugly, very quickly. After all, the whiskey fans and beer-guzzlers in the other end of Earl's basement actually looked forward to their turns in the room so that they could prove their support for the cause.

I wasn't stupid enough to think that if it were discovered that I'd infiltrated their group and a fight broke out, I had any kind of chance against the entire den.

I reasoned that if I were going to outsmart the nervous needle, I needed to break their rules without them realizing I was doing so, and I was pretty good at breaking rules. I glared into Tiny's peepers. "You guys don't know how much those sons-a-bitches piss me off."

Earl's head bobbed approvingly, while Tiny's jaw visibly tightened. Then, "Just answer the questions. Don't volunteer anything."

Then I got an idea: to do so poorly on the control questions that they wouldn't believe their own results.

"Are we in Los Angles?"

And there it was; the question that changed everything —a potential get-out-of-jail-free card. I scrunched my toes in my boots so hard that they felt as if a truck had just run over them.

"Yes," I said, hiding the pain and telling the truth for a change. All three of us glanced toward the needle. Due to the pain, it detected stress and quivered. Good. Each of us knew we were in LA, but the oft-reliable poly suggested my answer might have been deceptive. I relaxed my ailing toes as another mark found Tiny's notebook.

From that moment on I wanted the machine to suggest that I might be lying when we all knew I was telling the truth. If they knew their machine was inaccurate, they sure as hell couldn't declare me a liar—and I wouldn't get my ass kicked.

"Were you born in Minnesota?"

Thankfully, the department was good at overhauling backgrounds. By the time they were done replacing the truth with divorces and criminal records and seedy affiliations, you actually sounded interesting.

I'd already told the Klan boys that I'd been born in Minnesota and I gave them an address that they could verify, which they did. I paused about five seconds until Skinhead blinked. I squeezed my toes. Then, "Yes," I said. The needle twitched, thereby contradicting their own research.

After a few more questions, my toes begged for a break, so I shifted my attention to my butt cheeks. Before long, I developed a painful hemorrhoid. That war wound gave me another reason to chew my handler's ass.

"That's all for today," Tiny said.

Thank God! Skinhead and I rose while Tiny prepared for the next guy. In the hall, "How'd I do?" I asked.

"'Inconclusive.' I wouldn't worry about it. I get that grade once in a while too. Go get yourself a beer."

Good enough. At least for the time being, everybody still believed that I was a raving racist.

Oh, by the way, my name's Padget; Allen Padget. I had no idea that it would be a year before my next poly, but I did know that the trick was to stay alive until then.

2

THE PRESENT - DEL MAR, CALIFORNIA

Any ichthyologist can tell you that the deep pools in trout streams are deceiving because there's a lot more going on beneath the surface than appears. People could be like that too. Such was the case for six-foot-five bank officer Julius Patrick Crain—aka, JP—of CalWest Bank of Del Mar, California.

JP's sharp attire, flashy smile and delightfully affable personality shone bright to all those who met him. But below his calm surface where the truth resided, JP's motives brewed dark. He closed his new laptop and clicked his office radio to the business station.

"The state of California is worth four trillion dollars," the radio commentator said while JP listened closely. *"That's more than the value of most countries around the world."*

It sure as hell was. An expert mathematician, JP knew that each trillion was a thousand billions, and each billion was a thousand millions. That meant there were literally millions and millions of millions in the state, and a smart fellow who had the same initials as famous rich guys JP Morgan and John Paul Getty ought to be able to pocket one or more of those millions.

A familiar tick from his phone indicated that Sarah Burns,

the receptionist out in the lobby, probably had another mundane chore for him to do. *"JP? Can you help somebody get into her safe deposit box?"*

"Sure thing," he said with feigned enthusiasm. After all, he wasn't a millionaire just yet, and still had to play the corporate games until a worthy opportunity came knocking.

He dutifully marched to the lobby where he instantly recognized the nondescript middle-aged woman wearing tennis shoes and blue jeans and carrying an ordinary imitation leather bag. "Mrs. Clayton," he said, recalling her likeable and chatty personality. "It's so nice to see you. I understand you want to get into your deposit box?"

Mrs. Clayton glanced side-to-side like a cartoon spy and bobbed her head quickly. "For this," she said holding up a typical white envelope that appeared to be shaking in her fingers.

Since bank officers weren't supposed to ask questions about the various things customers kept in their boxes, JP ignored her comment and pointed toward the back of the bank. "This way. How's Mr. Clayton doing?"

She grinned. "Better than he realizes. God knows we've had our share of financial problems. He's tried hard, but he worries, gets frustrated. That leads to drinking and then worse. The neighbors have called the police. One time they took him to jail for striking me. But all of that has changed, now, thanks to what's in this envelope."

"I'm sure glad to hear that."

"He's basically a good man when he's not drinking. That's why I'm so happy. We finally got to take a really special vacation. A few months ago, we agreed that if he'd take me to London, he could go on a sportfishing trip when we returned—you know, those deep-sea trips they take out of San Diego. He always goes as a single so he can have some alone time on the boat."

"Oh, yeah," JP said as they reached the sign-in cabinet, which was intentionally positioned out of sight of surveillance cameras for insurance purposes. "I hear they catch some big tuna on those boats. That must be fun. So, when did you go on your trip?"

"A while back, but he didn't get excited about the fishing trip until a few days ago when he heard about El Nino. That's supposed to make it better."

JP unlocked a drawer and retrieved a file box that contained the signature cards of all the customers who had boxes in the vault. He found Mrs. Clayton's card and placed it on the table. "You know the routine. Sign here."

After she penned her name, he added his initials as a witness.

"When Stu gets to go fishing, he's like a little boy," she continued. "He gets excited and does the same thing every time. His favorite boat, the Pacific *Trawler*, leaves at 10 o'clock tomorrow night, but he'll go down to the docks a few hours early so he can reserve one of the little private bedrooms below the main floor."

"That sounds fun," JP said, returning the box to its rightful spot and then unlocking the thick vault door.

"You'll never guess what happened," Mrs. Clayton whispered.

"What?" JP playfully whispered back as they entered the vault, where a large, heavy table was built into one wall and several hundred safety deposit boxes of various sizes lined two other walls.

"I just have to tell somebody. When we were in London, I bought a few lottery tickets. I put them in my luggage and forgot I even bought them. But this morning after my husband went to the barbershop, I found them again and checked the internet." Once again, she fanned the air with her envelope. "At first, I thought I made a mistake, but I double-checked it. I'm not good at those conversion tables, but you must know this kind of thing. How many dollars are there in four million pounds anyway?"

Interesting. This was the kind of thing bank officers weren't supposed to know, but JP couldn't put the words back in Mrs. Clayton's mouth. Instead, he smiled and respectfully answered her question. "It varies a little from day to day but one pound is roughly a dollar and a quarter so that would be about three million American dollars."

A big smile splashed across her lips. "I thought it was something like that. That's why I came right down to the bank without telling anybody about the ticket. I want to put it in my safe deposit box, so I don't lose it."

"Well, congratulations. I don't blame you." Since it always took both a bank key and a customer's key to get into the customer's boxes, JP reached above his head for the top row where the Clayton's box was and inserted the bank's key. "We'll need your key, too."

"Oops, sorry," she said, pointing to her temple. She plopped her purse on the table and scrounged for the little red envelope that the bank gave the customers for their keys. "I've decided not to tell anybody about the ticket until my husband comes back from his trip. Otherwise, he'd get so excited, he'd cancel his vacation and I want him to enjoy himself first."

"That'll be one heck of a surprise."

"Here it is," she said handing him the key packet.

He pulled a stepping stool over so she could reach her box. "Here ya go."

She put one foot on the bottom step of the stool, then stopped and turned to JP. "Would you mind handing me my key from that little red packet?"

And there it was: JP's get-rich-quick opportunity. Obviously, Mrs. Clayton didn't realize that there were two keys in the red key packet. After all, they were very thin and a customer could easily make that mistake.

But JP could tell the difference, just as easily as if he were fondling pennies in his pocket. "Of course," he said.

Fortunately for him, banks never had surveillance cameras in the safe deposit box area. He opened the envelope, poured out both keys, palmed one and handed the other to Mrs. Clayton. "Here you go."

Standing on the top step of the stool, she turned around and inserted her key in the lock, thereby enabling JP to pocket the palmed key. "Uh-oh," she said. "My knees are too jittery to pull out the box and get back down this little ladder. Would you mind doing me one more favor?"

He smiled. "Sure thing." He waited for her to come back down the stool, reached for the box and placed it on the table. "I'm supposed to leave the vault while you do your thing," he said. "I'll be right outside the door. Let me know when you're done, and we'll put everything back where it belongs."

A few minutes later, she said, "I'm ready."

JP returned to the room, slid the box into its rightful spot, locked it all up and returned Mrs. Clayton's key to its envelope. "Here ya go, Mrs. Clayton. Is there anything else I can do for you today?"

"No, thank you," she said, slipping the envelope into her purse. "This was all I wanted."

That was all JP wanted, too. As Mrs. Clayton walked toward the exit doors, JP tapped the key in his pocket.

3

One thing I learned in my 40 years of police work, including my stint inside the KKK, was that when there were 7,000 officers and 2,000 civilians working for the LAPD, there was lots of room for problems. I'd certainly done a few things I wasn't proud of, both in my personal life and as an officer, but I also had a good quality or two.

For instance, I never liked all the labeling. I didn't like the "N" word. I didn't even like it when people referred to us as "cops," which was actually an acronym originating in the UK. C.O.P. stood for Constable On Patrol. So, for me, we were police officers, not cops.

Anyway, a person might wonder what would cause a particular officer of a huge department like the LAPD to actually want to infiltrate the Klan. In my case it wasn't particularly that I wanted to; it was either that or go insane from a horrendous accident that took place a year prior to my infamous lie detector test.

Way back then, I was a Police Officer II, or P-II, with a degree from a small mountain college and a three-year stint in the Marines. I'd been in the force for an additional three years and was about to make P-III, with an eye on becoming a sergeant. I had no idea that the proverbial shit was about to hit the fan and turn my life inside down and upside out.

I was no wimp and neither was my partner, Larry Montoya. He'd been patrolling in black and whites for nine years and had seen a lot of conflicts, particularly in the high-drama neighborhoods. An especially good shot, Larry had sent two gang members to their graves and a few others to the hospital. Everybody respected him.

Since we never knew when we'd be up against some drug-crazed assholes, we both pumped iron to strengthen our chances.

Up to that day, most of our time was spent breaking up domestic disputes and bar fights, plus dealing with minor crimes, traffic violations and auto accidents. Fortunately, I'd never had to shoot anybody—but that was about to change.

Now, I shake my head. I must have gotten complacent or overconfident because I sure as hell didn't anticipate the unstoppable runaway train that had my name on it.

It was late summer. Larry and I had been on patrol for an hour and made a couple routine stops before a dispatcher called all units to a 211 in progress in Lake View Terrace, where Rodney King would later be taken down. Larry hit the siren and flashing reds, while I handled the radio.

That store had been popped several times recently and once during our shift, but the suspects always got away before the department could get anybody over there. This time it was different. A woman who lived in the area had pulled into the parking lot just as the black suspect went into the store with a drawn gun. She immediately called 911 and we were there in mere minutes. From past experience, we knew the storeowner was also an African American.

Arriving at the scene, there was no sign of the female caller but an older, dark blue vehicle with no plates, presumably a get-away vehicle, was backed into a parking spot near the entrance. Larry parked where he could get a bead on both the front door of the store and the driver's side of the suspect's vehicle. We immediately drew our weapons and Jack-in-the-boxed out of the squad car.

To become a smaller target, Larry squatted and took cover behind our vehicle while I bolted to the side of the store with my two deadly friends—Smith and Wesson. From my vantage point I could watch both the front door and the only other exit door, which was at the back corner on that same side of the building. I reminded myself that if a gunfight was unavoidable, the most important rule was to "win" because nothing good happened to the man who ended up in second place.

Next, I wasn't about to send a stray bullet into somebody else's world, so I scanned the area that would be the backdrop to any confrontation or stray bullets. Across the lot there were two buildings side by side: a restaurant with a good-sized stucco wall and a printing store with lots of windows. If I was going to get a clean shot at the suspect, it would have to be with the stucco building in the background, which meant I'd have to take the shot while the suspect was still standing fairly close to the liquor store.

The next thing to do was draw the suspect outside so we could watch his every move and have a clean shot if we needed it. As soon as Larry saw the suspect, he yelled, "Police. Come out with your hands up. You can't get away."

By that time, the suspect probably knew that our backup would be there at any moment. Seconds later, with a bear hug around the owner's neck, the suspect nudged the owner out the front door and we had a hostage situation. Then I saw the suspect's gun upside the owner's temple.

I sighted the suspect's head but didn't shoot because there wasn't enough separation between him and the owner.

Larry tried again. "Drop the gun, asshole."

The suspect looked right at Larry. "No way. You gotta back off or I'm going to blow this guy's fucking head off."

"Do what he said," the petrified owner pleaded with Larry.

As far as I could tell, neither the owner nor the suspect knew that I was off to their side.

"You can't win this," Larry said. "Let that man go."

13

Suddenly the owner dropped down, pulled away and ran toward Larry, causing the suspect to panic and aim at the man.

In a split second, I knew that Larry couldn't shoot because the owner was between him and the suspect. It was up to me. I pulled my trigger and watched the suspect's head jerk to the side as the bullet sprayed his hair and brain tissue like water out of a sprinkler hose. His knees collapsed. His limp body dropped.

Still cautious, Larry and I moved toward the suspect with guns drawn. A closer look erased any doubts. For the first time in my career I'd killed a man—a man who probably had a family: kids, a wife, at least a mom.

While Larry called for a rescue ambulance and a supervisor, I stood motionless for a few seconds before I holstered my weapon. Then the owner rushed over and thanked me, but I found myself conflicted. A big part of me was pleased for having saved his life, but another part of me felt sorry for both the owner and the suspect.

I knew a lot of African American males had two strikes against them on the day they were born. There was a 70% chance that their mother was unwed, a 50% chance she'd dropped out of high school, and a 70% chance she was not employed.

In spite of all that, a fair number of them fought it out and made an honest living, while others felt hopeless and turned to crime. There was one of each of those stereotypes within my arms' reach, but only one was still alive.

By that time other patrol cars arrived. I got a few "attaboys" from the other officers as they set up a crime scene and kept the neighbors at bay.

Then a call came in on our car radio. It was bad news about my wife and our young son.

4

If JP Crain were going to steal Joann Clayton's London lottery ticket—and get away with it—he needed some help. In Escondido, a modest inland town, he rushed toward the home of his friends, Kyle Ward and Cassandra Sevvy.

Kyle was a great choice for a job like JP had in mind because his blood ran so cold that when he cut himself shaving he practically dripped bloodsickles. Cassandra was a good choice because, well, because she was gorgeous and well-built and would do nearly anything Kyle wanted.

At the correct stucco home, complete with a tile roof, JP knocked and let himself in just as Cassandra walked out of the bathroom, wet-haired and wrapped in a large towel. She "eeked" and hustled toward the bedroom. If JP hadn't had something urgent on his mind, he would have cursed that towel.

"You're early, man," Kyle said, coming from the kitchen. "You want a beer?"

JP nodded. "Yeah, but hurry up. I know how we can all get rich."

"You know me, I'm all for that, but why couldn't you tell me on the phone?"

"Cause it's going to take a little planning. I need both of you to pull this off."

A few minutes later, JP and Kyle sat in the living room on

15

a pair of recliners while Cassandra, now wearing blue jeans and a T-shirt, listened from the bathroom and fussed with her hair.

"This morning," JP began, "a bank customer put a winning lotto ticket in her safe deposit box, and I know how we can get at it."

Kyle pursed his lips. "Sounds risky. How much we talking about?"

"It's from the London lottery. About four million pounds or three million American dollars."

"That's a lot of money alright, but what are we supposed to do, dynamite the place, 'cause as far as I know those vaults are tighter than a virgin?"

"How would you know?" Cassandra teasingly asked from the bathroom.

"Just guessing, sweetie."

JP sat forward. "Everybody thinks that those vaults are secure, but if you know what you're doing, they're very vulnerable."

"No way, dude. Banks have surveillance cameras everywhere."

"You're both right and wrong, buddy. They do indeed have cameras all over the place, but the deposit box vault is the exception. It's an insurance matter. The banks don't have any way of knowing what's in the customers' boxes so they don't want the responsibility for the contents if something goes wrong. They don't even have a camera over the vault door to see who goes in and out of the vault."

"But don't you have to sign in to get inside the vault?"

"You would think so, but all they have is an antiquated card and box system. That's not under surveillance either. All we have to do is pretend we're signing a card and nobody will know otherwise. The only problem is you have to have two different keys to get into the individual boxes; the bank has one and the customer has one. And guess what. I've already got that handled."

16

"You do? How?"

"Because I have copies of both keys. As an officer of the bank I have access to the bank's key and I just happened to get the lady's spare key. The problem is we only have a brief window to snag the ticket before she's going to come back for it. I know how to permanently handle that, too, but I need both of you."

Cassandra came from the bathroom. "It sounds like you're talking about murder, JP. I don't like that."

"You can leave that part to Kyle and me, but when we're all done, I'll split the whole ticket with you guys 50/50."

Kyle twisted his head to the side. "Hold on there, buddy. I gotta admit that a big pay-off like that is worth breaking bigger rules, but if all three of us are needed to pull this off, then we should split the money three ways. That's a million each. I ain't even going to talk about it no more unless you agree to that." He turned to Cassandra. "You agree with that, don't you, sweetie?"

"A million dollars? Just for me? If I don't have to kill anybody and if you're one hundred percent certain we're not going to get caught, I could stand a million bucks. I could finally get me a good car."

* * *

The next day, JP waited for the late morning to implement the opening move to nab Mrs. Clayton's lottery ticket. At 11:45, Sarah Burns, the receptionist, clocked out for her lunch break, which required a different employee, Valerie Cole, to take her place.

In his private office, JP rose to his feet, stood in front of the large windows, turned to the side and opened a file, which was the signal for a slightly taller and younger Joann Clayton to return to her safe deposit box. Outside and a half-block away, Cassandra Sevvy got the signal. She drove to the prearranged corner of the lot, where surveillance cameras had a blind spot, and pulled a dark brown wig forward to cover the bulk of her forehead.

Minutes later, wearing minimal make-up and bland clothing, Cassandra made her entrance. Not coincidently, JP was standing off to the side. "Mrs. Clayton," he said instantly in his usually cheerful voice, "can I help you with something?" Cassandra turned her head toward JP and away from the greeter's desk so Valerie Cole couldn't get a good look at her face. "I need to put something in my safe deposit box."

"No problem. I'll take you back there."

At the sign-in cabinet, and safely out of sight of nosey surveillance cameras, JP retrieved the same box of signature cards as the day before. He pulled out a random card and slid it and a pen toward Cassandra, who pretended to sign the card. Then, JP faked a signature, returned the box of cards to the drawer and unlocked the vault door.

Safely inside, he inserted both his official key and the one he stole from Mrs. Clayton's envelope into her safe deposit box. With the box on the table, he snagged the white envelope with the lottery ticket from within the box.

"Did you bring the letter?" he whispered.

Cassandra tapped her purse and spoke softly. "Without fingerprints. What about you? Did you get registered for the fishing trip?"

"Yes. I called the dock a couple hours ago. What about Kyle? Did he get the other things we talked about?"

"No problem. He's ready."

With his partners squared away and the loose ends wrapped up, JP raised his voice to normal volume and spoke as he would to any other customer. "I'm not allowed in here when you open your box, Mrs. Clayton, so I'll stand outside the vault. Just speak up when you're done and we'll put everything back where it belongs."

While JP waited outside the vault, Cassandra placed her envelope in the box.

"Ready, Mr. Crain," Cassandra said.

5

"Into each life some rain must fall." For this officer, the rain of which Longfellow spoke came gushing from a horrific car crash near Glendale, on an otherwise sunny day. In that moment, life wasn't fair; not for my wife, Dorene; nor for our innocent three-year-old son, Junior; and certainly not for me.

After all, I'd just taken out a dangerous suspect before he could kill a storeowner or my partner. I should have been filling out paperwork. I should have been thanking God that I wasn't killed, thereby erasing my son's daddy and my wife's partner. I should have been planning an after-work gathering at a bar with a few other officers. But none of that was in the dark cloud overhead.

If I had known how the accident was going to change my life, I would have preferred to trade places with the guy I'd just killed. At least his rainy day was over before he hit the ground. But none of that was evident until my supervisor arrived at the scene.

Instead of heaping an "attaboy" on me, the sergeant adopted a super serious tone. "I need you to come with me, Officer."

That's type of thing doesn't happen very often, so I knew

something was wrong. "Yes, sir. What's up?" I asked as I climbed into the shotgun side of his car.

"You're needed at Glendale Memorial Hospital," he said while employing the siren and reds. "There's been an accident."

It didn't take a smart person to figure out that something bad happened to Dorene or Junior. "Do you have any details?"

"Not much, but it involves a car wreck."

For the next 17 minutes, I sat in silence while we wove quickly through traffic. All I could think about was Junior and Dorene. Then I got an eerie feeling and prayed they were both alive.

At the hospital we parked in the emergency lane and ran to the receptionist's desk where I was told to go to the third floor. I bypassed the elevator in favor of the stairs, bolted two steps at a time to the correct door and hustled to the nurse's station, where a doctor was told of my arrival. The few minutes that followed seemed like an eternity. The doctor finally escorted me into her office, where we both sat down.

"There's no easy way to say this, Mr. Padget," she said gently, "so I'm just going to come right out with it. I'm afraid your son has died in a car accident."

I felt like I weighed 400 pounds. "What about Dorene?" I whimpered, knowing that Junior was always with her.

The doc shook her head ever so slowly. "Not much better. She's in surgery now."

"Surgery?"

"Her brain is severely bruised. We had to cut her skull to relieve the pressure."

I couldn't breathe. My head dropped into my hands. "What are her chances?" I whispered.

"We don't know, but if she does recover, I'm afraid she may never be the same. All we can do now is pray."

So that was it. In that out-of-nowhere moment, a tough policeman who'd killed a bad guy less than an hour earlier dropped his head on the doctor's desk and wept.

Larry helped me get to the waiting room, where I prayed more and waited to find out if Dorene would survive.

After about forty-five minutes, another officer that I'd seen around but did not know showed up. "Officer Padget?" he asked.

I barely had the strength to nod.

"I'm Officer Margel. I just came from the accident scene. How's your wife doing?"

"We don't know yet. It's not good. She's in surgery now."

"Should I call her Dorene?"

"Please. We called my son Junior."

He nodded. "We're all sorry."

The police tended to stick together when things like that happened to one of our own. "I take it you've got news for me?"

He tapped his clipboard. "I have some of the details of the accident if you want them now. Otherwise we can get you a copy of the report when it's finished."

"I'd rather hear it now."

"Okay then. Witnesses told us that Dorene was heading south in the left lane on I-5 when a landscaper in a pick-up truck changed lanes right into her. The driver said she was in his blind spot and he just didn't see her.

"Apparently, she swerved onto the far-left shoulder and clipped the cement retaining wall pretty hard with the front left of her vehicle, causing it to spin and flip one and a half times. It landed on the roof. Junior didn't have a chance. He died instantly."

I knew that I was supposed to feel better because Junior didn't have time to suffer, but in a moment like that nothing feels better, just less worse.

"With the car as it was," Margel continued, "Dorene was trapped upside down. Other citizens struggled to get her out of the vehicle and kept her comfortable until the ambulance and the EM folks arrived. If she does pull through, it may be because of those people."

21

Once again, I was supposed to feel better, but I felt like throwing up. At that moment the same doctor that met me before came back and Margel excused himself. "How is she?" I asked the doctor.

"We won't know for a while. We did everything we could, but it's up to her now."

"I need to see her."

"Of course. We're taking her to the intensive care area right now. Once we get her settled in, I'll have somebody show you to her room."

I was never real big on religion, but I prayed some more and cried while I waited. Then something else occurred to me. Dorene would literally die of a broken heart if she knew what happened to her baby.

A little later an orderly showed up and escorted me to Dorene's room. It was worse than I expected. Her face was cut and bruised, her eyes swollen shut, and her head, wrapped in a mound of bandages, had grown to the size of a basketball. I held her hand. "Honey, it's Allen. If you can hear me, I want you to know that Junior is okay."

6

A fter JP and Cassandra took possession of Mrs. Clayton's lottery ticket, JP immediately jumped online and found the drawing in question. The ticket indeed held the correct numbers and correct date. The lone winner was entitled to 4.3 million pounds, or 3.5 million American dollars.

But JP and his partners still had several problems. If nothing else were done, Mrs. Clayton would return to the box to gather her winning ticket and all hell would break loose. The police would get involved. Her sign–in card would be reviewed. Fingers would point right at JP and an investigation would follow. Therefore, there was only one solution.

The idea of killing Mrs. Clayton took some getting used to, especially by Cassandra Sevvy, but JP had thought of everything, including making the death painless.

The idea was to make it appear as if Mrs. Clayton's killer was somebody she knew extremely well and who was very angry with her.

They eliminated the idea of a gun because guns were loud and Mrs. Clayton lived in an older townhome community where there were no surveillance cameras and other people could easily hear the noise.

They also eliminated strangulation because nobody

wanted to watch Mrs. Clayton fight for her life. Secondly, strangulation victims tended to fight hard. Mrs. Clayton's flailing arms at a time like that could scrape her nails across her strangler's arms or face, thereby scooping up DNA.

They eventually decided that the best way to quickly take her out was to hit the back of her head so hard with a heavy object that she'd be instantly knocked out. Additional strikes would finish her off and it would appear as if somebody who was very angry with her, such as a husband, had killed her. Fortunately, she wouldn't see the blows coming or feel much pain, and all of that could be accomplished in a few quiet seconds.

If they did everything correctly, the cops would examine the crime scene, conclude that the killing was personal and eye the people who were closest to her. Since she had already admitted that she and hubby had marital problems, primarily stemming from financial woes, the police would learn that too and Mr. Clayton would instantly become the primary suspect.

With the basic details determined, JP took the afternoon off, left his cell phone at home so nobody could put him in the vicinity of the Claytons' home, and met Kyle just up the street from Mrs. Clayton's complex at 2:30 p.m.

In Kyle's car they reviewed their plans one more time.

"Did you get the items we need?" JP asked.

"Yep. They're in the back seat in a briefcase. Got a heavy carpenter's hammer, a bottle of liquid cyanide and an eyedropper, too."

"What about the crackers?"

"Got them, but I think I'll just ask the woman for a cracker. If she has a box, it will already have her prints on it."

"Good thinking. What about surgical gloves?"

"Got 'em."

"Alright then. Remember, we want it to go as quickly as possible, so the harder you hit her the first time, the better."

"Yeah. I got it, JP. I just hope you thought of everything."

"No problem. If we do this right, the cops won't have any reason to look beyond the evidence we give them. One final thing. After it's all over, a forensic team will dust for fingerprints. We have to avoid touching anything of hers until after the first blow. Then we can put on the gloves and finish the job."

Kyle nodded aggressively. "Alright, let's do this."

Minutes later, they parked across the street and one house up from the Clayton's townhome. With Kyle toting his briefcase and both men wearing sport coats, JP used a stick to ring the Clayton's doorbell.

"I hear her coming," Kyle said. "Remember not to touch anything."

When she answered, JP took a half-step back so as not to be intimidating. "Hello, Mrs. Clayton. You remember me from the bank."

"Of course, I do. What can I do for you?"

"This is Kyle," JP said. "He's a bank examiner. I sorta screwed up the other day when you visited the bank. We have a new form I was supposed to get you to read and sign. Can we come in? It will only take a minute."

"I guess so," she said, stepping back.

Kyle tapped his briefcase. "It would probably be best if we went to the kitchen table for a moment."

"Certainly. I'll be happy to help."

"Could you sit here, ma'am?" Kyle said, knuckle-tapping the chair with its back to the sink and placing his briefcase on the counter behind her. That way JP and I can sit across from each other."

JP slid her chair out and sat in a side chair, making it easy for her to take the desired seat.

With Mrs. Clayton's back to Kyle, JP engaged her in conversation. "I'll bet your husband is pretty excited about his fishing trip," he said, while Kyle opened his briefcase and seized a large hammer.

"Oh, yeah, he loves those—"

Just then Kyle's hammer crashed into the top of Mrs. Clayton's head, causing her to grunt and immediately go limp. As her body teetered to the side, Kyle slammed six additional power blows, even deadlier than the first, hard into her skull. She hit the floor, obviously dead. It didn't even take 30 seconds.

"Gross," Kyle said, clinging to his bloodied hammer.

"Good job, dude," JP said stoically. "She didn't even know what hit her—just the way we planned it. She ain't even breathing."

"What now?"

"For starters, don't move. You stepped in a couple of the blood spots. Let's take off our shoes, then I gotta scrub my prints off the back of her chair. After that I want to find their printer to make sure they aren't using any fancy paper."

Minutes later they'd donned the doctor's gloves and erased any hint of their involvement in the crime.

After that, Kyle found a box of crackers in the kitchen cabinet. "What else?" he asked.

"Let's go to her bedroom. You get a pair of her husband's shoes and tap them in the blood on the kitchen floor, then put them by the door in the garage. While you do that, I want to look for the other key to her safe deposit box."

Upstairs it didn't take JP long to find what he was looking for. The little envelope with the key and her fingerprints all over it was in her jewelry box, on top of her dresser. He shook his head. "The first place I looked."

He placed the envelope on the dresser, lending the impression that it had just been used, which would lure the authorities to the safe deposit box and the note he and Cassandra had planted.

If all that worked out, the cops would find out JP was the officer who'd let her into her box. If approached, JP planned to say that Mrs. Clayton was distraught when she came in. That should pretty much deflect the suspicions where JP wanted them. Even if the police were thorough and wanted to verify whether JP was in the vicinity of Mrs. Clayton's home when she was killed, they'd probably check his cell phone records, which was why he left his cell at home. That information, coupled with the letter they put in the box, would clear JP and pin the murder on Stu Clayton.

With the envelope on display, JP met up with Kyle again. Kyle took the bottle of rat poison from his briefcase and carefully knelt next to Mrs. Clayton's body. Seconds later he had her palm print and fingerprints all over the bottle. "Okay, cuz, let's go to the garage."

There, they found one of Mr. Clayton's hammers. "I told ya," JP said. "Everybody has a hammer. Take this up to the kitchen, make sure you get some of her skin and hair on it, then drop it in the blood."

While Kyle was gone, JP pulled a sleeve of crackers from within the box. He doused several crackers with the rat poison and put the bottle and eyedropper on the bench.

All they had to do was retrieve Kyle's briefcase, put on their shoes and get down to the fishing docks to implement the final part of their plan.

7

From the day of the car wreck forward, I knew from personal experience that a father would rather have somebody rip out his heart and stomp on it than lose his innocent child; yet I'd also heard it said that there's no sorrow greater than that which a mother feels when she loses one of her babies. That implied that Dorene would somehow feel even worse than I did if she knew what happened to Junior.

Of course, that assumed that Dorene would survive and be of a similar mind as before, in spite of the doctor's suspicions. No matter how I moved the pieces around, there was no way to reassemble the puzzle that had been our former lives. All I could do was wait and shield Dorene from the loss of Junior—should she ever come around.

With tubes running through her like a science project and bags of dripping fluids barely keeping her alive, I stayed by her side day and night, holding her hands and talking to her. Meanwhile our next-door neighbors and Dorene's parents, Ryan and Tammy, who'd come in from Massachusetts, took care of the routine things that I'd completely ignored.

Somebody eventually brought me some clothes and toiletries and urged me to clean up, but I didn't want to leave Dorene, even to brush my teeth or take a leak, let alone traipse all the way down the hall to take a shower. I too was barely hanging on. I clung to Dorene and the way things used to be. I had no idea how I'd get by without her.

Several days transformed into yesterdays as doctors and uniformed nurses checked Dorene's vitals and dutifully changed her fluid bags as if she were an automobile on a rack at a Grease Monkey.

Each day I looked hopefully at the experts for any hint of optimism, but there was none. The tough policeman inside me receded further and further into a place of hopelessness. I knew I couldn't get Junior back but I desperately hoped against the evidence that somehow Dorene would come back to me.

Then on the fifth day, after they changed her sheets, I kissed her and held her hand. "Please, Lord," I prayed, "I know I haven't been your best work and I definitely don't have any business asking for favors, but Dorene has always believed in you. She deserves a second chance. Make her better. Amen."

But God wanted her for himself. At just after four p.m. her eyelids barely fluttered. Heartened just a smidgen, I placed my hand on her forehead. "It's Allen. I'm right here with you and I love you," I said.

Seconds later, her eyes opened to narrow slits. I leaned in and whispered in her ear. "Junior is down the hall, honey; you can hold him when you get a little bit better." As if that were all she wanted to know, the slightest quiver visited the corner of her mouth and she died peacefully in my arms.

Both saddened beyond measure and relieved that she didn't have to hear about Junior, I lowered my head and wept. I knew she was better off, but I sure as hell wasn't.

Almost instantly a nurse came in and took Dorene's vitals, but there was no hope. The nurse asked if I wanted her to pull a sheet over Dorene's head, but how do you do something like that? I wanted to be close to any version of her, even the dead and bandaged version.

Eventually Dorene was taken to a mortuary and I went home with my in-laws. In between gang-cries and threats to sue the landscaper for causing all of this, we occasionally recalled some of the good moments with both Dorene and Junior.

Ultimately, we had to discuss services and other ugly matters. Since Dorene and I never did get a will, I regretted that she had no voice in her services.

Ryan and Tammy wondered what I thought of sending Dorene and Junior back to Massachusetts, where the bulk of her family was, but I couldn't even imagine doing such a thing. As far as I was concerned Dorene and Junior and I were still a family and needed to be together—at least I needed that.

A couple days later, friends and family, including my brother and his wife, showed up. After a while we held a dual funeral with dozens and dozens of members from my police family lending support.

I also saw a young couple that I didn't recognize. The husband was nearly as upset as I was. Right after the initial services, I saw them get into a pick-up with *Hugo's Landscaping* on the door. I was too distraught to confront him.

An hour later Ryan and Tammy and I cried like babies while we watched cemetery workers lower two caskets into a hole of eternity for Dorene Louise Padget and Allen Mark Padget, Jr.

When it was all over, I couldn't walk away; couldn't say that last goodbye; couldn't face a future without a family that I should have appreciated a lot more while I had the chance.

Ultimately, I adopted a different perspective. My wife became angel-like to me. I cherished some of Dorene's kooky ideas. For instance, she wouldn't take all of the tax deductions she was entitled to because the government could use the money for needy people. Nor did she like to return things to stores. As far as she was concerned, if she bought it, it wasn't fair that they'd have to put it back on the shelf or send it back to the manufacturer.

Once in a while something like that drew a chuckle out

of me, but the pleasant memories of the past were always quickly broomed aside by the reality of the present.

8

MODERN DAY - CARLSBAD, CALIFORNIA

"Holy begeezer's," Danville said. "That's a lot of money, bro."

Stump grinned. He'd only known his half-brother a few years, but there they were, in a classy southern California jewelry store, shopping for an engagement ring for Stump's girlfriend, something about which neither had a whiff of knowledge.

"I can't tell diamonds from glass," Danville added.

Stump couldn't either—unless he dragged a diamond across a window. He handed the ring back to the clerk and pointed to the far side of the cabinet. "Can you show me that one in the corner?"

Stump had never known anything about his biological family on his father's side, until a few years earlier when Stump was trying to get a unique breakfast restaurant called Egg-Zaklee's up and running in his humble commercial building in downtown Carlsbad. After his bio-dad Xander Brooks found Stump and invited him to a family reunion, Danville took a liking to his older brother and essentially followed in Stump's footsteps. Now, 22-year-old Stump was just weeks from graduating from criminology college and Danville was two years behind.

A while later, Stump's former roommates, James and Yana, took over operations of Egg-Zaklee's and all they needed was a great hostess.

Stump lifted the next ring toward the light and checked the tag. Four thousand dollars seemed like a lot of money for a rock. Not knowing what else to do, he slid it on his pinky and spoke to the clerk. "I assume you can modify these to fit my girlfriend's finger?"

After getting a reassuring nod, he eyed a ring with both a big diamond and two green stones. "Can I see that one?"

This time, the diamond sparkled brighter. He handed it to Danville. "I sorta like the extra color. What about you?"

Danville shrugged, peeked at the price tag and let out a loud whistle. "Six thousand dollars? I could buy a car with that much money, bro."

"No way, dude." Regardless of the cost, Stump's girlfriend was worth it. He addressed the clerk. "Can I see that other one again? I want to compare it to this one.

"I don't want to be difficult," Stump said to the clerk, "but could you replace the emeralds with a couple rubies? My girlfriend's birthday is in July." The clerk nodded and retrieved a beautiful mahogany box from under the display case. One look and Stump knew precisely what he wanted to do. "Will you take a credit card?"

* * *

"It's just across the alley. It's called Egg-Zaklee's," Stump's girlfriend, Michael McFadden, said to the final customers of the day at her B&B in Carlsbad, California. "Just give them these coupons and order anything you want off their breakfast menu. My faves are banana omelets and jalapeno bread French toast, but it's all delicious and way better than anything I could make for you. There's no rush. Checkout time isn't for a couple hours yet."

From upstairs, Stump heard the foyer door click, meaning

he and Michael would be alone for a while. He liked being alone with her. In fact, he had liked nearly everything about her: her boyish name, the fact that she was seven years older than he, and that she had been an MP in the Maine Corps.

She worked at a bar up the street when Stump and his friends were trying to get Egg-Zaklee's off the ground. They recruited her because she had great people skills. She also knew things about the world outside of California, which the college-aged women whom Stump knew hadn't had time to learn. So, they recruited her.

Along the way, Stump and Michael liked getting professional massages and took walks on the beach. She taught Stump to jump out of airplanes and how to handle guns, both on the range and in real-life confrontations. They even worked together to get a corrupt mother/son combo sent to prison for scamming old folks.

But that wasn't all he liked about Michael. She filled a gaping hole in his heart.

As an only child of a single mother, Stump had never been able to get over his role in his alcoholic mother's accidental death in a house fire.

After that, Stump clung to any relationships he had with females, such as his first go-all-the-way girlfriend Maria. He'd also become close to Grandma Pauline, the mother of his adoptive father, Myles. But Maria found other boys to like and Grandma Pauline suffered from dementia and passed away. Then Michael showed up and they'd been together ever since. The bulk of their relationship was like that—one pleasant moment after the other.

The only significant bump in their road came last year, when he and Michael went on a Mediterranean cruise. During a stop in Greece, Michael tripped over a pile of bricks on the sidewalk and broke her ankle. By the time they got back to the states, she was addicted to pain meds. After a little tough love, in which Stump reminded her that his mother's death was a result of alcohol abuse and he couldn't put up with somebody else he loved doing the same thing. Michael sensed his sincerity, eventually recovered, and both were better for it.

Then, a while back, Michael had had an opportunity to buy her father's home, which was right across the alley from Egg-Zaklee's. Thereafter, Stump moved in, and together he and Michael turned her home into a B&B. With so much going for them, the "M" word slipped into the conversation from time to time and engagement became the next step.

Now, Michael was on the stairway at the B&B. "You in there, Stump?" she asked.

Before he could answer, she waddled into the bedroom, butt-naked and with a delightfully naughty grin that he couldn't ignore if he wanted to. There weren't many things Stump liked more than being taken for granted like that. The remainder of the morning was put on hold while they "appreciated" each other.

Later, Michael went online. "I thought so," she said to Stump. "They're reeling 'em in by the hundreds."

"Are you still interested in an overnight fishing trip—on the ocean?"

"Why not? We both deserve a breather."

Stump smiled. He'd never known a woman who'd gone on an offshore fishing trip, let alone inspired it. He loved Michael's adventuresome spirit.

"This is a rare opportunity," she added. "El Nino means warmer water and millions of thirty-pound albacore. The 'Limited Party' trips are the best."

"Oh yeah, why's that?"

Those boats can take 80 fishers at one time, but by limiting the number to 24, everybody has more room. It costs more, but it's funnerest."

"Funnerest?"

"Yep. I thought that made it sound even better than ordinary fun."

"Well, I gotta admit; I've never done anything funner than ordinary fun, let alone funnerest."

"So, you'll go? I can borrow some gear from Daddy."

"Yeah, but I should be studying for my finals."

She shook her head and scoffed in his face. "Oh b.s. If you're looking for somebody to believe that line, you might as well say it to an ear of corn 'cause I know better."

Stump deserved the sarcasm considering that he'd nearly flunked out, nearly dropped out, and lost most of his enthusiasm for school. He still loved solving crimes, but the majority of the bookwork was tedious, theoretical and mundane. In fact, he probably wouldn't have attended college if it weren't for his adoptive father, Myles, who wouldn't release any of Stump's trust money until he was 21.

It was either sweep floors at Wal-Mart or go to college. When he finally got access to his trust money, he was so close to graduation, he forced himself to hang in there in part because his mother would have wanted that.

But now that graduation was within reach, there was another problem: the best that could come from his degree was some sort of necktie job. Yecch!!! Given that he'd never worked for anybody else, and he didn't need a job, thanks to the revenue from his building, he wasn't certain he could fit into a traditional profession.

But that was a problem for another day and Michael wanted him to go fishing with her. By any objective measure, such a venture wouldn't change anything. "What about your dad?" he asked her. "Would he like to go?"

Michael smiled. "You've always been his greatest advocate, but we both know he has a bad heart, and would never leave his animals."

That was true. The man had several dozen cats. "How about James or Danville?"

"You can invite them if you want to," Michael said, "But, I'd like it just as much if it were just you and me."

"They probably won't go anyway, but I'll send a text to my brother."

"Okay. I just hope my wrist can take it."

"Your wrist? What's wrong with it?"
"Just a minor strain. It'll be fine."

9

I was told that following the day of the funeral, I constantly mumbled things like, "I was the one who should have died," and, "I was the one who took all the risks."

I don't know why I said those things. Maybe it was a way to remind myself that life was fleeting, fickle and precious. After that, I had an incredibly realistic dream in which I was a skydiver whose chute failed to open. The horror of the fall went on and on and on but the crash never came, which was a precursor to what the next few months were going to be like: all fall—no landing.

After the services, Ryan and Tammy stayed an extra week but all the others returned to their lives. Eventually, I was alone with an empty home and my head crowded with unwanted regrets.

In the meantime, my partner Larry did what he could to blunt the arduous investigative process that the LAPD employed to clear an officer after a shooting.

Over time, I used up all my bereavement leave and my sick days and my vacation time. I wept and drank and felt sorry for myself. I don't remember cleaning the house or changing the sheets or what I ate.

Throughout that time, I received a once-a-week personal call from Captain Donald Barbary, a veteran of 25 years, who had a reputation of being both fair and firm. Each time, he reassured me that my job would be there when I returned. He also reminded me that the department had an on-staff shrink I could meet with for free if I wanted to, but I didn't really see the point. I knew what the trouble was; life isn't fair and it hurts like hell when your loved ones get ripped away from you.

A full 60 days later I began thinking about work again, but the department couldn't just let me don a uniform, gun at my side, and act like everything was the same. A transition period was in order.

I dragged myself into work to discuss the path forward with the captain, which, ironically, prolonged the misery. Over and over I had to tell well-meaning associates how I was doing.

Eventually, the captain and I had a one-on-one, behind closed doors. He asked me the obligatory questions and got the obligatory responses, but the man was a captain for a reason. "Based on our previous phone conversations and our discussion here today," he said, "I have determined you're not ready to come back, not even on a part-time basis."

"You're probably right," I admitted, "but I've used up all my days off and don't have a lot of money in savings to get me by."

He nodded. "That's why we took up a collection. I had to pull a couple strings but the department said your co-workers could donate their vacation days to you. Everybody gave at least one day and a couple folks did better than that. You've got 37 vacation days back in your bank. That'll buy you well over a month. You'll still get paid and won't have to tap your savings or pay any of it back."

It's times like that when a guy appreciates the kind of people he works with. Humbled and grateful, I bowed my head. "Thank you. Thank everybody for me. I can use it."

"There's something else I'd like you to do. I want you to

meet with the shrink at least a couple times before you come back. The department will pick up the tab. If you feel like you need more meetings after you return, that can be arranged, too."

The next Monday, I was escorted into the office of psychiatrist Ralph Roybal, M.D. His office bragged of dark wood and bookcases and a large classy desk with one lone file on it.

He was a few years older than I—late thirties, I supposed. His shirt-tie-slacks combo, teamed with his dark-rimmed glasses and shaved head, gave him a no-nonsense, studious look. He rose and extended a hand. "Hello, Officer Padget." He pointed to a plush leather chair on the opposite side of his desk. "Have a seat."

"Thank you. This place resembles a high-priced law office."

His eyes bounced off his bookcases and back. "I guess it does, but don't worry, I won't be suing you," he said with a faint grin.

"I wouldn't have ordinarily imagined myself as suited for a shrink's couch," I said.

"Oh?"

"Up until lately, I could pretty well handle the curveballs that life threw my direction."

"But that's not always enough." He tapped at the file jacket. "I've been looking over your case. I'm deeply sorry about your wife and son. That had to be really rough, especially for a person who usually has control of himself."

"No shit. A guy instinctively knows that bad things like that happen, but you don't expect it to hit you, and when it does it rips you up a lot more than you would have guessed."

"I understand there was a car wreck. Can you talk about it?"

"That's about all I've been talking about for a couple of months now. My wife was in the far left lane of the highway when a landscaper changed lanes right into her. She swerved and clipped the concrete divider. The vehicle flipped. Our son died at the scene. Dorene lasted a few more days. I had to lie to her on her death bed so she wouldn't know that Junior had passed."

"You obviously loved them both. Did Dorene work outside the home?"

"Grade school teacher until she had our son."

"I understand that you saved a man's life on the same morning of the accident?"

"And killed another one. That was the first time I'd taken a man's life."

"So, you saved one person's life, killed another person and lost your family all at once? That's an awful lot of trauma for one day. What did it feel like to kill a man?"

"It didn't feel good. Guys like that start off with bad breaks in life and make things worse with bad choices. Eventually, they go too far. That's what happened. I had no choice. I had to spare an innocent man by taking out the other one."

"Your wife and son were innocent too."

"Yeah. Nobody spared them."

"Can I assume that you felt helpless?"

"Yeah, but logically I know there was nothing I could do about it."

"What would you say has been your primary emotion after that. Anger? Sorrow?"

"A little bit of both I guess, but the anger comes and goes. The sorrow never goes away."

"Aren't you angry with the landscaper?"

"On and off. When I want to blame somebody, I think of him, but I saw him at the funeral. He was a disaster. There were no drugs or drinking. He was self-employed and only had a minimal insurance policy. It covered the funerals and our car and some medical bills, but that's all he's got."

"It sounds like you've forgiven him?"

"Making him feel worse wouldn't make me feel any better. Besides, who among us hasn't missed a car in the blind spots of our side mirrors?"

"That's awfully benevolent. What have you done since the deaths?"

"Not much really."

"No long drives? No dinner with friends? Ball games?"

"Not really. I'm just a sad slug with no purpose."

"Alright then, that gives us something to work with until the next time. I'd ask you not to suppress your feelings or your memories of Dorene or Junior in any way. All of those feelings are legitimate and will give you a better perspective when things start turning around for you. And I *would* like to see you participate in some activities that you would usually think of as enjoyable. The idea is to find some other things to think about, even if it's in small spurts. Can you do that?"

"I don't know."

"All I'm asking you to do is give it a try. And if it works once, try it again. I'm also going to prescribe something for depression. Take it for a week and we'll see if it helps you to normalize." He rose and offered me his hand. "I'm genuinely sorry about your loss. If you need anything more from me, you've got my number."

All I could do was rise and nod, and schedule an appointment for the next week.

10

"What's your rush, Kyle?" JP asked his partner while they hurried home with a bottle of celebration champagne.

"Simple. I can't wait to tell Cassie how well we nailed it."

Of course they did. JP was smart and had planned every detail of Mrs. Clayton's demise. He grinned, mostly to himself. "Got you covered, my friend, but we still have a lot of planning to do. That's where most guys like us mess up. They wing it, don't think things through and end up in jail."

"I can't wait to hear phase II."

In this moment, Kyle's child-like exuberance was typical herd behavior. JP had seen it thousands of times in the bank when people wanted loans.

Ordinary people commonly lusted after new cars and spectacular houses that they didn't need. They'd go into debt for vacations and holidays and kids. When the interest expenses were added to the cost of their carefree spending, they took the loss in stride, all of which assured they would always be under both, financial pressure and the boss's thumb.

JP, on the other hand, had the aspirations of millionaires. These people were different. Not necessarily smarter - in fact, he was a lot smarter than the vast majority of them too - but he lived in southern California. He'd met performers and athletes and trust children and drug dealers. Many of them were dumber than a hardline phone - but they still managed to swim in pools of money.

And now he finally had his chance to join them, not so much for the money itself but it would symbolize that he outsmarted everybody involved. To do that, he needed to cash in the Clayton's lottery ticket and get away with it, all of which required a partner who would do as he was told and carry out some of the dirty work and that is what they were about to discuss. Of course, Kyle didn't know that JP was considering a last-minute double cross so that JP wouldn't have to share the proceeds of the ticket.

"Here we are," Kyle said pulling to the curb in front of his home.

Inside, Cassandra had three wine glasses ready for JP's opening toast. "Here's to a good start," he said holding his glass at eye level. "We have successfully secured the ticket. We took out Mrs. Clayton in a humane way. We made it look personal. We assured that the finger of blame points elsewhere, and we got out of there in five minutes. Everybody performed at a high level. Now we salute each other."

With that, Kyle gulped down a half glass, Cassandra took in a delicate swig and JP allowed a few drops to chill his tongue while he wondered what Cassandra's love juices might taste like—and would she be willing to split the lottery proceeds 50-50 with JP if Kyle were to fall victim to an unfortunate accident?

"Okay, my friends," he said setting down his glass. "Do either of you have anything to say before I tell you what we do next?"

"I do," Cassandra said. "I don't see why we don't just go to London now and cash in the ticket before anybody figures out what's going on. Then we can move to some romantic village somewhere."

JP nodded. "That's what most people would do, but they

don't know as much as we do. Whenever the cops are called in on a bloody case like this, they automatically look at the insiders first. They'll check out her husband, who could have any one of several motives; or her kids, who might be looking to rake in an early inheritance. If all those people have alibis the cops shift their attention to neighbors and coworkers and friends. They keep expanding the search until they find the perp. If that day never comes, the case becomes cold and sits on a shelf, waiting for somebody else to take another look—"

"But that could be ten years," Kyle interrupted. "By then we would be long gone."

JP shook his head. "This is why I'm the one doing the planning. In a situation like that Kyle, we could never come back or rest easy. Do you want to be looking over your shoulders the rest of your life, 'cause I sure don't?"

"No. I guess not. Not if I don't have to."

"That's right, and the best way to avoid that is to give the cops a credible killer. Once they close the case, nobody has an incentive to start snooping again—"

"And we can live happily ever after," A smiling Cassandra said before resting her wine class on her tantalizing lower lip and taking in another dab of the liquid.

"It's CYA people; CYA," JP added. "Bottomlining it for you guys, we have to hand the police a killer; somebody who cannot dispute our story."

"What you got in mind, JP," Cassandra asked.

"Your boyfriend and I are going for a boat ride."

"I was afraid of that," Kyle said. "I'm not sure how my stomach would hold up on the ocean. I've been tipsy on lakes and mountain passes when in cars."

For the next twenty minutes, they spoke of seasickness and how to recognize Stu Clayton on a packed fishing boat and how to isolate him and ultimately trick him into eating a couple poison-spiked crackers.

"After that," JP ultimately said, "The cops will focus on the man's family, just like we wanted and all we have to do is find a way to spend our money; a million each."

"That all sounds doable," Kyle said, "but, I have one last question, buddy. You've been holding onto that lotto ticket since we snagged it from that lady's box. I think it's time for Cassie and me to keep track of it."

JP grinned, "What's the matter, Kyle, don't you trust me?"

"Sure I do, but somebody once said 'trust and verify.'"

"That was Ronald Reagan."

"I don't care who it was. I just want to verify that you still have the ticket and I want Cassie and me to keep track of it just as much as you do."

"Don't worry. I have it in a safe place."

"So show it to me."

"Maybe it's at my home or in my wallet."

"Like I said, I want to see it."

"I don't like the implication."

"Well, I don't think you have it."

"C'mon you two," Cassandra said. "Let's compromise. JP, you show Kyle that you have the ticket at this very minute, and he lets you keep it for a few more days."

"I don't think he's got it, so I agree."

JP went poker faced. He looked back and forth between his partners and thought that Cassandra would look a lot better if Kyle weren't in the equation. Finally, he reached into his back pocket. Of course he had the ticket. That was the only way he could guarantee that it was safe.

11

A few days following my meeting with Dr. Roybal I found myself on antidepressants and in a Wal-Mart. I pushed a cart past the holiday aisle, which was packed with Halloween items. Remembering what the doctor said about *normalizing* I turned down that aisle.

Naturally, I thought about the previous Halloween, when Junior was two and Dorene dressed him up as a policeman so he could be "just like Daddy." The three of us joined another family from across the street and we all went trick or treating. Later that night, Dorene and I invaded Junior's stockpile of candy and used up our sugar high by making love.

Back in the Wal-Mart aisle I watched two boys, maybe aged five and seven, debate whether their mother should buy them costumes or paint for their faces. I caught myself smiling for the first time in days and realized my meds and the doc had become decent allies.

In the weeks that followed, I met with the doc on a regular basis. We talked about anger, injustices, normalizing and my occasional pleasant moments, which always got bumped aside by sadness, especially when I was alone. Overall, I was taking baby steps, but importantly, I wasn't getting worse.

When Thanksgiving arrived, I spent the day with my

partner, Larry, and his wife, Sylvia, along with their kinfolk of a couple dozen. I missed my family.

I drank a couple cervezas and enjoyed jalapeno dressing along with all the usual Turkey Day dishes and a few other random moments. When Dr. Roybal heard about that day, he authorized my return to work.

Thankfully, the captain teamed me with Larry again, probably because Larry would put up with my woes better than anybody else.

Larry quickly discovered that I saw everything through a prism of Junior and Dorene. If somebody performed a good deed, Dorene would have done it nicer. If a kid was cute, Junior was cuter.

A couple weeks later, the Christmas season landed in our laps, which generally made things worse. Patrol officers never got calls to visit happy people who behaved themselves. Instead there were extra shoplifters and more assaults, burglaries and domestic violence and an occasional murder thrown in for bad measure.

Out on the highways, the tragic traffic accidents ripped me apart. Once again, good ole Larry took on 70% of the ugliness.

Four days before Xmas, we were tasked with giving out presents that had been donated by various community groups for the poorer kids in our area. That felt pretty good and helped me to recall the most recent Christmases with Dorene and Junior, who was more interested in ripping wrapping paper off presents and playing with empty boxes than he was with his new pajamas and the pull toy that Santa brought him.

But the happy thoughts evaporated in the early afternoon when a call came in regarding four or five abandoned children. Larry and I were familiar with the address. The parents had a pattern of drunkenness, shouting and quarrelling.

The home itself was like most of the other frame houses in that vicinity—about 60 years old, just a couple of bedrooms and not in the best of shape.

From a half-block away, I could see the open gate to the chain link fence and several partially naked youngsters running back and forth between the street and the grassless front yard. A topless Caucasian girl, maybe six or seven, saw us coming and hustled through the gate towards the home. We parked right in front.

"Are you a cop?" a little Hispanic boy asked as soon as I slid out of our vehicle.

While Larry went to the front door, I answered the youngster's question in the friendliest voice I could muster. "We sure are. You guys all need to stay out of the street."

"Is that a real gun?" the same kid asked. "My daddy has a gun."

I knelt to him. "He does? Is that gun in this house?"

"No, it's at our house."

"And where is that?"

He held up two filthy hands, fingers wide apart, and shrugged for all he was worth. I assumed that his parents dropped him off and went drinking with the adults from the house we were at. I corralled the kids, closed the latchless gate and went to check on my partner.

At the front door, I caught a strong whiff of spoiled food and wet diaper. Inside, four kids of various ages, including a toddler, were huddled in the middle of the living room floor, apparently following Larry's orders. The kids from outside joined the group.

"Get your clothes on. Both of you," Larry said from the door to the front bedroom. He looked at me and rolled his eyes. "C'mon, now," he said to whomever he was wrangling. "Hurry up. Get out here and sit on the couch."

Seconds later two embarrassed and very young adolescents joined the living room gang, plus Larry and me. "Do either of you live here?" Larry asked the couch partners.

The young lady shook her head. "I'm the babysitter."

Larry remained calm. "What's your name?"

"Her name's Sheryl," the topless white girl said.

"How old are you, Sheryl?"

"Twelve."

I wanted to scream.

"And what about you?" Larry asked the boyfriend. "What's your name and age?"

"Raymond Sena. I'm 14."

I felt both irritated and saddened. That's when I heard a whimper from the back bedroom. I moved past the crowd of young folks and into the back room where I opened the closet door to find a naked boy of about four standing in his own feces. He cried and reached for me.

I quickly wiped his hands and feet with a pillowcase and hugged him, holding back tears of my own.

While we waited for back-up and social services, we obtained contact information from 14-year-old lover boy and sent him on his way with assurances we'd be by later.

Before leaving, we spoke with a few neighbors and learned that none of this was unusual. We posted a note on the door advising the parents who to call to find out about their kids.

Eventually the youngsters were tucked away, off-site, with clean clothes and warm food, but there was still no sign of the parents or any other responsible adults.

A lot later, the parents called. Lucky for them, my shift was over. I wouldn't have been very tactful when I explained why children were too precious to be treated like that.

12

From in the kitchen of Michael's B&B, Stump heard the upstairs toilet flush and then Michael descended the staircase. "What the hell is the matter with people?" she said, stomping toward him.

"Huh? What's wrong?"

"It's those last people for the day. I work my ass off for my customers, but they can't even flush the friggin' toilet when they poop. That's uncivilized."

"Maybe they were just trying to tell us that this place stinks," Stump said, trying to squeeze in a little levity.

"It's not funny, Stump. I got so angry when I flushed their toilet, I pushed too hard and tweaked my sore wrist."

"Sorry to hear that. You want to cancel our fishing plans?"

"No. It's not that bad, but those people were in their 40's. They should know better."

"You always feel better after lunch."

She sighed. "Maybe, but I still have to clean everything; the man-dribbles, the floor, the sink, the tub and everything else that those animals touched."

Forty minutes later, Michael had cleaned the guests' bathroom and began working on the bedroom. While tugging at the sheet corner she kicked something small under the bed. A closer look revealed a bottle of meds. "Those people are out of control," she whispered to herself. She checked out the bottle; about eight tabs of Oxycontin prescribed for the idiot pooper. Figured.

She knew from personal experience that this was not a drug to take lightly. In fact, a year earlier, she and Stump had nearly split up after she slipped on a sidewalk in Greece and got addicted to the exact same drug. Fortunately, Stump helped her kick the problem.

She shook her head, threw Pooper's bottle in the trash and resumed her work.

After Michael finished her chores, she found Stump, who was studying for a change. They crossed the alley and dropped in at Egg-Zaklee's. "Well, hello strangers," Yana said. "You guys here for lunchfast?"

Stump always liked that term. "Yeah, but before we take a seat do you think James would like to go on a two-day fishing trip with me and Michael tonight?"

"You can ask him. He's in the kitchen, but he won't go. We're having another party."

Those parties were Yana's claim to fame. A while back when business slowed down, she had suggested they modify the menus and obtain a cabaret license so they could hire small bands and dance at night. The college crowd had packed the place every weekend since — and many of them liked breakfast late at night.

"Hey, bro. 'Sup?" Stump recognized Danville's voice.

After Egg-Zaklee's was set up, Stump had shifted his attention to the two upper floors of his building. Eventually, the construction dust produced five brand-new apartments, three on the second story and two bigger ones on the top floor.

Yana and James had immediately moved to the top floor. Then when Danville announced that he wanted to move from Wisconsin to California, he and a roommate snagged one of the second story apartments. The others were all rented out at market rates, leaving Stump with a decent income.

"Michael and I are going fishing for albacore," Stump said to his brother. "You want to come along?"

"Albacore? What's that?"

"Just the filet mignon of tuna, bro. It costs more than most steaks."

"You borrowing a boat or something?"

"Naw. It's sportfishing. For a thousand bucks you go out with a couple dozen people on a 100-foot boat."

Michael nodded. "My father used to take me during El Nino, like it is now. It only happens once in a while."

"I'd like to, bro, but I've got to study, and I'd like to go to Yana's party."

"There's one thing for sure," Stump said. "You're a way better student than me."

"But our father says you have the instincts of an injured cat. That's why you've solved so many crimes."

Stump chuckled. "Really? I never heard him say that."

"Speaking of cats," Michael said to Danville. "Would you mind feeding my cats while we're gone? I'd ask Daddy, but he has enough to do."

"Sure. I can do that."

After lunch, having found no additional fishing partners, Stump and Michael crossed the street to her father's one-man cat museum.

In reality, Catts McFadden was Michael's grandfather. Her mother had dumped Michael on his doorstep like a basket of fruit right after Michael was born and they'd been together ever since.

When Stump first met Catts, the man had several dozen cats in a home that later became Michael's B&B. But first the government wanted him to cut the number to four. Not to be defeated, Stump convinced Catts to move into the vacant commercial property that Catts owned across the street from Stump's building. All they had to do was call it a museum.

At the faux museum, Michael rang Catts's bell. "I hope

he'll let us in," she said, half-joking, while Stump playfully waved at the surveillance camera.

Inside, the combination museum/apartment smelled as if Catts had fallen behind in his litter box duties. "Are you okay, Daddy?" Michael asked. "We can help you with your chores if you need it."

"I'm alright. I just need to open a couple windows. That's all."

"I worry about your heart, Daddy. A man your age has to take it easy."

"I'm only 79 and if I die, I die happy. That's all that matters."

"No, it's not, Daddy. Have you been taking your pills and your naps like the doctor—"

"Screw the doctors. There are more old grouches than old doctors, so he ought to be taking advice from me."

"That's not the point, Daddy. A mature man with stents in his arteries..."

While Catts and Michael sparred, Stump recalled the days when his grandma lived in a seniors' facility. One of the caregivers said some elderly people had a tough time forfeiting their independence. Stump suspected that Catts was like that and manufactured this belligerence to prove he was still strong enough to take care of himself. "Can I use your restroom, Catts?" Stump asked.

Inside the restroom, Stump quietly opened the medicine cabinet where a quick glimpse at Catts's 14-day pill organizer revealed that he was indeed taking all of his meds, which suggested he was probably doing everything else the doctor wanted too. With that settled, Stump wanted to end the mini war.

"Hey Michael," he said, returning from the restroom. "Did you ask your dad if we can borrow his fishing equipment?"

Catts turned to Michael. "My fishing gear. Why would you need that?"

"It's El Nino, Daddy. Stump and I thought we'd go get some albacore like you and I did a couple times."

Catts smiled for the first time since they arrived. "Do you remember that halibut you landed?"

Michael's smile matched her father's. "What a disaster."

Catts chuckled and spoke to Stump. "Everybody else was catching beautiful albacore but my little darling caught the ugly duckling of sportfishing: a twelve-pound halibut. You ever seen a live halibut?"

"I don't think so," Stump said, finding the new smiles contagious.

"They look like they've been beaten with the ugly stick. Both eyes migrate to one side of their heads and the other side becomes a belly."

"Everybody laughed at me," Michael added.

"True, so I sold her fish for five bucks and gave her the money."

"And I got a huge bag of Gummy Bears when we got home."

Stump smiled. "I guess that was before she became a Marine."

"Those were good days," Catts said, nodding.

"It's just for a couple days, Daddy. If you need anything, Danville and James are just across the street."

"Stop mothering me. You'd think I was a damn baby or something," he said, jaw-pointing toward the stairs. "The gear is down there. You'll probably have to get some new line for that old reel."

* * *

As Michael and Stump prepared to head down to the fishing docks, her wrist continued to throb. A scan of the medicine cabinet and the linen closet revealed they were out of Aleve. She considered making a trip to the drugstore but that would take a while and besides, there was a perfect Plan B at hand: the pill bottle she had found earlier. An Oxycontin would certainly solve her problem.

A quick internal debate led to the trash and then to the faucet. It wouldn't hurt to take just one.

As she washed down the pill, the phone rang. The Caller ID suggested it was the friggin' pooper man. "Hello," she said loudly, holding back a scolding.

Ten seconds later, she said, "Yeah, I found them, but I threw them in the trash, and the garbage truck came by and hauled the trash off. Sorry."

As soon as the lie left her lips, she listened for the dial tone and slipped the bottle with the remaining tabs in her travel bag just in case she needed them on the fishing trip.

13

Party. Party. Party, I thought, while driving around with Larry. Every time I turned around, families with kids were enjoying themselves while I struggled with painful memories. I would have given anything to have my wife and son back.

I also felt sorry for that youngster I found in a closet. But most of all I felt sorry for the kids of the man I killed on the steps of a liquor store. One afternoon I drove by his home. It was in desperate need of repair. Maybe if I hadn't killed their breadwinner, he could have painted the trim.

The next day, I felt like crap, went to the bank got a $500 cashier's check. Where it asked for remitter I had them say it was from Santa before I dropped it in their outgoing mailbox.

These people and millions more like them deserved better. So did women who suffered from domestic abuse. So did men who lost at life's lottery regardless of the reason. The holidays exacerbated all the injustices.

Then the department's coat-and-tie Christmas party rolled around. I forced myself to go. I arrived at the fancy high-rise hotel near the beach an hour before dinner.

In a well-decorated party room the pleasant tunes of a four-piece band entertained at least 150 people in dresses and ties—some of them already tipsy. The vast majority of the attendees were married or brought dates, but not me. Allen wasn't interested in anything like that.

I suppose that any other time I would have admired all the nicely dressed women, but at this point my animal instincts were duller than a plastic butter knife.

After a few minutes of awkward mingling, a waiter handed me a glass of champagne. Part of me wanted to get drunk because all of me missed my family.

When Larry's wife, Sylvia, asked me to dance, obviously out of pity, I politely obliged. After that, several other married women, including Rita Williamson, who was one of the few female officers in the department, did the same thing. Each time I went to the dance floor I felt like a zombie with good manners—I danced with somebody else's partner and then returned to nobody.

After I loitered a little more, Francine Vaughn, one of the office workers, wandered my way. Single, Francine had been with the force for about five years. She was in her late 20's, with long brown hair. I had admired her without ever indicating as much to anybody. "Hi, Allen," she said. "I'm glad you could make it. Are you with anybody?"

"Not really. I wasn't certain that I was going to come until a few hours ago."

"How are you doing, anyway?"

"My shrink says I'm doing better."

"I've never lost anybody, except my grandparents and some older relatives, but older people are supposed to go first. It must be really rough losing a wife and a child."

Although Francine was trying to be nice, comments like that made it impossible to concentrate on anything but my misery. "Well, we don't always get what we want."

A mellow voice came from overhead. "Ladies and gentlemen, our dinner is ready, so we'd like you to take your seats. We'll send you, one table at a time, to the line. We've got some prime rib and lobster and shrimp and all the trimmings."

Francine tapped me lightly on the arm. "Would you like to sit with my cousin and me? We're over there at table six."

Actually, that sounded like a good idea, if for no other reason than Larry and Sylvia were probably tired of gloomy Allen clinging to them on holidays. "Sure. Why not?"

Ultimately there were seven of us at the table. Officer Rita Williamson and her husband sat on one side along with a desk officer, Edwin Owens, and his wife. I got sandwiched between Francine and her cousin, Carmen—30ish, with shoulder-length blonde hair and a beautiful, tight blue dress.

Before long, everybody was getting to know each other. I welcomed the blah-blah-this and blah-blah-that because it enabled me to hide, at least temporarily, from my own reality. Carmen was the first person to engage me in a conversation. "Francine told me that you went to a small mountain college. Did you get to ski?"

Nearly every topic, including that one, had some tie to Dorene or Junior. In this case, I'd met Dorene at the college in question, but rather than draw everybody's attention to the void in my life I answered the specific question. "I wasn't very good, but it was a kick in the pants; really cold, too. I also made the football team, not because I was particularly talented, but it was a small school where second tier athletes could have a good time."

"Table six," the announcer said. "It's your turn at the buffet."

As the evening unfolded and we finished our dinner I mostly let others do the talking, but when the circumstances called for me to contribute something, I stuck with benign topics that had nothing to do with Dorene or Junior.

Then after we finished our sherbet, a few couples migrated toward the music and Carmen tapped the back of my hand. "Aren't you going to ask me to dance?"

She caught me off-guard. To that point I hadn't asked anybody to dance. When I did make it to the dance floor it was clearly benign and almost like a duty, but this was different. Carmen was single and attractive. It almost felt wrong.

But to not dance might have insulted her, and she hadn't done anything to deserve that. After all, we were only talking about a single dance. "Sure," I said. "I'd enjoy that if you would."

We barely reached the dance floor when the song ended and the band introduced a slower tune. It was awkward as hell, but I couldn't run away like a blushing fifth grader. I held her, wanting to draw her to me and to push her away.

"You said you work in a doctor's office," I said, hiding behind small talk. "What do you do?"

By mid-song we'd become a little closer to each other than I'd realized. I closed my eyes and imagined she were Dorene. Then just as the song was winding down, she reached up and whispered in my ear. "When you're ready to start seeing people again, give me a call."

Once again, I knew she was just trying to be nice, but I felt as if I were cheating on Dorene. Fifteen minutes later, I raced home, took a long shower and sobbed.

* * *

That year, New Year's Eve resembled the previous holidays: drunk drivers and dozens of victims, including neglected kids, abused women and men who'd been beaten up or shot. Like a sadistic mirror, those activities reflected the broader society where we were all victims in one way or another. I felt sorry for all of us.

At the lone party I attended, the excessive drinking by parents, both in and out of law enforcement, and their lack of connection with their children saddened me. I too numbed myself with liquor but for the opposite reason; I had no child to hug. That's when I asked myself an uncomfortable question that had been hiding behind my tongue ever since I went back to work: What good was I as an officer, if I couldn't perform my basic duties without melting like a piece of chocolate on a hot sidewalk every time I perceived somebody as wounded?

I decided to quit the department. That evening I wrote a resignation letter.

14

"This place is iconic," Michael said as Stump pulled into the parking lot at Fisherman's Landing. "We're a little early. After we check in, we can grab some dinner and still get back to the boat in plenty of time."

A half-dozen gulls from atop a long wooden fence watched Michael and Stump walk swiftly toward the primary building.

"I'm getting excited," Michael said, tugging on Stump's arm. "The registration area is inside the tackle store."

Inside, Michael pointed to an overhead TV screen with names of boats and numbers beside their names. "The captains report the fish count at the end of every day. Looks like everybody's kicking butt."

Stump picked up a brochure that indicated they were in the middle of one of the largest sportfishing flotillas in the world. "I can't believe I've never done this before."

"Is this where we sign in?" Michael asked a curly- haired, chiseled fellow behind a counter.

"Sure. If you want to go out tonight you have two choices. They're both going to 'the shelf.' The *Red King* is going on a three-day trip. It's an open boat so there will be about 50 fishers. It gets pretty crowded, but it's just $700 a person."

"We don't have that much time," Stump said.

"In that case, the only other option is the *Trawler*. It's going out for two days. It's a limited party boat. They only take 24 people, but it's $970 per person."

Stump almost whistled. "That's twice as much per day."

"Yeah, but you have a lot more room and you get free meals plus a private sleeping compartment."

"That's what we want," Michael said without hesitating. "Stump will need to rent some gear, but I brought my father's rod and reel. Can you replace the old line?"

Curly nodded. "No problem. I can assign your sleeping compartment now if you'd like. Would you prefer to be closer to the center of the boat, where it's more stable, or farther from the noisy engines?"

"We have headphones, so we'll go with the center area."

"Done. You'll need tag numbers. You are five and six. Who wants five?"

"I'll take it," Michael said.

A few minutes later Stump paid their bill. "We're going to go get some chow. What time should we be back?"

"No later than 8:15. If you're late they won't hold the boat for you or give you a refund."

"For two thousand dollars, you can be sure that we'll be back."

After dinner, with the night and day squeezing the last rays of daylight out of the horizon, they returned to the dock. Fifty yards off, the rumble of diesel engines declared which boats were warming up. "There it is. The *Trawler*," Michael said, pointing down a floating wooden walkway with side docks that moored dozens of smaller boats.

"This walkway is swaying," Stump said as they took their first few steps.

"You ain't seen nothin' yet."

At the *Trawler*, portable stairs led to a gate-like opening in a waist-high railing that surrounded the main deck.

Roughly the size of a volleyball court, the aft deck contained a bait tank about the size of four kitchen stoves pressed together. Half of the tank was covered with a sitting platform, complete with an upside-down bucket for a stool; the other side was wide open and full of water and a few four-inch anchovies.

Michael went right for a walkway on the far side of the two-story cabin. "This place is spotless," Stump said, eyeing the fore deck where several men were already drinking beer and bullshitting.

"Here we go," Michael said. A few steps up the walkway, they placed their thick rods in a couple of the countless rod clamps around the outside of the cabin. "Now we gotta stow our gear."

Stump grinned because Michael knew the jargon. He followed her to a narrow and dark stairway near the entrance to the eating area. They descended into the sleeping compartments, where they quickly located their room. Behind a smallish doorway, two equally smallish bunk beds took up the majority of the space. Otherwise it was standing room only. "I guess we won't be horsing around tonight," Stump said, "stowing" his travel bag on the lower bunk.

Back on the main level, and in the galley, three of six picnic table-sized booths were occupied.

In one of the occupied booths a crewman and a customer traded information while another customer, with a small circular bandage behind his ear, waited in the aisle for his turn. Michael grabbed Stump's hand and squeezed. "We gotta confirm our arrival and sign up for the jackpot."

The guy in front of them turned to Stump and Michael. "It's nice to see a lady on board. You guys ever do this before?"

Michael nodded. "I have, but it's been a long time. I had to borrow my father's old gear."

"First time for me," Stump said. "How about you?"

"I always come alone. It's cathartic."

"I get that," Michael said. "Until the fish start biting."

The man extended his hand. "My name's Stu Clayton."

"I'm Stump, she's Michael."

"Next," the sitting crewmember said.

After Stu checked in, Stump and Michael registered with Rusty, who handed Michael a shower curtain-like clip with a dozen tags, each with a large number five on it. "Everything you do," Rusty said, slipping Stump a clip full of sixes, "will tie to your tag number. Shall I enter you in the jackpot?"

"What kind of jackpot?" Stump asked.

"Most of the folks put twenty bucks in a pot. Whoever gets the biggest fish takes the pot."

"Damn right," Michael said.

After signing in, Stump and Michael migrated to the main deck where they could mingle with the others. At the bait tank, Stump observed a series of tissue box-sized wells surrounded the perimeter of the tank. "What are those for?" he asked Michael.

"Good question," she said like a wise teacher. "When the fishing gets hectic, the chummer sits on the stool and keeps 'chovies in those little wells so everybody can get to the bait without stepping all over each other."

"Makes sense," he said, noting that Michael was the only woman on board.

Eventually, a couple crewmembers methodically disconnected several thick ropes that held the boat to the dock and the captain putt-putted the boat toward the edge of the harbor.

Michael and Stump wandered to the side rail where a tall guy and his partner, who was smoking a cigarette, seemed to be whispering. "Hi, I'm Stump," he said to the tall one. "I saw the emblem on your travel bag when you came on board. I have an account at that bank in Carlsbad."

"Same bank. Different branch. I'm JP. This is Kyle."

"My girlfriend is Michael. She's done this before, but I haven't. What about you guys?"

"Nope. Just thought we'd check it out."

As Kyle flipped his cigarette butt in the water, Stu Clayton joined the conversation. "I don't know about you fellows, but I think it's difficult to cast the anchovy with the bait-casting reels. That was one of the reasons I just bought me a new Shimano spinning reel at a sporting goods store—that and it was marked down."

"I'd like to see that reel a little later," JP said.

Stump said he would too. This trip was going to be interesting, he thought.

15

A few days later, Larry and I drove halfway around the junior high and came across a handful of adolescents, smoking cigarettes across the street from school.

"I can't stand that shit anymore," I said.

"The smokers? Why not? We're lucky they're not doing weed."

"It's not just that. Most of these kids don't have any idea that they're wasting an opportunity and can never get it back."

"Half the kids fall into that trap, Allen. You know that."

"It's not just the kids. Their parents are oblivious too. I was the same way until the accident. Then I knew how precious Junior was, Dorene too. I still cry every night. I don't have a choice, but these people do."

"That's got to be pretty tough. We can go have a talk with them if it'll make you feel better."

"Won't do any good, Larry. Remember that call we made just before Christmas? Two kids, the same age as our smokers, were getting it on while all the younger ones were left to fend for themselves. None of those kids have good role models. They're all screwed."

"We can't solve all the world's problems, Allen."

"I keep thinking about the man I killed and his family and that closet kid. I can't get any of them out of my mind—or

Junior, or Dorene, for that matter. It's all so damn depressing. That's why I've decided to turn in my resignation."

Larry's head spun my way. "What the hell are you talking about, Allen? You've got to give yourself more time. I'll help cover for you until then."

"I know you would. You've been like a brother, but I just can't handle it. Every time I see some struggling kid or a woman who's been battered it makes me sad and angry. It happens every day and it's never going to change. I gotta look for another career, where I won't see so damn many sob stories."

"Are you sure about this, Allen? I saw you at the Christmas party. You looked like you were having a decent time. You probably just need a change of pace within the depart—"

"I'd still hear all the stories and feel sorry for the victims and miss my family. I give up. I've already written my resignation letter."

"Let's not be so hasty, amigo. You've got three years in. Don't throw that away. Have you thought about going into undercover work?"

Now that was a head thumper. I don't remember if I was familiar with the term "inflection point," but up to that moment in my career, I had assumed that I'd stay on course for 25 years or so, and climb the ladder, maybe make lieutenant someday.

"Not really," I said. "I've mostly thought of myself as a uniformed officer who puts bad guys behind bars."

"You could still do that. The important thing is, it would be challenging and distracting without the exposure to so many victims."

That was one thing I liked about my partner. He thought outside the box. "It's none of my business," he added, "but I think you ought to level with the captain, find out what he thinks. If you don't like what he has to say, you can always tender your resignation later. He'd probably meet you later today."

Sure enough, that afternoon, Larry dropped me off for a meeting with Captain Barbary to find out what he thought about my moving into an undercover role. The captain's door was wide open when I got there.

"Come on in, Officer," he said. "Close the door and take a seat. You want something to drink while we talk?"

For an authority figure, the man had a way of putting his subordinates at ease. "No thanks. I don't think this will take real long."

"Okay, then. I got my ears on. Are things getting any easier for you?"

"That's partly what I wanted to talk to you about. The truth is whenever we take domestic calls, I feel sorry for the kids and get angry with their folks. It's not getting any easier and I've been thinking about looking into some other type of work. Then my partner recommended I come see you."

"Well, I'm glad he did. I hate to see good people leave the force. You've been seeing a psychiatrist. Has that helped?"

"Somewhat. We talked about anger and sorrow. He made me realize I can't change the world and that's part of my problem."

"I see."

"Larry said something about the Intelligence division. I'm wondering what you know about them and if that might be a good fit for me?"

"Actually, now that you mention it," the captain said, "I think the PDID could be a good fit for you, depending on which subgroup you enter. You'd probably get a makeover—different hairstyle, different clothes, different car—things like that. Then you'd try to get inside their group, gather intelligence and help us get convictions."

"But it's mostly adults, right?"

He nodded. "Usually. I can send you to the lead handler downstairs if you'd like."

"I'd appreciate that. I like this idea because I wouldn't have to deal with dysfunctional families."

"Might just work. PDID usually requires a two-year commitment. By then you just might like the work, or at least climb out of the doldrums. I'll make a call to Lieutenant Aladar."

"Thank you, Captain. I appreciate that."

"In the meantime, I'm going to dismiss you from your next two shifts pending the outcome of the meeting."

At that moment, I would have run through a brick wall for the captain.

16

Barely away from the dock, a crackle came from an overhead speaker. "Welcome aboard the *Trawler*, everybody. I'm your captain, Greg Gregg. Even though this is a limited passenger boat most of you are doing this for the first time, so this trip is going to be better for everybody if we all work together.

"As most of you know, we're in El Nino. If the past few days are any indication, you're all going to catch your limit, so there's no reason to get aggressive or pissed off if something doesn't go just right. Most of the albacore are around 25 pounds.

"The water is gonna be a little choppy at first, but it should calm down by the time we get to the Shelf, where the biggest school is. We should be there sometime in the early morning. Then, we'll drop anchor and get after the albacore at daylight. Ernie Redman is our bartender and cook. Just tell him what you want, and he'll start a tab for you according to your tag number. If you feel queasy, don't puke on the boat—go to the rail and have at it.

"If you've never been on a trip like this before, we have to get some bait. We'll be at the storage tanks before long. The anchovies are good-sized and energetic. Later, Douglas will show you how to hook your anchovies. That's about it for now, so you probably won't hear from me again until morning. It looks like we're going to have a very good time and thanks for choosing the *Trawler*."

* * *

Following the announcements, JP slipped in the restroom to think his way through his plans to cash in the Claytons' Lotto ticket.

Thinking back, after he palmed Mrs. Clayton's safe deposit box key, given the typical lax security measures at the vault door, he could have just wandered back in at a later time, unlocked the box and helped himself to the ticket. He wouldn't even have needed to share the funds with partners. But there were several reasons that cake didn't rise.

For instance, Mrs. Clayton planned to tell her husband about the ticket as soon as he returned from his fishing trip. Therefore, they would come for her ticket in a few days and that would surely rally the police, who would figure out who escorted Mrs. Clayton to the box in the first place. Then the sign-in card would confirm it. A little more investigating would prove that Mrs. Clayton had been in London, where the ticket was sold. Therefore Mrs. Clayton had to be eliminated before she blabbed about the ticket to anybody else.

But that wasn't the only action that was necessary.

If the police didn't have somebody else to blame for her demise, they might find evidence that she'd been to the bank and put JP under their microscope.

Then JP remembered something he'd seen on TV in a sports bar; two boxers landed a knockout punch at the exact same time. The announcer said he'd only seen a "double knockout" once before.

Immediately after recalling that boxing match, JP knew precisely what he wanted to do: grab the ticket, erase both of the Claytons and make it look as if they'd taken each other out. That way nobody else would know about the ticket and suspicious eyes would never open, let alone glance in JP's direction.

Furthermore, the hammer near Mrs. Clayton's body would surely draw the police to her husband, so JP, Kyle and Cassandra were half-way home. Their final objective was to eliminate Stu Clayton, and make it appear as if Mrs. Clayton did it.

For now, all JP had to do was keep Kyle under control.

* * *

Back on the main deck and under the sky's generous sprinkling of stars, the *Trawler* trawled to the huge underwater bait tanks. Stump made small talk with Rusty, the crewman who signed them in. "I hope the fishing is good."

"Has to be. There's at least a hundred thousand fish in that school and they all love anchovies. Everybody will get his limit."

"What's the limit?" The tall banker asked.

Stump knew the answer to that one. "Five fish each."

"Correct," Rusty added. "But the captain will let you take an extra one or two. There will be so many albacore on the deck, it'll be like an incredible bloody gang orgasm."

"That's when the sharks show up," Michael said.

The crewman nodded. "She's right. When there's that much blood in the water Mini-Jaws can smell it from a half-mile away."

JP nodded. "Survival of the fittest, just the way it should be."

Mere minutes later the *Trawler* sidled up to several manmade floating boardwalks. Beneath them, a series of giant aluminum tanks held a half-million anchovies.

While a colony of seagulls and another colony of sea lions moved excitedly toward the boat and tanks, the crew gathered a handful of long-handled nets and opened one of the hatches.

Over the next ten minutes, they transferred thousands of 'chovies to the on-board tank with the chummer's seat. Then, like a gang of pirates they jumped back on board, thereby enabling the gulls and sea lions to scout the water for any escapees from the anchovy prison.

"Wow. They were so coordinated," Stump said to Michael, "I felt like I was watching a marching band."

"Yeah," she said, raising a slightly shaky finger, "if you don't mind, Stump, I'm going to walk around the deck a few times, just to stretch my legs. I'll catch up to you in a little while." When she turned around a fisher with a Chicago Cubs hat walk up to her.

"Hey, Babe," he said, "Can I buy you a beer?"

"First off," she said almost instantly, "the answer is no; and secondly, I'm not your 'babe.'"

"No prob, Babe. I'll check in with you later."

"Don't bother."

Michael's grit always made Stump grin.

17

Two days later, I was actually anxious to learn what undercover work, or the UC department in lay terms, was all about. The meeting was set for 6:30 a.m. I'll never forget that morning.

I got there a little early and went right to the lieutenant's office, where he was already sipping coffee.

"You must be Officer Padget," he said, coming my way with his hand extended. "Would you like some bean juice?"

"Bean juice? I'm sorry, Lieutenant, but I'm not familiar—"

He looked as if he'd caught a mouse. "Think about it. What popular breakfast drink is made from beans?"

Then it hit me. "Oh, yeah. I like it black, and no sugar."

Minutes later, at his desk, he leaned forward. "I heard about your wife's accident. I understand you're having a tough time getting back in the saddle?"

I nodded before jumping into my litany about traffic accidents and under-performing families. "When women or children are victims," I said, "it reminds me of my own losses. Worse, I can't fix any of it and it'll never get better."

"I've heard that before. Some guys just need a change. You got any other family or close friends in the area?"

"No family. I knew some of my wife's friends and I get together with other officers once in a while."

"Well, that moves you up my list. I prefer to hire single folks. That way, the bad guys can't use kids or spouses to uncover your cover. Nothing pisses off the captain more than investing a ton of time and money into a new recruit only to have his or her cover blown. That's why you have to sign a two-year performance agreement—so we get some legitimate return on our investment."

"I can understand that. I assume you want me to infiltrate some nefarious group. Who are we talking about exactly?"

"Good question. We've got guys in everything from motorcycle gangs to organized crime to political terrorist groups like the Palestine Liberation Organization—they want anarchy by any means necessary, including murder, kidnapping, bank robbery and bombing of government buildings."

"Where do I fit in?"

"Usually we assign our UC officers according to their profiles. Intellectual-looking types and young people infiltrate the left-wing organizations. But you're pretty buff. Your file says you played college football and did a stint in the Marines. You'd probably do best getting inside the KKK. We have a new opening there."

"You mentioned motorcycle gangs. What's that like?"

"Well, it's not as glamorous as you might think. These gangs need money so they sell drugs and guns and steal things they can sell. They have rallies and bust up towns and businesses. You'd have to get inside and find out what kind of mischief they're up to. It's not easy and it takes some time. You're asked to commit serious crimes, like armed robbery or rape, before you're 'patched.'"

"Any other risks?"

"Several. You'd have to hang out where they hang out and do what they do. Get drunk. Take drugs. It can get pretty dangerous, especially if you become addicted. If they figure you out, there's no telling what would happen. We lost a man about ten years ago. Completely disappeared."

"Well, that would give me something to think about besides my family problems."

"That's not all. They have orgies where two or three women service anybody in the club who wants it. That can mean a dozen guys or more. There aren't many condoms. It's gross and there's a decent chance you'd get a disease— hopefully, one that can be treated."

"I wouldn't like any part of that. I still have fresh memories of my wife and it just wouldn't feel right."

"That's another reason I steered you toward the KKK. We'd get you a cover job and set you up with a new identity and a small apartment so that if they check you out, you'll pass muster. You'd get to keep the meager paycheck that goes with your job."

"How do I get into their group? What am I looking for?"

"There haven't been any cross burnings or lynchings for a long time but we never know when that type of thing might rise up again. More recently, most of their troublemaking is as counter-protestors to other protests. The tension attracts the press. They stand on sidewalks and hand out pamphlets to recruit new members. We'd probably have you show up at one of their rallies and hope they invite you to a meeting."

"There must be some negatives."

"Of course. There's danger if your cover is blown. You'll usually be surrounded by at least a dozen bad boys. If they get wind that you're in law enforcement, your life could be in danger, but there's something else. You've never been hated like you will be if you join the Klan. Some of our people can't take that."

I shrugged. I knew it wouldn't be easy or safe to penetrate the Klan, but hey, the danger would enable me to substitute deviousness for sadness and pretend to be against the Klan's enemies—blacks and Jews—while all along, my real hatred was for the Klan. I liked the clandestine layers involved.

"I'd have to think about it a little bit," I said, "but to level with you, I think I could get into something like that."

"Alright then. I see a good fit too, but before I make any commitments, I'd like to have a talk with the captain and your psychiatrist, maybe some other people. If that all works out, you'll have to take a polygraph. Then you'll be on your way to the KKK."

The sooner, the better, I thought.

18

It wasn't easy to admit, but Michael's stroll around the deck wasn't entirely inspired by a need to stretch her legs as she told Stump. In fact, it wasn't about that at all. She knew from her trip to Greece with Stump that the euphoria she'd been feeling from the poop-man's Oxycontin pill she'd taken earlier in the day was bound to wear off within a few hours. Then what?

As she walked up the side of the boat, she hurried and worried and hosted an internal one-person debate.

Could she really limit herself to one pill as she previously thought?

If the medication wore off in the middle of the night, would it be difficult to sleep like it was in Greece?

Was she going to have withdrawal?

No matter how badly she might need a second pill, wouldn't it be a lot easier to end the problem before it got worse?

What if the pain in her wrist resumed?

What would Stump think or do if he knew she had a whole bottle of pills prescribed for somebody else?

If she really thought she was only going to take one pill, why did she subconsciously toss the entire bottle in her travel bag?

Suddenly she realized that she had walked completely around the deck and reached the entrance to the galley. Just a few feet farther, the narrow stairway led down to their sleeping compartment. For some reason she felt compelled to slip on down there and verify that the pill bottle was still there—in case an emergency arose.

* * *

With Michael out of sight, Stump noticed that the water had gotten choppier and that small groups of anxious fishers had gathered in the galley and around the deck to trade scuttlebutt.

He particularly wanted to see what was going on in the galley. While waddling up the deck, he glanced off in the distance where the lights of a half-dozen similar boats also dipped and rolled like drunks.

In the galley he joined two elderly men, Doc and Harold, in a booth. "I can see why people get seasick," Stump said. "Is the rocking always like this?"

Harold grinned. "Sometimes it's much worse. The belly of a fishing boat is rounded as opposed to the V-shaped hulls, which cut through the waves better."

"It can be clumsy at first," Doc added, "but you'll get used to it."

"There you are," a familiar voice said from behind Stump. Michael slid next to Stump. "Hello, gentlemen. What's going on here?"

"I was just about to ask your boyfriend if he's getting used to the waves," Doc said.

Stump nodded. "It's not easy. Just when I think I've got my balance the boat leans in some direction I didn't expect."

Harold smiled. "Actually, a boat has three ways it can mess you up. Roll is when it looks like it wants to roll over on its side; yaw is when it pulls to one side or the other; and pitch is like a teeter-totter."

Stump smiled. "I've always liked learning things from mature people."

Doc pointed at Stump. "What do you do to fill your time?"

"I'm going to graduate from Carlsbad Criminology College pretty soon. Michael runs her own B&B."

"What about after graduation?"

Stump sighed. "I'm not really sure. I like solving crimes, but you can't start out as a detective. You have to be a policeman for two or three years just to qualify. Some people like that but I'm not big on taking orders because I've always been self-employed."

"An entrepreneur, huh?"

"Not really. When I was 13, I was given a large trust for solving a murder. I've been able to invest the money and earn a living off it."

Michael shook her head. "That's not all he's done. He's already solved five murders and a cold case, put a serial rapist in prison, opened a breakfast restaurant which he gave to somebody else, and sent an evil woman and her worthless son to jail for exploiting vulnerable seniors."

"Wow. No wonder you want to be a detective."

"That's what I wanted to do—that and work my way into the homicide department—but then I found out that most of the solved murders are committed by exactly who you'd expect."

"And that's too easy for you?"

"In a way. Some homicide officers like the easy cases. They call them grounders."

"Like an easy out in baseball?"

"Yes. Most of the solved cases are like that. The detectives are smart, but they don't get to do very much actual investigating."

"There should be some other opportunities for somebody like you," Doc said.

"Yeah, there are. I've considered forensics or becoming a PI or going to a smaller community. I just don't know."

"Have you thought about working for the FBI or becoming a postal inspector?" Harold asked.

"Postal Inspector? You mean catch drugs in the mail?"

"It's much more than that. Any crime that involves the mail is a federal crime. We could be talking about guns, documents, blackmail or child pornography. Anything like that."

"Those things sound interesting."

"My brother's neighbor is a postal inspector. One time some stolen bonds were mailed into his district. By the time it was all over he ended up in Vegas drinking and partying with the criminals just to see who else was involved in their scam. When he had all the evidence he needed, he called in the FBI and the bad boys went bye bye. I can get you his number if you'd like."

Stump pursed his lips. Then, "Yeah. I guess I would. I never heard of that."

19

I waited for Lieutenant Jack Aladar to do his homework and finally got the call I'd been hoping for. He asked me to set the next week aside for orientation. I agreed and called all three of my cheerleaders—the captain, my shrink and Larry Montoya—to personally thank them for their support.

Monday morning, right after my shower and shave I went to my closet and actually smiled. What does one wear to enter the world of the KKK? I selected dark slacks, a dress shirt and black tie.

Dressed like a Mormon missionary on a door-to-door campaign, I landed in the lieutenant's office just a few minutes before eight. Predictably, he was already there. So was his civilian secretary, Cynthia Koyle, a 40ish, well-dressed professional who introduced herself and announced my arrival.

The lieutenant welcomed me aboard before we snagged a couple cups of bean juice from the small kitchen area that doubled as a copy room. "If you're smart," the lieutenant said on the way back to his office, "you'll be real nice to Cynthia. She's been around here for over twenty years and knows everybody and everything."

I would have done that anyway, but I still wanted to show

that I got the point. "That's nice to know," I said, not realizing what a great ally Cynthia would later become.

Back in the lieutenant's office, I waved a hand in front of my abdomen. "I didn't really know what to wear today."

"That's good enough, but you'll want to gather some items that support your cover story. We'll get into that tomorrow. But generally, you can grow a beard or change your hair style or get tattoos. Almost anything is okay so long as it fits your character."

Back in Cynthia's reception area, the outer door opened. "Good morning, Sergeant," she said to a newcomer. "They're in the lieutenant's office."

Seconds later, a tall African American, dressed in a sergeant's uniform, walked in. "Officer Allen Padget," the lieutenant said, "meet Sergeant Robert Jillian. He'll be your trainer. Sergeant, here's your newest project."

"The KKK guy, huh?" the sergeant looked right at me. "Do you hate niggers?" he asked.

Confused, I hadn't the slightest idea how to respond. "No. Of course not—"

"From now on you do. Start getting it in your blood. Mexicans, Jews and Catholics too. You won't get anywhere with the Klan if you're wishy-washy about the one thing that matters most to them."

He had a point. I nodded. "Yes, sir."

The lieutenant, half smiling, looked my way. "The sergeant has got a room ready down the hall. When you get a chance, check back with Cynthia. She'll have some papers for you to sign."

Ten minutes later Sergeant Jillian and I sat on opposite sides of a large table in a conference room where he checked the back of a three-ring binder that he had brought with him.

"How long have you been doing this?" I asked.

"Been training for four years. It's an 'as needed' situation. The rest of the time, I'm in the streets."

He opened his notebook, revealing a hodgepodge of papers

and causing several to slither to the side. "The first thing you need to know," he said, tapping the papers back in place, "is we can't micromanage you. You'll have to think on your feet, so you'll do a lot better if you let things come naturally. Does that make sense?"

"Yes, sir. I think so."

"Good, then call me a nigger."

"Really? But I'm not sure—"

"You want to do this or not?"

"Yes, but I'm just not used to—"

He opened a file jacket and ran his finger down a page. "It says here that you played college football. That right?"

"Yes, at a small mountain school, mostly just for kicks."

"What position?"

"Center."

"Did you play in any games?"

I nodded. "Quite a bit."

"So, when you were in a game, how'd you know what to do when they called a particular play?"

"We practiced all week."

"Correct, and this exercise is like that. You've got to practice saying those racist vulgarities until they roll off your tongue naturally so that you're prepared when you're in the game. Stand up. I want to show you something."

"Now?"

"Yep," he said, standing too. Taller than me by four inches, he moved belly to belly and touched his toes against mine. "Now, call me a nigger."

It was one of the most awkward moments of my life, which was precisely what he wanted. "You're a nigger," I said.

"No good. Too meek. When you get inside a den, you're pretending to be a racist. You're going to speak in a tone and language they use. If you don't sound like you mean it, they'll throw you out on your ass."

"I can understand that."

"Okay, then," he said, backing off a couple steps. "I want

you to close your eyes and clench your fists as tight as you can and think about somebody who has pissed you off."

I recalled a drunk who once hit on Dorene when we were out to dinner.

"Now, suppose that guy was a tall black man and you were really pissed. Got it?"

"Yeah," I said with my eyes still closed. "A drunk black guy hit on my wife and it pissed me off."

"Good. Now visualize yourself in a garage with your Klan friends. When you open your eyes, I'll be one of them and you're going to tell me about the nigger who got rude with your wife. Got it?"

The sergeant was correct; this was just like my football days in college. He was a quarterback. He just called a play, and I had a certain job to do. "I think I can do it."

"Okay, then. When you're ready, open your eyes and tell your Klan buddy what that experience was like."

I nodded, balled my fists and imagined that drunk reaching for Dorene. I opened my eyes and spoke to an imaginary Klan member in a braggadocious tone. "When that black bastard reached for my wife, I shoved his slimy ass to the floor and told him he was damn lucky I didn't rip off his head and shit in his lungs."

The sergeant grinned. "Oh, that's a lot better. You were more believable. If you can do it once, you can do it twice. Now, remembering that you're a hardcore racist, this time you're telling your pals about a black woman at the motor vehicle department who did you wrong. Open your eyes and tell us what that was like, and don't forget to put the emotions in it, not too much, but just make it believable."

Once again, the quarterback called the play. I closed my eyes and made up my story before I spoke to my sham listener. "The parking lot was packed, then I saw somebody backing out of a spot in my direction. I hurried over there, but some black bitch coming from the other direction squirted into my fucking spot. I wasn't gonna put up with that bullshit from her, so I pulled behind her car so she couldn't get out. I pulled my .45 from under my seat, removed it from the holster and waited until she opened her door and came my way with her smart-ass attitude. The second she opened her big mouth I raised my weapon. 'I got a few rounds in here that'd fit right between your eyes,' I told her. 'Now get back in your car and think about what you did.' As soon as she got in her car, I laughed my ass off and drove away so she couldn't get my plates."

"That's fantastic," the sergeant said, chuckling. "I was able to picture the whole thing. I want you to practice talking to pretend Klansmen like that. Then when the day comes, you should be able to handle it."

I was glad he gave me the football imagery. He made a very awkward situation manageable. For better or worse.

20

Below deck, where the perpetual grumble of the engines made it impossible for anybody to eavesdrop on JP and Kyle, they gathered for some last minute brainstorming regarding Stu Clayton's demise.

"You were right about one thing," Kyle said. "That Stu guy was easy to find."

"I told you so. I've been thinking about things like this since my Uncle Willie went to prison for embezzlement."

"Yeah, I remember you speaking of him."

"My mom's brother. After seven years he got out and nobody ever found the money. People said he made off with two million bucks. That's nearly 300,000 dollars a year tax-free and he didn't have to kiss some boss's ass. That's the best part."

"What happened to him?"

"He kept his mouth shut, never admitted it and lived high on the hog until he died."

"Seven years, huh? That would be a bitch, but it might be worth it for two mill."

"Well, as long as you and Cassandra keep your mouths shut, we won't have to worry about that. I'm a lot smarter than my uncle was and I sure as hell don't plan on going to prison."

"I hope not, JP because we're talking about a couple of murders here. If we get busted, we ain't getting out in no seven years."

"Gotcha covered, man. Cassandra too. You guys just do what I tell you and we'll all have enough money to live on for at least a decade."

"I can tell you one thing; the sooner I get off this boat, the better."

"I get it, but you can't send out signals like that. We need to act like everybody else. Blend in the best you can."

"You keep saying that too."

"All we gotta do is remain calm and look for a chance to be alone with that Stu dude, and I already know how we're going to do it."

"You still thinking about beer and crackers?"

"Yeah. I already found out he likes beer, so we keep him up as late as we can by giving him free beers all paid for by a bogus expense account. Sooner or later, we all get hungry for something salty."

"And that's when we introduce the spiked crackers."

"You got it. The tricky part comes after the poison kicks in. We gotta get him down to his sleeping compartment, but I got that figured out too. Just remember to keep your fingerprints off everything he owns, oh and wear a long-sleeved shirt when we're ready to do the deed. If he puts up a fight. We don't want to have any noticeable scratches or bruises on our arms."

"Okay, got it. It all sounds workable."

"Damn right, it is. I'm smarter than the cops. They have to play by certain rules. Like 'proof beyond a reasonable doubt' and we've made sure all the evidence points elsewhere. They might ask us a few questions after it's all over, but we gotta play dumb. We just gotta wait him out. If nothing else, we can sneak in his room in the middle of the night."

"I realize we're talking about a back-up plan here, but

what if he doesn't want to eat one of our poisoned crackers? How're we going to 'force' him to eat it?"

"Got that covered. We sneak into his compartment when everybody is sleeping and the noise of the engine is at its peak. I shove a weapon in his face and convince him we're holding his wife hostage. Remember, we were in his house, I can describe the inside of it perfectly. He'll believe it and do anything we say. Including eat a couple crackers."

"I guess you're right."

"Sure, I am. All we gotta do is act like everybody else, enjoy a few beers and wait for the right moment, the later in the evening, the better."

Kyle nodded. "Too bad your Uncle Willie didn't do some better planning."

"No shit. He could have avoided seven years in a cage."

* * *

Due to the lack of entertainment options, Stump and Michael elected to walk around the deck for a while. After a couple casual laps and conversations with various people, Stump was mildly surprised by her tendency to chuckle at unfunny comments. He assumed he'd underestimated the level of pleasure she derived from the experience. Getting her away from the B&B was certainly a good idea.

Then around nine, Michael suddenly wanted to call it a day, but Stump still had some energy so he went with her to the sleeping bunks and picked up one of his books to study.

Back in the galley, he took a seat facing the bow and flipped through a couple dozen pages before a man came from behind him. "Whatcha reading?"

It was Stu Clayton, who'd Stump met during the sign-in. "Oh, hi," he said, showing the man the cover of his book. "It's about deviant behavior, but I was just about to take a break. It gets pretty dull."

"Well then, mind if I join you?"

"No prob. I'll have plenty of time for studying on the way back. Besides I wanted to ask you something. I noticed the round Band-Aid behind your ear. Is that for motion sickness? Would you have an extra one if I need it?"

"I could do that, but if you haven't gotten sick by now, you're probably safe. The waves aren't supposed to get any bigger. Just keep food in your stomach and you should be okay."

A while later JP the banker and Kyle the smoker eased into the galley. "If you guys wouldn't mind our company," JP said, "I'd be glad to buy us a round of beers." Stump declined so Ernie the bartender produced three brews.

"That's nice of you," Stu said to JP. "Thanks."

"Sure. It's no big deal. I have an expense account."

Stu nodded. "I think you said you're in banking or financing. Are you a Certified Financial Planner?"

Stump could have answered that question, but had no reason to butt in.

"No. My organization funds major construction projects."

Stump wrinkled his forehead and wondered why a banker would overstate his status by using terms such as, "my organization" and "major construction projects." That would be like a student claiming he was "in research."

Oh, well. Stump had met exaggerators before.

After a couple more rounds of beer, nearly everybody else on the boat had wandered down to their sleeping compartments. Stump yawned. It was his turn to follow suit. "It's been a long day for me too. I think I'm going to grab some snores while I can."

He eased down the stairs and into their compartment, causing Michael to stir from the upper bunk. Trying to be quiet, Stump dug through his bag for his headphones and eventually wiggled into his bunk, where he burrowed his head in his pillow and allowed the movements of the boat to rock him. In that moment of peace Michael stirred again and then rolled over as if she were having trouble sleeping. Odd considering that she'd been in bed a couple hours and ought to be zonked out. A few songs later, Stump's headphones had reduced the rumble of the diesel engines to a soothing purr and he entered a very deep sleep.

21

It's not easy to become a raving racist, even when the cause is noble, but that was the only way to get inside the KKK where we could legally break them up. After coming to grips with my new paradigm, I studied the history of the Klan.

They originated right after the Civil War when certain hardcore southerners didn't like the outcome. The sheets symbolized the ghosts of confederate soldiers who lost their lives on the battlefields and had come back for justice.

After a few years of ruthless lynchings, cross burnings and the destruction of black families and churches, Ulysses S. Grant sent in troops to wipe out the Klan, which worked for 45 years.

The group was revived in 1910s and '20s and before long they grew to five million members, many of them in California cities near me such as Anaheim and Fallbrook.

By the time the late '70s rolled around, their membership had declined substantially, but not disappeared. That's when I showed up.

On the morning of the second day of my orientation, insider Cynthia Koyle pulled me aside. "If you want a piece of free advice," she whispered, "don't refer to the lieutenant and sergeant as 'Jack and Jill.' The sergeant will pull rank; a second offense and he'll write you up for insubordination."

It hadn't even occurred to me until she brought it up, but the names Jack Aladar and Robert Jillian did indeed invite the juvenile moniker.

I thanked her for the warning before she handed me a sheet of paper with several addresses on it. "This is a list of local businesses that work with us. The first one is a motel. Go register there and get a new driver's license with that address. You don't really have to stay there, but we want it to look like it was your address for a time. As soon as you receive some mail at that address, move to the next place. Naturally, we pick up the tab."

"Sure. What's the point?"

She reminded me that about the only place for people to gather background information on each other was at the DMV, where a person with a single dollar and a license plate number of any vehicle could get the name and address of the vehicle's owner.

At the same time, most public records only went back five moves. So, I had to move that many times for my current address to fall off the radar.

"If you ever have to justify why you moved so much," Cynthia added, "just say the places had roaches or were too noisy—stuff like that. But memorize your story so you'll say the same thing every time you're asked about it."

I nodded. This covert activity was exactly what I needed. I meandered into the conference room and observed the sergeant thumbing through his disheveled notebook. When it came to undercover work, the man knew his stuff, but he would never win a "most organized" award.

"Morning, Officer," he said, gripping a newspaper clipping from under his notebook and sliding it my way. "Our printing department created this for you."

I scanned the headline: *Father of Three Murdered: Klan Suspected.*

I took another glance at the clipping. It looked like the real deal. "So, it's phony?"

"Yes, but it's perfect for what we're doing. Go ahead. Read it."

I hand-ironed the article. It said that a black man named Robert Brease was walking on a dirt road in Mississippi and was purposely run over six to eight times until he was killed. With no witnesses and no known enemies, it was suspected that the local Klan was to blame, but they denied the kill, opting instead to praise whoever did it as a *right-headed patriot*.

"Sounds awful," I said, raising my head.

"Keep the article. When the local den tries to recruit you, you're going to slip it to them and imply that you were the killer."

I couldn't escape the unpleasant irony. I was supposed to "pretend" that I'd proudly killed a black family man, when a few months back I did exactly that during a liquor store robbery and felt no pride whatsoever. I still felt sorry for that man's family.

"Memorize it," the sergeant said. "Sooner or later your new friends will want to know the particulars of the event. When that happens, you should shut down the conversation as if you're avoiding a confession."

Once again, this man who couldn't keep control of his notebook made a lot of sense.

By the third day, I knew why the lieutenant surrounded himself with pros like Cynthia and the sergeant. I strutted up to Cynthia's desk with a bouquet of flowers I'd picked up on my way in. "You were correct," I said.

"Flowers for me? They're beautiful. What do I have to do?" she said with a naughty smile.

"It's what you've already done. You characterized the sergeant correctly—a straight shooter, always plays by the book. After I got over the awkwardness of the first couple meetings, I felt more comfortable."

"Well, thank you, from both of us."

I silently thanked Dorene, too. She was the one who taught me that people like to know that they're appreciated.

22

With but a few fishers left on the front deck, and only one table occupied in the galley, JP offered his two boothmates another beer.

"After all," Kyle said to Stu Clayton, "they're on the expense account."

"Why not? A poor guy like me doesn't get many free beers."

After serving up the beers, Ernie Redman took one last look around the galley. "Okay, gentlemen; you guys are on your own. Just get your own beers and write down how many you took and your tag number. We'll get caught up tomorrow."

JP discreetly nodded to Kyle. Finally, they could erect an invisible but impenetrable wall around themselves and a multi-million dollar lottery ticket that waited for them 70 miles back on shore. "If you gentlemen will excuse me for a quick minute," JP said, "I gotta get something. I'll be right back."

He carefully carried the box of crackers that he and Kyle lifted from the Claytons' home by its corners to avoid planting his prints on it and quickly returned with the box. "We might as well have these with our beer," JP said, thrusting the box fairly close to Clayton's face. "Have you ever tried these? Smell 'em, they're pretty good."

Clayton basically had to take a hold of the box, thereby assuring his fingerprints would be on it. He feigned a sniff. "Yeah. My wife buys this kind."

"Go ahead," JP said to Clayton, "pour some onto this napkin. Clayton nodded and poured some out, causing JP to take a cracker from the right side of the cracker collection, thereby signaling Kyle where the untainted specimens were.

Getting the message, Kyle also took a couple crackers from that side. "Why don't we have one last round before we call it a night?" he said. "After all, the beer is free."

"Go ahead, Stu," JP said. "Have a couple crackers while I get the beers. I'd just have to throw them out later."

Like an opportunistic fish, Clayton took the deadly bait— two crackers. "Good idea. A fellow has to keep a little food on his belly to keep from getting seasick, but I'm going to have to hit the bunk pretty soon, too." He grabbed three more crackers, including one that JP and Kyle had tainted. JP nodded to Kyle.

After Clayton crunched down the tainted cracker, JP knew they had only a few minutes before the cyanide would kick in.

"Before we hit the rack," he said, "would you mind showing me that new reel you said you bought? I've never seen one of those."

"Yeah. I'd like to see that too," Kyle added.

"I guess so. It's time to call it a night anyway."

Below deck, the dual diesel engines hummed loudly as they descended the stairs and reached Clayton's sleeping compartment. Clayton and JP went inside the little room while Kyle stood watch in the doorway.

When Clayton knelt to open his tackle box he slowly rose and lifted his hand to his forehead. "I'm dizzy. Got a horrible headache."

"Probably too much beer," JP said. "Sit on your bunk for a minute."

Clayton gasped for a breath and backed onto the edge of his bunk. "It's not that," he gasped. "I can't...breathe."

JP nudged Clayton's shoulders. "Lie down, Stu. I'll have Kyle get somebody."

Instead, Clayton pushed back, "I gotta...get out of here. Need...help."

JP pushed back. "You can't get out quick enough. I'll have Kyle do it."

JP opened the door to talk to Kyle, but Clayton was desperate and tried to squeeze through the door opening. As Clayton coughed and choked, JP tugged at the man's shoulders and Kyle got a sense of what was going on. Kyle shoved Clayton back inside while JP tugged.

By that time, Clayton must have figured out that his beer-drinking buddies were the source of his misery. Choking on the foam that erupted from his stomach he coughed and weakly yelled for help.

"Oh no, you don't," Kyle said, pushing Clayton back into his bunk where the injured man kicked at the wall in hopelessness.

JP grabbed the man's pillow and forced it over his mouth.

Clayton was getting weaker but not too weak to kick Kyle in the face. "You son-of-a-bitch," Kyle said, throwing a punch into the choking man's gut while JP put all his weight and strength into the pillow and forced it to smother Clayton.

The coughs and kicks weakened while JP snuffed the life out of his victim and Kyle wiped saliva from his own mouth with his shirtsleeve.

Finally, Clayton's foot shuddered futilely and the choking stopped. Then the kicking stopped too. The man's chest was motionless.

But JP wasn't taking any chances. He pressed the pillow into the man's face and watched for any motion, but there was none. It was over.

In any other situation, Stu Clayton's last few breaths, the deep groaning and kick or two might have awakened people nearby, but the loud rumble of the diesel engines out-matched all other sounds combined.

JP exhaled loudly. "Thank God for this noise."

Kyle nodded. "Now what?"

"Go back to the galley. Get the crackers. Hurry and remember, we gotta avoid laying down any fingerprints."

Kyle raced up the stairs and then back with the remaining crackers and a box chock-full of Joann Clayton's prints. "Put it on the floor," JP said. "It'll look like our boy kicked it over."

Finally, they dragged Clayton's body to the back of the door, so it looked as if he tried to get out. Then they backed into the hall and eased into their own sleeping compartment. The only thing left to do was wait until somebody else discovered the body.

Since there was no evidence to the contrary, and nobody else knew about the lottery ticket, there was no reason for doubting eyes to open let alone look elsewhere for answers. Investigators would ultimately have to conclude that Stu Clayton killed his wife and vice versa.

And that meant JP, Kyle and Cassandra were free to cash in a multi-million dollar lottery ticket. A flight to London was now in order.

23

On the fourth day of my orientation, the sergeant examined a page from his unruly notebook.

"We'll find a way for you to meet somebody from a den and hope they invite you to attend a meeting," he said. "Always accept their invitations but avoid forcing yourself on them. They see through that kind of thing. After they meet you, they'll probably drop by your job or apartment to see if they want to invite you to additional meetings and events. Go to as many of them as you can."

I nodded.

"Once you get inside a den you'll be laid back. Adopt their language, but don't be the most vulgar guy in the den. For that matter, you always want to be a middle-of-the-pack guy."

He turned a couple pages, then added, "There is a red line you can't cross under any conditions. You're not allowed to commit violent crimes nor condone them. If something like that is planned, notify the lieutenant or me so we can get some other people to the location and break it all up before it starts. But if some spontaneous violent crime is about to go down and you can't call us, you'll have to make an arrest. Of course, that would mean that you are of no more use in that role and we don't want that unless it can't be helped."

"I get it," I said, anxious to employ all I'd learned.

"Another thing: You obviously have apprehensions about name-calling and using profanities, so I want to reiterate that whenever you're driving around, you should look at the people you see. Imagine what a Klan member might say about them. Then say it yourself right there in your car. The idea is to 'become' this other Allen we've created."

I agreed and hoped that the hate-speak would somehow become easier.

At the end of the day, he pulled a paper from the back of his notebook. "I'm supposed to give you this evaluation form. You can fill it out in private, but the information gets back to me anyway."

"No problem. I know exactly what I'll say. I think you'll make an excellent replacement for the lieutenant some day or to take on the lead role somewhere else—provided you have a good administrative assistant like Cynthia to keep you organized."

He smiled for a change. "You ought to see my garage." He shook my hand. "Good luck with your new gig. The best advice I can give you is to come out of your shell—and stay alive."

It had been a remarkable four days, but I wasn't finished yet. I needed a new identity and a cover role.

As part of my backstory, I planned to say that before I came to LA I'd migrated from Minnesota to Massachusetts to Mississippi, which might lend me an opportunity to slip in a remark about the newspaper article.

To look my part, I gathered some old-new clothes from Goodwill and bleached a couple tennis ball-sized spots into my inch-long, frizzy, brown hair; one spot over my right ear and the other on the back of my head. I then dyed the side spot bright orange and the back spot a light green just to prove I was at least half-crazy, and therefore prime Klan material.

Then, Lieutenant Jack Aladar got me a job in a silk-screening shop, which was owned by Jack's neighbor, Charles Abbott. In a bit of serendipity, Charles happened to have a 22-year-old eye-catching daughter, Beck, living at home. I had no idea at the time, but Beck would eventually become a life-long blessing.

Ultimately, the cover job was a win/win situation. Beck's dad got some cheap labor and I got to pocket the extra paychecks I made.

I also kept changing my address and gathered three tattoos: the classic skull and crossbones on my upper left arm, an American flag with the words "No Regrets" written vertically on the flag pole on my right arm, and a four-inch "Mama's Boy" for the middle of my chest. I only had a few more things to do before my first contact.

* * *

"Thank you," I said to my fifth landlord—a middle-aged woman—in as many weeks. By the time I reached this woman's building, all evidence of my past had been expunged from public records. This would be my last move, at least for a few months.

Just before I signed the lease, I caught her peeking at the orange splotch in my hair. She shrugged as if she'd seen worse. "Here's your keys," she said. "You can move your things in as soon as you want but keep the noise down after 11."

"Got it," I said, knowing we'd keep her in the dark for her own good. "I'll be bringing my furniture over pretty soon." Thankfully, Cynthia Koyle had arranged for a couple day workers to pick up some half-decent used furniture at Goodwill. After that, if any Klan members should happen to suddenly drop by, the meager apartment would support my backstory.

Psychologically and emotionally, the overarching plan to change departments worked pretty well. Although I never completely escaped the pain of losing Dorene and Junior, I had a whole bunch of new shit to think about; best of all, none of it involved domestic violence and I no longer needed head meds. To a tiny degree, I was on my way back.

24

The noisy and powerful engines of the *Trawler* suddenly relaxed, causing Stump to awaken and recall where he was.

Then, an ear-splitting crunch of heavy steel caused his eyes to spring open. Oh, yeah; the captain had mentioned in previous announcements that they'd drop anchor once they reached the fishing grounds. He checked his iPhone for the time. 4:44. It would be at least an hour before the fishing would begin. He decided to slip down the hall to take a leak and then catch some more sleep.

When he returned, Michael had emigrated to his bunk, which could only have meant one thing: morning boat sex. Due to the ocean swells, the below-deck darkness and the small bunk, it was like doing it in a bobbing coffin. It must have turned Michael on too because she really got into it.

After the genital fusion and a very crowded nap, Stump caught a welcome whiff of fried bacon.

"Good morning, everybody," the captain said over a speaker in their compartment. "You'll be happy to know that there's a huge school of 25-pound albacore beneath us. There are thousands of them, so get your tag clips and come gather in the galley. In fifteen minutes, we're going to have some last-minute instructions before we begin trolling."

If Stump hadn't heard other people speak of schools that

size, he would have doubted the announcement. Instead he grabbed his jeans and leaned against the wall to avoid falling over if an ornery wave were to try to trip him.

He rummaged through his bag for his favorite hat, a red one that his father had given him with the words "Jackalope Slayer" on the front.

Minutes later as they left their compartment, he glanced at Michael's purse, which was open and on the edge of her bunk. "Do you want to hide this?"

"Yeah, thanks. Just tuck it under the blanket."

As he did so, he observed a pill bottle but didn't give it much attention.

Upstairs he observed a few similar boats bouncing up and down several miles away.

On the upper deck a colony of squawking seagulls had laid claim to the handrails and kept their eyes on the bait tank, where crewmember Beardo had parked his butt on the upside-down bucket and was repeatedly dipping a long-handled net into the tank for lively anchovies, which he immediately threw over the aft rail.

"Chumming," Michael said to Stump as the boat gradually rose a foot and then rolled gently to one side, then back again. "They're trying to get the school to come to the boat."

"Listen up," Rusty said over the speakers. "When multiple guys have fish on their lines at the same time, spooked fish dart in various directions or even dive deeper, but if we work together, we can keep the damage to a minimum. First, when you get hooked up, call a crewman and try to keep your line directly in front of you.

"If you do get tangled with another fisher, a crewman may tell you to move left or right; chances are, you'll have to raise or lower your rod over the next guy's rod to get untangled and get your line in front of you again. In some cases, a crewmember may have to take your rod away and straighten out the mess themselves. In rarer moments somebody's line may be cut to save somebody else's fish. Just remember we

105

want everybody to catch as many fish as possible so don't take anything like that personal. Simply get more bait and try again. There's no reason to get emotional about it."

Stump tilted his head toward Michael. "Do grown men really need to be told how to behave?"

"Trust me," she said, both smiling and nodding. "When things get tense it's like war."

"When we get your fish to the edge of the boat," Rusty added, "a crewman will gaff it and pull it on deck. We'll need to know what you want us to do with your fish. We can gut them and leave them whole or just keep the fillets, so begin thinking about that."

For a moment there, Stump wished the announcement phase would come to an end before the fish all got away, then he silently mocked himself: there was no place for them to hide.

"One last thing; Ernie is making breakfast in the galley. Don't everybody rush him at once, but when you place your order, give him your tag number and he'll call you when your meal is ready."

Just then a loud steel-on-steel cranking sound indicated they were taking up anchor. Stump licked his lips. He hadn't been so anxious in months. Michael seemed giddy too.

A moment later, the anchor had been stowed and the captain revved the engines, prompting the other crewmembers to take up positions around the deck.

Rusty returned to the mic. "The first thing we have to do, gentlemen, is bring the school to the boat and to do that we troll. The idea is to make it look like the first fish has homed in on food. With any luck other fish will want to check it out. Beardo will toss anchovies behind the boat, to confirm that there are anchovies available. When we catch that first fish on the trolling rigs, the other trollers must bring their lines in as fast as possible because everybody else will be getting an anchovy and casting their lines behind the boat too. Now, to get things going, we need numbers one through four at the back rail. You're our first trollers. If you don't have your own trolling rig you can use one of the boat's rods."

People watched as three trollers wandered to the back of the boat. The crewmembers handed each one a rod that was so thick it reminded Stump of a broom handle. A huge reel with extra-heavy-duty line was attached to the butt of the rod, and a gigantic lure, the size of a kid's shoe, dangled from the tip. Rusty escorted Number One to the corner on the stern side, where he held the rod tip over the rail and released the reel's lock, allowing the lure to feed out as the boat putt-putted forward. When the lure was 40 feet back, Rusty flipped the lock back into place and handed the fisher the rod. "If you get one, yell 'hook-up' as loud as you can."

"Number Four," the captain said over the PA. "It's your turn to troll. If you don't come forward, we're going to give your spot to the next man up."

Michael spoke to Stump. "If he doesn't speak up pretty soon, it's my turn."

After Rusty and Douglas got the second and third trollers squared away, Douglas turned toward all the others. "Who's got five?"

"I do," Michael said. "I'll need a boat-rig."

"Alright, everybody," Douglas said, "I spoke with this woman last night. She knows what she's doing. Watch her and learn."

Stump grinned. Michael had been teaching him boy-things since the first time he met her.

"I don't know about that," she said to Douglas while the boat lifted slightly with the roiling Pacific, "but I'll give it a try." She took the port side corner, held her rod tip over the rail and let her giant feathery lure fall into the white water behind the slow-moving boat. When the lure was out the proper distance, she locked the reel back into its rightful position and instantly got a hit by a large albacore.

"HOOK UP!!!"

The captain cut the throttle.

25

By the end of the '70s, most of the Klan's radical violence had been replaced by political protests. The operative word in that sentence is "*most.*"

The membership numbers may have been way down, but there were still plenty of mouthy thugs who thought action spoke better than words, and that group attracted cameras.

By that time the Supreme Court had endorsed forced bussing to desegregate the schools, so it was no surprise that the Klan wanted to thwart any efforts to implement the Court's rulings, especially when a large event along those lines was to take place just down the road from Disneyland, where lots of people could see the action and potentially join the den. One such gathering lent me the opportunity for my initial contact. I still remember the chill on my back and the mass of goose bumps that sprinkled my thighs when the day came for me to move from the theories of a small classroom to the realities of the streets. I slid into my blue jeans, popped a small diamond stud earring in my newly pierced ear, and completed my costume with a white short-sleeved shirt.

By that time, I'd bought a 1971 baby-shit-brown Ford LTD because no self-respecting Klansman would drive anything other than a stout American car or truck.

During my drive to the park I reminded myself that I

was doing all of this because a group of victims had injected themselves into my life. I was especially tormented by the memory of the man I killed—a black man—the very type of person whom the Klan boys could do without regardless of any hardships that might befall the dead man's family.

All of that was because of me and my gun at a liquor store, but at least on this one day, I had a chance to push back. With any luck, I might be able to get inside their group and curtail some of the hatred that would otherwise be visited on other minority families in the Los Angeles area.

I made my way to the park where the pro- and anti-bussing forces were already yelling at each other. I sneaked one last look at myself in the mirror and grinned at my colorful hair before marching toward three distinctively different groups.

One faction, about 40 strong, consisted of relatively happy family types—blacks and whites, moms and dads and kids, some on skateboards and bicycles. A tall white guy with a bright yellow shirt handed out homemade signs with sensible messages such as "Equality in Schools," and "Fairness is Fair."

A more ominous group, about a dozen in number, mostly white males, stood loosely together a half-block away. Camouflage cargo shorts and sleeveless shirts bearing vulgar sayings made up their garb. A few had donned holsters with huge hunting knives. They too had signs such as, "Niggers Stay Home," and "You Aren't Welcome."

The police made up the third group, because there was a good chance the event would turn violent. Thus far, the insults were flying back and forth but nobody was getting in the other team's faces.

Anaheim was out of my usual district, so I didn't see any officers I knew, which basically meant I wasn't going to get any special treatment. I reasoned if I did get in some sort of ruckus, I'd play it like a Klansman would until I could get alone with an officer.

Having assessed the situation, I walked toward the group

I least related to—the Klan guys. I homed in on a man with a shaved head, a big knife in his belt and a handful of yellow pamphlets.

I slowed my pace and waited for him to look me in the eye. Finally, he spoke. "Hey, brother," he said, "can I talk to you for a minute?"

I hesitated so as not to make this too easy for him.

"C'mon over," he insisted, while thrusting one of his pamphlets my way. "I just want to talk. That's all."

"I don't know. I probably shouldn't get involved."

"C'mon. We don't harass good folks like you," he continued while two of his team members hurled epithets toward the bigger group. "Let me ask you something. Do you have any children of your own?"

I was supposed to be a fatherless bachelor, so I brushed the truth into the recesses of my mind. "No. Who are you guys?"

"Before I answer that, do you think it's fair for kids who take their schooling seriously to be butted aside for outsiders who don't take care of their own schools and don't pay their fair share of costs?"

"Not really. Is that what's happening?"

"You damn right it is, brother, and a lot more. How are our kids supposed to get a good education when other people send their ignorant offspring in and slow down the learning? That isn't fair, is it?"

"Doesn't sound fair to me."

He grabbed a paper towel and wiped some sweat beads off his head. "That's what this reconstruction crap is doing to us. The sanctity of our schools is being threatened. Our neighborhoods are next. Hell, half the time those people don't even bathe. We're against that kind of thing. Aren't you?"

"All I know is I have to work for a living while other people get to live off the government. That isn't fair either."

"You got that right, brother. Good white people like us are carrying the load for everybody else."

Just then the heavy end of an empty beer bottle crashed

into his left eyebrow, knocking him down and nearly out. The policeman in me instinctively turned to see three young guys, about college age, with long hair and a bad attitude. "That'll teach you assholes," a plump one said.

I looked for some officers to come calm everything down but none of them were paying attention, which didn't surprise me because I knew from first-hand experience that the police could turn a blind eye to anything they didn't "want" to see.

"He didn't do anything to you guys," I said to the bottle thrower.

"Bullshit. You assholes have been talking smack all day long. It's time somebody shut you bigots up."

"There's a difference between words and assault, you morons."

"You want a piece of us, big man?" Chubby said, curling a finger and daring me to engage in a fight.

It was completely weird. Morally, I was on their side, except for the assault, but my role required me to try to get into Skinhead's den. I knelt to help my injured *friend*.

Skinhead rose to one knee with a new golf ball-size welt and a bleeding gash over his eye. "Where the hell are the cops?" I said.

My injured "pal" sighed. "They're a bunch of pussies. They always let our side take a few hits before they do anything about it."

"You've got that right," I said. I knew a few officers who did exactly as he said, but they certainly weren't *pussies*. "You can never count on the bastards when you need them."

"C'mon, big mouth," bottle thrower said, stepping in our direction.

Finally, a couple officers hustled toward us. I didn't know either one of them, but then, why would I? There were many thousands of us in the LA area and this wasn't my usual district. I pointed at the bottle thrower and said something I thought Skinhead might say. "Arrest that fat prick. He hurt my friend."

111

Then it was the bottle thrower's turn to yell at the police. "Why the hell do you pigs let these racist assholes hang around? You know they just want to incite a riot."

"Fucking sack-of-shit cops," Skinhead yelled while pointing at the officers. "Admit it. You saw what they did and let it happen."

The taller officer shouted back, "You let us worry about—-"

Skinhead looked my way. "Thanks a lot, buddy," he said, extending his hand. It's nice to know who a guy's friends are. My name's Earl Someda."

"I'm Allen. Allen Padget."

26

The first announcement of a "hook-up" set a well-coordinated set of activities in motion.

Michael grinned wide and went tense.

The captain cut the throttle.

Crewmember Douglas yelled out, "All trollers, get your lines in."

Crewman Rusty scooted to Michael's shoulder to coach her if necessary.

Beardo distributed frisky anchovies into the water behind the boat and around a series of bait wells on the top of the tank where fishers could get to them easily.

Stump watched Michael draw the thick rod to her and then "bow and reel" as she had instructed him.

At the bait tank, at least ten seasoned fishers had already mined the little wells for the liveliest anchovies, baited their hooks and quickly raced to the rail to cast their offering to any other albacore that might be rising to the surface in search of food.

In awe, Stump and several others held back, preferring to get an overview of the process and to watch Michael.

"Hook-up!" somebody else yelled from the starboard side, while his buzzing reel begrudgingly forfeited a few yards of line to the first baitfish.

"Follow your fish," Rusty said to Michael as the lines of other fishers were hitting the water on either side of hers.

Seconds later, more than a dozen fishers, each with their lines in the water, stood shoulder to shoulder, most of them at the stern.

"Hook-up!" loudly pierced through the buzz and another deckhand hurried to help.

After a few minutes, crewmembers helped the more timid fishers bait their hooks. "Butt in wherever you can," Douglas instructed one of them.

Stump ignored his desire to do the same thing and opted instead to watch Michael duck under rods and follow her fish up the side of the boat, while Rusty watched over her shoulder in case she needed advice.

"C'mon, you slimy S.O.B.," Michael yelled at her fish.

While they all danced and rolled with the sea, more bait fishers hooked up, and most of the albacore wanted to go anywhere other than toward the boat. From random places instructions rained down.

"Go under him."

"Pull and tuck and reel."

"You need a fresh bait."

"Watch that hook. You almost caught me in the eye."

"Pass your rod over this man."

"He's going to the bow. Hurry. Follow him."

Stump looked back to Michael, whose smile was amazing. Her hips shifted from side to side in perfect sync with the rocking boat. Her next tug-and-reel exercise brought her exhausted fish to 20 feet from the boat. It tried to dive but Michael would have none of it. She tugged again. "Oh, no, you don't. Mama's gonna have you for dinner." Her rod was less strained. The fish was noticeably weaker.

"Gaff, gaff. I'm gonna need a gaff," she yelled as she drew her fish even closer.

Beardo jumped off the bait tank, seized a long pole with a coat hanger-sized hook on the end and dangled the pole over the side of the boat, hook at the ready.

Michael drew the swimming silver demon to within five

feet. It made one last attempt to roll out of the way, but just as it exposed its belly, Beardo's gaff came in from underneath, snagged the fish and in a split second a hand-over-hand exercise brought it bleeding and flopping onto the deck, thereby earning Michael a healthy spattering of cheers.

While Mr. Albacore spent his last energy flopping in protest on the deck, Michael pumped her fist in the air and gave out a loud Marine cheer. "Oorah! And that's all there is to it, fellas."

Noting her million-dollar grin, Stump wished he had his camera, but instead added some oral support. "Way to go, Michael. I knew you could do it."

Rusty used a pair of pliers to remove the lure from the fish's jaw. "You've got at least fifteen pounds of steak here," he said to Michael. "Gimme one of your tags." Seconds later, with the number five stapled to the fish's shiny gill, Rusty asked, "What do you want us to do with it?"

"Fillet," she said loudly without hesitation. "Definitely fillet."

Rusty grabbed a magic marker from his tool belt and added a big F to the tag.

"Hook-up!" This time somebody on the bow got the call.

A quick scan of the boat revealed that five or six people had snagged fish and Stump was one of a handful who still hadn't dropped a line in the water, the others being the tall banker, JP, and his friend Kyle, who were tucked away in a galley booth as if they were bored.

Having seen what success looked like, Stump grabbed his rod and went for the wells around the bait tank. His hands spent several minutes chasing little fish around before he caught an enthusiastic wiggler.

By that time, it seemed like a chorus of people were yelling either "hook-up" or "gaff," and nearly a dozen tagged albacore flopped angrily in a slithering carpet of blood on the deck.

Stump pushed the hook through the 'chovie's gill as

everybody else was doing and hustled over the killing field and to the back of the boat. He delicately dropped his bait into the water. With his reel in "free spool" the line fed out while his 'chovie dove for deeper water. Then it suddenly rocketed deeper. An albacore had taken his bait. "Hook-up! Hook-up! Hook-up!" he yelled as he locked the spool down and set the hook.

27

My reaction to the knot on Skinhead's noggin essentially red-carpeted me into the den, but when he encouraged me to attend an upcoming membership drive, I downplayed my interest and said I probably wouldn't be there.

Since that introduction meeting was several days off and none of the Klan members knew anything about me yet, I spent a good chunk of that time at Dorene's and my home where barely numbed memories still tugged at my heart.

In my better moments, I attended to minor chores such as forming a company, transferring the title to my home into that company's name and adding a few decorating touches to my undercover apartment. By that time, Cynthia Koyle had obtained a confederate flag, which I hung on my bedroom wall. Smaller touches included a well-worn Protestant version of the Bible, and a framed version of the phony article that the department had printed, which suggested I'd killed a black man in Mississippi.

In between those moments, I got familiar with the silk-screening equipment at my cover job and caught myself glancing at the boss's cute daughter, Beck.

Ultimately, the evening of the membership drive came around. I dressed conservatively, tucked a snub gun behind my back and slipped into my turd-colored Ford LTD, which had seats the size of my living room sofa. As I drew closer, I was surprised the meeting was in a residential area. I rolled to the curb across the street from the host's home and slowly wandered to the front door, where an attractive brunette introduced herself as Gloria, Skinhead's wife.

A stairway led down to a masculine man-cave replete with dark woods, thick carpet, leather chairs and a classy bar where a handful of guys already had beer mugs in hand.

"Allen," Skinhead said, hustling over to shake my hand. "Glad you could break loose. Got room for a beer?"

"Yeah, sure," I said, noticing he still had a healthy shiner.

"Hey, Royce. This is the guy who saved my ass. Get him a beer from the kegerator."

"Oh, yeah, I recognize that kooky hair."

I scanned the walls while Royce drew my beer.

Then Skinhead glared at my earring. "None of the guys around here wear those."

"The babes dig 'em, but just the left ear. Right ear means you're a faggot," I said.

"Here ya go," wavy-haired Royce said, handing me a mug of brew. "We've been telling Earl that he should find a better way to catch beer bottles."

"I think the damn cops just let it happen," I said, looking over Royce's shoulder and then back to Skinhead. "Is that an antique safe? You got gold in there or what?"

"It belonged to a bank where my uncle worked. I use it for some of my better guns. Sometime, when we have more time, I'll show them to you. I have a few that are 'very special.'"

I raised my eyebrows, assuming he meant something illegal such as a sawed-off shotgun or a hand-made pistol or an M-16 assault rifle from the Viet Nam War.

Just then, another person descended the stairs. "That's Robbie Roberts," Skinhead said. "He owns the bar where I get my keg. Hey, Robbie. Over here. I want you to meet Allen Padget. He's the guy who saved my bacon at the demonstration."

If the facts were as Earl presented them, their keg-for-money exchange was probably illegal. Licensed liquor stores were allowed to sell kegs to the public, but bars weren't.

Robbie shook my hand and gathered a beer. "Hey, Earl, there's a couple other guys wandering around outside. They asked me what was going on. I told them you'd come talk to them."

"We always got room for one more. I'll go see if they want to check us out."

While Earl was gone, I met another recruit named Myron Thorn. A tall man with a flat-top haircut and a reddish goatee, he said he'd just moved to the area from Texas and was looking to join a den. Behind him, a wall was filled with pictures of famous people such as Mark Twain, Elvis Presley and some of the Brooklyn Dodgers, along with former politicians such as Robert Byrd, George Wallace and several presidents. The implication was that all were Klan members.

A short time later, several other regulars showed up, as did the two guys from outside, who introduced themselves as the Wilson brothers. They said they had casual interest in finding out what this group was all about.

Then, with 11 people in attendance, Skinhead opened the meeting by grabbing a large brass bell from the top of his safe and clanging it a few times. "Okay, everybody, now that we've all had a chance to introduce ourselves, let's get this event underway." Everybody took a seat, except Royce, who held his position behind the bar for anybody who wanted a refill.

Earl introduced a few of the regulars before he got around to Carlton Bisk, who said, "I wish I woulda been around in the '20s when know-it-all niggers were dragged from their homes and beaten. A hanging here and there kept their entire tribe in line."

"A lot of us feel that way," Robbie Roberts said," but the national boys say it ain't just about the nigras no more. It's about anybody who doesn't have the proper spirit. Like Jews, Chinese and Catholics."

"What's wrong with Catholics?" one of the Wilson brothers asked, thereby triggering a lesson from Robbie.

"The Catholics' Bible has seven extra books. They believe in the three P's: the Pope, purgatory and penitence, but real scripture doesn't mention those things. No man, not even the Pope can take on Christ's authority: Only Christ's mercy can bring salvation."

Two other guys nodded but the brothers remained stiff and motionless.

After a few more minutes of talking about rallies and soft-pedaling the Klan's basic philosophies, Skinhead wanted to thin the crop. "That's a basic overview of what we do, gentlemen. If you don't think this is for you, this would be a good time for you to bug outta here. The rest of us are gonna shoot the shit and have another beer."

The Wilson brothers rose. "I might have been sympathetic with some of your views," the older one said, "but we're Catholic, so I can't get behind anybody who thinks my views don't count."

Skinhead shrugged. "You got that right. The sooner you get outta our sight, the better."

The brothers plopped their mugs on the bar and bolted for the steps with Skinhead right behind them.

"What about you?" Royce asked Myron. "You want to hear more?"

"I don't need to hear more. I was in another den, in Texas. I know the score. That's why I'm here."

"What about you, Allen? You got your fill or are you staying?"

I elected to take a less direct approach. "I was looking at a couple of those pictures of Lester Maddox and George Wallace. I thought those boys denied they were ever in the Klan."

Robbie nodded. "Wallace never officially joined, but he regularly addressed rallies."

"I always suspected he was one of us," I said, choosing my words carefully.

Skinhead rejoined us and handed applications to Myron and me. "Now that we've gotten rid of the shoe clerks, me and Royce got some cool things to show you new boys."

Together, they reached for the wall behind the bar and pulled a five-by-eight section forward. Skinhead glanced at me. "Ready?"

"I nodded approvingly as he and Royce slowly flipped the board, thereby revealing the back side where a large confederate flag was flanked by a score of framed articles and pictures of cross-burnings, lynchings and raised weapons. I strolled toward the board and knuckle-tapped one of the framed articles that spoke of an auto accident in Alabama where a black man was killed on a dirt road.

"This reminds me of an article that I have at my place," I said.

28

"Yahoo!" Stump yelled as his rod bent and his reel forfeited line to his tugging fish.

Douglas stepped forward and tapped the next guy on the rail. "We have to go under you."

Seconds later, Stump's fish raced under the boat and to the opposite side. "No problem," Douglas said. "Lower your rod tip. We're going to work our way around the bow."

Trying to win a tug-of-war, Stump moved to his left and danced with the sea while he sidestepped under several people and sometimes somebody going in the opposite direction.

In those moments, Stump forgot everything else about his life. He was no longer a student about to take his finals, no longer the boyfriend of a Marine, no longer somebody who may have been on a track to matrimony. Instead, he was a great fisherman trying to land Moby Albacore, the most elusive sportfish in the entire history of the sea.

Rusty arrived with a gaff, handed it to Douglas and leaned over the rail. "I can see him. He's getting tired."

"He's not the only one," Stump said, "but I ain't giving up now."

"Just a little more," Douglas said.

Then Michael pinched Stump's butt. "Way to go, Stump."

Stump lifted the rod high, then bowed and reeled as fast as he could, just like Michael taught him. The fish came within a few feet of the surface.

"One more," Douglas insisted, dangling the gaff.

Stump's arms ached. A swell lifted the boat and then dipped. Stump bowed and reeled as fast as he could. His fish had had enough. It rolled. Stump could see its belly. Suddenly the gaff plunged under the fish. The hook on the end came up hard in the fish's neck. A second later Douglas's lightning fast hands had Stump's fish on deck, flopping and bleeding like its predecessors. With blood on his shoes, and arms that must have looked like those of an ape, Stump traded high-fives with Michael. "You were right," he yelled, "this is a kick in the ass."

Douglas knelt near Stump's fish with a ready stapler. "Gimme one of your tags. How do you want your fish?"

Stump plucked a tag from the shower curtain clip. "Michael says to get fillets."

"You got it. Now go get another 'chovie and catch this guy's bigger brother."

Stump swayed with the boat and scoffed. "No way, dude, I gotta rest my arms."

An hour later Stump had recovered and boated another fish when a crackle came from the overhead speakers. "Okay, everybody, I'm afraid we have a little bad news. All this blood has attracted a shiver of sharks. We've got about 20 of them swimming around. We're going to use this opportunity to drop your fish into the freezer and wash off the deck while we move elsewhere. I just spoke with the captain of the *Sea Scout*. They're six miles north and having success with no sharks in the area. It'll take us a short hour to get there. If you don't have a fish on right now, please put your rods away. This would be a good time to order something from the galley or to catch a nap."

Although others moaned in protest, Stump looked at the deck-turned-battlefield-red and knew what somebody had meant the night before when he said the whole experience was like a bloody gang orgasm.

"Son-of-a-bitch!" one of the few remaining fishers yelled loudly. Most heads turned to see the man lift the bodiless head of an albacore over the rail. "A goddam shark got the body of my fish."

Having grown largely accustomed to the gore, Stump glanced at the hanging head, with its eyes still open. Oh well. Sharks had to eat, too.

* * *

Minutes later and down in the sleeping compartments, the reverberation of the diesel engines drowned out Kyle and JP's conversation. "Nobody misses that guy," Kyle said, speaking of Stu Clayton. "How are we going to make the cops think his wife killed him if nobody knows he's dead?"

JP shook his head. "Use your common sense, Kyle. The man came by himself. Nobody knows to look for him. If we draw attention to him, we're dead meat. We have to be engaged with what's going on up on the deck. Just act like everybody else, catch a few fish and wait it out. The best thing that could happen to us is nobody finds him until we get back to land. Eventually, somebody is going to clean up the compartments and that's when they'll find him. The cops will think his wife poisoned him and we're home free."

"I sure hope so."

"Trust me. I know how these people think. All we gotta do is act like everybody else. If we both catch a few fish, nobody will suspect anything."

"Okay. I get it. I already landed one, but——"

"All you gotta do is bring in a couple more. There are so many out there, you can do that in a couple hours. Then we'll both have as many as everybody else."

"Alright. I just want to get off this boat."

"Me, too, but the best thing to do is blend in. I'm going

back up, now. You come up in a few minutes. We'll order breakfast. Talk to people. Get into it. Act like this is the best thing you've done in years."

"Okay. I get it. I'll see you up top."

Back on the blood-drenched deck, the galley seats were taken, so JP stood near the lady-fisher and her boyfriend, where they watched the crew wash the blood off the dead fish with a hose before dropping them through a hatch in the floor and into a huge freezer compartment.

"Congratulations for getting that first fish," JP said to Michael. "You obviously knew what you were doing."

"It's been a while, but it's like riding a bicycle; it's hard to unlearn."

"Yeah, I guess so. How many have you caught so far?"

"Between Stump and me, we have six. You might think we're nuts, but we'll be using a lot of the meat to feed my father's cats. He runs a little cat museum and shelter in downtown Carlsbad."

"We'll freeze some too," Stump said.

Just then Kyle showed up and a colony of gulls plopped into the bloody waters behind the boat. "What the heck's the matter with those birds?" he asked nobody in particular.

"Simple," Michael said. "They're in search of fish guts or anchovy pieces."

"They better be careful or the sharks might get them."

"If you gentlemen will excuse me," Michael said stoically, "I'm going to slip below." She tapped Stump's hand. "I'll see you later."

Stump tilted his head. It seemed that Michael had lost some of her enthusiasm.

29

After the initial meeting in Skinhead's basement I informed the lieutenant about the location of the meeting, the secret wall panel, the illegal selling of alcohol and the safe with possible illegal weapons. None of these appeared to be big-ticket crimes but they could be lumped in with other charges later.

While I waited for the KKK boys to make the next move, I continued to wear my earring, lift weights and report to the silkscreen shop.

One day, after my shift, I'd just gotten to my car, when Kenneth Cargill climbed out of the driver's side of a nearby van. "Hey, Allen. We wanted to see if you filled out your application." By that time Skinhead piled out the other door of the van.

"Hi, guys," I said, feeling as if I'd just caught a dangerous animal with my bare hands. "Yeah, I filled it out. It's at my place."

"What do you say we spin by there and pick it up?"

I downplayed my enthusiasm. "Well, I was thinking about going to the grocery store. There are usually some ladies shopping this time of day and I might get lucky."

"Does that work?" Kenneth asked. "Picking up women at a grocery store, I mean?"

I pointed at the side of my head. "I keep telling you gents, certain chicks dig the hair and earring and would rather go out for dinner, maybe have a glass of wine, than have to go home and cook. But I can do that some other time."

"I'll ride with you," Skinhead said. "Kenneth can follow us."

On the way to my staged apartment, we spoke of all the groups the Klan boys disliked, which amounted to just about anybody other than white Protestants.

"What about your wife and the other wives?" I asked for multiple reasons. "Do they like what we do, or do they just go along with it?"

"A lot of them have grown accustomed to a certain lifestyle and don't want no outsiders threatening that. As a matter of fact, my wife was thinking about setting you up with one of her sister's friends if you check out."

I smiled. "I told ya, Earl. A few of them like the earring."

He chuckled. "And that goofy hairdo of yours. I wouldn't a guessed they like that, but they think those things make you *interesting*."

"Well, not all of them, but enough to have a good time here and there—as long as they don't got no diseases."

"You can get around that."

"Not me, man. Big Allen thinks it's rude to wear a hat in church and Little Allen thinks it's rude to wear a hat in bed."

Skinhead snickered. "That's one of the benefits of being married."

"Yeah, but that's like watching reruns on TV. There ain't many surprises. When it comes to women, I like variety." I lied while pointed out the windshield. "My place is just a few blocks up the road."

When I opened the door to my unimpressive, one-bedroom apartment I watched them glance at the few items I'd planted just for this occasion. "Sorry, I ain't got no beer, but I already told you fellows that I was planning to go to the store."

"No problem," Skinhead said while Kenneth scanned the kitchen table where I had stacked a Bible on top of a few papers.

"You guys gotta check out my flag," I said. "It ain't as big as the one behind Earl's bar but it dresses up a bedroom." So did the .38 and a black holster that I'd draped across my headboard.

After they scanned the place, we returned to the kitchen, where I handed Skinhead the application. While he looked it over, Kenneth flipped through the Bible, presumably to verify it was the non-Catholic version.

"What's that?" Skinhead asked, pointing to the framed article that I had placed on the end table.

"Oh that?" I said, reaching for the frame. "See for yourself."

I sat silently as Skinhead read the article and Kenneth looked over his shoulder. After reading a few lines, Skinhead raised his eyes my way. "Are you saying this is about you?"

Sergeant Jillian had prepared me for that exact question. I smiled mischievously. "That's exactly what I'm trying to avoid saying, Earl."

"Oh, really? I think you did it."

"I ain't saying yes."

Kenneth raised a finger. "Yeah, but you ain't saying no, either."

"Well then, Kenneth, let's just agree that nobody knows who did it."

"True, but an innocent person wouldn't have a reason to frame a clipping like this."

"Hey," Skinhead said. "You wanna go over to Robbie's place for a couple beers and a little premature celebrating?"

"Celebrating?"

"Yeah. You're practically a member of the den already."

"I guess I could drive. I got plenty of room in my LTD."

On the way to the bar, Skinhead and Kenneth claimed to know the Klan's rising star, Tom Metzger. If I wanted to drop names, I could have told them I knew the police chief, but I elected to keep that morsel of truth to myself.

When we got to the bar, Skinhead put his hand on my shoulder and guided me past eight or ten loud tables and to the bar. After a couple beers and some big talk, two young ladies, both blondes, wandered my way.

"I told you," the shorter-haired one said to her gal-pal before speaking to me. "We saw your hair colors and wondered if it was just powder."

Uh-oh. Flirting. Even though I'd been bragging about my conquests at grocery stores and elsewhere for a couple weeks, they caught me off-guard. Nevertheless, I'd intentionally taken on this character to escape my former woes and this was a good chance to trade places with my off-beat image. A quick glance at Skinhead and Kenneth revealed toothy smiles.

"It's real hair," I said. "You can run your fingers through it if you want to but go real slow 'cause it turns me on."

They both giggled and rubbed my frizzy hair as if it were a fortuneteller's glass ball. "I just love your earring," the long-haired one said, "but why do you have just one?"

I smiled at Skinhead as if to say *I told you so.*

"I can't answer that out loud. I'd have to whisper it to ya."

"Okay," she said leaning forward where I got a whiff of her hair. I'd forgotten how much I liked clean-smelling hair.

"The left ear means I like girls," I whispered. *"The right ear would mean I like boys."*

She tapped my chin. "Well, I think it's cute. We have to go now, but if you'd ask me for my number, I'd give it to you."

I grabbed a napkin and a pen. "Sure. My name's Allen."

"I'm Rayleen. I'm available this weekend," she said as she wrote her name and number on the napkin before walking off with her pal, which earned me a couple backslaps.

A little later Skinhead said, "I got a little confession for ya, Allen. When you were at my house for that meeting, we wrote down your license plate number and found out some things about you. I'm supposed to ask you why you've moved so much."

I smiled inside and thought of Cynthia Koyle. "I got tired of noise and cockroaches."

30

Back on shore, two County detectives and two uniformed officers in a patrol car responded to a call from Julia Grundell, a 60ish manager of a townhome community who'd said she'd discovered a dead resident.

Detective Ricardo Flores pointed to a woman standing in the driveway of the home where the corpse was found. "That must be Mrs. Grundell," he said to his partner, Detective Linda Jenkins.

All four officers converged on the woman. "Thank you all for coming," the manager said in a crackly voice. "I don't want to go in there again, if I don't have to."

"No ma'am," Detective Flores said. "That won't be necessary, but we'd like to ask you a few questions now if it's okay. Then you can give us your contact information and we'll come see you a little later if we have any further questions. Who is the victim?"

"Joann Clayton," Mrs. Grundell said, shaking her head. "She was a nice woman."

"Does she live alone?"

"No. Her husband is Stu. He's nice too."

"Any kids?"

"I think they have a married daughter who lives out of state."

"Do you know how we can reach any of them?"

"He's an architect. I think I have his number back at my place."

"Was there any sign of him, either yesterday or today?"

She shook her head and released a deep breath. "No, but I don't think he'd do anything like this."

"We just have to ask these things, ma'am. How did you come upon the body?"

"Some of our residents instruct the delivery companies to drop off packages with me when the residents are not home. I got one of those yesterday for Joann. After dinner, I called to tell her about it, but she didn't answer. So, I tried again this morning. But that didn't work either, so I brought it up myself to put inside their front door." She put her hand over her mouth and nearly sobbed. "But then I saw the blood—and hammer. That poor woman."

"But you never saw anybody else at her property, or anything unusual?"

"No. Not really. Nothing like this has ever happened in this community. Up until now we never really had to watch out for that sort of thing."

"Okay. That will be all for now, Mrs. Grundell. Give these officers your information—including Mr. Clayton's number—and we'll come talk with you when we're done if we have any additional questions."

"I just hope everybody else around here is safe."

While the uniformed officers secured some yellow tape to indicate that the home was a crime scene, the detectives moved to the front door where they examined the frame and the door itself.

"Nothing out of the ordinary," Flores said.

Detective Jenkins shrugged her shoulders. "Looks like the perp either had a key or was allowed in by the victim."

"If this area is as safe as the manager suggested, the victim might just leave her door unlocked. The perp could have walked right in."

"Yeah, but why here?" Jenkins said. "And why her?"

"Dunno. Let's have a look around."

In the living room, Jenkins said, "Given the tidiness in here, if this was a robbery, the perps probably got what they wanted without much resistance, and if that's the case, it's probably not a robbery gone bad."

"Unless she knew the robber and he didn't want her to identify him," Flores said as they reached the kitchen.

"Now we know this was no robbery," he said pointing toward Mrs. Clayton's head. "Robbers don't ordinarily bring hammers with them. Or bash their victims' heads that many times."

Jenkins nodded. "We can eliminate a professional hit, too. A pro would have used a gun and silencer. This was personal."

"It looks like all the action was right here, in the kitchen," Flores said, putting on rubber gloves and picking up the bloody hammer. "Let's bag this. It's got tissue and hair on it. Forensics can check it for prints."

Jenkins gloved up and bagged the hammer while Flores leaned over and looked closely at the wounds.

"There's something else we can assume. It would take a hell of a lot of force to do this much damage to a skull. Our perp is probably an adult male who was very angry."

"Like a jealous husband. I'll look around, to see if there's anything else unusual we should examine."

A little later Jenkins returned. "I found a couple things. The closet contained both male and female clothes and the master bath had multiple toothbrushes and an electric razor."

"That pretty much confirms that hubby still lives here."

"The only other things I found were her purse, and this weird little envelope and key on their dresser."

"That's a safe deposit box key."

"Really? I wouldn't know. I've never owned anything valuable enough to need one."

"Since that key is the only thing out of place around here, our victim may have been at the bank recently."

"That could mean any number of things."

"What about the purse?"

"Nothing out of the ordinary. But there are some car keys and her checkbook. It's from CalWest Bank on North Del Mar."

"We'll go over there later. For now, let's see if we can figure out where hubby is, starting with the garage."

"I take it you'll want to search any cars in there?"

"Always, always, always."

In the garage area, "Just one car in here," Flores said to Detective Jenkins. "Maybe the titles to their vehicles are in their bank box. Then we can put whatever husband drives on look-out. Why don't you look over her car while I check out the storage cabinet?"

"Got it. I'll start with the trunk."

On the workbench Detective Flores spotted a bottle of rat poison and a colorful brochure with some pictures of boats on it. He opened the cabinet at the end of the workbench and saw a few pieces of fishing gear. "It looks like Stu may have gone deep sea fishing out of Fisherman's Landing. Why would a man pop his wife and then go fishing?"

"Maybe he's dying and doesn't care," Jenkins said. "Or he expects to get caught and wants to take one last fling before he spends his life in prison."

"Could be. For now, he's our lead suspect. We need to find out if he's on one of the commercial boats. Why don't you call the docks, beginning with Fisherman's Landing? We might get lucky and find him right away."

"What if we do find him? Should we call the boat back in?"

"Don't think so. Those fishing boats go so slow they wouldn't be back until sundown. Besides, if we made them come back, and he's our boy, he might figure we're on to him. There's no telling if he's got a weapon. He might hijack the boat. I think it'd be better if we get out there in a smaller speedboat. We can get there by midafternoon and get back here before dark."

"Sounds like a plan, but those boats could be in Mexican waters. What about jurisdiction?"

"The crime originated here. We'll be okay. But we might ask the harbor police if they can spare a boat and driver."

"Okay, got it."

"While you're checking the docks, I'll have somebody else get a court order so we can get into our victim's safe deposit box."

31

Just as expected, my bogus newspaper article ensured I was accepted as a member of the den. The ceremony, if you want to call it that, was rather lackluster. It had been arranged in the same way as all the routine meetings. The leaders picked a day, place and time—usually in the evening, mid-week—and employed a clumsy communication chain in which they had two people call two other members, who in turn notified two additional members and so on, until everybody had been informed of the event. I was watching a brand-new episode of the TV series "M*A*S*H*" when I got my official invitation to join their club.

On the night of my induction, we gathered in the back room of a shoe store in the North Hollywood area. Only half of the members showed up. Of those, Kenneth and a loud-mouthed guy they called Doorknob because he could wrap his entire mouth around a standard doorknob, were sporting earrings—on the left ear, of course. After some typical opening comments, I was unceremoniously handed a homemade sheet-robe and a classic conic headpiece.

After I paid a symbolic ten-dollar initiation fee called a "Klectoken," we all donned our sheets and spoke admiringly of the initiation rituals of generations earlier, when burning crosses and toxic speeches were the norm.

By comparison, we guzzled beer while I took a loyalty oath and declared that I was not in law enforcement, which was absurd because any officer who was trying to infiltrate a den would certainly lie about it.

As the '80s clicked ever closer, I attended mostly benign weekly meetings where there were no secret handshakes or nods or sayings. Instead, we shared booze and talked about our adversaries while Doorknob constantly urged the newer guys to help him burn a cross in the yard of a Catholic church. Fortunately, nobody took him up on it.

Beyond that, I lifted weights with Kenneth and two other members on a fairly regular basis. That was when they began referring to me as "Padge."

Meanwhile, back at my silk-screening job, I had gotten to know the boss's daughter. Although I was attracted to Beck, the memory of Dorene and Junior was still too fresh to justify investing any time or emotion in a relationship.

On the other hand, my Klan buds and their wives introduced me to a handful of their lady-friends and relatives.

Predictably, a few of those women were very free-spirited and basically threw themselves at me. They didn't care that I had a meager job. Nor were they looking for a meaningful relationship. They simply wanted to have some fun with an affable oddball who sported colorful hair, tats and an earring.

Naturally, my character would have loved all that action, and there was no emotional connection to the women, so I went along with it and enjoyed more one-nighters than I ever would have imagined. The first couple times that I made love with naughty Klan-friendly women, I felt like an actor in a porno movie, just going through the motions. I also understood why the department preferred to hire single guys for undercover roles: A line such as "It's part of my job" simply wouldn't fly with police wives.

Other information had been revealed along the way. For instance, I figured out that the KKK boys weren't exclusively comprised of society's D students. In fact, only a few of us were lower-middle-class people. The others held respectable positions in their fields or owned their own businesses.

Additionally, both political parties were well represented. Of course, the Klan had always been a home for Bible-thumping Democrats who routinely bragged that they were superior to the *mud people*.

But the Dems weren't alone. Heartless Republicans didn't want to subsidize poorer groups via taxes or any other means.

This lack of empathy was particularly evident in black schools, which were inferior by any measure. I wondered how a society could expect students in those circumstances to attain a good education, or get a diploma, or develop the ability to land decent jobs.

For those who managed to make it to the workplace, it was harder for them to feel accepted, harder to get raises and harder to get promotions.

Throughout those days, it was incredibly difficult for me to pretend I liked the sheet-heads, but that was also part of what made it all work for me on a personal level. Society needed people like me to undermine these hateful groups and I needed a reason to make my life worth living.

So, outwardly I professed hatred for blacks, Jews, Mexicans and Catholics, but the Klan was my real adversary. The uncomfortable paradox was that some of my hate-speak was coming more naturally.

Another interesting thing happened in those months. Tom Metzger, the local rising star of the KKK, had figured out that he could get on TV talk shows by constantly agitating against the Jews for immoral capitalistic greed. Blacks were also attacked for having no souls. As a result of Metzger's success, David Duke declared him the Grand Wizard of California. I didn't know it then, but I would later meet Metzger's son.

Eventually, the den landed an opportunity to garner more attention when a radical left-wing militant group of students planned a protest against the federal government for its imperialism.

That sparked Tom Metzger to call a counter-protest because we could get good coverage. Naturally, the prospect of a new counter-protest stoked certain internal fires among our membership. We ranted about kicking some black guy's ass or how much trouble the Jews had caused.

By the time all the pot-stirring was over, it appeared that everyone wanted to be at the event. We all agreed to hand out fliers the day before.

As for me, the counter-protest presented an opportunity to suppress loneliness and appreciate the fact than I had become one of the group and could eventually pull the carpet out from under the whole nefarious gang.

The only thing left to do was report the upcoming counter-protest to my handler, Lieutenant Jack Aladar. I had no idea he'd have a knock-me-down revelation of his own.

32

By early afternoon, Captain Greg had followed the recommendations of the captain of the Sea Scout and located another huge school of albacore. This time, everybody on the *Trawler* knew how to play the bizarre game of fishing-pole-go-over, fishing-pole-go-under.

As before, a troller hooked the first fish; then the chummer and other fishers bombarded the water with spunky anchovies, most with sharp silver-coated hooks in their gills. Almost immediately the instincts and curiosity of the school took over. Fishing reels sang as a new batch of albacore flopped bloody on deck.

Before long, Michael and Stump had accumulated nine fish, with Michael besting Stump five to four. Even more impressive, some of the better fishers already had more than their limit. "After all," Rusty said in their defense, "most of the fish get cut into fillets so it's impossible for the Mexican police to tell how many fish got chopped up."

"Besides," JP added, "we paid a ton of money to come on this voyage and fresh albacore is nine bucks a pound at the store. I want my money's worth."

"Another thing," Kyle said, "since we paid for a two-day license, we should be allowed to keep five fish from each day."

That made a little sense to Stump. Of course, there was one other reason to relax the rule. There were so many friggin' fish in these schools it was ridiculous, and there had to be hundreds, if not thousands, of other schools. If everybody ended up with twice as many fish as the limit, it would be less damaging than a long-tongued anteater slurping up a few ants from a field of a thousand anthills. It simply wouldn't matter.

After the basic message of abundance had soaked into the collective heads of the group, the fishing became even better. Captain Greg played his guitar from the upper deck. People grabbed a leisurely cup of coffee and shot the breeze in the galley, knowing they could get right back in the frenzy whenever the mood struck.

Others realized there were just as many fish at the bow as the stern, so they fished from up there, leaving everybody with a lot more room.

With all the fishers at ease, the crew washed down the deck regularly, which was less likely to attract another shiver of sharks.

By that time the ocean had calmed down too. No matter where Stump went on the boat, he unconsciously dipped and swayed as needed.

"This is fishing nirvana," he said to Michael when she returned from a short visit to the sleeping compartment. Then Stump watched the Chicago Cubs fan walk toward her.

"Good news, Babe. You get another chance. Whaddaya say?"

Stump chuckled. In addition to Michael's stint as an MP in the Marines, where she had hand-to-hand combat training, she had also worked in a bar for a couple years. In other words, Michael knew how to deal with guys like that.

"Do you take 'jerk pills' or does rude behavior just come naturally to you?" she asked.

"Now that's not nice. How 'bout a beer?"

"I told you before, I'm taken."

"By that Boy Scout? You should drop the loser. Go with the 'cruiser.'"

"The cruiser, huh? You?"

"You bet. I ain't never had no complaints."

She plopped her hands on her hips. "Well, let me tell you something, Mr. Cruiser Man. If this boat capsized and you and I were the only two to survive, I still wouldn't have a beer with you. Now leave me alone."

Stump almost laughed at the guy but grinned instead. He liked the fact that Michael could take care of herself when she needed to.

After giving Michael a thumbs-up sign, he went to the bait tank, picked out an excited 'chovie, delicately slipped the hook through its gill and lowered it over the rail. It swam quickly away from the boat for fifteen yards but not quickly enough to escape the maw of a hungry albacore. He set the hook like an old salt. "Hook-up!" he screamed with the calmed confidence of someone who'd been there, done that.

Without a coach, he methodically drew his fish to the boat. Then, when the time was right, "Gaff. I need a gaff," he yelled.

By the time Rusty arrived, Stump's fish rolled over, as if it were a dog earning a biscuit in the park. Mere minutes later a tag to a gill indicated that fish belonged to Number Six and another "albie" was on its way to a below-deck hold.

After that, Michael went off on her own again only this time she seemed to be agitated. Then Stump realized he was standing next to the moron with the Chicago Cubs hat. "I know what you've been doing, dude, and you're messing with the wrong woman."

"Oh really? Zat a threat?"

Stump could have mentioned Michael's background but an ornery part of him hoped that Michael would have a good chance to plop the guy on the deck like a defeated albacore. "Oh, no. I'm just giving you fair warning not to do something you might regret."

"Yeah, I ain't worried about a Cub Scout, like you."
The dude had it all wrong, which was the point.

* * *

In her sleeping compartment, Michael sighed and reached for her bag. She'd already taken three of the original Oxycontin, each time convincing herself that it was the final one. Then that asshole Cub idiot pissed her off. He was lucky she didn't put a smackdown on him.

But now she was suddenly sleepy and her wrist wasn't completely healed. The only way to get out of her funk was to find that bottle of relief she brought with her and get one last pill. Then she could throw the whole bottle away and tough it out the rest of the trip.

She found the bottle, poured a pill into her hand, tossed it in her mouth and washed it down with bottled water. That done, she waited for a few minutes, then threw the pill bottle back into her bag and returned to the main deck.

33

As was the norm for most of the officers in the undercover roles, the majority of my contacts with my handler, Lieutenant Jack Aladar, were via twice-weekly phone calls. Ordinarily we discussed my actions, progress, and findings of the previous days before we went over plans for the days to come. Then, once a month, I met with Jack in his office, usually around 6:00 a.m.

Proud of myself for having learned that Metzger wanted our den to carry out a counter-protest, I met the lieutenant on a Wednesday.

"How you holding up?" he immediately asked.

"It's still rough but getting better."

"What else do you have for us? You still on good terms with Earl Someda?"

"Skinhead? Oh, yeah. He trusts me and likes me, but I wouldn't say I'm his go-to guy yet. Kenneth fills that role."

"Has anybody new entered the equation?"

"Some guy named Martin Seawald dropped by."

"Tell me about him."

"He's tall, from the Midwest. Didn't seem very interested."

"Be sure to keep me informed if he should come back. We'll do a background check, just in case. What about Kerry Conklin?"

I'd mentioned Conklin a few weeks back. A pudgy guy, with a wife and five kids, he'd said he moved from San Francisco. "So far, he's on-again-off-again," I said. "Doesn't get to every meeting."

"You got anything on him?"

"Not really; he's one of these deep water types. He doesn't ring any loud bells, but you just know there's some stinkin' thinkin' going on under the surface."

"Noted. How about Thorn? How's he behaving?"

"Myron's another one who's hard to read. He's a middle-of-the-pack guy. Sorta quiet."

"Anybody else strike you as dangerous?"

"Yeah. I think Doorknob is up to no good."

"Steven Houser? Like what?"

"I think he got a buzz out of that article the department made about me and wants to do the same thing."

"Run over somebody with a vehicle? Did he say as much?"

"Not in so many words. It could be just bluster, but he suggested we get together at midnight and go hunting for some black people we can harass or even run over—either that or help him burn a cross in the yard of a Catholic church."

"What did you say?"

"I didn't want to discourage him, in case we want to arrest him, so I just nodded."

"Good. Like you said, he could just be talking big. Let's see if he pushes the matter, then we might be able to pin some conspiracy charges on him. Anybody else embrace the idea?"

"Kenneth more or less nodded, but nobody else indicated anything one way or the other."

"Any other unfinished business before we refill our cups and move on?"

"Yeah. Now that you mention it, Skinhead says that Tom Metzger is making a name for himself."

"What's Mr. Metzger up to now?"

"It's just gossip but Skinhead claims Metzger is particularly upset with the Jews."

144

"We've noticed that. Do you have any knowledge of his upcoming plans?"

"Not really. From what I can tell, the entire organization is so disorganized it's a miracle they get anything done."

"How so?"

"Their meetings seem impulsive. There isn't much structure to anything they do."

"That's true nationally, too. We think that's one of the reasons they're losing membership. Anything else?"

"Yeah. Skinhead said they're planning a march this coming Saturday. Metzger and his allies think the publicity will gain us the attention of other like-minded people, hopefully to join us and grow our number."

"The one at Disneyland?"

Jack's comment caught me completely off-guard. My news was as fresh as the first batch of donuts at a bakery in the morning, but somehow Jack already knew of it. "How did you know that?" I asked.

"It doesn't matter."

That too was a strange reply. Why the secrecy? Regardless, I didn't want to press him. After all, he'd treated me well most of the time. This was the only secret or negative thing to have happened since I met him.

"That'll be all for today," he said. "Get back out there, keep your eyes and ears open."

That night, while watching TV, it hit me. There must have been another UC officer among the den members. Either that or the lieutenant got a tip from one of his counterparts.

From that time on, I suspected there was another officer in the den, which begged another rhetorical question. If they already had somebody else inside the den, then why did they need me?

34

Buzzing toward the fishing grounds in a stout, unmarked motorboat, Detectives Jenkins and Trent and Sergeant Flores were still an hour away from the *Trawler*. Flores spoke with their driver, Officer Davos of the harbor police. "At least the water is fairly smooth."

"Yeah," the weathered officer said, "it's usually worse." He turned toward the back seat. "How 'bout you two? You doing okay?"

"I'm glad I get to ride in the front seat on the way back," Jenkins said.

"Just remember, if you gotta up-chuck, do it over the rail, or you get to clean up your mess when we get back to shore."

Detective Trent spoke next. "How we gonna play this, Sergeant?"

"Good question. When we get a little closer to them, we'll need to verify their position and confirm that Clayton is on board, but I don't want to alarm anybody. That's why I told you guys to dress casually."

Just then a call came in. "Yeah, he's here," Davos said to the caller before handing the phone to Flores. "It's a Detective Richards."

"Good. He must be at the bank. Hey, detective. You got any news for us?"

"Yep. We got the warrant like you asked and went to the bank. You'll never guess what we found in that woman's safe deposit box."

"Let me guess. Clayton cleaned it out."

"No, sir. In fact, it looks like his wife was the last one in there. Aside from titles to their cars and a deed to their home and a couple other benign documents, there was an envelope right on top, with a very brief letter from Mrs. Clayton. I can read it to you if you'd like."

"Yeah. Let me put it on speaker first," he said, causing Davos to tap a button in the dash. "Okay. Go ahead, Detective."

"Here goes. 'To whom it may concern, If I'm dead, my husband did it. He hates me. Wants our house to himself. I'm scared.'"

"Is that it?"

"Yep. Short and to the point."

"It doesn't prove anything, but it pretty much supports what we already suspected. Thanks for your efforts, Detective. Good job."

After disconnecting the sergeant returned his attention to those in the boat. "As it looks now, we could have means, motive, a weapon and the note. With all of that, we might squeeze a confession out of Stu Clayton."

"But how are we going to do that without spooking him? If he's got a gun, he could take the whole boat hostage or go on a shooting spree."

"That's why we're going to get him to come to us."

* * *

Back on the *Trawler*, a happy-faced Michael got two sodas from the galley and found Stump, who was thinking about studying. "Let's go to the upper deck," she said. "We can sit on the benches, away from the noise, and enjoy a little peace."

Nearly anything was better than more studying. After a brief tour of the captain's bridge, they sat on the padded benches, sipped their drinks and let the better part of a calm hour belie the organized chaos on the main deck.

Eventually, Stump removed his Jackalope cap and rubbed his head. "I've got hat hair," he said. "Do you think they'd mind if I take a shower?"

"Probably not. As long as one of the restrooms stays open. Why don't you ask Captain Greg?"

Stump nodded and rose, but before he reached the captain a message came in over the ship-to-shore radio. *"Base to Trawler. Do you read me, Trawler?"*

"Yes, base. Captain Gregg here. I've got you. Go ahead."

"Can you talk in complete privacy, Captain?"

"There are a couple customers on my upper deck, but I can clear them if you need me to."

"Please do, Captain."

A moment later, as Stump descended the ladder from the upper deck, he observed the captain pull the door to his cubicle area closed. Something unusual was up.

Down on the main deck, he and Michael were left to speculate what the incoming message was all about. "Maybe there's a storm coming," Stump suggested.

Michael looked all around. "I doubt it. There are only a few clouds and they're small."

"Now that I think about it, they wouldn't have chased us off because of a weather forecast. I guess we'll find out soon enough. I hear that Ernie makes an excellent albacore steak sandwich."

"That sounds good. Maybe he'll give me his recipe."

* * *

"Okay, Sergeant," Captain Gregg said. "We're all alone. What can I do for you?"

"Thanks, Captain. There's been a homicide. We have reason to believe that the perpetrator is on your craft. We're coming out to get him, but we're going to need your help. Based on our GPS it looks as if you're out by the Shelf. That correct?"

"Affirmative. We're over a good-sized school of albacore."

"What about Mr. Stewart Clayton? Can you see him?"

"We get a new batch of guys every trip, Detective. I only know a few of them by name. Right now, nearly everybody is fishing, but I've got our registration roster right here. I can tell you that he signed up early and I show that he signed up for the jackpot. So, he's definitely onboard. Do you want me to fetch him?"

"No. No. No. The less he knows, the better. Just keep doing what you ordinarily do. We're about 8.4 nautical miles from you. Should be there in about 20 minutes or so. I'll call you with instructions then. We're planning on faking a break-down a couple miles from your location, so you can pretend to offer assistance. That way Clayton won't know that the police are on to him until we've got him under control."

"I understand, Sergeant. Let me know when you're ready."

"Good enough. Out."

35

A couple days prior to the counter-protest I was still trying to make sense out of the fact that Jack was gathering information about the Klan from somebody besides me. Who was it? The most perplexing part was the secrecy, which made me wonder if they were spying on me.

Meanwhile, I employed my new silk-screening skills and made myself a few T-shirts that boasted large American flags and a popular slogan of the time: My Country - Right or Wrong. I planned to wear one to the counter-protest.

On the morning of the rally, a few of my den-mates arrived at the designated location before me. Being just a half-mile from the Disneyland entrance, thousands of people would see us, and some might want to join our den.

"Hello, Allen," a female voice soon said from off to my right. I turned to see Kenneth's wife and her sister, Jerri Grove, who was one of a handful of young women who'd been introduced to me by den members.

I'd slept with most of them at least once, primarily because that was what my character would have done, but to be perfectly honest there was some basic ego gratification too. After all, I'd only been with one woman for quite a while before that and it was nice to know I had some appeal to other women.

Anyway, Jerri was more domestically inclined than the other women. She spoke regularly and fondly of relationships and families and seemed to be testing my willingness to enter into a monogamous arrangement, but that was impossible. Aside from the fact that I wasn't who I was pretending to be, my job was to gather data, some of it against her brother-in-law, and I couldn't do that if she or anybody else were constantly in the picture.

I tried to figure out how to back out of the situation, but how do you tell a nice person who would do practically anything for you that it won't work?

"Hi, Jerri," I said, focused on another dilemma. This whole rally/counter-protest event had the potential to get real ugly, as was proved at the last event when a beer bottle banked off Skinhead's eyebrow.

The emotionally wounded person inside me, who was probably overly sympathetic to victims, didn't want anybody to get physically hurt, not even the Klan members or their supporters.

"I don't know if Kenneth told you," I said to her, "but this place isn't safe."

"I know," she said. "I've been to these events before. I just wanted to see you."

She obviously hadn't given up. Then I got an idea. "I don't have much time, Jerri," I said, pointing at a large nearby bush, "but can we go over there and talk for a minute."

Once there, I said, "I'm probably mistaken but I keep getting the feeling that you want us to have some sort of relationship. That would never work for me. I'm sorry if I've led you on, but I'm the kind of guy who likes to play the field. I get tired of the same woman and it would happen with you. I don't want to fall in love, and I could never be faithful to you. I'd cheat all the time. You deserve somebody much better. I think you'd make someone a great mom and a great wife, just not me. Okay?"

She paused a moment. Then, "Yeah. Thanks for being

honest, Allen. I'm disappointed—and sad—but I wish everybody could do that. It would make things a lot easier."

That "being honest" comment reeked of irony. My whole life was a lie—a lie for the good, I'd argue—but a lie nonetheless. In fact, at that moment there were only a few absolute truths in my world: first, I didn't want to hurt Jerri; second, I still wanted to thwart my den-mates whenever possible; and third, I would never go back to black-and-whites.

As I wandered back toward the gathering spot, I almost laughed. In spite of all the brazen talk at our meeting, only about half the den members showed up, mostly the hardcore ones—Doorknob being the most obvious. But there was a flip side to that coin.

For me to gather dirt on these guys, I needed them to be where I could interact with them. Of those who made it, most wore hefty boots, just in case they had a good chance to kick somebody's head in. I could only imagine a few of those fellows instigating something like that, but graves and prisons were packed with ignorant people who got drawn into unexpected, out-of-control violence. All of these guys were capable of that.

We took up a position near a traffic light where drivers had to stop. By that time, several media types had seen the action. One of them asked me if I wanted to talk on air, but I referred them to Doorknob. He was always willing to open his big mouth.

As the cars stopped, I told those with their windows down that I was with the Klan and passed out handbills that invited them to come join us. Of course, that provoked a lot more people than it pleased.

It's not an exaggeration to say half the people hated me enough to call me names or spit at me. I hated being hated and would have liked to tell those folks that I was actually on their side, but that wasn't going to happen.

As the day unfolded, I remained in character and observed

my counterparts while wondering if one of them was a mole, just like me.

Eventually, we called it quits and were told that our next meeting would be the following night. We were going to get together and compare notes to determine how much success we had had. Unbeknownst to me, a polygraph expert, nicknamed Tiny, would be there too.

36

"Listen up, everybody," Captain Gregg said over the loud speaker. "I'm afraid we've got a broken-down boat a few miles away. Since we're the closest boat to it, we've got to pull up all our lines and provide assistance."

The message was barely completed before people who were as content as sleepy kittens mere minutes earlier roared in protest. "Haven't these idiots heard of tow boats?" somebody snapped.

"Yeah, and we already lost a couple hours today."

"Let somebody else forfeit their time," the Chicago Cubs fan shouted.

While others bemoaned their collective fate, Stump and Michael leaned up against the side rail and watched a speck on the water slowly grow bigger and eventually take the shape of an ailing boat. "This is sorta interesting," Stump said after a few minutes.

"I'm glad you think so, but I agree with some of these other people. I came to fish, not to go for a boat ride. I'm sleepy. I'm going downstairs."

"No, Michael. Don't go," Stump said. "We can do something else if you want."

"This is boring to me and I need some sleep. I don't want to be bothered, okay?"

"Really? How can this be boring?"

"I don't have to explain it. I just want to be left alone. I'll find you later. Alright?"

Stump nodded. "I guess so. Let me know when you feel better."

Hmph. How the heck could she be bored? Just a while ago she was happy just sitting on the upper deck. Now they were in rescue mode. That should be interesting. Maybe she was dealing with monthly issues. Naw. She just went through that a couple weeks ago. This was something else. Oh well, she was well past 21 and entitled to make her own decisions. He might as well just do what she asked and return his attention to the rescue mission.

"I'll get the fenders," Beardo said as he opened a storage compartment and pulled out a couple heavy-duty Styrofoam tubes about the thickness of a telephone pole. Using fancy knots, Beardo tied one end of the Styro-tubes to the cleats of the boat and dangled the tubes over the edge.

Stump didn't know a lot about boating, but it appeared as if they were going to draw the two boats together, and these Styrofoam tubes were like bumpers to keep the boats from banging into each other.

As the *Trawler* slowly drew closer to the immobilized boat, Stump noticed four people on the smaller craft, three males and one woman, all in casual clothes. There was no sign of fishing poles so they must have just gone out for a sightseeing cruise.

Eventually Captain Greg had closed the gap between the boats. He backed off the throttle and brought his vessel alongside the smaller boat. Then, Rusty tossed a rope to a man wearing a straw hat, presumably the owner of the smaller boat. Beardo and Rusty slowly tugged the boat to the bumpers and Douglas tied off the ropes.

Almost instantly, Douglas opened the rail gate and Beardo hung a ladder over the edge for the newcomers. The man with a straw hat stayed with the smaller boat while the other two men, one apparently Hispanic, and a ponytailed woman, who looked like she'd been up all night, made their way onto the deck and boldly kept going to the ladder that led to the captain's bridge.

Stump recalled when he and the others had boarded the *Trawler*. Other than the crew, nobody rushed to the upper deck as these people did. This was something other than a broken-down boat. He needed to get where he could hear or see what was going on.

He drifted up the walkway and stopped just below the feet of those on the upper deck. They appeared to be talking about a missing person.

A few minutes later the captain paged Rusty to the upper deck, and then requested the cook's breakfast clipboard.

Stump nonchalantly migrated back toward the ladder and waited for Rusty to gather the papers.

A half-minute later Stump followed Rusty up the ladder and sat on one of the padded benches, pretending to ignore the goings-on.

Almost instantly, the newcomers were pointing at names on the breakfast list. Stump could tell by their tone that they were authorities of some kind and must have been looking for a particular person.

Then the captain picked up his microphone. "Attention, everybody. We're looking for Number Four. Stewart Clayton. Is Number Four down there?"

Stewart Clayton? Stump remembered meeting that man when he and Michael first signed in and later in the galley before they went to bed. But now that he thought about it, he hadn't seen the man since. Whatever the problem was, it was likely to explain why Number Four didn't take his turn trolling earlier in the day.

For the moment, just about everybody looked around at belts and tags, but nobody pointed out Number Four. Stump wondered if Mr. Clayton could have fallen overboard—or been pushed—without anybody noticing.

With no sign of Number Four, one of the new arrivals stepped to the edge of the upper deck where he could speak with the fishers below. He quickly produced a badge and spoke loudly.

"Can I have everybody's attention, please? I'm Sergeant Ricardo Flores with the police. The other people who came on board with me are also detectives. We're here on official police business and want everybody to stay back and away from the stairs leading down to the bunkrooms until further notice. Failure to comply could lead to your arrest for impeding a police investigation. Now, everybody move as far away as you can from that area." He turned to Stump. "You too, son, you'll have to join the others."

While the fishers followed orders and Stump descended the ladder he smiled for having figured out that the newbies were detectives. Then he realized that Michael was down in their sleeping compartment, right where the detectives were headed. She could be in danger.

He had no choice; he had to get her out of there. In spite of the directions to the contrary he bolted down the stairs, two at a time, and pushed his way into the tiny room and flicked on the light. From the top bunk, Michael sighed and rolled his way. "What do you want? I asked you to leave me alone."

"Sorry Michael," he whispered, "it couldn't be helped. The police are coming down here to find Mr. Clayton. It could be dangerous. We gotta get out of here."

37

Red. Red. Everywhere red.
A pool of blood the black man shed.
Ankle deep, my mind's eye said.
Red. Red. Get out of bed.
Legs wouldn't move. I cried instead.
Looked down again and he was dead.
Black man's babies held his head.
"But Daddy, Daddy," naked one said.
"We have no clothes and we need fed."
He looked at me, as cold as lead
And on my hands, the black man bled.

Suddenly I awoke, both sad and relieved that the nightmare was over. As at previous times, my entire bed was damp from all the guilt-sweat. All I could do was remind myself that I "had to" kill that man. I took a few deep breaths and slowly headed for the shower.

* * *

Sometimes what we don't say rings louder than a bullhorn on a mountaintop. That was the case the next morning. After I put in a couple hours at the silk-screening shop, I called the lieutenant with a report.

Like me, Jack was disappointed that half my den buddies had failed to attend the rally, but when I advised him that they'd called for a follow-up meeting to analyze the results, he urged me to be there and see if there was any other news to be gleaned. And that's when something dawned on me.

It was obvious by Jack's comments and demeanor that he had not heard of the follow-up meeting. That was different from the last time that I fed him some hot news only to find out he already knew all about it.

I reasoned, if there were indeed another mole in the den, that person hadn't said a word about the follow-up meeting to Jack, at least not yet, probably because whoever it was hadn't attended the rally where the announcement was made.

I still didn't know if any of this "other mole" idea had legs, but if I ever were to need an ally, I could assume the other mole was from the group of people who did not attend the rally.

That afternoon I punched out, made sure I wasn't being followed and drove to my real home. There, I eventually glared in Dorene's dressing mirror where a formerly naïve and happily married father had been replaced by a less-happy fellow with rainbow hair, an earring, tattoos and a one-of-a-kind T-shirt—and who'd been playing bunny rabbits with female friends of the local KKK.

After a shower, I threw a frozen TV dinner into our very first microwave oven and grinned. A couple years prior, when those things first came out, I thought they were stupid, but Dorene was more in tune with the future than I was. Eventually, she won me over and I hadn't used our other oven since she passed. Obviously, rethinking those days made me miss Dorene.

While I had a little time, I watched some TV and turned the volume up to offset the stillness of a childless home.

When I arrived at Skinhead's place, I observed a different vehicle in the driveway, a 10-year-old, black '68 Ford Mustang GT fastback that mirrored the classic one Steve McQueen drove in the movie "Bullitt." I glad-eyed the vehicle before slipping into the home and down the stairs to the basement, where I was ready for a conversation about the previous day's activities, but instead Skinhead led me to a back room. There a big guy with a polygraph machine sat at an old kitchen table.

"What's going on?" I quizzed.

"A lie detector," Skinhead said. "We all take them from time to time. This is Samuel Goode, but we call him Tiny."

Caught completely off-guard, I offered my hand to Tiny but got a wimpy cold fish handshake in return. "Sit down," he said matter-of-factly while he pointed to a vinyl-covered chair across the table from him.

I wondered what the hell to say.

Skinhead handed me a small paper cup with water in it. "We take an oath not to talk about these tests with new members, but don't worry, you'll do fine."

It would have looked suspicious to put up any resistance, so I took my seat across from Tiny. Skinhead sat at the head of the table between us.

"You ever take a poly before?" Tiny asked.

I thought about my orientation process, back when Cynthia had set me up with a professional polygrapher. I almost snickered. I'd barely entered the room and I already had to lie. "No. I wouldn't have a reason to do that. What do I have to do?"

"Everybody is nervous at first, but the key is to relax. You can loosen your clothes before we begin. After we plop a couple sensors on your fingertips and chest, we'll wrap your upper arm with a blood pressure strap. Then I'll ask you a series of simple questions. You'll know all the answers so just tell the truth because if you lie, well, just don't lie."

"Sounds fun," I said, adding another lie-link to the chain that was sure to follow.

A couple minutes later I had so many wires and sensors and straps attached to me that I looked like I was on life support.

"You fellows ready?" Tiny quizzed as he pulled out a small notebook.

Skinhead nodded. "I am," he said, before looking at me.

"Sure. Okay by me."

38

After a little explaining and back on the main deck, a groggy Michael shook her head and went to the bow, while Stump slid just around the corner of the stairway where he listened to the detectives discuss what to do about Mr. Clayton.

"We gotta check his sleeping compartment," the sergeant said. "If he's not down there, he went overboard. Tanner, you guard the stairway while Linda and I go below."

This was getting interesting. While the detectives moved into position, Stump inched closer to the stairway to the sleeping area.

When the detectives reached the stairs the sergeant took over. "Everybody ready?" he asked his partners.

Stump sure was. He assumed that they'd already drawn their weapons.

* * *

At the bottom of the stairs, Detectives Flores and Jenkins located Clayton's room and squatted to make themselves smaller, just in case their suspect had a weapon. Flores knocked. "Mr. Clayton? Are you in there?"

Getting no reply, Flores tried again. "Mr. Clayton, this is

the police. Come out so we can speak with you. Make this easy on everybody."

More silence. He tried again. "We know what you did to your wife, Mr. Clayton, and we know you expected to get caught so come on out now. You can't win this."

Detective Flores chin-pointed to his partner and mouthed for her to give it a try.

Still crouched, the woman duck-walked to the doorframe. "Mr. Clayton. This is Detective Linda Jenkins. I promised my children I'd be safe today. If you don't come out, we're going to come in. You wouldn't want a mother of three children in a confrontation like that, would you?"

Complete silence prompted her to try again. "Mr. Clayton. Can you hear me, Mr. Clayton? Make some noise, sir, so we'll know you're in there."

With no response, Detective Flores scooted to the far side of the doorframe and grasped the knob. "Last chance to do the right thing, Mr. Clayton. You don't want to put everybody on this boat in danger, do you?"

With only one thing left to do, Detective Flores held his weapon in his right hand and moved his other hand to the door handle. "Ready?" he whispered to his partner.

Double-handing her weapon, Jenkins nodded her approval.

Flores slowly twisted the handle until he felt the latch disengage.

With nothing but silence in Mr. Clayton's compartment, Flores used his weapon to push slowly at the door until he saw a man's torso on the floor. Flores knew who it was. Since the man didn't move or moan, the detective reached a hand to Clayton's neck. The chilly body answered the obvious unspoken question. Mr. Clayton was dead.

The detectives rose to their feet and holstered their weapons. The body was fairly close to the door so they forced it back just enough so that they could slide into the little room without moving the body any more than necessary.

Inside the tiny room, they quickly noticed dried caked foam at the man's mouth and an opened package of crackers.

"Looks like this man has been poisoned," Detective Jenkins said, softly. "I can get a bag. Forensics can prove it."

Flores nodded. "Yeah. I saw a bottle of poison in his garage. I'm guessing his wife's prints will be all over everything. This certainly changes things."

Jenkins nodded and tapped the pillow. "It looks like he ate bad crackers, laid down and then it hit him. He tried to get out of here but only made it to the door."

"Rough way to go."

"What now?"

"We need to preserve the evidence. We've got to get this boat back to the dock where Forensics can look it over."

"Wonderful," she said sarcastically. "That's all my stomach needs. A long boat ride. I gotta let my husband know."

"Sorry, detective. It can't be helped."

"Yeah, I know. I feel like I've got the world's worst hangover."

"This certainly sheds some light on a few things. Based on that note we already know that Mrs. Clayton suspected her husband was going to sneak up on her sooner or later so when he went fishing she knew he'd need some snacks so she launched her own pre-emptive attack."

Jenkins nodded. "One bite of his cracker and he was doomed. She wouldn't even have to deal with his body. And, revenge was her motive."

"If all of that is true," Flores added, "we've got us a double homicide. Hubby killed her and vice versa."

She shook her head. "Poetic justice, I guess."

"About all we can do now is talk to the people on this boat just in case somebody saw something 'fishy,' if you'll forgive the poor choice of words."

She smirked but said nothing.

"All right, then," he resumed. "Why don't you fill in

Detective Trent and dismiss Officer Davos. I'll go advise the captain that we're going back to the marina."

"Have you ever been hungry and afraid to eat because you can't keep anything down?"

"That's a dilemma alright. They might have a spare bunk around here. You could lie down for a while."

"Naw. That wouldn't do any good. I'll just have to tough it out and drop a little weight."

A few minutes later Captain Greg made an announcement. "Sorry, folks," he said over the speakers, "but this boat has become a crime scene and the subject of a police investigation. We have to go back to the marina. Until further notice passengers may not go below deck without authorization. While we're en route, the detectives want to talk to each of you, one by one. So, we're going to talk with the crew first, then you people will be called to the upper deck in order of your tag numbers."

"That's going to take seven fucking hours," the Cubs fan grumbled.

"Just to get to the marina," Rusty said. "Throw in another block of time for us to tie down the boat and distribute the fish."

At that moment, in a salt-on-wound gesture, the man with the straw hat started up the engine of the smaller boat and blew out of there, indicating it was operational all along. Angry comments immediately dwarfed the rumbling diesels.

"What a screw job."

"This pisses me off."

"I want my fucking money back."

39

I was never prone to insubordination, either during my years in the Marines or as a police officer, but I came damn close the day after my backroom poly. Anxious to get to a meeting I'd arranged with my handler, I kept thinking of that "Jack and Jill" comment that Cynthia Koyle had made. As far as I was concerned at that moment, both Jack Aladar, the bean juice lieutenant, and his part-time, disorganized trainer, Sergeant Robert Jillian, deserved the term—only I was the one who *fell down and broke his crown*. They were damn sure going to hear about it.

I was waiting at the lieutenant's door when he arrived just before six.

"You want some coffee?" he asked.

"No," I said curtly.

"You mind if I get some?"

"No."

A few minutes later we sat on opposite sides of his desk. "I can tell something is on your mind," he said. "What's up?"

I forced myself to stay calm. "To tell you the truth Lieutenant, I'm pissed off."

"I can see that. What's the problem?"

"You and Jillian. That's the problem. I got dragged into the goddamn backroom."

"What box? I don't know what you're talking about?"

"Alright, let me make it clear. I went to that follow-up meeting we talked about and got ambushed by a fat-ass man-tank, and you guys never prepared me for my own execution."

"I don't know what you're talking about."

"That's the problem, Lieutenant. Your lack of oversight coulda killed me. If I wanted to get fucked, I woulda found a woman."

"Let me remind you of something, Officer. I am still your supervisor and I won't have you talking to me like that."

"With all due respect," I said sarcastically, "you may not have your position for long if word gets out that your subordinates end up in meat grinders."

"What meat grinder? Let's back up a minute. You said something about a backroom. What did you mean?"

"For Christ's sake, Lieutenant, I got dragged into a backroom, hooked to a lie detector and damn near got thrown to a pack of wolves."

"A lie detector test? By the Klan?"

"Damn right, with 16 bad boys down the hall who could've ripped me to pieces if I'd failed that test. Jillian should have warned me."

"Let me see if I understand you. You went to that meeting, thinking it was a review of the rally, but they hauled you in a backroom and gave you a lie detector test? Is that it?"

"A goddam gorilla was running the show, Lieutenant. Later, when I got to drinking beer with the rest of those sheet monkeys, they told me Tiny was one of the best in the business. I could have been killed in there."

"Well, this might surprise you, but this is the first time I've ever heard of them doing that. It must be something new."

"Not entirely. One of those guys said they'd been doing it for a while."

"Well. This is the first time I've heard of it. No wonder

you're so shook up. I would be too. I take it you passed the test?"

At that moment, I realized that he really didn't know about the Klan's new toy. That made me feel a little better. "Skinhead said it was *inconclusive*. You won't believe what I had to do to confuse their little machine. Let's just say the department is going to reimburse me for a giant tube of hemorrhoid cream."

He paused for quite a while to think about my experience and what he ought to do about it. Finally, "Alright then. Now that we know what the problem is, I'll do some homework and set up a training program. We'll get our own poly guys in here to tell us what to do in situations like that. We'll need you to work with Sergeant Jillian."

"Yeah, alright. Speaking of the Sergeant, he could use some help getting organized."

"Good to know that. I'll have Ms. Koyle organize his notes. You said that the questioner's name was Tiny. You got anything else on him?"

"They said his real name is Samuel Goode. He's built like a brick shithouse and drives a fastback Mustang."

"Never heard of him. That's one of the reasons we need you. Okay, before I let you go, there's one more thing. If you ever talk to me or any other officer like that again, you'll regret it. Is that clear?

* * *

After I fell into a Grand Canyon-sized crack in the almighty system, the Lieutenant called in Warren Fitter, the polygrapher who tested me when I changed departments.

I couldn't ignore the irony. A professional poly examiner was going to tell us how to beat his own tests.

Of course, that was 40 years ago. Back then, many people held an elevated regard for the lie detector. But in the years that followed the tests were proven to be so unreliable that employers could no longer use them on employees and courts never accepted test results as evidence of guilt or innocence.

Anyway, one thing we all agreed on was if the department wanted to give our own people a poly, they should do it before we taught them how to outsmart it.

Finally, near the end of the training, Mr. Fitter suggested that I get some tacks and hide one between my two biggest toes when I attended meetings. I was encouraged to practice manipulating the tack into place on demand and stepping on it whenever I was taking the test again and needed to elevate my stress level.

After that, he gave me several pills that were guaranteed to make my blood pressure erratic. The idea was to take them with me to meetings and if I got wind there was a test, sneak into the restroom, down a pill and be the last one to go into the box. "If you're stressed the entire time," Fitter said, "there's no way for them to tell if you're lying or not."

I nodded because that was basically what I figured out when on my own.

40

After the smaller boat departed, it was obvious that Mr. Clayton had died on the boat. Sergeant Flores posted Detective Jenkins at the head of the stairway to prevent anybody from going below without her approval.

At the same time, smart alecks suggested a sea burial for the corpse. Others said the cops should have tossed the body into the smaller boat and let the fishers keep fishing. The tall banker said they should have let some of the guys on the *Trawler* go back with the smaller boat. "I would have gone," he said, "and it's morbid to stay out here any longer than necessary."

In spite of the tension, Stump wasn't as upset as the others. For one thing, dealing with the sea and reeling in fish was almost too easy. Secondly, he preferred intellectual challenges to physical challenges and that was exactly what the detectives had brought with them. Stump wondered if the death was caused by a crime or suicide or an illness. This was the kind of puzzle he loved.

"Why didn't they take the dead man back in that little boat?" an elderly man asked nobody and everybody. Stump knew the answer to that one: Police don't like to disrupt crime scenes until the forensic people check for evidence.

Before long, the detectives set up an area on the upper deck and interviewed the crew, one by one. Then they turned their attention to the customers.

After the detectives spoke with fishers One, Two and Three, Michael got the next call. She appeared to be feeling better.

While she was on the upper deck, Stump quizzed two of the men who'd already been interviewed. They were asked about their backgrounds, whether they saw Clayton arguing with anybody and if they had any idea what happened to him. Once those routine questions were put to bed, the detectives shifted their attention to the next person. There wasn't much to it.

A few short minutes later, Michael must have experienced the same thing, because she was already descending the ladder. "That was fast," Stump said to her.

"They're moving along at a pretty good pace," she said with an unexplainable grin. "What do you suppose that means?"

"I don't know. One of the guys said Stu Clayton was poisoned, but something doesn't add up."

"Whaddya mean?"

"They pretended that their boat was disabled so that we would go to them, but they had to be out here for a reason, and that reason involves Mr. Clayton."

"Maybe they knew somebody was going to kill him?"

"Don't think so. I heard them just before they found the body. They were completely stunned by his death."

"I don't know about that, but I do know that my wrist is acting up again."

"Number Six."

Stump pivoted toward the ladder to the upper deck and hustled his way to the padded bench.

Detective Trent glanced at some papers on a clipboard. "It says here your name is Stump. 'Zat right?"

"That's my nickname. My legal name is Neal Joseph Randolph."

"Your girlfriend said you're in crime school?"

"Carlsbad Criminology College, to be exact. I'm graduating pretty soon."

"Did you know Mr. Clayton in any way?"

"Not until we got on the boat and registered for the jackpot. He signed in just before Michael and me."

"Did he seem distressed?"

"Not particularly. He was alone and sorta quiet, but I didn't make much of it."

"What about after that? Did you interact with him?"

"We all just milled around, getting to know each other a little bit. I don't think I talked to him again until late at night."

"Oh, yeah? What happened?"

"It must have been about 10:30. Four of us sat around one of the tables in the dining area. The other guys were drinking beers. Eventually, I went to bed."

"Who were these other guys?"

"Kyle and JP. JP is the tall guy. They're numbers eleven and twelve."

The detective flipped a page. "Did they all know each other?"

"I don't think so. Their conversations were more like people getting to know each other."

"Was there any arguing?"

"No. Definitely not. The opposite."

"Did Mr. Clayton eat anything?"

"Not that I know of. Like I said they had a few beers though."

"But you left the three of them alone?"

"Yeah. There was a long ride ahead of us so there wasn't much else to do."

"So, they were the last ones in the galley?"

"They were when I left, but others might have wandered in after that."

"What about out on the deck? Was anybody out there?"

"I didn't see anyone. There could have been some people on the bow, but I didn't look."

"But you didn't see any tension between Mr. Clayton and anybody else on the boat. Is that correct?"

"Except for that Cubs fan hitting on my girlfriend, there wasn't much tension anywhere on the boat until the sharks came to the blood and we had to move, but whatever happened to Mr. Clayton had to have happened before that."

Detective Tanner looked at Sergeant Flores. "You got any questions for Mr. Randolph?"

Flores shook his head and spoke to Stump. "Your girlfriend was right. You do pay more attention to detail than most people. Good luck with your career."

* * *

At the back rail where the diesel engines provided enough noise to muffle nefarious conversations, JP and Kyle gathered to go over their story one last time.

"Looks like they're getting close to us," Kyle said.

"No problem. We've covered everything. Remember, they already have their suspects. They don't know about the lotto ticket, nor do we have any known motive to kill either of the Claytons. If we tell the identical story and keep it simple so we don't contradict each other, they won't have any reason to suspect us. Just remember, we were at the bait tank the first time we met the man; later we had a few beers before we went our separate ways."

"Got it. What about at the end of the night? That kid knows we were the last ones to see Clayton alive."

"We have to acknowledge that. Just say we went down to the bunks around 11 o'clock. He went to his compartment; we went to ours. He seemed fine when we left him."

"Agreed. He was fine when we all went to bed."

"Number Eleven," The detective called from the upper deck.

JP raised a finger and walked briskly toward the ladder. "That's me."

41

After my infamous poly, things settled down for a few months. There was still plenty of racist talk floating around, but I pretty much came to the conclusion that the group was more like a pack of obnoxious barking dogs than a deadly band of coyotes. In all actuality, the typical Klan member of that era was more benign than his predecessors of decades earlier.

In spite of all that, there was always the possibility that the burning fuse of tension would ignite an explosion of some kind. Then, during one of our traditional gatherings—this time at Kenneth Cargill's shoe store—Skinhead said that the big shots were disappointed in our membership numbers.

Since Skinhead never did say who he was talking about, I assumed it was either Tom Metzger, who had been building a name for himself in California, or David Duke, the Imperial Wizard, or a national governing body down south that they referred to as a "Klanvocation," which was one of their made-up terms born a generation earlier.

Regardless of who was behind it, the whole idea met with mixed responses. Carlton Bisk, Max Merryweather and shoe store owner Kenneth thought it best if we kept the den to a few people whom we could trust; contrarily, Doorknob,

Myron Thorn and Skinhead thought the more, the merrier. Predictably, I sided with them.

"The leaders want a hundred percent attendance at the rallies," Skinhead said. "You're all encouraged to bring friends and wives, too. We want to make the impression that we're a huge organization and getting bigger by the day."

Then he unexpectedly turned to me. "Allen, we're hoping you can make us a batch of catchy T-shirts with crosses and flags and the like."

Not sure if Charles, the owner of the silk-screening shop, would want that kind of business, I made the most benign comment I could think of. "I'll check on it, but it depends on what other projects we're working on."

After the meeting broke up, I hung around with Skinhead, Kenneth, Max and Doorknob in hopes of gathering some additional information. Then Doorknob made a proposal. "If you guys don't have anything better to do, I've got something fun in mind."

"I'm game," I said.

"Me, too," said Max.

As the others dispersed, Doorknob hit me with a stunner. "Let's climb in my truck and go looking for a couple niggers to push around. I got a shotgun behind the seat if we need it."

Max nodded at Doorknob. "Let's do it."

This was one of those situations that Robert Jillian had prepared me for back in my orientation sessions. In theory, the best thing I could do in a moment like this was back out and report the potential problem to dispatch so they could get the boys in blue to take care of it before any damage was done, and I wouldn't have to blow my cover. But I'd just said I'd go along. Furthermore, they already believed that I'd done something similar once before.

"I've seen a few of those black bastards hanging around on Hollywood Boulevard," I lied. "Maybe we can go teach them that they don't belong there."

"Good enough," Doorknob proclaimed.

A minute later, Max found the middle of the seat and I took the window. Then Doorknob slid behind the steering wheel, reached under the seat and retrieved a brand-new bottle of Jim Beam. "This ought to add to the excitement," he said, untwisting the cap and taking a glug.

"Right on," Max snapped.

"Now we're talking," I added, hoping things would get better before they got worse. I decided that when the bottle got to me, I'd take the smallest swigs possible and then try to take over driving duties if Doorknob got noticeably drunk. It just took a few seconds for the bottle to make the trip my way.

As a former street officer, I knew this was a quintessential example of how people got in trouble.

Then, I implemented a plan of my own. As we passed the bottle back and forth and drifted through the streets, I pretended to be tipsy. Eventually I rolled down my window and yelled at pedestrians and people in other cars.

The idea was to make it sound to Doorknob and Max like I was crazy-drunk so I could yell at a real officer if and when we saw one. It took about 20 minutes before we came upon a couple officers that had pulled somebody over.

"There's a cop," Max said, as we got closer. "You'd better keep it quiet, Padge."

But there was no way I was going to do that. "Fuck them," I said with the kind of bravado they could relate to. When we reached the officers' car, I stuck my head out the window and let them have it. "Fuck you, ash-holes," I slurred at the officer talking to the other driver. "Why doan you muther fuckers pick on somebody your own size?"

If I was correct, they'd detect the drunken behavior, let the other guy go and be on our butts in less than a minute.

"Oh, shit," Doorknob said as I saw the first hint of red lights. "They're coming our way. Cap the bottle, Max, and stick it under the seat."

"We could ditch 'em," I mumbled, "if we had Tiny's Mustang."

"Yeah, but we don't."

Thank God Doorknob pulled over and I stuck with my imitation of an obnoxious drunk. I'd heard plenty of anti-police lines in my day. "Kiss my ass," and "Screw you, pig" were added to the mix. They immediately knew we'd been drinking so they handcuffed us and called for back-up.

While we waited, I continued to act drunk and encouraged my drinking buddies to plead not guilty and to demand an attorney, rather than defend themselves, but it was all just to protect my cover.

After being processed, I waited until the next morning when Maxwell Merryweather, Steven Houser, aka Doorknob, and I got an arraignment hearing and were told we were being charged with drunk and disorderly conduct and disturbing the peace.

Eventually, I had a one-on-one conversation with a court-appointed attorney. A few hours later, all of the charges were dropped. Max thought it was because of illegal search and seizure, but it was really because the department had to get all three of us off to protect their mole. Meanwhile, Doorknob assumed that the cops had failed to check behind the seat where his shotgun was kept, but that too was false. In fact, both the booze and the shotgun had disappeared.

42

"Hi there, Babe. Wanna have that beer now?"

Stump wondered what the hell was the matter with that idiot. Maybe he was just messing around, but either way, he was damn lucky Michael didn't knock him into next week.

"You again?" she said, obviously disgusted. "I'd rather have the stomach flu."

"C'mon. We both know you're no angel," he said, grabbing her elbow and nudging her toward the galley.

Touching her was a big mistake. Her Marine Corps training took over. In a split second, she shot her right arm around his neck, pivoted slightly and rolled him over both her hip and the railing and into the water, earning loud applause and a few cheers from Stump and others.

"Man overboard," Douglas yelled, throwing a life preserver ring behind the boat like a Frisbee.

The captain cut the throttle. Then Michael shook her head and jumped overboard, too. By that time additional life preservers flew toward both of the wet ones.

While the captain turned the boat around, people came from the galley and the crew went into action. The rail gate was opened, a ladder landed in its spot and both Douglas and Rusty held upside-down gaffs on call. Meanwhile, Stump moved to the rail so he could keep an eye on Michael.

A minute later the *Trawler* made it back to the swimmers. By that time Cubbie had secured two life preservers, one for each arm. Michael also had one. "Take him first," she yelled at the crew.

After a few more minutes, two drenched fishers were back on board, with the Cubs fan lying on the deck breathing deeply as if he'd just swum the English Channel.

"Why'd you jump in too?" Rusty asked Michael.

She sighed and squeegeed her body. "The way his arms were flapping when he hit the water, I could tell he couldn't swim. I had to make sure the dumb shit didn't drown."

A few more compliments revealed that Michael had earned a lot of fans.

Stump looked at the pathetic Cubs fan, who rose to one knee, still gasping for breath. "I warned you, dude."

Michael threw her arms in the air and stomped toward the stairs. "I gotta change my friggin' clothes," she huffed.

"You gonna be okay?" Stump asked. "That dead man is in the cabin next to ours."

"I got no damn choice, Stump."

Detective Jenkins stepped aside so Michael could drop down to her quarters.

Douglas waved at the captain, who returned the engines to their usual slowpoke pace, and the boat bobbed onward.

* * *

With Michael changing clothes and the *Trawler* back on course, Stump nudged his way next to Detective Jenkins. "I warned that guy not to mess with my girlfriend. She's an expert marksman, too."

"Looks like she handled herself just fine. Too bad that had to happen."

"Who do you think did it?"

"Did what?"

"Killed Mr. Clayton."

"What makes you think someone killed him? He might have died from natural causes or taken his own life."

"Nah. That ain't it. Since you won't tell me who you think did it, how about I tell you who I think did it and if I'm right you just nod your head."

"Why don't you just tell us what you know?"

"Sure. For starters, nobody on this boat knew about the death, including you, until you opened his door. Therefore, nobody on the boat had a reason to call you prior to that. But you were on your way out here anyway. I know that because my girlfriend and I were on the deck when you first called our captain. A few minutes later he instructed everybody to bring in their lines.

"Then we went to your boat, which we now know worked just fine. You guys must have dressed casual so nobody would know you were the police. Then when you boarded our boat, you went right to the upper deck. Some random person wouldn't have done that. That confirmed that you were authorities of some kind, and on a mission; but you guys didn't want anybody to know who you were or why you were here until you could get in position to see if anybody acted weird when you called for Mr. Clayton.

"I'm guessing that he was a suspect for some other crime—a real serious one, otherwise you wouldn't have jumped through so many hoops to get to him."

"Interesting speculation."

"It's not speculation. It's true, and that's not all I know. After the announcements failed to locate Mr. Clayton, you did the only logical thing: looked for him in his cabin, but you were surprised to find him dead. I talked with him just before he went to bed and he wasn't acting strange then. So, his death was a surprise to him, too. And now we know he died of poisoning—"

"Wait a minute. We never said anything about poisoning."

"Not officially, but I heard you mention it to the sergeant when you were both below deck. You said something about crackers, too. Don't worry, I haven't told anybody. Anyway, we can assume that Mr. Clayton brought the crackers from home."

"And how do you know that?"

"Easy, the boat doesn't provide any crackers, so somebody brought them on board. The key thing is, we already established that you came out here because you thought he committed a very serious crime. I suppose he could have had a run-in with somebody involving a business transaction or something like that, but how would that person get Mr. Clayton to eat poisoned crackers?

"His death was more likely to be a personal matter and any criminology student knows that before you go looking for outlaws, first you gotta look at the in-laws. So, I'm guessing he had a run-in with his wife. It ended badly and you came out to get him, but then you found him poisoned, presumably by his wife. Ironically, they each killed the other. Am I right?"

"Maybe. Maybe not."

"But you haven't denied any of it, so I must be pretty close."

"You said you saw him just before you went to bed. Did you witness any suspicious behavior?"

"Not really. Our cabin is right next to Mr. Clayton's, but we went to bed before he did. We both listened to music on our headphones, so I never heard anything after that."

43

Call it two years or 700 days or 60 million seconds, it doesn't really matter. The result was the same. My family, my home, my car, my perspectives on life and work all got kicked to the curb when my wife and son died.

There was very little room for real fun. But then the end of 1981 rolled round.

By the time the leaves started to fall, I felt like one of those leaves: Spent. Useless. Looking for a place to rest.

Then, on the Monday preceding Turkey Day, I drove to the silk-screening shop. Outside, an angry, cool wind shook the last stubborn leaves from near-naked trees. I wished I'd worn some warmer clothes.

That was when the owner of the silk-screening shop, Charles Abbott, approached me. "Say, Allen. If you don't have any plans for Thanksgiving, our family would love to have you join us."

I didn't know it, but this was one of those rocks-landing-in-a-lake moments. To this day, the ripples have not stopped.

As an alternative, I could have spent the holiday alone or at a bar; or I could have looked up my long-time partner, Larry, and fused with his family again, but that would lead to a bunch of war stories, many laced with victims.

Another option had occurred to me. I probably could've

wrangled a meal and a date out of one of the Klan ladies, particularly Jerri Grove, but that was a square-peg-round-hole kind of relationship that I didn't want to pursue.

However, Charles's family was benign. Even if we were to slip into a little shop talk about the silk-screening business, the worst thing that could happen is somebody would fall to sleep from boredom. But that wasn't the only reason his proposal appealed to me. He and wife Eleanor had an interesting daughter. A good looker, smart and six to seven years younger than me, Beck had been by the shop quite a few times. Brief conversations indicated she was the kind of person who could cheer up the last few people on the deck of the Titanic.

In spite of Beck's ever-glowing cheerfulness, I held apprehensions about being with her for an extended period because, as an undercover officer, I was not allowed to reveal my actual identity. That meant Beck thought I really was a goofy-haired, well-tattooed silk-screener. I wondered how a guy like that would relate to a talented lady who was already in the workforce as an RN and doula. Somebody like that would be a good communicator and common sense dictated that sooner or later she'd ask me some questions about my past. Then what?

I knew from my training that whenever somebody tried to lure awkward background information out of me, it was best to give a brief answer and employ the "porcupine" technique; that is, throw the prickly question right back in his or her lap.

For instance, if she were to ask where I was raised, I'd respond, "A suburb of Boston. How about you? Have you lived in California all your life?"

That way she'd be the one on the witness stand and I wouldn't have to lie to her—as much.

I decided that if she were to ask how I got into silk-screening, I'd answer briefly, and turn the tables. "I saw an ad in the newspaper. I understand you help deliver babies. What's that like?"

When the big day arrived, I would have liked to show up wearing casual dress clothes and driving my SUV, but that would have belied the character I'd been portraying for months. Instead, I drove my KKK-mobile and wore blue jeans and one of the American flag T-shirts that I'd made in her father's shop.

Once there, and after the initial niceties, Charles and I floated to their back room where we drank a couple beers and watched football while Beck and Mrs. Abbott, who preferred to be called Eleanor, bounced around in the kitchen.

Eventually, we gathered at the dining table, where good-mannered Beck asked me one of those probing questions. "My father tells me you're a good worker. Is that something you learned from your parents?"

Hmm. "Pretty much," I said, having caught the porcupine and prepared to toss it right back. "I'm originally from Boston. I wasn't much of a student, so my dad made me work. I mowed lawns. Things like that. What about you? I hear you're a college grad. Did you like school?"

"Yeah. I like to read—and interact with people. Was it cold up north?"

That darn porcupine was back. She wasn't supposed to do that. I tried again. "Yes, especially when the wind blows. Based on your tan, I bet you really like the outdoors. Do you get to the beach a lot?"

"Not as much as I used too. You said you weren't much of a student, yet you seem to use good grammar. Who taught you that?"

Ouch. I felt like I had a complete prickle of porcupines poking my ribs. I looked at Charles, who was enjoying some dressing, and then Eleanor, who seemed to be waiting for my reply.

"That was because of my maternal grandmother," I said, trying to think of another question I could bounce off her. "She made all her grandkids memorize long poems and use good grammar. Who would you say influenced you the most when you were younger?"

"They're right here at this table. I was always required to get good grades. What made you leave Boston?"

Damn. Damn. Damn. There it was again. Every time I volleyed the ball of conversation her way, she bounced it right back. That could go on forever.

I decided to break the pattern and reveal some of the background information I'd rehearsed back in my orientation days. I couldn't say anything about the KKK or being a mole, but I could still lend a little more depth to the conversation.

So, I offered up longer, more substantive answers to her questions, always shielding who I really was. It took quite a while to spin my various yarns, but Beck paid close attention and smiled quite a bit, especially when I told her I liked having orange hair. Finally, I got around to the day where I supposedly learned of the silk-screening job in her dad's shop.

"I'd been staying in a motel," I said, "but I really wanted my own apartment. Then I heard that your dad had an opening. I'm grateful that he gave me the job."

After all of that, it was finally Beck's turn to fill in some blanks, but if I'd made a thousand guesses, I never would have anticipated her reply.

She smiled first. Then, "So, how long have you been a cop?"

44

Eventually Michael dried off, changed clothes and returned to the main deck where her new fans complimented her — both for throwing the Cubs fan overboard and for saving his life. Harold of Harold and Doc suggested she should have let him drown.

After a couple calm hours in the sun, Stump and Michael grabbed a tuna burger. Near the end Stump mentioned the detectives. "It's like they're just going through the motions."

"I don't really care right now, Stump," she said. "After throwing that jerk in the water, my wrist hurts again and I need an aspirin—but that friggin' dead guy is in the room next to ours. It's creepy but I'm going downstairs anyway. I'll see you later."

"Another aspirin? You've gone for aspirin three or four times. Are you sure you're alright?"

"You're keeping count? I don't like that. I just want to be left alone. Okay?"

"I guess. If you're going to be long, I would like to get my book and do some studying."

She ticked her tongue. "Just wait here, I'll get it for you."

As Michael walked off Stump wondered if she felt guilty for thumping Cubbie. Fortunately, either way they'd be home in a few more hours and all of this would be in the past.

After getting his book, Stump tried to study, but it wasn't easy to concentrate. Eventually, he gave up and drifted out to the main deck where Detective Jenkins was guarding the stairs to the bunks. "I bet the stench of diesel fuel doesn't help your stomach."

"It's not pleasant, but I'm getting used to it."

Together they watched Beardo open the hatch to the below-deck freezer and climb down there. Within minutes he passed semi-frozen fish upwards to Douglas, who slid them to the port side of the boat where Rusty had attached a stout butcher-block table to the boat rail and produced a huge knife. With the skill of a million-dollar surgeon and the speed of a gang member, he made a shallow slit up the fish's back and back down the belly. In a split second he peeled off the skin and tossed it over the rail to squawking gulls.

One more drag of the knife removed the gourmet-quality fillet, which he stuffed in a clear plastic bag. After flopping the fish over he duplicated the process, tagged the bag and sent it back to where it came from.

He then grabbed the carcass by the tail and flipped the remaining hideous, meatless tuna-creature overboard, causing crazed gulls to morph into a bunch of shrieking sea buzzards.

"One down. A hundred to go," Stump said.

Detective Jenkins smiled. "That fish was as big as a turkey."

"Can I ask you something, Detective? Do you like your job?"

"Me? Sure, I do," she said while another fish found Rusty's table. "But it can be tough sometimes—like when you're in the middle of the Pacific Ocean on a fishing boat and your kids are hours away."

"That sounds rough. What about this case? Would you mind if I check in and follow how it progresses?"

"You can do that if you wish, but about all we can do is give you the same info we give the media."

"That's cool. I'd be interested in following a real

investigation as opposed to the ones I read about in class. They just don't come to life."

* * *

After several dozen fish succumbed to Rusty's knife, Michael returned, happier than before. Together she and Stump went to the bow, where they laughed and talked for a couple hours while a starry sky replaced the daylight. By the time they reached Fisherman's Landing the boat had been cleaned from head to toe sans the sleeping compartments.

At the dock the captain led Detectives Flores and Jenkins toward the tackle shop while Detective Trent stayed with the crime scene. Meanwhile fishers gathered their gear and deckhands retrieved the processed fish from the hold.

One at a time a collection of tired folks, soldiered up the boardwalk toward the tackle shop where Sergeant Flores and Detective Jenkins had already huddled with two ambulance attendants by a gurney, obviously for Mr. Clayton.

"Attention, *Trawler* passengers," an overhead voice said. "This is Captain Gregg. Each of you will get a refund for half your money. You can come inside the tackle shop, or, if you paid with a credit card, we'll make the adjustment tomorrow and send you a confirmation by email."

"It's still a screw job," somebody mumbled.

"Seems fair to me," Stump said while he and Michael rested their gear against the building and waited for their fish. Finally, Beardo, Rusty and Douglas pushed a stout laundry cart full of fish toward the gang of fishers. It took all three of them to roll the heavy cart into an area of the sidewalk in which numbers one through 30 formed a large circle.

While Beardo and Rusty went back for another cart, Douglas picked up a whole albacore by the tail and checked the tag on its gill. "Number 15," he said before he placed it on the ground over the corresponding number.

After doing the same thing with the remaining whole fish,

Douglas pulled a series of strong plastic bags, each filled with fish steaks, from the cart. "Number Five," he said placing one of Michael's fish on her number where it could wait for her other packages.

After the first cart was emptied, a second cart took its place. Some folks took their fish and headed for home while others wandered into the tackle shop for their refunds. Then, something caught Stump's eye.

"Look at that, Michael," he said. "JP and Kyle are going to their car, but there are three whole fish on the ground covering up Kyle's number."

"They're probably coming back for them."

"I don't think so. Just a minute. I'll go check." Stump jogged toward them. "Hey, you guys. Hey. You forgot your fish."

JP and Kyle turned around. "I don't want those slimy things," Kyle said, "so I told the crew to give them away."

"Oh. That explains it. Sorry for butting in." He hustled back to Michael. "No problem. They left the fish to the crew."

"Do you really think I give a damn, Stump? 'cause I sure as hell don't."

"What. Where is that coming from, Michael? You've been agitated a lot lately. All I did was make sure a guy didn't forget his fish."

"Yeah, right. You worry about some guy you don't even know, but when that jerk harassed me, you didn't even defend me. What kind of boyfriend does that?"

"You're wrong, Michael. I talked to that guy several times."

45

My symbolic loss to Beck's superior communication skills was like the very first cell that crawled out of the sea. It injected new life into me. Up until that time, I hadn't realized how badly I needed a genuine and playful laugh-out-loud moment.

A smile filled her face when she confessed, "I knew that you were an officer the last three times I saw you at my father's shop. I intentionally asked you questions about your past just to listen to your yarns. I thought you were cute."

Cute? Me? That was something I hadn't heard before. In a sense, the doula in Beck had effectively helped in another birth. This time she brought forth a 200-pounder, who needed someone to talk to, and gave him a new start and a spiritual lift. She might as well have spanked my fanny.

In the weeks that followed, Beck came by the shop about three times a week and made a point to visit me while she was there. She was always well-dressed and cheerful and smelled wonderful. I smiled both inside and outside whenever I was with her.

Eventually, I told her all about Dorene and Junior, which prompted her to wrap her arms around my neck, comforting me and validating my feelings, all of which reinforced why she was in such high demand in her work: She made people feel good.

It was at about that time that I got a call from my handler, Jack Aladar. In his office, he said he had a new, short-term assignment for me. "Have you heard anything about the Bus Stop movement?" he asked.

"Yeah. I've been reading about it in the newspaper. It's another one of those bussing issues. The county wants to integrate the schools, but it's all been tied up in court."

"Not anymore. We got word yesterday that it's a go. The district plans to bus a thousand minority kids out of the inner city and into the schools that are *too white*."

"Too white? Who determines that?"

He shrugged and raised his eyebrows at the same time. "Believe me, somebody has been doing the studies and this has the same kind of racial overtones that you've witnessed in your other capacity."

"Understandable," I said. "What do you need me to do?"

"Some of the parents and community leaders don't want the black kids to make it to the white schools. Others snuck into the bus lot last night and let the air out of tires. We're putting an end to that with dogs and patrol cars."

"But..."

"Those people aren't going to give up easily. The last few days they have been gathering at various schools. We think they're going to pick one or two schools at random and then do everything they can to keep the busses from getting into the parking lots. They'll form human roadblocks, toss nails and sharp objects under the tires, throw eggs at the windshields. Things like that."

"Can't you get some patrol cars over there?"

"That's another part of our problem and why we need you. We can't afford to place officers at every single school. It would take up too many resources, so we need to know where they're going to gather each day before they get there. That way we can squash the activity with one or two officers, before it gets out of hand."

"I take it you want me to see if I can get on the inside of that group?"

"That's correct. We want you to pretend to be a disgruntled parent. You'll act like you don't want the black children in the same schools with your white kids, then when they tell you of their next meeting place, you feed us the information we need in a timely manner and we can stop it before it even starts."

"I guess I could do that. So how do I make first contact?"

"We're expecting them to be at one of the schools tomorrow morning. When we find out which one, we'll call you and you can bolt over there and do what you did with the Klan boys. Once you're in the loop, you can help us bring this to an end before somebody gets hurt and we get bad press."

"Okay then, I'll be looking for your call tomorrow morning."

"It should be sometime about 7:30. Until then, it would be great if you could recruit some young woman to pretend to be your wife. The two of you can act like a couple of hostile white parents."

Oh, I knew somebody, all right.

Later the night, the prospect of recruiting Beck to assist me in disrupting the Operation Bus Stop people brought me to a symbolic line in my mind that I'd not yet been willing to cross. In my post-Dorene days there were many times when I asked myself when, if ever, it would be appropriate to allow somebody new to slip into my head or heart. It had been over two years since I lost Dorene and thus far I hadn't reached that point.

Furthermore, there was no reason to rush anything. I was not yet 30 and the laws of probability suggested I'd fall in love again, sooner or later. Some dating and another marriage were certainly possibilities.

But the question remained: When would it be appropriate to be with another attractive and interesting woman?

Whenever I asked myself that question, the overly simplistic answer always was, "whenever it feels right." But feelings are tricky things. Millions of rebounders, be they victims of death or divorce or some other partnership-splitting event, have succumbed to such feelings only to later find out that the wounded persons were no more than an outlet for somebody else's animal urges, all of which made vulnerable people "feel" even worse.

Of course, I was talking about quality relationships vs. flings. When it came to having meaningless sex romps, those were easy to keep in perspective. It was like watching your favorite team hit a home run, but still lose the game. It didn't mean anything.

Then Beck showed up and a blurry line appeared.

A big part of me craved the company and intimacy of an intelligent woman like her. I respected her and liked her on a level I hadn't experienced since the pre-Dorene era. I really didn't know if it was too early to genuinely like a woman, but I was finally willing to find out.

46

"I'm sorry I irritated you, Michael," Stump said, merging onto the highway, "but if you think I didn't speak up for you, you're wrong. When that asshole first started hitting on you, I warned him to leave you alone."

"Or what?"

"There was no 'or what,' Michael. You've always said you can take care of yourself, and you did a damn good job of it. By the time I knew what was going on you'd already flipped him over the rail. What was I supposed to do? Kick him in the teeth when they brought him back on board? He was out of breath and couldn't even stand up."

After a pause, Michael sighed, "You're right. I know you care. I'm sorry."

"I think we're both exhausted."

"That and I'm worried about Daddy and taking it out on you. I shouldn't have done that."

"Well, then, let's just forgive each other and have a nice make-up session when we get home."

"I'm not in the mood for that tonight, Stump. After being jammed in with a bunch of human sardines for two days, I just want to stretch out my arms and get a real shower."

After a quiet ride, they arrived at the B&B. Sweat and humidity had essentially glued Stump's clothes to his body.

"If your wrist still hurts," he said, "I can bring your things upstairs."

She reached for her bag. "Thanks, but I can get it. Anyways, you've still got to deal with the fish."

He blew out a loud, tired breath. "True that. I hope your father's cats appreciate all this."

After their gear was inside, Stump went across the alley to Egg-Zaklee's and packed a hundred pounds of tuna in a couple large boxes inside the restaurant's freezer.

When he returned, he traipsed up the stairs and heard the shower running. On the bed, Michael's half-empty travel bag contained a nearly empty pill bottle. If it weren't for their trip to Greece, it wouldn't have caught his attention. He forced back an uneasy feeling.

* * *

"How'd you sleep?" he asked Michael the next morning when their alarm went off.

"I dunno. Not real well."

"Sorry to hear that. I think I'll return your dad's fishing gear. Would you like to go with me?"

"No. I just want to get the house ready for the next guests."

"I could get a couple cinnamon rolls while I'm out."

"Fine."

On the way to Catts's place, Stump stopped by Egg-Zaklee's. "Hi, Stump," Yana said at the door. "I saw the tuna in the freezer. You must be a really good fisherman."

Stump smirked. "Not really. During El Nino, there are so many fish you can't miss. I can take some of them to Catts's place right now and get the others later. Can you get me a couple cinnamon rolls too?"

After unloading Catts's gear and a bunch of albacore steaks, he got a text message indicating the engagement ring he'd ordered was ready. Perfect. That might just perk Michael up.

Twenty minutes later, and six thousand dollars poorer, Stump sat at the kitchen table with Michael. "We haven't gone shooting for a while," he said, pulling off a piece of his roll. "We both like that. We could do that later, or go out to dinner or something after your guests check in."

"Maybe. Right now, all I want to do is get my work done. I'm tired of cleaning up after customers. It gets old."

"But you get paid for it, and you don't have to cook for them, and you're usually done for the day by noon. That's not real bad."

"So says the man who has no job and still can't find much time to study for his finals."

Ouch. If Stump were in court and asked about his schooling, he'd have to admit that he did the least he could to get by. But this was no time for negativity. He had something else in mind. "I got you a present today. Would you like it now?"

"A present? You know me. I'm always open to that idea. What is it?"

"I was going to wait until later. That's why I tried to get you on a date," he said reaching inside the back of his shirt. He knelt next to her and opened the ring box. "Michael, you are the only woman I've ever truly loved. You make me higher than the trees and happier than a tail-wagging puppy."

A toothy smile spread across her face as he proceeded.

"You make me understand what 'forever' really means and why flowers are incredible. You tickle my funny bone and challenge my mind. You put the wind to my back and beauty before my eyes. But none of that matches the feelings you stir inside me."

Her head began to bob.

"For all of that and the countless blessings yet to come, I'm asking you to marry me. Will you?"

Her arms shot around his shoulders. "Of course, I will, Stump. I love you, too."

After Michael slid her ring over her finger, they marched up the block and back, sharing the good news with her father and the Egg-Zaklee's gang.

The remainder of the day, they traded hugs and kisses and warm eyes while they carried out their duties. Then they celebrated at a late dinner where Michael endlessly admired her ring and ultimately apologized for being grouchy earlier.

"I understand," Stump said, sipping his first glass of wine in over six months. "You don't get a lot of stimulating things to do—except for throwing a guy over the rail of a fishing boat."

After giggles and long meandering talks, they ultimately went home, where Michael slipped into the master bath while Stump checked the doors and lights. Pleased and contented, he meandered into the bedroom where he looked toward Michael's dresser where he saw the same pill bottle that he saw earlier, only this time it was empty. A quick look at the label resulted in a sinking feeling.

OxyContin was the same pain drug Michael took when she and Stump were in Greece, but the only pain she'd mentioned lately was her hurt wrist during the fishing trip, which she later declared to be okay.

Now that Stump had been forced to think about it, Michael had been exhibiting several symptoms of opioid abuse lately: agitation, mood swings, sleeping troubles. Just the thought of it sickened him.

When she came out of the restroom, he held the bottle behind his back and confronted her. "I'm worried about you, Michael."

"Worried? Why?"

"This."

47

When the Operation Bus Stop issue arose, I didn't know if Beck would want to play the role of an angry mother whose child was about to be force-fed a new batch of schoolmates. But I did know that she still lived with her parents.

I wondered about them. What would they say if Beck were willing to go along with the department's clandestine idea?

Not wanting to cause a family tiff, I called Beck's mom to get her take on my idea. At first, Eleanor said that Beck was entirely free to make up her own mind, but she soon slipped into protective-mom mode and wanted to know how dangerous the event would be. After I assured her that this was not the kind of event that was likely to get violent, Eleanor said, "Well, I don't think you'd let anything bad happen to her." I agreed.

After that, Beck's father backed up Eleanor, which left only one other person to consult. Beck said something about the whole concept being more interesting than hanging around a house filled with TV-watching old people.

That night, I cleaned up my tiny apartment, read a couple articles about Operation Bus Stop and hit the rack early. As I faded out, I wondered what Dorene would say about my crazy new life and the not-entirely-innocent rendezvous I'd set up with Beck.

The next morning, I took the shit-brown LTD to my real home to get my SUV, which fit the new role better. While there, I doubted I could ever bring another woman into Dorene's home, especially into the master bedroom.

At 6:30 I'd made it to the home of a perky woman wearing a plaid blouse, tan slacks and a big smile, all of which fit Beck perfectly. She slid into my SUV. "If this is a date," she said, "it's the weirdest one I've ever been on."

The "date" comment caught my attention. I pulled into a donut house to wait for instructions from my handlers. "Are you nervous?" I asked as we sat at a table with our treats.

"Not particularly, but I know that some moms can get very protective when somebody threatens their children. All I gotta do is act like that."

"Like your mother?" I asked with a grin of my own.

"Why? Did you talk to her? What did she say?"

"At first she said she didn't want to interfere in your business, but then she made me promise I'd get you out of there if anything gets violent."

Beck's eyes rolled like a couple of green, helium-filled balloons. "If I didn't have to pay off my schooling, I'd get my own place, but right now free rent is hard to beat."

Of course, it was.

After we discussed the why, what, and how of the Bus Stop matter, we were free to talk about a few personal issues, like why she was so skilled at the porcupine game.

"Simple," She said. "Doulas have to draw information out of timid clients, so I learned to ask open-ended questions, where they have to open up."

"Well, you're better at it than anybody else I've ever met."

"What about you? What was your real past like?"

And there we were, with her in charge of the conversation again. I gave in and leveled with her about my past. "I screwed up a lot with my wife," I admitted. "I'm not saying it was all my fault, but we were young, and I'd always been in pursuit of tough-guy interests: football, the Marines and the police force. It can be difficult for people like me to turn off the authority figure role when we go home."

Her head bobbed. "I'm guessing that the spouses don't need straightened out like the perps do?"

"You got that right. That's why a disproportionate number of police marriages end in divorce."

"I bet that's tough on the male ego."

"Fortunately, Dorene knew how to peel me back when I got out of line." Just then my pager went off.

I rushed to a phone, called in and was told that a school bus was heading for Palm Breeze Elementary just a couple miles away and they were expecting protesters.

As we rushed toward my vehicle, I wondered if a young gentlewoman like Beck, who always knew how to make people feel better, could actually play the role of a pissed-off, obnoxious racist.

"Shouldn't I drive?" she asked.

That was an interesting comment. "Why do say that?"

"Bigots probably attract other bigots. What if we see one of those Klan people you know? They think you drive that other car. If I'm the driver, we can say we're friends and I have kids who are affected by this forced bussing nonsense, so I asked you to come with me—in my car."

"Good thinking," I said and flipped her the keys. As we pulled onto the school grounds, we noticed several passenger vehicles parked in the Busses Only Zone, presumably to make it more difficult for the busses to park and the students to get off the busses. "That must be our group," she said. "I'll park like that too."

"Fine. Are you sure you want to do this?"

"Sure, I am. The black kids deserve good schools, too. If this helps them, I'm all for it."

"Okay, then. Just act like an angry parent would act, and keep your eye out for whoever is in charge."

We'd barely pulled to the curb when a tall man about our ages hustled our way. "You folks here to stop the busses?"

"Damn right, we are," I said as Beck and I slid out of the vehicle. "Who do we report to?"

"That couple over there. Dick and Jolene," he said, pointing to a duo who looked so clean-cut they could have passed for Sunday School teachers.

"Good," I said. "I want to give them my number."

"There's the busses now," somebody said, as two busses approached the school's parking lot. "Don't make this easy for them."

"Damn right," somebody else yelled while others added comments.

"Let's form a human barricade."

"They want to ruin our schools."

"Keep 'em out."

"We don't need black kids here." That particular female voice was very familiar. I turned to see Beck smile before returning her attention to the incoming busses. She pointed her finger and screamed louder than before. "Keep those mother fuckers out of here."

I actually laughed out loud for the first time in two years.

48

Michael appeared to be caught off-guard when Stump showed her the empty pill bottle. "Oh. If you think I'm taking those," she said, waving a dismissive hand in the air, "you're wrong. They were left behind by our last guests. You can see his name on the label."

"I'm not buying it Michael. I saw this same bottle in your bag before, only it had at least one pill in it. Now it's empty."

She sighed. "Okay, I admit it. I found the bottle before we went fishing. It had a few pills in it and I took one when my wrist hurt. But I just threw the rest of them in the toilet. I'm done with them now."

Stump wished that were true, but he suspected otherwise. "I call b.s., Michael. You've been sniffling lately."

"So what? I have a little cold. What of it?"

"You must think I'm an idiot, Michael. Excessive sniffling is a symptom of opioid abuse. You've been lethargic too. And you didn't want to see your dad or—"

"Well, I'm sorry if I don't live up to your expectations."

"I'm not done. You've been acting like you did after we got home from Greece—anxious one minute, euphoric the next. You've been locking the bathroom door lately. You sneaked down to our sleeping compartment a lot on the boat."

She glanced off to the side. "Shh!! Our neighbors will hear us."

"I don't care about them, Michael. I care about you. I saw alcohol ruin my mother's life. I heard all the excuses and all the broken promises about quitting. I won't go through that again. Do you understand that?"

She didn't answer.

"I've told you before how my mother's death changed my whole life. I can't let that happen again to somebody I love. You're going to ruin everything if you don't face this and deal with it. You get that, right?"

After a long pause, Michael looked him in the eyes, sighed and bowed her head. "Okay, I admit it. I've taken a few pills but only when I really needed them. You don't know what it's like to have chronic pain. I just needed a little help, but I know what I'm doing. You need to trust me."

He glared in her eyes and shook his head. "That's your answer? Chronic pain. A little help. I still ain't buying it, Michael, but I'm going to give you a fair chance to fix this on your own, but if you don't take care of it, I'm going to have to make an ugly decision and I don't want to be put in that situation."

"Don't worry, Stump. This all looks worse than it is. I promise. You can trust me. Honest. Now let's go to bed. I know what'll make you feel better."

"Not now, Michael. Not now."

* * *

"There he is," Joe Lakley said to JP the morning after one of the most successful fishing trips in mankind's history. "Catch anything?"

They sure did. In addition to netting a handful of valuable fish, JP and Kyle got one hell of a lot closer to cashing in the Claytons' lottery ticket. This too was all a part of the smart one's plan to "make everything look normal." Now JP, Kyle and girlfriend Cassandra were all in the bank and JP was squeezing his boss for some time off so that he and his partners could go cash in the ticket. After that, they planned to return, work a few months and nonchalantly move on when the investigation was over and forgotten.

"Incredible," JP said, answering his manager's question. "That's what I wanted to talk to you about. I would never have guessed it, but I really needed that time off. Now we want to go someplace else — this time to London. My partners took their vacations and I'd like to do the same thing for ten days. I have enough vacation time."

Joe knitted his brows. "Now? You're not talking about right now, are you?"

"Pretty much. We're planning to leave in a few days."

"But I can't authorize that, JP. We have an audit coming up, remember? I need you to cover for me while I'm in meetings. Why don't you put off this idea for a month or so, then we can talk about more time off."

"That won't work. My friends already got the time off. You can get somebody else to fill in for me."

"Not on this short notice, I can't. Like I said, I can't spare you right now."

"But this is important to me and I've never asked you for any favors."

"I'm sorry, JP. I just can't do it. You knew this was coming up and you shoulda planned better."

"My planning isn't the problem; it's your inflexibility that's the problem. I have vacation time and I'm entitled to take it. You've got people who can fill in if you ask them."

"Can't do it."

JP pursed his angry lips together for a couple seconds. Then, "In that case, I quit and that means you'll have to go get somebody to take my place anyhow. So, you're in the same situation. Asshole."

The news surprised Kyle. "But you said you were just going to use up some vacation time," he said as they rode to the house he shared with Cassandra.

"I tried to, dude, but that butt stain wouldn't let me do that. Now he has to find a replacement anyway."

"But we could have just waited a couple weeks," Cassandra offered from the back seat. "What if somebody puts two and two together—you know, two people died and their banker, who knew both of them, quits his job?"

"She's got a good point, JP."

JP shook his head and slapped the steering wheel "I hate that fucking job. Besides these people aren't detectives. They just do what they're told."

Kyle lit a cigarette and blew the smoke out a crack in his window. "But what about the cops? They might figure it out."

"No way. They go where the evidence leads them and we've stacked that deck with four aces."

"Regardless, dude. It's not good optics. You're the one who's always lecturing us, and then you go off and do something stupid. It draws attention to all of us."

"We'll be okay. I'm smarter than those people."

"Oh, yeah, like when you said how much poison it would take to kill Clayton. You screwed that up too."

"Why?" Cassandra asked. "What happened, Kyle?"

"There wasn't enough poison on the cracker to kill him quickly. The guy put up a fierce fight and damn near kicked the walls down." Kyle thumb-pointed to JP. "The 'smartest man in the world' here was wrong. We had to hold him down and smother him with his pillow."

"Oh, my God."

JP shook his head. "So what? The Medical Examiner will find the poison in his gut and declare that he was poisoned. And the only bottle of poison that any of them know about is back in the man's garage with his wife's fingerprints all over it. Piece of cake."

"We just lucked out because it was late at night and the engines were so loud and people were wearing headphones."

"He died, didn't he? That's the important thing. And you

were no better. You shouldn't have left your fish behind. Nobody does that."

"All of this sniping isn't doing any good," Cassandra said. "But my kids better not get hurt 'cause I don't want them growing up without their mommy."

"Trust me, I've got it covered."

Kyle blew some smoke out the window. "What are we going to do now?"

"Simple. We're going to London."

49

After Beck's tongue-lashing, the busses stopped 50 yards back from their usual loading area, tempting our impromptu gang of angry parents to move closer and hurl rude epithets at the intruders. I had to fight back a stubborn smile because Beck was the best cusser in the group.

While the busses clearly symbolized a threat to a previously stable community, strictly speaking the protest was stupid. Neither the kids on the busses nor the bus driver had any say in the matter. It was a lot like a wolf howling at the moon because it wouldn't go away.

To catch the favor of the coordinators, Dick and Jolene, I too let a few well-placed zingers fly before three patrol cars took a position between the busses and our group. After they splashed their reds all over us the officers leapt out of their cars and moved quickly toward us. I didn't know any of them.

Suddenly it occurred to me that if Beck were to lay into the police with that energetic locker-room talk of hers, they might just use her to set an example. In an instant she'd be handcuffed, thrown in the back of a squad car and hauled away. How the heck would I explain that to her mother? I quickly caught her attention and tapped my forefinger to my lips.

The priceless mischievous grin on her face made me want to see pictures of her as a youngster.

A minute later a black officer produced a bullhorn and made it perfectly clear that our gang of misfits could either get out of there or cool off in jail.

Like I said, most of these people looked more like church-goers than criminals, especially the ladies who'd probably never seen the inside of a jail. I caught Beck's attention and gestured toward my SUV.

After the busses reached the curb right in front of the school entrance, Beck and I drove off, both grinning. "Your language caught me off-guard back there," I offered.

She shrugged. "Well, you said you wanted me to act like a pissed off mom, so I gave it a try. I had a lot of fun. Can we do it again tomorrow?"

"I think so. I'll have to check with my handlers. I can get back to you later. Can I ask you something else? I'm thinking about dyeing my hair again or shaving my head, instead. What do you think?"

She stared at me for a few seconds as if she were pondering one of the greatest mysteries of the planet. "No dye. Keep the hair. Women go to beauty parlors and pay big money to get curly hair like yours. If you really want my opinion, I'd say let it grow out more."

"What about an Afro?"

"Not sure. Those look good on some guys, especially when they wear bellbottoms and colorful silky shirts at disco clubs. Do you dance?"

"Let's just say I 'pretend' to dance."

"Good. Maybe we could *pretend dance* together sometime. Now I have a confession for you, about Thanksgiving. I was the one who asked my father to invite you to our home."

"You were?"

"Yep. I heard him talking to your boss and figured out you were an officer. After that, I wanted to get to know you better. You should keep the earring, too."

"What? My earring? What about it."

"It looks good on you."

"I'll try to remember that," I said, "Can I ask you something else? It's about that man I shot."

"I guess so, what about him?"

Even though I had broached the topic previously, I never emphasized how badly I felt for that man's family. This time I put it all on the table. including the nightmares. "Technically," I finally said, "I know I had no choice in the matter. Two other people were in a high-risk situation and I had to take the guy out, but I feel like the elephant that can't forget. What's your take on the matter?"

"Well, I understand your concern for the young-uns, but you're blaming the wrong person. You said that your perp hadn't had a real job for years. Sooner or later he was bound to need money. If he was willing to aim a gun at somebody to get that money, he left you no options. The way I see it, you're a hero."

"But what about his family? I made life harder for all of them."

"No you didn't. He did that, not you."

"So you don't think I should have given them money for Christmas?"

Her eyeballs nearly popped out. "Are you kidding me? You can't buy your way out of guilt and you shouldn't feel guilty in the first place. Society needs people like you. You're a good man, so stop beating yourself up for doing your job, and that's final."

Even though I couldn't shake off my blues that easily, I appreciated the implication that I was totally and completely exonerated, not just in the eyes of the law, but also in her mind. She always knew how to make people feel better, even a policeman.

I glanced at my watch. Somehow three hours had disappeared.

After dropping her off at her parent's place, I drove to my house to switch out the SUV for the LTD and headed for the silk-screening shop, just in case any of the KKK fellows were to drop by.

Late that night my head was both muddied and clearer, thanks to Beck. Then I got a call from the wife of the Operation Bus Stop people. "Allen. This is Jolene. We're gathering at the middle school tomorrow at 7 a.m. I hope you'll help us barricade the driveway before the busses arrive."

"Sure thing. I hope my wife wasn't too offensive."

"No way. We needed that. Please bring her along."

I immediately called Jack Aladar, to inform him of the plan. He'd had enough and wanted to overwhelm the protesters so they'd drop the entire program. This time he was willing to arrest people.

Knowing that the department was ready to clamp down on the wrong-doers, I buzzed Beck and told her she'd have to stay away.

The next day I showed up at the proposed site, where several patrol cars had already taken up strategic positions. I parked up the block and joined a few other spectators. Minutes later one of the officers used a bullhorn to inform everybody within earshot that any protestors could expect to be arrested for disorderly conduct, trespassing and other charges. That pretty much ended it all.

Over the next few months, I saw Beck more and more and we eventually made it past the "just friends" stage. Since we couldn't be alone at her parents' home and I still resisted the idea of bringing another woman into Dorene's and my place, we spent some time at my crummy little apartment.

At the same time, I cut off the rack romps with the Klan women, but that didn't mean that all was well.

In fact, there was a little extra risk to both Beck and me if the Klan assholes wanted to poke around.

That was the first time I thought about seeking another transfer.

50

Frustrated as he'd ever been, Stump had to find some way to get his mind off of Michael's poor choices. He wasn't in the mood for studying but he could make a couple phone calls. When back on the fishing boat, Stump heard of some potential career options that sounded interesting and he knew just who to call to get some additional unbiased information. His adoptive father, Myles, had retired from a stellar career as a detective for the LAPD. Then a couple years after Myles's mother, Grandma Pauline, passed away, he and Katherine moved back east.

Although Myles and Katherine weren't going to make it to Stump's graduation, Stump promised to keep them in the loop and with graduation less than three weeks off, he had two reasons to call.

A few minutes into the call, Stump said, "Don't worry about it, Myles. I know you have a scheduling conflict, but I wanted to tell you that you were a pain in the butt sometimes, like when I wanted my trust money, but you told me I'd understand some day and that day has come. I've got some good investments and some automatic income. I don't meet many people who can say that. So, thanks for putting up with me all that time. You always treated me a lot better than you had to."

"That's awfully nice of you to say, Stumpster. We'll send you a little something in the mail for graduation. If you get any video or pictures of your big day, send us a copy."

"Will do. There's something else I want to ask you, Myles. I met an old guy on the boat who said something about postal inspectors. He said that they're kinda like the FBI, the Secret Service and the ATF, but I never heard of them. It got me to wondering if the federal agencies might be a good fit for me. What do you think?"

"Those are all good agencies, Stump, but the short answer is, you wouldn't like the early years and you wouldn't make the cut."

"Why not?"

"You're smart enough, but your grades won't cut it. Most of their folks are A students. Beyond that, you wouldn't get to pick where you live for at least five years, and it wouldn't be on the beach in sunny California. Do you want me to go on?"

"Er, no. I get it. You were right. It ain't for me."

"I still think the LAPD is a good shot. After a couple years in patrol cars, you can apply for detective. By then your work experience might outweigh your grades."

Just then a text message came in from Yana. Come to Egg-Zaklee's ASAP.

"I gotta go, Myles. Yana needs me to drop by the restaurant— probably about the two tons of fish I put in their freezer."

"Alright, Stumpster. Give our regards to everybody. Your mother would be very proud of you."

"Thanks, Myles. See ya."

Before checking in on Yana, Stump made a similar call. "Hi, Xander," he said when his bio-dad answered. "Just thought I'd check in."

"I'm glad you did. Are you and Danville doing okay?"

"Yeah. He's a better student than I am. So that's good. Are you guys still coming to my graduation?"

"Brianne and I will be there. Same thing for my folks — Grandma wants to see the ocean — but the other kids will see you at the family picnic later in the summer."

"I'm looking forward to that. Michael and I just got back from a fishing trip. A guy got killed on the boat."

"Oh, my god. That sounds dangerous."

"Not to us. It's still under investigation, but it looks like the guy's wife poisoned him with some crackers. But here's a strange twist. I think that before he got on the boat, he killed his wife."

"That's a new one. Why would somebody go on a fishing trip after killing somebody else?"

"I think it had to do with optics. If he disappeared too quickly, everybody would know he was guilty, but if he could hang around a while and make it look like he was already at the docks when she died, he'd have an alibi."

"That kind of thing has always intrigued you. How are the job prospects going?"

"I still don't know. Myles wants me to join the LAPD, but I'm going to look into a couple other options before I make a final decision."

"It's always a good idea to know your options. I hate to cut you short, Stump, but I promised Brianne we could go look at some furniture. We'll get back to you before the graduation."

"I gotta go too. Yana needs something and I still gotta do some boring studying today if I can."

Minutes later Stump walked to Egg-Zaklee's, where Yana met him at the front door. Obviously frazzled, she pointed a finger in his face. "The health inspector dropped by for a surprise inspection this morning. He didn't like all those stupid fish in the freezer. They're not USDA inspected. He's coming back at four o'clock. If you don't get those damn fish out of here, he's going to close us down. As it is, he wants us to clean out the entire freezer. Do you know what a pain in the butt that is? I knew we shouldn't have let you put those stinky fish in there."

* * *

Just across the alley, Michael placed a call. "Hello," she said when a receptionist answered. "This is Michael McFadden. I'm a patient of Doctor Osgood's. I've sprained my wrist and the pain won't go away. I was wondering if I could get an appointment for him to look at it pretty soon and prescribe something for the pain so I can function again. It's a minor emergency."

51

With the Bus Stop episode comfortably in our past, Beck and I saw each other more and more and eventually, I leveled with my handlers about her. After they heard of the porcupine exercise and how smart she was, they wanted to meet her. So, we went out to dinner and they were comfortable that she wasn't the type to get easily tricked into revealing who I really was.

Then Jack Aladar actually said that since most of the den members were married or in relationships, it wouldn't look strange for me to find a partner too. From that moment on, I just had to avoid exposing Beck to the den members and their acquaintances. For example, if somebody were to propose a double date or something like that, I was to make up a plausible reason why Beck and I couldn't go.

Meanwhile, to give us an alternative to hanging out in my ugly apartment, Beck got her own place and I was a regular visitor. I still spoke of Dorene and Junior, probably more than I should have, but Beck usually indulged me.

I can only remember a couple occasions when I got under her skin. Once, I referred to one of her clients as a "prego." After she tongue-lashed me for using such an "unprofessional" term, I stated that my low-mindedness was one of the reasons I was able to infiltrate the Klan. She simply

215

rolled her eyes and said she was going to start calling me a "cop," which she knew I'd never liked. Once again, she beat me at my own game.

A similar squabble arose one day when she said something about hypocrites, and I pointed out that she'd displayed some hypocrisy of her own.

"How so?" she asked in a testy tone.

"You say you don't like off-color words. You even include words like 'friggin.' Heck, you don't even like 'dumb blonde' jokes."

"So what? I think those words are uncouth and show a lack of communication skills."

"But other times, such as at the Bus Stop event, you nearly made my earwax melt, not to mention some of your bedroom talk." I knew I'd regret that last bit as soon as I said it.

"Well, the first example doesn't count because I was just playing a role, like you do when you're in Klan mode. As for the bedroom, if it'll make you happy, I'll just shut up from now on. Is that what you want?"

"No. No. No. Don't get me wrong. I didn't say I don't like it. I'm just saying there's some hypocrisy in there."

"Well, I disagree. One situation is private and the other was not the real me."

On the flip side, some of Beck's straight-laced jargon was amusing. For instance, one day we went for a long drive and eventually came upon a rest area. Beck turned to me and asked, "Do you have to go potty?"

Potty? Really? For crying out loud! We were both full-grown adults and I was a KKK infiltrator, a former football player, a Marine, a policeman. We urinated or emptied our bladders or took a leak or a wiz or simply used the bathroom. But we sure as hell didn't 'go potty,' or tinkle. At least I didn't.

From a more distant vantage point all this silliness was good for me. It provided me with a bridge from past gloom and doom to a more uplifting future.

Meanwhile, I continued to attend Klan meetings, each time

with an instant stress pill in my pocket and a tack in my shoes just in case there was another impromptu polygraph.

For the most part, the meetings were simply repositories for big talk between rallies, which only rolled around once every six weeks or so. All along, I continued to report to my handlers and to wonder if there was another mole in the den.

Then everything shifted in ways I hadn't imagined.

52

Stump wasn't prone to snooping in other people's business, but it had been two days since he and Michael had the dustup over the empty bottle of pain meds.

He didn't know exactly how many pills she'd taken but he got a peek at the bottle when it was in her bag. It had at least two pills in it. If that was all she took, she may have already straightened up before any damage was done. But the other possibility was much uglier. As unpleasant as the idea was, he decided to keep a watchful eye out both for a new supply of drugs and any erratic or suspicious behavior. Meanwhile, he had other things going on.

He still didn't have any definitive job plans for after graduation so after driving through Cardiff-by-the-Sea, or "Cardiff" as the locals called it, he parked in the street and walked a half-block to a stucco building much like his. The main floor was a gift shop, but Stump was headed for the upstairs offices. He had considered becoming a private eye and he had secured an appointment with a Mrs. Fairfax, owner of Cardiff Investigations.

After he introduced himself to the plump, 50ish woman, she led him to the conference room. "So, you want to become a professional snoop?" she asked.

"I'll be graduating from Criminology College in a

couple weeks and my own father was a police detective. He worked for the LAPD, mostly on non-homicide cases, so I have pretty good idea what detective work is like, at least as it relates to crimes. But I'm looking into some other possibilities."

"Have you done any investigating that doesn't relate to crimes?"

"Yes, ma'am. One time my friend James and I found bond money for residents of lower-income families to fix up their homes."

"Anything else?"

"Michael—she's my girlfriend—and I found a jar of rare coins and an old stock certificate that made a huge difference in the lives of some elderly people. I also found a hidden room in which a missing girl died a long time ago. Would you mind if I asked you what some of the problems are in private firms like this, compared to the police departments?"

"Sure. For starters we're less glamorous than the big departments, like the LAPD. There are no award banquets. No big promotions. Some firms offer healthcare plans, sick days and vacations, but each firm is different. Generally, none of them offers as much money or as many perks as the government does."

"But I wouldn't have as many rules, either."

"That's basically true. You don't need a degree, or any college for that matter. But you can't get a license until you go through a certain amount of supervised experience."

"Like baby-sitters?"

"It probably seems like that, but we have some talented people on our staff. You'd probably like a lot of it. Anyway, since you have a four-year degree in Criminology, you'll have to work under supervision for two years before you can go rogue."

"But I wouldn't have to work in patrol cars."

"That's true. We don't have any of those. Our people use their own vehicles and get a tax deduction for it."

"That might be okay. I just want something that challenges me, is flexible and doesn't require a whole lot of paperwork."

She shrugged. "You never beat the paperwork. That's how we know what to charge our clients. But most of those other things fit."

"What kind of cases would I work on?"

"Routine things mostly: background checks, missing persons, dysfunctional relationships, both personal and business."

"Is there anything more exciting? Crimes maybe?"

She grinned. "I can tell you've watched your fair share of television. You might get a criminal case where somebody thinks his brother was wrongly convicted. Things like that. One of our guys, Fred Dracetti, is a retired deputy sheriff. He has solved a string of DNA cases. Once he gets the evidence, he turns it over to the authorities, who usually reopen the cases."

"That's sorta rad."

"We've worked cases that the police set aside because they ran out of leads or knew who did it but couldn't *prove* it beyond the reasonable doubt standard. The families pay us to keep digging. There are other specialties. Nina Balkins, for example, works with divorce attorneys. She can find hidden assets that people don't always want their spouses to know about."

"I don't think I have any built-in business like that. Does it ever get dangerous?"

"Not usually. There's no uniform so most people don't even know what you're doing. Another thing. Private means 'private.' We're bound by the same guidelines found in attorney/client relationships."

"I like the idea of solving cases that the police have set aside. What do you know about that niche?"

"There's definitely room for people to do that. In fact, only half of all murders get solved, so there are thousands of cold cases piled up in warehouses. Same thing goes for many unsolved rapes and burglaries and assaults. A lot of those cases could be solved if somebody had an incentive to look into them. The challenge is to find somebody who's willing to pay you for your efforts."

"How much money would I make?"

"Depends. If you want steady work, you can get a decent salary. We charge our clients a minimum of $50 an hour. You'd get about half if you did the bulk of the routine work."

"That doesn't sound like very much."

"Bigger cases pay more. Sometimes we charge a flat fee. So much to find a missing person. So much to catch a cheating spouse. Things like that. When you solve a case like that you get most of the money in a lump sum, but we get a piece of the action to cover expenses."

"That seems fair."

"There's good and bad aspects to all jobs. I'm sorry to cut you off, but I've got to get back to my own work now. If all of this appeals to you, you're welcome to fill out an application."

"Thank you. I'll take one with me, but I still have to check some other places out before I make a decision."

53

"What do you know about the Nazis?" Lieutenant Jack Aladar asked me in his office.

A sinking feeling filled my gut. "Not a lot," I said. "Just what I've read in history books and seen on TV. I'm familiar with the concentration camps and the mass executions of Jews during the war. But that's about it. I never needed to hear any more than that to know I hated the entire movement."

"The reason I ask is that a new American Nazi group has formed nearby. They're looking for new members. Since the KKK and Nazis subscribe to similar philosophies, the members of either group often overlap. You can expect an invitation to join them."

Once again, I wondered where the man was getting his news, because I hadn't heard anything like this, and I'd been attending all the meetings.

"I take it you want me to accept the invite and penetrate their group?"

"That's the plan, but my sources tell me that this particular group makes your KKK buddies look like Girl Scouts."

"All right. I'll do my best."

"Good. Until then, study up, just like you did with Sergeant Jillian during your orientation."

"Got it," I said, already harboring mixed feelings. I hated

being hated when I was pretending to be a Klan member, but I loved the idea of obstructing a group like that if I could.

When I left the meeting, I thought about my former partner and his claim that a UC gig would give me a bunch of new things to think about. Considering my experiences with the KKK, the Bus Stop gang and now the Nazi Party, I had to admit I got everything I had bargained for.

Now I wondered how to proceed.

For starters, I couldn't think of the Nazis without thinking of war. In addition to my stint in the military I was previously a college student in the Viet Nam era when each day's body count dominated the network news. I was among those who didn't mind ignoring some of the stories because it was so depressing.

Anyhow, I went to the library and checked out a half-dozen books to learn more details about the Nazis and their infamous leader. As it turned out, a government error enabled Hitler to join the German army in WWI, in spite of having flunked his physical.

Once in battle, Corporal Hitler almost lost his eyesight and speaking ability due to a mustard gas attack. Later he was disappointed in his country's performance and sought to restore its status.

A generation later, he gained control, threw out old policies, created new ones, traded in his brown uniform for a grey one and assigned himself a brand-new rank: the First Soldier of the German Reich.

As I read on, I forced myself to study the concentration camps, where Jewish men were taken from their families. If those men were strong enough, they were forced to work at hard labor for up to 14 hours a day, sometimes with bare feet in snow. If they weren't strong enough, they were beaten, then shot or gassed in crematories.

All along, the women and children were abused in every way a human being could imagine. When they no longer served those purposes, they too were executed.

For breakfast, prisoners were given a bowl of diluted soup and a small chunk of bread. For dinner they had more soup and any bread that they hadn't eaten for breakfast. At night, five men in a heatless wooden shack shared a single bunk bed and one blanket. Anybody who complained was taken away by sadistic guards who routinely chanted "Heil Hitler" and "Sieg heil," which loosely meant "Viva victory."

The more I read, the more I came to believe that the Jews who died early were the only ones who had something to be thankful for.

As I continued to limp through the pages, my own conflict remained. I didn't want to be like the Nazis in any way, even if it was just in a UC role, but at the same time I had a chance to make their lives miserable. Very few people had an opportunity like that. I felt like millions of Jewish spirits were urging me on.

Eventually, I'd gobbled up about all the horrible information I could swallow and returned the books.

Mere days later, all hell broke loose in Greensboro, North Carolina when the local KKK den and the Nazis of that area joined forces and attacked the left-wing Communist Party at one of their marches. When the blood stopped spurting, five marchers lay dead in the streets in what came to be called the Greensboro Massacre of 1982.

That massacre served as a catalyst for the LA Nazis to locate some allies. That next week, five fellows, in perfectly cleaned and pressed Nazi officer uniforms, sans the swastika on the left sleeve, showed up at our next den meeting.

The Nazi garb made the KKK's white sheets and hoods look like a child's Halloween costume.

The well-decorated leader, Dexter Braun, held the rank of SS-Schar führer, which was the equivalent of a Platoon Army Major. He said they'd improved on the public image of Hitler's Nazi Party by downplaying the swastika and replacing "Sieg heil" with "White power."

His rigidity and discipline would have been impressive if it weren't so damn sickening.

The five Nazis spoke highly of a proposed allegiance between the two groups and how that would enable each group to claim they had more numbers and unity than they actually had. Eventually, Braun asked us if anybody would be interested in visiting one of their hangouts and possibly joining their ranks. They even had uniforms waiting for us.

The majority of the Klan boys raised their hands, but I knew from past experiences that a number of them would disappear when the time came for action. This time, that would be a good thing. The last thing LA needed was extra Nazis floating around.

That next weekend, three den members and I carpooled with two of Braun's subordinates to a nice home in northern Hollywood. In a large garage, complete with a giant-sized swastika flag on the back of the door next to a framed poster of Hitler, several tables had been butted together around the walls, as if for a garage sale.

Twenty complete uniforms, including pressed trousers, brown shirts, shined black leather Jack boots that ended just below the knee, and chin-strapped caps were lined up on the tables like perfect soldiers, waiting for their assignment. A pegboard bragged of spotless belts, ties, shoulder straps and collar patches of various ranks.

Before I knew it, all four of us agreed to join and I found the right-sized pieces to complete my uniform. When I saw myself in their dressing mirror, I hated everything that uniform stood for and considered getting out of UC work altogether. Instead, I pursed my lips and followed orders.

Minutes later we faced the Nazi flag and a Hitler poster while we were taught the salute: right arm straight and raised, palm down. We practiced saying "Heil Hitler" and "White power." It took a while before Braun was satisfied with the volume and sincerity in our tone.

Finally, they had a good way to test our seriousness; we

had to pay for our own uniforms. As a poor silk-screener, I had to pay for mine via the installment plan.

A couple weeks later, we held our first public event, in North Hollywood Park. I loathed it even more than I hated the KKK rallies. I wanted to spit on myself.

Thank God, Beck kept it all in perspective. She made me hide my uniform in a utility closet.

54

Two down, two to go. The week of finals sneaked up on Stump like an unwanted bill, primarily because studying never seemed like the most important thing he could do with his time. Of course, there was always the proverbial "other hand," and in that regard he'd always managed to do just enough to live inside the pass-or-fail line.

Having just squeaked through two of his last four finals, all he had left to do was duplicate the results for Advanced Sociology and Theories of Deviant Behavior. After that, he could attend the graduation ceremony and put college behind him forever.

With the wind finally at his back, and a few more days to study, he had a few minutes to check on the status of the Clayton case. Detective Tanner Trent, whom he'd met on the boat, took the call.

"It's been a couple weeks," Stump said, "and you guys said I could stay in touch."

"*Oh, yeah, I remember you. We interviewed every person on that boat and you were the only one who figured out that we were the police before we introduced ourselves.*"

"Yeah, that's me. So how's the case going? Have there been any surprises?"

227

"As a matter of fact, we just declared the cases 'closed' and I was about to release the information to the press."

Cases. That confirmed one of Stump's theories; he had suspected there were two murders. The term "grounder" came to mind. "That was fast."

"Sometimes things just fall into place."

"What were some of the key things you considered?"

"Since we're releasing some of the details to the press shortly, I guess I can tell you that much. It all started when we got a call about a bloody murder scene. The victim was Clayton's wife. She took a lot of repulsive hammer blows to the skull. The weapon was right next to her body, complete with his prints."

"I see what you mean. That doesn't leave much room for doubt. What was the motive?"

"Money and revenge. We found a note from her in their safe deposit box at CalWest Bank. Apparently, the Mister had been threatening her and wanted the equity in their home for himself."

"If he wanted their house, why did he leave his dead wife in the home and go fishing? He must have known he'd be a suspect."

"He needed a plausible alibi. We figured they had a big fight. He lost control, went to the garage, got his weapon and took her out. But then he knew he was going to be caught unless he had an alibi, so he raced down to the docks and signed up for that trip so it would look as if he was far away when she got killed. The timelines were close, but there was enough other evidence to close the case."

"But he didn't seem uptight."

"Some people hide their emotions. Prisons are full of perps who others misjudged."

Stump nodded. He'd met several murderers and two of them, a biker and a maintenance man, were actually likeable people.

"But there was one thing Clayton didn't know when he boarded that boat," the detective continued. *"Mrs. Clayton had already implemented a plan of her own. Tired of his cruelty and threats, she saw his fishing trip as a convenient way to end the abuse before he*

could come back and take her out. It was a form of self-defense. She basically admitted it in a note she left at the bank."

"Really? She came right out and admitted that she killed him?"

"Not in those exact words, but she intimated that she'd had enough of his abuse. We didn't know precisely what she meant until we got there; then it was easy to put in context."

"So she poisoned the crackers?"

"In addition to being a decent snack they are a good antidote to motion sickness. She knew he'd get into them sooner or later. We even found matching poison in their garage and her fingerprints on the cracker box."

"That's pretty thorough, all right."

"As you know, Clayton was deceased when we got to the boat. That meant they killed each other, like a double knockout in boxing."

"That's all very fascinating. Thanks for sharing all this with me and letting me follow along."

"You bet. It's good to see talented young people who are interested in law enforcement. Now if you'll excuse me, I promised a few reporters I'd get back to them when the case was closed."

Stump hung up, and once again he learned more from interacting with people than he did from his lame-ass schoolwork.

And he reminded himself that none of that mattered at the moment. Graduation was just days away and he still had to pass his final two classes. Unfortunately, there was only one way to do that: study.

* * *

The next morning, Stump slipped down to the dining area in the B&B with his books, but as usual, he found himself less interested in his studies than the idea that two people could actually kill each other. He'd heard of that happening in duels of the olden days, but this time the deaths took place

229

in two completely different places and at two completely different moments.

Then while his mind was intrigued and wandering, he recalled something Detective Trent had said, namely that the note that they discovered came from a safe deposit box at CalWest Bank. Stump once had an account with that chain. In fact, lots of people had connections to a big chain like that, including JP, who worked there and had a travel bag with the bank's logo on it.

He also recalled that first night on the boat when JP and Kyle were drinking beer with Clayton. Eventually, they were the last ones in the galley and Clayton died sometime later that night. A suspicious person might raise an eyebrow.

But, it could all be just a coincidence. After all, the bank had lots of branches and thousands of customers at each branch. Stump wondered if the detectives had considered any of that before reaching their conclusions.

Something else bounced into his head: JP and Kyle seemed out of place on that trip. Among other things, they hung out in the galley more than anybody else. And another thing: They weren't at all upset when the trip had been prematurely terminated.

On top of all that, Kyle didn't even take his fish with him. Everybody else looked upon their hard-caught fish as valuable, but it didn't even matter to Kyle. He appeared to be more interested in going home than anything else. And another 'nother thing: At one point, JP said he was in "financing" instead of banking. That seemed strange to Stump at the time, but it might have been more meaningful than it first appeared.

None of this proved anything. It didn't even rise to the level of a genuine hunch. Heck, flukes happened all the time. Besides the police had already found means, motive and opportunity plus prints and a confession with no conflicting evidence that Stump knew of. No wonder they closed the case.

Still, it would be more interesting to ask a few additional questions than it would to crack a textbook.

55

On my way to the next den meeting, I expected the bulk of the conversation to revolve around our new kissing cousins, the Nazi troop. I worried for Beck. All that brotherly love raised the stakes for both her and me. As a precautionary measure, I'd taught her how to tell if she was being tailed and to call me if she were.

I got to Burbank and then to Carlton Bisk's home, where I saw something in the driveway that I'd been anticipating for a long time—the infamous Mustang that was at my first poly nearly a year earlier.

That meant Samuel Goode, aka Tiny, was back.

Fortunately, I was prepared this time. I drove a hundred yards past Carlton's home, made a U-turn and parked where I could keep an eye on the comings and goings. I ripped out my wallet and mined one of the inside pockets for the tack and the stress-inducing pill that I always kept with me. I downed the pill, then I removed my right shoe, slid the tack inside my sock in between the Little Piggy that went to market and the one that stayed home.

While I waited for the pill to take effect, I thought about the training I'd undergone to deal with this situation. I could expect Tiny to say that the machine can accurately distinguish truth from lies, but I'd already learned that all a poly could do is measure the difference in stress levels as the participants moved through the various questions.

Since most of us couldn't turn stress on and off on an as-needed basis, our stress levels fluctuated within a range, depending on the circumstances. It was the questioner's mission to determine what caused the needle to fluctuate within an individual's range.

When criminal suspects were hooked to the little machine, a common but flawed tactic of questioners was to ask a vaguely threatening control question, like "Have you ever stolen from a friend?"

Not long after that, the questioner asked a more threatening question. For instance, if it was believed that the subject was a guilty arsonist, they might ask, "Did you set the fire?"

A person who was more stressed by the first question probably didn't set the fire. Conversely, the person who was more stressed by the second question was likely to be guilty. Either way, at that moment the interrogator could inform the test taker that he or she had failed the test whether it was true or not. Sometimes they got a confession right then and there.

But, as stated, the poly was beatable by a trained test-taker, such as myself. I reminded myself to use the tack to escalate my stress level on the benign questions so that, when they got around to asking whether I was in law enforcement, an active needle wouldn't mean anything.

Some 15 minutes later my fingers vibrated slightly. I pulled to the curb of Carlton's home. Inside, I joined the familiar gang sitting in the living room.

"Royce is in the backroom with Tiny," Skinhead said to me, prompting my first lie.

"Oh, really? I forgot we even do that." Meanwhile, the pill had more time to take effect.

As the evening unfolded, we exchanged comments about the Nazi group while Skinhead escorted guys in and out of the exam room.

By the time they called for me, I was feeling delightfully jittery. I stood proudly and followed Skinhead into the room.

After the predicable warning about the machine's mind-reading capabilities, Tiny jumped right in with one of those control questions.

"Do you work in a silk-screening shop?"

We all knew I did so I punctured my toe with the tack. "Yes," I said ignoring the pain and stealing a peek at the needle. It jumped noticeably as if I were highly stressed by the question and therefore lying. Perfect. It took the needle several seconds before it returned to its starting point.

Even though my toe was unhappy, I got a kick out of confusing the hell out of them. After a few more questions, I knew I'd beaten them again.

The only thing I hadn't counted on was there was no easy way to dislodge the damn tack when my turn was over. I had to avoid hobbling as I made my way to the restroom and discovered a damp red blood blotch on the toe of my white sock—a war wound of sorts.

When the meeting was over, I had a few new things to report to my handler, so the next morning I joined Lieutenant Aladar to fill him in. While we were milling in the hallway, a deliveryman wheeled in the department's very first batch of desktop computers. I was among those who didn't see the point. As far as I knew, about all computers could do was store files and info cards on perps, but our file cabinets had been doing that job just fine for decades.

56

After wandering over to Egg-Zaklee's for an early breakfast and a few half-hearted glances at his textbooks, Stump called the detectives again. This time Detective Jenkins took his call. "Do you remember me?" he asked. "I was the one who—"

"I know who you are. What can I do for you?"

"Detective Trent said that both cases are closed, but can I ask you something?"

"Make it brief."

"I understand that you folks found a note in the Clayton's safe deposit box at CalWest Bank. Is that right?"

"That's right."

"I didn't think to ask him at the time, but there are quite a few CalWest branches. We're not talking about the Del Mar branch, are we?"

"That sounds correct. Why?"

"One of the guys on the boat worked at that branch. I saw a logo on his bag and talked with him about it."

"Meaning?"

"I dunno, exactly. I could tell that the banker and Mr. Clayton didn't know each other when the boat went out to the bait tank, but they did have a long conversation later that night before Mr. Clayton died."

"I'm not sure what you're implying, but we interviewed that banker just as we interviewed everybody else. There was no reason to suspect anything. He had no motive. Besides, if everybody who had a connection to that chain were considered suspects, we'd have tens of thousands of them. Regardless, we found an abundance of additional solid evidence to support our conclusion."

"Like what?"

"If you must know, we verified prints, talked with the Claytons' adult daughter and found out the couple had been known to quarrel loudly. That note in their box was important too. We always follow the evidence. It's the most reliable technique in solving crimes."

"You're probably right. I just thought I'd ask."

"I wouldn't worry about it if I were you. We had an abundance of concrete, corroborating evidence."

"Yeah. Okay. I've got other things I should be doing anyway. Thanks for your time."

Before concentrating on his books, Stump sent Michael a "good morning" text and suggested they take some time out later in the day to visit her father. Her fairly quick one-word response—affirmative—lent him some comfort. So did the fact that he hadn't seen any signs of her pain pills lately.

He moved to another table in the back of the restaurant where it was easier to concentrate and forced himself to review several chapters in Deviant Behavior. This time it may have taken ten full minutes before his mind wandered again.

In spite of the fact that the detectives were very confident in their case, Stump held an uneasy feeling about JP and Kyle. He couldn't get over the fact that they were the last ones with Clayton before he died or their suspicious behavior throughout the voyage, especially after the police prematurely terminated the trip. It was one of those "you had to be there" situations. He couldn't stand it anymore. He called Detective Trent again.

"Hello Neal," the detective said. "I hope you have something new to say. We can't keep talking with you about a closed case."

"I know that, but regarding the double knockout theory, I

think there was another possibility. You might want to look into it."

"*We told you before, we put this baby to bed, Neal. We're not going to wake it up because a college student has a hunch. A hunch doesn't outweigh pages of forensics to the contrary.*"

"Well, would you at least hear me out?"

Stump heard Trent sigh. "*Make it quick. I've got other things I need to do.*"

"Thank you. JP and Kyle didn't fish very much compared to the others. Why would they go to all that trouble and then sit out so much?"

"*How do I know? Maybe they were seasick or intimidated.*"

"They were the only ones who weren't grumbling about getting back to shore when you guys took over our boat."

"*None of that matters, Neal. We're not going to reopen a case on something that vague.*"

"But Kyle left all his fish behind. Who does that? It was as if he just wanted to get out of there."

"*Look. We know you want to become a detective, and you'll probably make a good one someday, but you'll discover that some cases are easier than others. Now unless you've got something a lot stronger, I've got to go now. Maybe we can work together some other time, but this case is closed. 'Bye, now.*"

When Stump hung up, he had to admit that if he compared their information with his it was like plopping a bowling ball on one side of a fulcrum and a pebble on the other side.

Nonetheless, a pebble in a tennis shoe can be very pesky until it is removed. And that's what he needed to do. Completely remove the last pebble of doubt regarding whether JP and Kyle could have been involved in either of the deaths. And to do that, a quick drive to JP's branch office was in order.

* * *

Later at the Del Mar branch of CalWest Banks, Stump walked up to the receptionist, scanned a group of business cards on her desk and grabbed one bearing the name Julius Patrick Crain. "Hi. My name is Neal. Is JP available? I met him on a fishing trip and need to talk with him."

The receptionist shook her head. "No, he's not, and he's not coming back."

"Really? Why not?"

"I don't know, actually. It was real sudden. He came in with two friends, said he had a bunch of vacation time, and mentioned an evening flight to London."

"London? Why London?"

"I sure don't know. He just upped and quit. He didn't even give the usual two weeks' notice."

"What about the friends? Was there a male who smoked?"

"As a matter of fact, there was. I could smell it on him."

"I'm looking for him, too. Do you know how I can reach any of them? It's real important."

"I never saw either of them before. I think the woman called the other man Ward."

"Ward, huh? Could that have been his last name?"

"I wouldn't know."

"Who was the woman? Does she work here?"

"No. She appeared to be Ward's girlfriend. Sorta tall, but I don't know how to reach any of them."

"Okay, thanks," Stump said, turning around and grinning. He took a little pride in putting the names together and discovering that a flight to London was in the mix. People didn't usually go on impromptu long trips, nor did businesspeople leave their jobs without giving notice. Those things didn't prove anything, but they moved Stump's goalpost, at least a small amount.

Regrouping, he knew that one Julius Patrick Crain, alias JP, and JP's fishing buddy, Kyle Ward, along with a tallish girlfriend, comprised some sort of team that planned to leave the country in a couple days. But why? And if these people were in on the Claytons' murders, what the heck was their motive?

There was one way to find out.

57

I spent the next several years going to meetings of both the Nazis and the Klan. All along, I gathered inside information and set up violent guys, mostly from the Nazi group, and never had to go to court as a witness, which would have blown my cover.

Anyway, in the spring of '83 Beck agreed to marry me. I still thought about Dorene and Junior, but it had been five years since the accident, and I was finally able to keep it all in perspective. My present moments were every bit the blessing my past was.

After a wonderful honeymoon to Japan, Beck and I returned home, where a month later, Jack Aladar summoned me to his office. I was told to wear "very" casual clothes.

Intrigued, I did as asked and arrived at just past eight on the day in question.

"I need you to take on a small side job," he said after we got down to business.

"Me? What's this about?"

"Yesterday a woman named Phyllis Vann came in and said that her friend Naomi Price wanted to know if Ms. Vann knew anybody who could delete Naomi's husband."

"Uh-oh."

"There's a relatively common procedure for something

like this," the lieutenant continues, "so we asked Ms. Vann if she would be willing to wear a wire and try to get Price to reaffirm her wish."

"Vann must have agreed."

"Correct. Before we sent her back to Price's home, we told her to get Price to repeat her goal, only this time we needed Price to make a specific offer on her own so we could avoid being accused of entrapment."

"Did Vann get it?"

"Not well enough. We plugged her in and tailed her to Price's home. Once inside, Vann said she'd been thinking about Price's request. When Price reaffirmed her wishes, Vann said she knew a guy from her exercise club who might do the job, but she didn't know how much to offer him."

"But Price didn't take the bait?"

"Not completely. She was certain she wanted hubby dead, but she never would say how much she wanted to pay the executioner—and without that, any decent defense lawyer could say she was just kidding."

"What happened next?"

"Fortunately, Vann eventually said she could ask her exercise buddy if he was interested and then send him over there and the two of them could cut their own deal. That's where you come in."

Now it made sense. "You want me to play the role of a hit man and see if I can coax an offer out of her. Why me?"

Jack smiled. "Simple, with your build and tats you look more like a hit man than anybody else who's available. It should only take you an hour or so. You'll be wired and have plenty of back-up."

"Sure. Sounds fun. When do I go over there?"

"Just as soon as we hook you up. Just remember, the key is to get her to make a specific offer. Then give her a couple chances to back out so the intent is clear."

I agreed and a little later my half-sleeved sweatshirt and tattered blue jeans stood in contrast to the upper middle-class home of James and Naomi Price. Wired, I verified that the back-up team was ready to record the event.

I walked past a flower garden to the doorbell and drew a couple boisterous, ankle-high Peekapoos to the inside of the glass outer door.

A minute later an attractive, thin brunette in a skintight, yellow exercise outfit with a matching sweatband came to the door. She picked up one of the dogs and looked me over pretty good. "Yes?"

With canine snarls as background noise, I asked matter-of-factly, "Your name Price?"

"Could be. Who are you?"

"Phyllis Vann sent me."

She glanced up the street before she pushed the door my way. "Come in."

Once inside, she held her arm out toward one of two lush green sofas. I sat in one. She took the other. "Did Phyllis tell you what I need?" she asked.

"Not really. She just said it would pay well, but the less she knows, the better. Why don't you just speak for yourself?"

"Okay, then, how do I know you're not a cop?"

I almost smiled before I pointed at the KKK tat on my upper arm that I had gotten a few years back. "Cops don't like guys like me. How do I know you're not just a blowhard?"

She crossed her arms and grinned. "I guess that makes us even."

"Alright then, what you got in mind?"

"You gotta gun? Can you get one?"

I scoffed. "Oh, I got a few of them. Who's the loser?"

"I may not look like it," she said, smiling, "but I've got two assholes. The second one parks his car in my garage at night. His name is Jimmy. He's been cheating on me for years. He cheats on his girlfriends, too. If a woman moves, he'll fuck her."

"I take it he's grown tired of you?"

She scoffed and swiped her hand in front of her torso. "Nobody gets tired of this. Not even Jimmy."

"You still haven't said what you have in mind."

"Killing him, of course. I want to teach him a lesson. Too bad we can't do it more than once."

I'd heard about the proverbial "woman scorned," but this was the first time I'd met her. "You got a plan?"

"Do I look like a bimbo? My husband is as predictable as gravity. He's coming back from one of his 'business' trips tonight. We'll have dinner, some wine, sit in the hot tub for precisely 20 minutes and then screw—he has a very brief routine for that, too."

"Too bad for him."

Her naughty smile made me suspect she had enjoyed just as many conquests as her promiscuous husband. "Tomorrow he'll be up at seven," she added. "He'll work out, take a shower, make a few calls, jump in his Mercedes and park at the back of the lot at his favorite liquor store precisely at ten. Then he'll buy the same old wine and scotch he always buys."

"Okay, I'm with you. What then?"

"Simple. When he returns to his car, you'll be in your car, right next to his, and end his routine. I only have one requirement."

"A requirement?"

"Yeah. After you kill him, I want you to shoot his dick."

Hmm. This was a good chance to imply I was on her side. "Neither of us wants that," I said. "If we make his penis disappear, that'll make it extremely personal and the cops will race right back to you, and that could lead to me and I don't like that game."

After a brief pause she smiled. "Good point. Damn. I woulda got some special pleasure out of separating him from his little wandering fireman. Oh well, I guess I can compromise."

"Why don't you just file for divorce? By the looks of this place, you'd still get plenty of money and you could avoid dealing with the cops and everything else afterwards."

"Buncha reasons. He'd figure out how to hide as much as he could. I'd only get half of what's left over. It would take too long...and it wouldn't be as satisfying."

"Alright. I think I can pull this off. But you better be damn sure this is what you want."

"Oh, I'm more than *damn sure.*"

It was almost too easy. I had everything I needed except for a specific offer. "And?"

"Oh, I guess a fellow like you needs a little spending money. How's a thousand up front and a thousand when it's done sound?"

That was good enough to make the arrest, but I wanted to make her reaffirm her intent. "It sounds like you're looking for an amateur. That's how it sounds."

"Okay then. How much do you want?"

"You just make another offer and I'll let you know if you've got my interest."

"Okay? How 'bout two up front and one when it's done."

"You're boring me, lady. You can afford a lot more than that."

"Alright, alright. I get it. Three up-front. Two on the back, plus a bonus."

"A bonus?"

"Yeah. A damn good one, too. You do your job right and I'll give you an all-night bonus that you'll never forget."

I grinned. She probably got a lot of things that way. "Sorry, but you ain't my type."

"Try me."

Just then the dogs barked and two of our detectives burst through the front door with weapons drawn.

Months later, Mrs. Vann traded in her yellow outfit for an orange one and got forty-six months of free rent, compliments of the citizens of Los Angeles.

58

Stump couldn't stop thinking about the double knockout theory. No doubt, the detectives had nailed down means, motive and opportunity. All the t's were crossed, the i's dotted. They also had Stu Clayton's prints on the hammer and Joann Clayton's prints both on the cracker package and the bottle of poison. Then there was that letter in their private safe deposit box. Mrs. Clayton had predicted her demise. That couldn't have been a coincidence. No wonder the police closed the cases so quickly. All the pegs were in the right holes.

But none of that eliminated the symbolic pebble in his shoe—the other eyebrow-raising facts, both on the boat and at the tackle shop. The more he thought about it, he'd rather work his ass off and confirm that JP and Kyle were innocent than snuff out any hopes the Claytons' heirs had to find out that their parents hadn't killed each other.

It wasn't impossible to develop an alternate theory. He simply had to think in terms of means, motive and opportunity.

Starting with the easiest of those, nearly everybody, including JP and Kyle, had the means to get a hammer and a bottle of poison.

Opportunity was a different matter. JP and Kyle clearly had an opportunity to take out Stu on the boat, but Stump didn't know if they could have played a role in Joann Clayton's death, so that issue was fuzzy.

The motive was also unclear. The big three were revenge, sex and money and it could have been any one of those. Either of the Claytons could have had an affair, and that could mean that sex and revenge were both possibilities.

At the same time, all of this was taking place with a bank in the background so it wasn't a stretch to consider money as a possible motive.

But that concept had some flaws, too. As far as Stump could tell there wasn't any indication that the Claytons were affluent. Therefore, their home may have been their most valuable asset—and JP wouldn't have killed them to get their house. Estate laws would get in the way. Ditto any life insurance policies. JP wouldn't have been a beneficiary to anything like that.

Still the undeniable fact was that the Claytons had accounts and a safe deposit box in the exact same branch where JP worked and banks have those boxes for a reason: People store valuables in those boxes.

Considering that the detectives had seen inside the Claytons' box, if there ever was anything of value in there, whatever it was had disappeared before the detectives got there. Therefore, if the Claytons truly did store something of value in their box, and neither the detectives nor the Claytons had possession of it, then somebody else had it, and that is where JP warranted suspicion.

When assisting customers in the vaults, bankers would have to hear numerous stories about the contents of the boxes. If something like that happened while JP was in the vault with one of the Claytons, the money motive was definitely in play for JP.

Unwilling to give up, Stump did a quick Google search where he found several JP Crains, but only one Julius Patrick Crain in southern California. A little visit from a stranger might just pull some useful information from JP's own mouth. First, Stump needed to call his brother and borrow Catts McFadden's fishing rod again.

An hour later, with the prop fishing rod in the back seat and on their way to JP's address, Stump spoke to Danville. "Here's what you do, bro. To start out, take the rod with you to his door. He's really tall so you'll know if you have the right guy. Tell him you work at the dock. Say that somebody left the rod there and the clerk in the tackle shop thought it belonged to JP or Kyle and you're there to return it..."

After Stump spelled out the rest of his plan, they arrived in JP's neighborhood where Stump got out of the car and Danville proceeded to JP's home.

Mere minutes later Danville returned with a cat-caught-the-mouse grin on his face. "You were right, dude," he said to Stump. "After that JP guy said the rod wasn't his, I fed him that crock about me being from England and that we didn't have any tuna fishing there."

"I knew it'd work, bro. Did you ask him if he'd ever been there?"

"Yep. Just like you said and it worked perfectly. He said he's going there Wednesday evening."

Stump nodded. "That confirms what the receptionist told me."

"Then I told him I liked American Airlines, but they've gotten too expensive. That's when I asked him which airline he likes."

"Please tell me that he answered the question."

A grin of grins spread across Danville's face. "Piece of cake, dude. It's Virgin Airlines. He's going to leave Wednesday night on Virgin Airlines."

Stump raised a tight fist in the air. "Way to go, bro. I knew you could do it."

With that little nugget of information tucked away, Stump decided to take one more run at the detectives, this time in person. If he couldn't persuade them to overlook their previous conclusion and investigate JP and Kyle, he'd have to consider trailing his suspects to London, all of which would impair his ability to take his last two finals.

* * *

"Thanks for seeing me, Detective Trent," Stump said, this time sitting across the table from the man. "I know you're tired of me and I don't mean to beat a dead horse, but I've uncovered some new information that might change your minds."

"Such as?"

"JP and Kyle were the last ones with Mr. Clayton before he died. They had a good opportunity to kill him."

"With poison? You already said they didn't know each other when they all got onboard. Now you're telling me they had a bottle of poison with them and had nothing else to do so they decided to kill the last guy to go to bed."

Ouch! When he put it that way, Stump's theory sounded much weaker.

"Unless you have something better than that," Trent added, "I want you to listen to me one last time so we don't have to keep going over this. We checked everything out. When we arrived at the first crime scene there was no evidence of a break-in. That implies that Mrs. Clayton knew her killer. The poor woman's head was shattered and blood-soaked by a hammer that was right next to her body with Stu Clayton's prints on it. That means it was personal. There was no doubt about it—Mr. Clayton had means, motive and opportunity to kill his wife. Therefore, we had a very strong reason to suspect him. But that's not all.

"After discovering that he went fishing, we went to pick him up. That led to discovering he had been poisoned in his sleeping compartment. And his wife's prints were on the cracker box and a bottle of poison in their garage. Nobody else's prints. Just those of the Claytons."

"But—"

"But nothing. We talked to everybody who knew them. According to their daughter, they had a few intense marital spats from time to time. Furthermore, there wasn't any evidence to implicate anybody else. No DNA. No motive. No prints. Nothing. Now unless you have something else, a blockbuster that trumps all of that, I have other cases."

"But perps can mess with crime scenes."

"What part of 'case closed' don't you understand?"

"The part that leaves another possibility on the table. Would it make any difference if I told you that JP quit his job and is planning to go to London?"

Detective Trent paused for a moment, then shrugged. "That's interesting but it's no big deal. Thousands of people go there every day. The Claytons themselves went there a while back."

"Really? Doesn't that strike you as odd?"

"Not particularly. We're talking about two completely different timeframes here. There's no connection."

"Couldn't you at least call their daughter to see if they know who Julius Crain and Kyle Ward are?"

Trent sighed. "I'll think about it, but for now I've got plenty of other things to do."

"I'd ask you to check their phone records, but I know you have to get a subpoena for that. Still, you can check their criminal records. Would you mind?"

59

My one-time venture into the role of a hit man proved I could fit into other forms of UC work, but over the next few years the vast majority of my time was spent gathering data about both my den-mates at the KKK and the Nazi troop.

It was common for both of those nefarious kissing cousins to attend the same public gatherings. Ordinarily the events attracted a lot of yelling and name-calling. Oddly, whenever violence broke out, the public usually started it. Somebody would throw a rock or spit on one of us and we responded in kind. In those situations, I opted to shove a person or two, just for the optics, but I was very careful not to hurt anybody. Then in '87 one of those events triggered another odd encounter.

After a protest rally a few of the KKK guys wanted to grab a beer. I went along in case I could gather any intel. A few too many beers prompted the predictable braggadocio and Myron Thorn, a long-time member with a flattop haircut and a well-groomed goatee, decided he wanted go kick the snot out of a black person or two.

I basically had to go along and hope I could get a call to dispatch so they could have the boys in blue arrest Myron, should he get violent.

The two of us jumped in his old truck. That was when I recalled that he was a softball coach. "Too bad you ain't got no bats with you," I said, hoping to find out just how dangerous this little journey was.

He smiled. "I got it covered, man. They're right behind the seat."

The red flags sprang up. If I couldn't find some way to get a call in to dispatch or my handlers, there was a decent chance I'd have to arrest Myron and blow my cover. For the time being, I sat tight and wondered if this would be the end to my den days.

During a long hour of chest-thumping, Myron got louder and louder, and I said just enough in the right tone and demeanor to preserve my image. Then I noticed a black guy/white woman couple refueling at a gas station. They were prime candidates for the kind of whupping Myron was talking about, but at that moment, Myron looked my way and said something about his truck not running quite right and drove right on by.

I didn't know how Coach Myron could have missed seeing the couple, but it meant I wouldn't have to intervene and thereby risk blowing my cover. After that, we cruised a little while longer, then called it a night without any additional drama.

* * *

The next odd thing came up a year later in '88 when Geraldo Rivera had a TV show. At the time, his producers wanted to air a program about hate groups. Our den was close by, so they asked us if we'd consider attending.

Skinhead contacted Tom Metzger, the California Grand Dragon. Metzger liked the opportunity and encouraged our attendance.

That got us to talking about Metzger, who had stopped paying taxes in the 1970s. In '79 he and some other Klan boys harassed some illegal Mexican immigrants in Fallbrook, south of LA.

The next year he won the Democratic Party's nomination for the U.S. House of Representatives in a San Diego neighborhood. Fortunately, the party wouldn't allow him to take office, but that didn't shut him up.

In the mid-'80s he founded the White Aryan Resistance (WAR), an openly racist skinhead organization. By that time, Metgzer had brought his hot-headed son, John, into the mix.

With all of that as background, Rivera's producers eventually decided to focus on "young" hate groups.

The skinheads and Metzger's son—a 20-year-old with enough hate in him to make his racist father proud, were tapped to be on a panel. I was one of several guys from our den who agreed to act as bodyguards for the panelists.

On the day of the taping, while milling around the studio before the program, we met up with a young leader from the American Front. The director of the Skinheads of National Resistance was also called in. The tension was immediately obvious and a precursor to an all-out brawl.

Just before the big scuffle broke out, the younger white guys were seated on one side of the stage. On the other side, a tall African American named Roy Innis represented the Congress of Racial Equality. The last man on the panel was a member of the Jewish community.

Predictably, a bunch of arguing pitted the three young men and their supporters against nearly everybody else. After a few warm-up questions to raise the tension, Mr. Rivera allowed audience members to ask questions of the panel.

A woman asked Metzger's kid why he felt compelled to attack anybody with whom he disagreed, to which he replied, "Because I'm tired of Kikes complaining all the time." Then he pointed a limp thumb in the direction of Roy Innis, the lone black man in the group, "and I'm sick and tired of Uncle Tom here, sucking up and trying to be a white man."

Innis had had enough. He rose from his chair, wrapped his

hands around Metzger's neck and lifted the terrified youth to his tiptoes. Then, a 20-person punch-up broke out.

Audience members and security personnel attacked the stage. Fists flew. People reached for weapons. The audience yelled. Then a folding chair rose above the heads and smashed down on Mr. Rivera. While he was reeling, one of the WAR guys cold-cocked him, breaking his nose and drawing blood. That provoked even more people. It took ten extremely hazardous minutes for the security crew to get the matter under control.

As for me, I held back a couple of skinheads who were approaching the stage from their front row seats. Then I got in a staring match with a tall stagehand/bouncer whom you can see in the video that has since been placed on the internet.

After all was said and done, I preserved my undercover status and avoided hurting anybody, but I had a memory that would last a lifetime. Meanwhile, I hoped that the event might someday play a role in bringing Tom Metzger down.

60

Some issues are black and white; others are varying shades of gray. As far as Stump was concerned, when it came to murder, all of the gray should be removed. The police did a damn good job on the Clayton case, but Stump had suspicions and questions that they hadn't considered — like why London was so damn important.

Snubbed by Detective Trent, Stump had to choose between doing what he "ought" to do—focus on his schoolwork and pick up a diploma at the upcoming ceremony—or do what he felt "compelled" to do—forgo his finals for the time being and find out if JP et al had anything to do with the Claytons' murders, which would require a few days of international travel and could all end up being a big waste of time.

Somebody else might have considered that a tough choice, but not Stump. Studying was like taking medicine while solving crimes was like curing diseases. Besides, he'd been in this kind of situation on other occasions and always recovered.

For instance, in 10th grade he had to go to summer school to make up for all the classes he'd cut while trying to send a bad guy to jail. Another time, in his first year of criminology school, he missed some tests because he was busy solving two cases at the time. Later he persuaded the college to set up make-up tests when he insisted all of that proved he was detective material, even though he didn't always fit some of the orthodoxy.

This case was similar. He believed that JP and Kyle could have murdered one or both of the Claytons and catching somebody like that was more important than a couple of tests that could be rescheduled if necessary.

With his strategy in place he needed a partner. He waited until he and Michael were alone at the B&B before broaching the topic. "Say, Michael, do you have a lot of bookings in the next week?"

"For the B&B? Why?"

"I know this sounds crazy, but I have to go to London for a little while."

"London, England? Are you nuts?"

"I've been following up on that hunch I told you about. I'm convinced those two guys on the boat could have had something to do with the double murder. I'd like you to go with me."

"That's crazy. Let the police handle it."

"I tried, but they brushed me off."

"Well, that ought to tell you something, like it's none of your business."

"Sure, it is. We're talking about a couple murders here, and nobody else is going to chase down this lead. If those guys are guilty and I don't stop them, they're going to get away with murder. I can't ignore that."

"Well, I can, and I'm not going on a wild goose chase. Why don't you take your brother?"

"Can't. He's got finals."

"Well, double damn duh, Stump! So do you. What about your graduation? That's just a few days off. You can't go to London and get back in time to take your last two tests, let alone graduate."

"I'll talk with them when I get back, Michael. They've

made emergency allowances for people before. I'll get them to do the same for me."

"Yeah. Right. Good luck with that. In the meantime, Xander and everybody else is coming in to see you. What are you going to do about them—just let them flop in the wind?"

"I've thought about that. Xander gets free airfare. He can come some other time. Besides, I bet he'd want me to go get those guys."

"I don't know about that, but I do know that those two yahoos would recognize me and I don't want to leave Daddy right now. He's been walking slower lately."

"Yana and Danville can keep an eye on him. C'mon. I really want you to go with me."

"No. No. No," she said shaking her head aggressively. "Ain't happening."

"What if I got on my knees and begged you to come?"

"Dammit, Stump, listen to me. There's no fucking way. Is that clear enough for you?"

Head, meet two-by-four. Stump finally got the message. Michael didn't usually get that huffy. . .unless. "I gotta ask you something, Michael. Are you still taking pain pills?"

Red with anger, she grabbed her head and hurried for the door and screamed, "Stop accusing me of things." She slammed the door behind her.

Now what? Maybe Michael was genuinely working on the matter and just needed to be left alone for a while. She could get that alone time if he'd go to London for a few days.

Regardless of the other issues, Michael was correct about the likelihood that JP and/or Kyle would recognize her—and she wasn't the only one. There was a legitimate chance they'd recognize Stump, too. If Stump were to tail those guys to London, he'd have to get some sort of disguise.

Still wanting to take a partner, he hustled over to Egg-Zaklee's to see if James could break away from the breakfast grill for a while. There, Stump observed Danville studying on a back table. "Nose in the books, eh, bro?" Stump said.

"Yeah, you know the grind. What you up to?"

"I came to see if James wants to go with me to London. I still think those two guys on the boat could have been behind one or both murders."

"Really? I've been to London before. I'd go."

"I dunno, dude. Our father might throw a fit."

"So what? He'll have a long time to get over it. But you and I may never have another chance like this."

"Really, are you sure? What about your schoolwork?"

"What about it? You've done things like this before and it always worked out. Besides, if I'm going to be in law enforcement, I have to catch bad guys."

"I don't want to be a bad influence on my younger brother."

"Oh, yeah? Well I know a wise person who said if you're going to be a detective, you don't get to pick when the cases come your way."

"Dude, it's no fair using my own lines against me."

"Then count me in."

"Alright, but we better tell our father what we're up to."

"He'll probably be pissed at first, but my mother doesn't want me to drop out, so I think they'll roll with it just so long as I agree to get back on track."

"Yeah. Parents are like that. They'll do almost anything to keep us in school."

"Alright, let's call 'em when we're on the plane or in London. That way they can't do anything about it."

Stump smirked, "You're my bro, alright. Oh, by the way, you're gonna have to shave your mustache."

61

By 1983, I'd sold the old house and bought a new one with Beck, who had a baby a few months later. We named him Jonathan Baxter Padget.

After that, I considered getting out of undercover work, but I was pretty good at it and liked thinning society's herd of misfits. Furthermore, I didn't qualify for retirement and most of the non-desk jobs were just as dangerous as what I was doing, so the whole notion of "getting out" wasn't very practical.

Instead, I promised Beck that I'd play it safe because I wanted to see our son grow up. I wanted to laugh out loud when he blew out the back-end of a diaper; I wanted to watch him play baseball; I wanted to see him fall in puppy love, and I wanted to teach him to drive.

Then, 1992 rolled around. I'd been in UC work for 14 years and had secretly disrupted many of my den's plans, which was one reason they were getting weaker. But all of that was about to come to an end.

At a typical den meeting, we were told that Tom Metzger had called for a huge, four-den summit in a private lodge, 40 miles out of town. Fifty men, including Metzger himself, were expected to attend.

This was precisely the kind of event that spawned bluster

and caused the more brazen guys, including yours truly, to openly pack heat.

On the designated Saturday, a dozen of us met at Kenneth Cargill's shoe store for a carpool. It took four vehicles to accommodate both our group and two kegs of donated beer. I was teamed up with Royce Perry, Carlton Bisk and Steven Hauser, aka Doorknob.

Along the way, the anticipation rivaled that of a kid's Christmas morning. Doorknob predicted that we were going to pull off the first Klan murder in two decades. Bisk said he knew a black cop who "would look good in a casket." By the time we got to the lodge we'd thrown enough bullshit around to fertilize a large farm.

As the first den to arrive, we hauled in the beer and scoped out the place. A large open space took up half the main floor. A huge kitchen, a poolroom, a coatroom and a couple restrooms finished it off. We rolled in three racks of folding chairs from the coatroom and wondered where the other dens were.

"Okay everybody," Royce Perry eventually said, from in front of the rows of folding chairs we'd laid out. "We've got some news for you, but first we'd like you to grab a seat in the front two rows."

I took the far left seat of the front row.

"The truth is," Royce said moving away from me slightly, "we're the only den that's going to be here today. Someone in here has been up to no good, and nobody's going anywhere until we straighten it out."

His tone indicated that he meant business but Doorknob thought Royce was talking about a personal issue. "What's a matter, big guy?" he asked. "Has your wife been sleeping around again?"

The implication that one of the guys in the den had "been with" Royce's wife caused the man's jaw to tighten and his face to glow red. "Fuck you, Doorknob. This is much bigger. Somebody here has betrayed us, you moron."

This wasn't good. They must have figured out that I was a mole. Others went silent while Royce slowly roamed around the room, glaring at people. Eventually he looked at me. It appeared that I was finally busted, but I held steady for a few more seconds and took mental inventory of my weapon.

Then he took another half-step away from me before turning toward Myron Thorn, the coach. "Why don't you tell them what I'm talking about, Myron? I'm sure you want them to hear it from your own lips."

Myron glanced around. "Is this a joke, Royce? I don't know what the hell you're talking about."

While all the eyes were aimed at Myron and Royce, I reached down to my pant leg and unhooked my ankle holster.

Just then, Royce cold-cocked Myron, who grunted and reeled backwards, lending me a moment to snag my weapon. By that time Royce had jumped on Myron. "I know who you are, you fucking bastard," he said, landing several more punches and then reaching for a knife that he kept in a sheath at his belt.

Suddenly, I had to end the threat before things got really ugly. By the time Royce grasped his knife, I had moved forward, double-handed my weapon and looked for a clear shot at either his head or heart. But it wasn't there and painful memories of the man that I'd killed at a liquor store a few years back pressed me instead to blow a hole through Royce's right knee.

He screamed, released the knife and reached for his wound.

Heads pivoted my way. Not wanting to give anybody a chance to escalate the tension, I waved my weapon back and forth so they all could see it. "Everybody put your hands up unless you want to be next."

Hands rose, most of them reluctantly.

From the floor, Royce had slithered off Myron and clung to

his limp, bleeding knee. "One of you motherfuckers get me some help," he screeched through clenched teeth.

Realizing that Myron was the elusive mole I'd always wondered about, I moved into an open space in front of the chairs and stole a quick glance at the creek of blood oozing off his chin. "Can you draw your weapon?"

He spit out a loose tooth and rose to his feet. "Damn right I can."

While I held the others at bay, Myron reached for the holster that he kept behind his back. "All right, everybody," I went on. "You need to know that I'm a police officer with the LAPD. Myron here is a deputy sheriff. If you want to see your kids grow up, I suggest you do as we say."

"Get me a goddamn ambulance, you assholes."

"In a minute, Royce."

While others mumbled, Skinhead shook his head. "I knew it."

"Quiet, Earl. Everybody keep your hands high where I can see them." Thankfully, they did as requested.

"Now I want Earl, Carlton and Doorknob to take one step forward."

While they did that, Royce rolled around on the floor moaning, but for the moment, I had a lake full of bigger fish to fry.

I kept my eyes on the troops and spoke to Myron. "These three gents all have weapons. Since Carlton is closest to you, we'll have him drop his weapon first. Then you kick it over my way. We'll remove the cartridges in a minute."

"Got it."

After a very cautious few minutes, each of the initial three den-mates was disarmed and had been patted down.

"Okay, you three," I said, "I want you to slowly move into the corner, behind Royce."

With the most dangerous fellows tucked in the corner, Myron and I could focus on the others. "Now Kenneth, Martin, and Max, it's your turn. Keep 'em high and step forward." That done, we performed the same exercise with everybody else and ultimately bunched everybody behind Royce where we could see all of them at the same time. We could finally breathe just a little.

With our guns still drawn, I stood at a window on one wall, while Myron stood near a window on the other wall and rubbed his jaw. We essentially had them in a crossfire.

"Okay," I said to Carlton. "Now I want you to remove your shirt and use the sleeves to squeeze off Royce's wound."

After that, I took a seat a full 15 feet back from the mass of guys while Myron called for back-up and an ambulance. While we waited, Myron looked my way. "How'd you know?"

"That you're a deputy sheriff? I always knew there was another mole. Then there was that day when you and I went out to pop somebody's head with a bat, but when we came to those people getting gas, you ignored an obvious opportunity. When Royce struck you, that confirmed it. Since I'd never seen you at a Xmas party or even in a hallway in a police building, you had to be based somewhere else. The best bet was the sheriff's office."

Myron nodded. "Good point. Looks like we're outed now."

We sure were.

62

After Danville agreed to go to London, it occurred to Stump that every once in a while a person had to make life-altering decisions. For him, this was one of those occasions. It was either get a diploma or investigate a murder. Since he chose not to get the degree, he called his case the *Zero Degree Murder*.

With his strategy in place, he jumped online and found the Virgin Airlines website to make reservations for two on an enormous 300-seat jet called a Dreamliner.

The tricky part was to avoid being recognized by JP or Kyle. Stump knew from previous trips that the airlines allowed slower people to board first; then they loaded the plane from rear to front. Another thing he knew was most people liked to sit toward the front of the aircraft so they could deplane first.

By the time Stump completed their reservations he and Danville had two seats on the nine p.m. flight in the rear of the plane and poor Danville was recovering from a painful appendectomy that would enable them to be among the first group to board, thereby limiting their time in the lobby where the suspects might spot them.

With all of that locked down, there remained a risk that JP would recognize Stump from the fishing trip or Danville from their lost fishing pole encounter at JP's home, so Danville shaved off his mustache before he and Stump zipped over to the mall and into the Beard And Things store. There, a clerk helped Danville pick out a baseball cap and a set of bushy, dark brown sideburns made from real human hair.

Stump went for a slightly more professorial disguise. Once again, real human hair formed a light brown mustache with a matching goatee. A touring cap and a pair of classic black frame glasses finished the costume.

Now, inside the airport and not knowing how much luggage JP and Kyle might bring, Stump and Danville decided to limit their baggage to one backpack each in case the suspects did the same thing to make a fast exit from the London airport.

With their costumes in their bags, they checked in, showed their passports, went through the screening process and scooted through the concourse to the nearest restroom. There, they donned their new facial hair before wandering down the concourse to a near-empty seating area fifty yards from their eventual gate.

At seven p.m. and way ahead of their flight time, they walked toward the windows where Stump snagged his phone and speed-dialed Michael in hopes that she'd calmed down following the tongue-darts she'd shot his way the previous day.

She didn't answer, so he sent a very brief text instead. Love u miss u.

While he had his phone out, he placed the call he and Danville had put off. "Hi, Xander," he said to their father a moment later.

"Hello back, eldest son. I bet your nose is bruised from sticking it in your books. We're looking forward to seeing you both."

"That's what I called about. You should cancel your flight."

"I don't actually have a flight. I fly standby for free. Remember?"

"Yeah, but isn't Brianne coming too?"

"Yes, and your grandparents. My mother is looking forward to walking on the beach."

263

"Those are the ones to cancel."

"*What are you talking about, Stump? Why would we do that?*"

"Well, I'm on a case and I won't be here."

"*A case. With the police?*"

"No. I think two guys committed a murder, but the police think somebody else did it, so I have to go to London to check it out."

"*London? Can't you do it after graduation?*"

"It's a long story, but the answer is 'no.' We're in the airport now."

"*That's a bummer. I'll have to ask if my mom still wants to go to see Danville and the ocean, or if she'd rather wait until we can all be together.*"

"Well, that's another problem; Danville's going with me. I paid for his airfare."

After a silent pause, Xander said, "*Is he with you, now? May I please speak with him?*"

"Sure," Stump said handing his cell to his brother. "Your turn."

"Hello, Father. I'm going to London."

Stump finger-combed his fake mustache while he listened to his brother wrestle with the old peeps.

"Yes. Yes. I promise," Danville eventually said. "I'll work it all out when I get back. I gotta go now. Love you. 'Bye.'"

Stump grinned. "How'd they take it?"

Danville smiled. "I told you, dude. My mom made me promise not to drop out. I just hope you're right about us getting back in school."

"Me, too, bro. Me, too. Now we need to discuss our strategy in case we get split up."

Still a good distance from nosey ears, they discussed how they could watch for their suspects and perhaps get pictures of them leaving the country. "The way I see it," Stump said. "Considering the time change and the flight time, it'll be past noon when we get there. The riskiest time is when we get off the plane. If JP and Kyle don't have large bags, they'll want to get out of there in a hurry. We'll have to be right on their tails, because if they get away, we probably won't be able to find them again."

"Got it," Danville said, "but I'd bet that we're the only ones who didn't bring luggage."

"I hope so. That way, if we get separated from them in the London airport, we can find them at baggage claim."

Fifteen minutes later they'd watched at least a hundred people soldier past them and toward the gate, but no sign of JP and his partner. After a while, Stump speed-dialed Michael again. As before she didn't answer, probably by choice.

Stump had still not seen JP or Kyle when a message dropped down from overhead speakers. *"Welcome to Virgin Airlines, ladies and gentlemen. We're going to begin boarding now. Families with children and anybody needing special assistance can come forward now. After that we'll begin boarding the aircraft. Once again, it's time for families with children, or anybody needing special assistance to board the aircraft."*

To Stump, "special assistance" included anybody who claimed to be recovering from an appendectomy and that person's travel partner. He nudged his half-brother. "That's us, bro. Let's go, but move slow."

Stump didn't like misleading everybody about Danville's fake appendectomy, but solving a murder was a noble cause and it was imperative that they take every precaution to avoid being recognized by JP or Kyle.

When Stump stepped inside the gargantuan aircraft it occurred to him that the cabin should have been called an auditorium. He and Danville walked past the first-class section, in which several dozen lucky people would enjoy extra leg space and plush lounge chairs that could easily serve as nap beds. Remembering that JP was a head taller than most people, Stump hoped the dude had purchased first-class tickets to get some leg space and thereby remain in the front seating area.

Back farther, the remaining two-thirds of the seating area

resembled a movie theater with three sections separated by two aisles.

Stump had reserved the aisle seat on the outer section on the right side of the plane for himself. Danville had the same thing, but on the left side. That way they'd each have a good view up the aisles and one or the other should be able to keep an eye on the suspects. When needed, they could discreetly send messages back and forth via their cell phones.

At his seat, Stump watched a parade of passengers jam their backpacks, laptops and travel bags into ever-shrinking overhead bins. Most gathered reading materials, iPads and headphones for a very long flight.

Before long, and on the other side of the plane, a couple attractively tanned young ladies worked their way back to Danville's row. Danville rose to allow his new row mates—perhaps age 21, perhaps single and perhaps sympathetic to a fellow recovering from an appendectomy—to wiggle past him and into the row.

Stump sent a text. "*You lucky dog.*"

Like the cat who caught the fat mouse, Danville grinned in Stump's direction and mouthed, "Thank you."

63

For the second time in my career, I had let the system crawl up my backside to make certain I handled the shooting of a KKK member and subsequent activities correctly. Only this time, the incident took place outside our jurisdiction, so it was more cumbersome and annoying.

As the previous time, a lot of things were considered, both external (What was the crime scene like? Were drugs or alcohol involved? How did the events unfold?) and internal (Was I having marital problems? Did I harbor any grudges? Was I having financial problems?). There was also a lot of discussion regarding all the weapons in the room and any alternatives I had to shooting Royce.

Condensing my response, I said something to this effect: "A deputy sheriff was getting beaten, a bad-ass weapon was about to be used on him, and there was no telling what an entire group of police haters, several with deadly weapons and criminal records, would do if given another second or two. I had to end the threat and end it immediately."

Apparently, the panel agreed because I was eventually exonerated. By that time, a slew of charges was brought against half of the den members, both for what happened at the lodge and in the years before that. Eventually, a handful of convictions were obtained. Royce got the worst sentence:

seven months in jail, five years' probation and life with a limp.

Naturally, the den essentially disbanded, which had some other bennies. As a rule, most of the officers in UC capacities burned out within five years for various reasons. Since I was north of 40, I'd passed that point years earlier and still liked certain aspects of it.

The department gave me a choice of applying for detective, going into another branch of UC work or returning to patrol, perhaps on a motorcycle. The idea of riding a motorcycle was interesting, but patrol wasn't for me for the same old reasons. One evening Beck and I bounced the other ideas around.

Beck pointed out that I was good at being sneaky and detectives were essentially on call 24/7, so I decided to shift into some other type of UC work.

I shared the decision with my ever-present handler, who met me in his office and caught me off-guard with another odd request. "I have an opening in the vice squad," he said, "so I can place you there, but first I could use a favor."

Vice sounded workable, but—"What kind of favor?"

"It's another one-time job. Nobody else can take it on. Either they don't fit the profile, they're on other cases or they can't be away from home for very long. You, on the other hand, with your tats, will seal the deal."

I looked at my arm. "You said something about being away from home?"

"It's not entirely *away from home*," he said. "We've locked up Billy Chase, a known car thief who supplies cars to chop shops."

"I've heard a little about those guys. The thief gets a grand or two for a half-hour's work and the bosses sell any parts that don't have serial numbers."

"Or they acquire an identical wrecked vehicle, get the title and change the serial numbers around on the stolen vehicle and sell it whole. It's a very profitable enterprise. Anyway, the court set Billy's bail so high, he couldn't get anybody to post it."

"I see. What do you want me to do?"

"Simple. Be his cellmate. Befriend him. See if you can get him to reveal any information about his buyer. Whoever that is must be employing several of these car thieves."

"But a guy like that isn't going to chirp right away."

"That's the problem. You'll have to stay in jail until Billy trusts you."

"I dunno, Lieutenant. I might go coo-coo in a cage."

"It's not all the time. We'll get you out for phony court hearings, meetings with your attorney. Things like that—and of course Beck can come see you on visitors day as long as it appears credible."

"How long is my sentence and what am I in for?"

"Six weeks, tops. If Billy doesn't trust you enough to open up by then, he probably never will."

"I've got a wife and kid to think about. I'd miss them."

"As I said, we'll get you out for a few hours a couple of times every week so you can still be with your family regularly."

"What's my cover story?"

"You're a public nuisance. A drug dealer and repeat offender who skipped bail and can't get out until all his misdeeds are settled. That'll give us lots of reasons to call you away."

I didn't really know what to think. I liked the idea of busting up the chop shop, and there would be a lot of down time in a cell. I'd either enjoy the peace or go nuts. "But after that, I go to Vice? Right?"

Jack nodded. "So help me God."

And that was the deal. Before I gave the idea a final nod, I spoke with Beck, who said that anything was better than hanging out with the KKK and Nazis at rallies. A few days later Billy Chase got himself a cellmate; a belligerent drunk named Pierce Allen who got thrown into jail for selling drugs, jumping bond and a whole bunch of other shit.

Naturally, I couldn't just walk right into Billy's cell and demand he reveal his contacts. I had to play him a while, gain his confidence before I could go for the juice.

We slowly got to know each other and asked the inevitable benign questions: "What are you in for?" and "How'd you get busted?"

Billy believed my cover, but then, why wouldn't he? There were thousands of people in the L.A. criminal justice system and many of them had similar stories.

Over the couple weeks that followed, we traded tales about how much we hated cops, other crimes we knew about and our girlfriends, who came by on visitor days.

By that time, he'd admitted he was a car thief, so I said I had a cousin who worked near a four-story parking lot and could make a couple luxury cars disappear. "The trouble is," I said, "we don't know where to take them."

"Whatever you do," Billy said with confidence," ya gotta dump 'em quick, before the owner even knows they're missing."

Over the next few days I pulled a few pointers out of him without pressing him but definitely gaining his confidence.

Meanwhile, I only got to see Beck on visitors day and one other time each week at a random time "to talk with my attorney" and "to appear in court." At first it was erotic, like a conjugal visit, but I missed the long talks, home meals and all the rest.

After three full weeks, Billy Chase finally opened up. I'd been bitching about the risk/reward ratio of dealing drugs and segued into a proposal. "My girlfriend has checked with my cousin," I said. "He'd be willing to hook a luxury car here and there. If you'd tell us how to dump them off, we could give you half of our first few deals."

Before answering, he looked up and down the cellblock. That was when I knew I had him. "Guy's name is Phil Meeks," he said. "You can find him at Jackie's Grill, two blocks from the courthouse. He'll tell you what kinds of cars to look for and where to take them. Just say I sent you."

Billy Chase could count on that.

Two days later, I had another one of my "mysterious" court hearings, only this time I didn't go back.

For the next few days, Beck was particularly loving and cheerful. I assumed it was solely because of my return home, but then one evening when I climbed in bed, I unearthed a book from under my pillow—a book of baby names. Beck was two months pregnant with our second child.

The next day I made an appointment to have my KKK tat removed and wondered what Vice would be like.

64

On the monster jet, a few more minutes passed before a 50ish couple picked their way back to Stump's row. The man pointed to the seats between Stump and the window. "Hi, there. Looks like we're your neighbors."

Stump stepped into the aisle while "Cindy" slid into the window seat and "Barry" eased next to her. Before returning to his seat, Stump glanced over to his happy-faced brother and the longhaired beauties. If Stump didn't already have a rad fiancée, he might have filed a formal complaint with the seating gods. Instead he took advantage of his viewpoint and remained standing while dozens of passengers squeezed into the aisles and then into their seats.

Eventually, and with no sign of his suspects, a hint of cold anxiety tapped his spine. What if he and Danville were mistaken? What if JP and Kyle had decided to take a different carrier or go on a different day, or give up on the entire mission? He watched the door anxiously.

At just past nine, and with ninety percent of the passengers on board, Stump hadn't seen his prey. He concluded that he'd rather get his diploma than take a purposeless flight half-way round the world. He sent Danville a text message. *"I haven't seen them. U?"*

"no"

"wanna abort?"

"no way, the ladies like me."

"so do ladies at beach" Stump said, just as JP entered the plane and added a beige cowboy hat to his height. He looked like a skyscraper compared to everybody else.

After confirming that Kyle was there too, Stump thumbed another brother message. *"Check the buckaroo."*

"got him"

With his main question answered, Stump puckered his lips, let out a heart-felt sigh and eased into his seat while JP and Kyle took seats in first class.

Danville sent another text: *"very small backpacks."*

Good. That implied that the suspects had additional luggage and would have to stop off at baggage pick-up in London. Further, there were restrooms up front so it wasn't likely that JP or Kyle would wander into the main seating area much, if at all.

With all of that settled, Stump wondered about Michael and her dad. She'd been worrying about him lately, and when she worried, she was vulnerable to poor choices. He placed another unanswered call before opting to leave yet another text message. *"Miss you. Will call later. Bye."*

Like everybody else Stump settled in and marveled at how 80 tons of steel could leap into the clouds and take hundreds of people halfway around the planet. Hours later, at midnight California time, and eight a.m. in London, nearly everybody was sleeping in the darkened cabin. A stray mustache hair tickled Stump's nostril. He brushed it aside and made one last attempt to reach Michael, but her phone was dead or, more probably, she flat-out didn't want to talk with him.

Eventually, daylight peeked through windows and people, including Stump, began to stir. Once in a while somebody from first class wandered to the back of the aircraft to use the restrooms and stretch his or her legs. Then at midmorning London time, and with roughly two hours yet to landing, "it" happened on Danville's side of the plane: JP roamed toward the rear restroom.

If it would have been Michael or James over there, Stump wouldn't have worried so much because they'd both been battle-tested in furtive activities. Stump quickly sent his bro a simple "heads up" text, after which he wished he and Danville had discussed this kind of thing more completely.

A bit on edge, but in a good seat, Stump pretended to be messing with his iPhone while JP, sans his cowboy hat, slowly passed row after row until he uneventfully slipped past Danville and into the restroom.

Good. With fingers mentally crossed, Stump hoped JP's return to his seat would be equally benign. A few minutes later, Mr. Tall rejoined the cabin, crept forward past the people in the very back row, and stopped right at Danville's shoulder, where JP pivoted toward Stump's brother and the young women.

If Stump had been chewing gum, he would have swallowed it because Danville and JP had met once before and if JP were to put two and two together, Stump's entire investigation could be at risk. He tried to listen past the constant muffled roar of the jet engines and tune in to a conversation that had already begun on the other side of the jet.

He couldn't make out what they were saying, but almost instantly a female giggle implied that JP had stopped to flirt with the young ladies. Stump mentally urged JP to move on, but it appeared JP's ESP receiver didn't get the message.

Minutes ticked away while JP's arms flailed and the flattered young women giggled in unison at what must have been some well-rehearsed jokes. Then Kyle wandered back and joined the conversation. Thank God.

The mini-gathering drew the attention of a flight attendant who soldiered her way into the mix and pointed back up the aisle, after which both JP and Kyle returned to their seats. Then, as if Danville was reading Stump's mind, he rose and slipped into the restroom. Stump sent the first text.

"how'd it go"

"GR8 katie likes me"

"what about JP"

"he likes me 2"

"but was he suspicious"

"don't think so u want me 2 ask him"

"r u screwing with me"

"yes u worry 2 much"

"somebody has 2"

"i gotta get katie's number"

Just then, the restroom door opened. Danville looked Stump's way and gave him a thumbs-up. No longer suffering from an appendectomy, the guy was cooler than Stump expected.

Stump smiled. Previously, Danville had told Stump that whenever he got a woman's number, he called her right on the spot to find out if she had told him the truth. Katie must have passed the test.

After that, Stump waited until the last hour of the flight to send Danville several text messages regarding tailing JP and Kyle to the baggage claim area.

When the plane finally touched down, they unbuckled their belts a little early and hustled up the aisles as far as they could while the other passengers were still shuffling their gear. From there, they waited for the first-class passengers to deplane, then waited for another two-dozen folks to deplane. When it was finally Stump and Danville's turn in the exit tunnel, they wiggled past another dozen passengers before they broke into the concourse. "I don't see the hat," Danville said. "Do you?"

Stump shook his head. "No, but they have to be going to the baggage pick-up area. We need to get there as fast as we can."

They hugged a wall, raced past slow pokes with carry-on luggage, and reached the men's water closet. Stump pushed mustache hairs away from his nose and pointed. "One of us should see if they're in there."

"I'll go, bro."

"Try not to let them see you."

While Danville ducked into the restroom, Stump tucked behind a couple other men who were waiting for their female partners.

A turnstile full of people spun in and out of the restroom before JP and Kyle finally walked out. Seconds later Danville joined his bro and from 20 meters back they followed a hat to the luggage area. Stump got a picture of his suspects' backs as they passed under a sign that said, "Welcome to Heathrow Airport."

Half-a-forever later, JP and Kyle snagged their luggage, traded some dollars for euros and worked their way out to the curb, where a private vehicle, either an accomplice or an Uber driver, picked them up.

Stump hailed a taxi. For the next fifteen minutes in the back seat of Chester's cab, they followed JP and Kyle, who finally stopped at a government building and piled out.

"Pull over," Stump said to Chester. From 50 meters back, "What is that building?" Stump asked excitedly.

"That's the Settlement Office for LottoLondon, mate. Someday I hope to cash in one of me own tickets there."

65

The '90s brought on new challenges and some almost-fun assignments. After Billy Chase provided the road map to off-loading his stolen vehicles, one of my co-workers made contact with Phil Meeks at Jackie's Grill.

Naturally, Meeks was tight-lipped, but he was already cooked. Once we knew we had the right guy, the department put a tail on him. Two days later he led us right to an inland chop shop, near a large junkyard on Sawtelle Blvd.

Thirty days of surveillance produced enough evidence to bring down one of the bigger car-jacking enterprises in Los Angeles to that point.

By that time, I'd been promoted to Sergeant-II and stepped across the threshold into the world of Vice.

Beck and I discussed the new group of street victims to which I'd be exposed. In some cases, they were every bit as neglected or abused as those I saw in patrol, particularly teenage runaways of both genders that turned to prostitution. They became easy prey for both pimps and johns. A few even got killed.

Another less-obvious "bad guy" of the times brought wrath and pain to the sex-driven people of the streets: the HIV/AIDS virus. By that time the disease had a history of infecting and killing LA citizens, mostly gays, blacks, and bisexual males. Ultimately, it invaded the lives of celebrities and famous athletes such as Magic Johnson, an all-star basketball player. Many doubted he'd live another decade. Meanwhile the U.S. death toll from the disease reached the hundreds of thousands.

So, a journey into Vice wasn't going to be a cupcake party, but Beck and I still thought it was the best place for me at the time, which meant another orientation process and a few more surprises.

When discussing human sexuality, I wasn't completely naive. I'd been in college during the free-love period hippie era, I'd had my share of girlfriends along the way, and had been married twice; but I confess, Vice revealed a human depravity I hadn't completely expected.

As previously mentioned, I knew there were a few high-risk things going on in the streets, but I thought prostitution was mostly about horny guys picking up women who had no other way to make a decent living—you know, the "consenting adults" theory, but there was a lot more to it than that.

For one thing, I'd underestimated the violence certain johns inflicted on their dates. Another set of bad boys preyed on the johns—and neither set of victims was prone to report the matters for fear they too would become entangled in the almighty system.

One of the first practices I learned about was named after Darryl Strawberry, the famous professional baseball player. Around 1990 he was arrested for possession of cocaine and soliciting sex from an undercover policewoman.

It wasn't difficult to figure out that he and other rich guys could get their hands on drugs and trade those drugs for sex. Fair or not, we called the sex-for-drugs trade-off "the Strawberry."

Another bizarre situation involved cross-dressing prostitutes. Before I share their story, let me make something clear: If guys want to dress up as women and get friendly with each other, I don't have a big problem with it. I'll leave the judging up to God.

But when they bring that behavior into public places, they're just like anybody else. Openly lewd behavior makes the public uptight. When that happens, Vice gets the call, and justifiably so.

We called the cross-dressing prostitutes "drag queens." Some of them were downright striking. Their clothes, tasteful make-up, pretty wigs and jewelry, attracted certain johns who preferred that kind of date. But a number of their customers didn't figure out what was going on until the "woman" spoke in a deep voice.

Other, more naïve johns didn't get the message until the genital touching phase began. Once in a while, the sudden "surprise" resulted in an assault. Regardless, that particular group of prostitutes had plenty of dates.

But then there were the more radical queens: the wildly ornate ones. It was common for certain queens, who had the whiskers of a five-day beard and smelled like cigarettes, booze and locker rooms, to wear low-cut dresses that revealed enough chest hair to impress a shag carpet salesman.

Their clients got a thrill out of a lot of makeup, odd wigs, jewelry and mismatched accessories. That was the point: to give the paying customer a completely bizarre experience, visually and otherwise.

These more colorful queens had their favorite sidewalks, frequently along Ventura Boulevard in the San Fernando Valley. They hung out, on display, until a potential customer pulled to the curb and opened his window. Then the street jargon began. "Do you want a date?"

Seconds later, in the front seat, the menu and pricing were discussed, leaving but one unresolved matter: before the two of them drove off to some semi-private spot to carry out their arrangement, the queens said, "Give me a sloppy kiss."

It was actually a very clever ploy to find out if the john was really a Vice officer. A true john was there for the kinky behavior and would indeed trade spit with the hairy-chested, whisker-faced queen; but the officers didn't want to play tongue-tag with people who could be carrying any one of several diseases.

So, when the customer/john turned down the juicy spit-kiss, the queen knew the score, and withdrew the original offer.

It wasn't long before I heard of a legendary occasion before my time, when a young officer went along with the wet kiss proposal in order to get an arrest—big mistake. The ridicule that followed led to his transfer to another state.

Finally, regarding all the street people, I had to regularly remind myself that most of them wouldn't have resorted to such extremes if there weren't a market for it. Some people call that capitalism. Some people called it gross. I thought of it as tragic.

66

The discovery of the lottery office was like the early morning sunrise erasing shadows of doubt.

"Can we wait here for a little while?" Stump asked cabbie Chester.

"Anything you want, if the meter runs, mate."

"Fair enough. Is there a costume shop nearby?"

Chester shrugged. "You'll have to Google it."

"Why do we need that, bro?"

"Simple. JP and Kyle have already seen you with dark sideburns. If they see you again, they might recognize you and we can't afford to arouse suspicion. We gotta get you a new look."

"How 'bout a deerstalker hat, a hound's-tooth coat and a briarwood pipe?"

"Sherlock, huh? I was thinking of making you look like Lady Gaga."

Chester chuckled. "I like American humor."

"This lotto thing could be the key to everything," Stump said.

"Can you buy a London ticket in the U.S., bro?"

"Don't know, but why would you? We have lottos too and you don't have to go around the world to cash them in."

Danville shrugged. "Somebody else could have bought it for them."

"Could be, but when those two were on the boat, they weren't acting like affluent rich people. After all, JP was working nine-to-five. Twenty-four hours later, everything changed. JP suddenly quit his job and they were both bound for London. That's something a rich person might do. I think there's a more likely possibility. Detective Trent said that the Claytons went to London a while back. If that's true, they may have bought a winning ticket. One of them could have easily taken it to the bank for safe keeping, the same bank where JP worked."

"So, you think JP robbed one of the Claytons?"

"Mrs. Clayton in particular, but it wasn't a typical robbery. Have you ever seen a safe deposit box?"

"Yeah. My folks keep passports, car titles and the deed to their home in one."

"That's right. You have to have two keys to get into a box. JP already had access to the bank's key, so somehow, he got hold of Mrs. Clayton's personal key around the same time that Stu Clayton went fishing. Not only that, JP had to murder her after robbing her so she couldn't identify him."

"Another possibility is they got into her home, then killed her and found the key."

"Could be, but either way our suspects definitely could have murdered her and gotten her key. After that, they murdered Stu Clayton too and made it look as if Mrs. Clayton did it."

When the M-word ricocheted off the inside of Chester's cab a few times, he rubbernecked toward his mirror. "You blokes don't have guns with you, do you?"

"Not here, dude, but we have them at home."

After Chester breathed a sigh of relief, Danville glanced in Stump's direction. "You gonna call the detectives back in the states?"

"Not yet. They'll just brush us off again. We gotta get some stronger evidence first."

"There they are, now," Chester said enthusiastically, pointing to the doors on the lottery building.

"Hello, gentlemen," Stump said, snapping several pics of JP and Kyle. "I bet they call for another Uber. We'll follow them and see if we can make sense of this."

A few minutes later, a two-vehicle parade snaked through a half-hour blend of narrow streets and multi-lane roads before ending up at the Holiday Inn Express.

"All right, this must be their home base, at least for one night," Stump said, gathering more pictures. "Now we gotta go back to that lotto settlement office. I have some questions for them."

"I'm enjoying this, chaps," Chester said, "and I hate to be a meanie, but the bill is getting high. I need you to settle up and then we can reset the meter."

"No prob, dude," Stump said, passing a credit card forward and grabbing his cell. "I'm going to get us a room in that Holiday Inn."

When back at the lotto office, Chester happily waited with the meter running while Stump and Danville entered the building, fanned a picture of JP and Kyle, and found the elderly female clerk who had spoken with them an hour earlier.

"Yeah, they had a winning ticket," she said in a delightful accent, "but we don't keep drawers full of money here. We have to do a little homework before we release the funds."

"That's one good thing," Stump said. "How long does it take to complete your investigation?"

"We have to verify the ticket, make sure there are no other winners, and make arrangements with the bank and the tax man. All that can take up to seven days."

"Good to hear that. Can you tell us the amount?"

"Oh yes, that's public information. This one was just over four million pounds."

"That's what I thought. How about when and where the ticket was purchased? Do you have that information?"

"We've got that, too. They bought it at the Square, four months ago."

Stump's eyebrows rose. He glanced at his brother and back again. "Really? Do people usually wait this long to claim their prize?"

"Not ordinarily, unless they see a barrister first."

"I didn't think so. That's very interesting. Thanks a lot."

On the way back to the cab, Danville spoke first, "My mom always scratches her tickets right away."

Stump slapped his brother's arm. "We're in London, dude. You mean, 'me mum' not 'my mom,' and mine, too. She couldn't wait to see if she won. I can't imagine a smart banker like JP taking four months to cash in a ticket. They balance their drawers and check their vaults all the time. When it comes to money, they don't leave loose ends lying around. I'm virtually certain that the winning ticket belonged to the Claytons and they got killed for it." Stump glanced at the time. "It's almost four o'clock here so it's eight a.m. in California. The detectives should be starting their day." He punched at his cell.

"*What's up, Mr. Randolph?*" said Detective Trent. "*I don't have a lot of time.*"

"I know that, sir, but my brother and I followed JP and Kyle Ward to London, and we have a lot more evidence that says they killed the Claytons."

"*Not that again.*"

"Yes, sir. We've been at the settlement office of the London lottery. Our suspects turned in a winning ticket, and I'm pretty sure they got it from the Claytons."

"*We'd need a lot more than your speculation to reopen a closed case.*"

"I think I've got that, but first would you mind if I ask you about their criminal records? You said you'd look them up."

"*I haven't gotten around to it yet. What else you got?*"

"Well, the winning ticket is for four million pounds. The interesting thing is it was purchased four months ago."

"*So?*"

"So, we know when and where the ticket was bought,

and you said the Claytons went to London a while back. It shouldn't be too difficult to find out if any of our characters were here when that ticket was purchased. There might even be video of who bought the ticket. Anyway, if the Claytons bought it, then JP and Kyle should have to explain how they ended up with it and why the Claytons ended up dead."

The detective didn't reply.

"Hello. Detective Trent? Are you there? I may have been disconnected. Hello?"

"*Uh. No. We weren't disconnected, Mr. Randolph. It's just that you're correct. We did know that the Claytons went to London, but we didn't think the dates were relevant. Now I think I'm going to have to call their daughter. If the dates match up—*"

"If you could get JP's credit card information and cell phone records, you might find some other useful evidence."

"*Well, I'd like to say that you don't have to tell me how to do my job, but apparently I underestimated you.*"

"Thank you. You have to hurry. The settlement office is verifying the ticket, so you only have limited time to stop them from making a payout, assuming you have the jurisdiction to do that."

"*That's no problem. We work together in cases like this.*"

"There's one more thing. When I went to JP's bank a few days ago, I learned that they have an accomplice. Kyle's girlfriend. You can get Kyle's address from the sign-up sheets at the fishing dock. That lady might live with him."

"*Okay, I have to admit you've caught my attention. Is there anything else before I make my calls?*"

"Yes, sir, my brother and I have lots of pictures. Would you like me to send them to you?"

67

During one of my earliest stints in Vice our supervisors wanted to arrest some johns. None of the policewomen were required to dress up as street prostitutes but some of them got a kick out of it. For those, short tight skirts, heels, classy wigs, well-placed jewelry, and a little too much make-up were the norm.

Ventura Boulevard had plenty of worthy sidewalks where a wired policewoman could troll for horny dudes while a couple of back-up teams watched and listened from plain vehicles, a half-block back.

The policewoman's job was to let the customer come to her and to get him to make it known that he wanted a service for a fee. Then she'd say a prearranged code phrase and we'd squeeze the guy. On that specific evening I was down the block in the back-up vehicle, with engine running, when Officer Cheryl Buddrow was the bait.

"Black Chevy," she said, letting us know a potential john was pulling to the curb.

"Hi. Would you like a ride?" the potential customer asked.

"Maybe. What do you have in mind?"

"I could use some action. How much?"

"Fifty for a hand job. A hundred for a BJ or front door. Two hundred for back door."

"Good enough. I could use some pussy. Get in."

"You gotta pay me first."

At that point, the guy handed her the money, which triggered the code phrase. "I know a dark place up ahead."

We converged on the john from two directions quicker than we could invade a donut shop. A minute later, the perp was cuffed, read his rights and on his way to jail. En route, like many of the naughty boys he begged us to let him go because his wife wouldn't understand. You can probably guess how much sympathy we gave him.

Meanwhile, as his vehicle was being impounded the next back-up vehicle took our place. By that time, the real prostitutes could read the tealeaves and sought out some other location to peddle their wares for the evening.

In the end, any john that cruised Ventura Boulevard that night got screwed one way or the other. By the time we called it a night, we'd arrested nearly a dozen men.

The process was similar when the department heads wanted to send a message to the streetwalkers. A male officer wearing a mic would slip to the curb and wait for the working prostitute to offer his or her services. After a discussion of the menu, the money slid from one hand to the other and the trigger phrase hailed the processing crew.

Admittedly, the public didn't cry many tears for those engaging in these activities, but the prostitutes, be they men or women, under-aged or not, were frequently robbed—or worse—and couldn't really report the crime because they didn't want to be in a police car for any reason.

With all these interesting characters filling the sidewalks, the day-to-day routine usually flew by, but do not assume that Vice was always easy or safe. Enter Officer Lucille Branson.

One evening, officer Branson, an eight-year veteran, had worked the street 'til around one a.m. Tired, she returned to the station and cleaned up before she piled into her vehicle and drove home. Along the way a car full of four adolescents tailed her from far enough back that she didn't realize they were interested in her.

One of the young men, a 15-year-old, wanted to impress his new 14-year-old girlfriend by showing her how he could hijack a nice car.

Eventually, Officer Branson turned onto her block, hit the garage door opener and parked in her driveway. As was her routine, she pulled her favorite handgun from the door pocket and tucked it under her left armpit before opening the car door.

Her foot barely hit the cement when the 15-year-old sprang from behind her trunk, gun in hand, and demanded that she step aside. Instead, she instinctively dropped to her knee and yelled for him to drop his weapon. Stunned, the young man shot and sent a bullet through her left breast and out near her shoulder blade. Amazingly, as she went down, Officer Branson's aim was literally deadly. One shot through the perp's heart resulted in his instant death. His buddies and girlfriend squealed out of there—all of which awakened the neighbors, who called for help.

With an entry wound to her breast and a one-inch hole in her back the officer nearly bled out by the time the ambulance arrived, but fortunately, she lived to tell her tale. In fact, she became a regular speaker to warn rookie policewomen why they always had to be on high alert, particularly late at night.

Officer Branson wasn't the only person who had a near-death experience while working Vice. I'd been on the squad nearly two years when it was my turn. We'd gotten an anonymous tip that a well-built fellow, wearing tight jean-shorts and a tank top, had been cruising the sidewalk, posing as a male prostitute and they thought he might be dangerous.

Long about 11:00 p.m. I was pretending to be a john. As I always did, I had my snub-nose pistol tucked next to the left side of my seat. We'd already busted several ladies of the evening when I saw a male candidate who fit the description of the man we were looking for.

With two officers in an unmarked car across the street and half a block up, I cruised up to him with my window rolled down. "Are you lost?" I asked.

He looked me over. "Not really. You up for a little fun?"

I nodded, "How much?"

"Same as most. Fifty for hand. A hundred for mouth. Two hundred for butt."

"I can swing a hundred," I said.

"Let me see the money."

I slipped what looked like a dozen bills from my wallet and flashed him a hundo.

He let himself in and looked over his shoulder. Then, "Turn around."

Uh oh. This guy was astute. My back-up guys were just up the block. If I turned around, they would have to do the same thing and if my rider were to see that, it would blow the whole sting. Fortunately, I was wired and could tip off my team.

"You looked over your shoulder. Are you a cop or something?" I asked.

"No. I'm just being cautious. Go up here two blocks and turn left."

From there we made several impromptu turns. Each time he looked back and I checked my mirrors. Nobody was following us. We ended up slowly cruising a dark residential street with a large bushy hedgerow.

Suddenly, he pivoted my way and swung his right hand, complete with a five-inch Bowie knife to within two feet of my face. One thrust and I could have become lunchmeat. I slammed on the brake causing a complete and abrupt stop.

While he regained his balance, I shot my right hand to his wrist and temporarily stalled him. "Need back-up, need back-up," I yelled out. The perp was strong and determined. He pulled back and almost broke loose.

Fortunately, for me, I had always been a weight- lifter. With one foot on the brake and my right hand wrestling with his knife hand, I reached my left hand to the side of the seat for my gun, only it had slipped forward when I hit the brakes. I dragged my knuckles across the carpet at the side of the seat and tried to scoot forward toward my weapon, but he tugged hard to break my grip on his wrist. If he were to get his knife hand free, I might not see the next day.

We wrestled for a minute or so before flashing reds washed the bushes and caught my attacker off-guard. In that spit-second my left hand joined my right and I broke his wrist. A simultaneous loud screech and a dropped knife indicated the struggle was over. A few seconds later my partners shone flashlights and guns in his face.

Predictably, I had more paperwork than usual that night.

68

A quick call to the Claytons' daughter verified that Joann and Stu Clayton had indeed been in London at the time the London lotto ticket was purchased. While this didn't prove a crime, it definitely justified more investigating.

Detective Trent called the tackle store at Fisherman's Landing, which produced Kyle Ward's address. A check of the county records indicated that somebody else owned the property in which Kyle lived. A call to the owner dug up the names of two tenants: Kyle Ward and Cassandra Sevvy.

After that, Detective Trent ordered criminal records for Julius Crain, Kyle Ward and Cassandra Sevvy. Next, Trent made arrangements to meet the president of the Del Mar branch of CalWest banks.

The next morning, at the bank, he was invited into the office of Mr. Joe Lakley, a balding, white-shirted man in his early 60s. "Yes, sir," Lakley said to Trent. "I've been told it's okay to speak with you."

"Thanks. We're investigating a murder and I'd like to ask you a few questions, in confidence of course."

"Of course."

"To begin with, I'd like to know if Julius Crain took any extended time off between March 15 and April 1."

"Julius, huh? I'm not surprised."

"Oh? Why do you say that?"

"A few days ago he wanted a couple weeks off but we're in audits now. I couldn't spare him. He got angry and quit — after five years of good service. I hated to see him go."

"I see. What about that time period I mentioned? Did he take any time off?"

"I don't think he did, but I can double check that. What else?"

"I'd also like to know if Crain was at work the afternoon of June 12, at about four o'clock."

"I can have my assistant look that up, too. Anything else?"

"Yes. Can we see video of the people who've been inside your vault with the safe deposit boxes over the last two weeks?"

"I'm sorry, Detective. We have surveillance cameras in the lobby and parking lots, but none in the vault for insurance purposes."

"Well, people sign in, don't they? Can we see that list for March 15 to June 13?"

"Sure. That's easy enough. We keep the records right near the vault."

"Okay, then. While we have a look at those records, would you have someone check on those other questions?"

A few minutes later, an assistant produced a list of answers. "As you can see," she said, "JP worked all of March and April."

"Are you sure?"

"Yes, sir. Checked it myself."

"What about the afternoon of June 12? Was he here in the bank all day?"

"He worked in the morning, but not the afternoon. He didn't come back until after a fishing trip, when he quit for good."

"Okay, then, that's all I need for now."

Having confirmed all the suspicions and evidence that young Mr. Randolph had given him, Detective Trent had no choice: It was time to share the new information and the photos with his superiors.

* * *

"Yes?" a pretty woman asked, eyeing two strangers on her porch.

"Good morning ma'am. I'm Detective Linda Jenkins. This is Detective Tanner Trent. Are you Cassandra Sevvy?"

"Yes. What is this about?"

"We have some questions. May we come in?"

"Is this about my kids? Are they okay?"

"It's not about that, ma'am. We just have a few questions for you."

"Can't it wait?"

"Afraid not, ma'am."

The woman sighed and stepped aside. "What's so important?"

"Have a seat, ma'am," Jenkins said.

Tanner lifted an attention-getting finger. "Do you mind if I look around, ma'am?"

"For what? What do you guys want?"

"Detective Jenkins will get to that while I look around—- that is, unless you have something to hide."

She waved a flippant hand in the air. "Go ahead, and don't get aroused by the underwear on the floor."

"No ma'am, this isn't about underwear."

She shook her head and looked at Jenkins. "Well?"

Jenkins pulled up a picture on her iPhone and showed it to Cassandra. "Do you recognize this gentleman?"

Cassandra froze.

"We've spoken with your landlord, Ms. Sevvy. Both your name and Mr. Ward's name are on the lease."

"Alright. Alright. He's my boyfriend. Is he okay?"

"As far as we know." Jenkins swiped her phone screen a few times. Then, "What about this tall man with the cowboy hat?"

"That's JP. He's a friend. So what?"

"Can I assume that you know where these two gentlemen are right now?"

"Not really."

"I see," Jenkins swiped her screen a few more times before revealing another picture. "This is them walking under a sign in a London airport. Does this refresh your memory?"

Cassandra didn't answer.

"Well, it doesn't really matter. We checked the criminal records of all three of you. Turns out, your boyfriend has spent two years in prison for assaulting another woman. Did you know that?"

"It wasn't his fault," Cassandra said with a less cocky voice.

"Is that what he told you? I'm under the impression that he was charged with attempted murder and took a plea deal. Why would I think that?"

"I dunno," Cassandra said, looking distraught. "I wouldn't know anything about you people."

Just then Detective Trent returned, pulled Jenkins aside and traded whispers. Jenkins nodded and resumed her conversation with Cassandra. "We'd like you to come to the station with us, ma'am, to answer a few more questions. Would that be okay?"

"I'd rather not."

"I understand that, but it's either that or we'll get a warrant. Then officers will bang on your doors and make a big scene. It would be in your interest to keep this easy on all of us."

She shook her head. "But I have two kids. They're playing at the neighbor's house."

"Do you think your neighbor would watch them for a while longer? If not, we can get a social worker."

Cassandra released a breath of frustration. "She might help me. What is all this about?"

"Alright, then. I'll go with you when you ask her."

69

There's no telling how many people engage in depravity in their private lives but some of LA's citizens derived special satisfaction by carrying out their fantasies in public places.

Such was the case in North Hollywood Park, in 1994, when everyday citizens wandered into the public restroom and found themselves in the nightly gathering spot of odd impromptu man-on-man hook-ups. Many of the condom-less participants held a don't-give-a-damn attitude about dangerous diseases.

Regardless of the risks, the activities probably wouldn't have drawn the attention of the police if they'd taken place in the back rooms of any one of several "friendly" bars in the area, but that wasn't the case and we got a call to end it.

A typical daytime examination of the restrooms in question revealed that all the light bulbs were missing. After our eyes adjusted, we observed a long urinal and several stalls with doors removed.

The nest of human cockroaches that got their kicks from this kind of place developed a code of conduct that governed their behavior, usually at night.

For instance, fellows who wanted a "date" with a random like-minded stranger stood at the urinal, in the dark, penis in hand.

Eventually, another guy wandered in, eyed the first man, and listened for the flow of liquids, which indicated whether the first man was simply there to take a wiz. But, if there were no flowing tinkles, and the new guy wanted to get frisky, he too stood at the urinal and tapped the original guy's thigh; and the date was underway. From there, they hustled to a car in the parking lot where they were free to get familiar with each other.

Before long somebody else would wander in, and the pattern would repeat. Some fellows went back several times per night.

On one of my first shifts I wore a tight T-shirt, shorts and tennis shoes. I was a few years shy of 50 at the time.

I pulled into the lot just past sundown. Two other officers, working as back-up, had already parked an unmarked car in which they sat close together, lending the impression they were engaged in some of the typical activity one might expect. Wearing a wire, I walked nervously toward the restroom.

As the only one in the darkened room, I stood near the urinal, my hands at my zipper as if I were dangling my privates and ready for some action. It didn't take long for my first perp to show up, but I got a hell of a lot more drama out of the moment than I expected.

A clickity-click, clickity-click, clickity-click escorted him to the doorway. Not knowing what to think, I stayed in character, stood at attention facing the wall, my hands in place.

The new guy, a bit shorter than average, slowly eased next to me. I reminded myself not to move, so there was no doubt who made the first contact.

Seconds later, he tapped my thigh. I didn't pull away or encourage him. Then, he did it again. Getting no resistance from me, he reached for my manhood. I remembered the "clickity-click" and thought he might have something extra kinky or even dangerous in mind.

Not wanting to take a chance, I turned, leapt on him and overpowered him so he couldn't get away. More clickity-click indicated that he still had his weapon or toy or whatever it was. He squirmed and screamed for help, which my partners picked up over the wire. I squeezed the bad boy into submission and held him immobile as he writhed and pleaded for sympathy.

Just then, my partners came to my rescue. Holding flashlights and drawn guns, they lifted the perp to his feet. That was when I first saw his arm braces. The poor man could barely walk and wore aluminum braces. I'd essentially knocked a disabled guy into the next week.

For the time being, my partners held their tongues and processed the man just like they would have processed anybody else, but later in the shift, I understood more completely the comedy and tragedy masks of ancient Greek theater. While my partners laughed repeatedly about my wildly exuberant takedown of an obviously frail foe, I felt like crap for having been so rough with the man.

Ultimately, the clickity-click man proved to be a Catholic schoolteacher. He was convicted in court of lewd behavior and spent six months in the county jail and lost his job. After that his wife dumped him.

In the end and generally speaking, I never could figure out why men would do things like that, especially considering the health risk, but we made enough arrests that the word got out and the participants took their activities elsewhere, at least for a while.

* * *

Over time, I came to like the Vice gigs, in part because the busts were instantaneous, and there weren't many children in the mix.

Most of the perps were fairly harmless, but we always had to be on alert just in case something unusual went down. Such was the case in 1996.

Once again, the action was at North Hollywood Park.

As before, a daytime inspection revealed a urinal plus two doorless stalls and no light bulbs. This time, we eased into the parking lot around 10 p.m.

I checked my wire and lumbered to the entrance of the men's room. At that time of night, the place was as dark as an underwater cave, but I could hear heavy breathing and shuffling near the stalls. I stood near the sinks to give my eyes a chance to adjust. If there were illegal activities already playing out, I wouldn't need to step up to the urinal. A half-minute later I detected someone standing in the far stall; then I saw another guy, then another.

Two of them had dropped their pants to their knees and stood tightly, front to back, if you get my drift. The fellow in front faced somebody else who had taken a seat on the stool, presumably to perform oral sex on the front man. "You want to get in line?" one of the guys asked me.

Yeah, right. I didn't know if I should laugh or throw up. "Just a minute," I said, as if I was all for joining their little orgy. "I've got a friend outside. He'll want to participate too."

"The more, the better."

Outside I hustled up the sidewalk so the pants-at-the-knees gentlemen couldn't hear me urge my partners to immediately bring flashlights and cuffs.

An hour later all three participants had been booked and a trio of seasoned officers had another tale to remember.

After that and as the years unraveled, there were always opportunities for me to infiltrate various groups such as motorcycle gangs and radical environmentalists who liked to burn down new housing developments while they were under construction. But I was getting older and didn't fit the desired profiles very well so none of them appealed to me.

I also had chances to go into Juvenile Crimes and Narcotics, but I still didn't want to be around young victims, so I passed on those, too. Then an unexpected breeze of fate blew a new situation my way.

70

A short time later Detective Jenkins led Cassandra Sevvy into a conference room and began to drill down. "Before we begin, I'd like to read you your rights."

"My rights? Why? I haven't done anything."

"That's what we want to talk about, ma'am. We just want to be sure you know your rights."

Cassandra crossed her arms. "Hurry up. I have to get back to my kids."

After the usual spiel, Jenkins asked the same questions as before, partly to see if Ms. Sevvy's story would change and partly to earn a few "good-cop" chips.

Over the course of the interrogation, whenever Cassandra gave evasive or inaccurate answers to the questions, Jenkins showed the woman another picture or revealed something else that the police already knew, all of which was designed to make her think they essentially already knew *the truth, the whole truth and nothing but the truth* so that she couldn't get away with lying about the few minor details that had not yet been discussed.

Then "bad-cop" Trent replaced Jenkins for the squeeze. Having observed Cassandra's fidgety fingers, he thumb-pointed over his shoulder. "See that mirror behind me? We've been watching you from the other side."

Cassandra shook her head. "I don't know about that."

Trent leaned forward. "I'm an expert at body language, ma'am, and I gotta tell ya, your jury will love to hear what I learned while watching you."

Cassandra's eyes widened and her jaw visibly tightened.

"No comment? Okay, let's go over a few things again. You've identified two men: Kyle Ward, your ex-con boyfriend, and Julius Patrick Crain. Is that right?"

"How many times do I have to answer the same questions?"

"Just until we get all the answers. Let me show you a couple more pictures to refresh your memory of what we already know. Here's one of your teammates in front of the settlement office of the London lottery. Any idea why they'd go there?"

"No, not really."

"I gotta couple pictures of them on the plane if you want to see them. They flew first class. Isn't it nice to have all these pics? It takes all the guesswork out. Let me show you something else," he said, opening an iPad and starting a video. "This is a surveillance video at CalWest Bank in Del Mar. See this woman walking across the floor with your friend JP? Her name is Mrs. Clayton."

Cassandra sat still, said nothing.

"Now look at this next video," Trent said. "It's from the next day. Here's another woman who also paired up with Julius Crain. This woman is taller. About your height, I'd say. But she never signed in. Any idea why a person would go to a bank vault and avoid the sign-in process?"

"No. I don't know much about banks."

"Well, here's the interesting part. I saw a wig in your bedroom closet that looked exactly like that woman's hair in the video. You know what else was in your closet? Some clothes that just happen to match those in the video. Our forensic team will be bagging it up as evidence before long. We both know when they confirm our suspicions that you're screwed, don't we?"

A shroud of silence encased Cassandra.

"Not only that, but we've got video of you walking to and from the vault. Do I have to tell you about opening the box and the paper you guys planted inside it?"

Cassandra's brows furrowed and her head dropped, telling Trent he could tighten the noose.

"We've got a lot more, ma'am. Like video of Mrs. Clayton buying a lottery ticket in London. And your friends trying to cash in that exact same ticket. Do you see what's happening here, Ms. Sevvy? Those two gentlemen seemed to have drawn you into some bad behavior of your own. Let me show you what they did." He slid her a picture of Mrs. Clayton's smashed-in head on the kitchen floor.

Her hand shot to her mouth.

"Did you know they were going to do that? Stu Clayton suffered a gruesome death, too, Ms. Sevvy. I can show you a picture of the crusty foam in his mouth when he died if you'd like to take a look at it."

She shook her head wildly. "No. No. No. I don't want to see it."

Trent paused. Then, "From here on out, Ms. Sevvy, things will go a lot easier on you if you stop covering for those eight-balls."

After a few silent seconds she lifted her head. "I thought they were just going to steal the ticket. I didn't know anything about a murder."

"Even if I believed that, it doesn't really matter. In the eyes of the law, Ms. Sevvy, you're just as guilty as they are."

Her stunned eyes grew larger.

"It's like this, ma'am. Right now, the guys are out of the country having a good time. If they don't come back to face the judge, that leaves you to take the entire rap. Your jury will hate you, find you guilty of premeditated murder. A life sentence is in your future. The DA will see to it that you're locked up in a prison so far away from here that it will be too inconvenient for your family to come visit you. It's like being on an island surrounded by bad girls who will use you as a play toy. Have you ever been blackmailed by a heartless nasty person, Ms. Sevvy?"

"No," she said, shaking her head slowly.

"It goes on all the time in those places. Strong, drug-crazed women will demand that your mother sneak in some cocaine or cash or a weapon. If you don't pull it off...well, let's just say you'll be so scared that you'll beg your mother to pack her private areas with whatever it is the bad girls want and sneak it in.

"If you and mama get busted, mama will go to prison too; the warden will award you with a couple months of solitary confinement. You'll sleep directly on a cold cement floor—no pillow, no blankets. The next morning you'll pee in a drain in the center of your cell. When you finally get out, you'll go back to your cage where you'll stay for the rest of your miserable life. You wouldn't want any of that, would you?"

Cassandra shook her head.

"I'm going to level with you, ma'am. "Right now, we're trying to decide if we should charge all three of you with conspiracy, bank robbery and two counts of first-degree murder, which would easily mean life in prison with no possibility of parole—"

"I swear, I didn't know anything about that poor woman until they'd already killed her."

"That's kinda what we thought. It's like this: we've already got a very strong case, but we'd like to have a confession. If you'll level with us, totally and completely, we can talk to the DA about putting you in a better facility and giving you a decent chance to get out in 20 years or so. With good behavior, you might even cut that in half. If you help us fill in all the blanks and provide the details regarding each person's role in all this, you just might have a chance to get out of jail before your youngest kid graduates from high school. You'd like that, wouldn't you?"

"But I don't want to go to jail at all."

"Then you'd have to take your chances in court and hope that neither of your boyfriends puts the blame on you. And with all this video of you in the vault...well, let me put it this way. When that jury sees what your friends did to Mrs. Clayton's skull, I doubt there will be any mercy for any of you. Face it, you helped plan it all, you were a primary character in a bank robbery, and you are just as culpable for two murders as your friends are."

Cassandra buried her head in her hands and wept.

Trent paused for a moment to allow her to come to grips with her vulnerability before lowering his voice. "This is the only deal we're going to offer you, Ms. Sevvy. It's your choice. Do you want to see your kids again? Take it or leave it."

Cassandra bowed her head and continued to cry. "What do you want to know?"

"Alright then," he said, messing around with his iPhone and setting it in front of her. "This is a recorder. Why don't you start at the beginning? Tell us how all this started and don't leave anything out or we'll withdraw the deal."

After endless sobbing and Cassandra's half-hour story, Detective Trent turned off the recording and Detective Jenkins helped Cassandra write it all down.

Meanwhile, Detective Trent placed a call to an Inquiry Agent in London to enlist their help. He gave them Neal Randolph's number to help them locate Julius Patrick Crain and Kyle Ward.

71

With a couple hours of daylight left and waiting to hear back from Detective Trent, Stump and Danville, who was sporting a new hoodie, wandered to a pub across the street from their hotel and took a table near a large window where they could also watch for JP and Kyle.

"If I were home now," Stump said, after ordering a beer and some chips, "I'd be cramming for my last two finals."

"I'd be right with you, bro, but now I understand why you've had issues with the classroom. This shit we're doing is a hell of a lot more exciting than reading textbooks."

"Well, don't tell that to our father. He and your *mum* will think I'm a bad influence on you."

"LOL, bro. *Me mum* already floated that idea."

From off to the side, their waiter slipped a couple beers on the table. "That'll be six pounds, mates."

Stump nodded, flipped the man his credit card.

Danville reached for his mug. "I'm glad I only have to be 18 to drink beer here," he said before taking a glug. "Hey wait a minute. This beer is warm."

"Americans, eh? You want a couple ice cubes?"

Stump grinned and reprimanded his naïve brother. "That's how they do it here, dude. Get into it."

Danville took another sip and scrunched up his face. "It's like drinking warm piss."

"I wouldn't know," Stump said before making yet another futile attempt to reach Michael. He hung up and glanced out the window where a little car waited to turn into the hotel's lot.

"That's JP and Kyle, dude. We gotta get over there."

Outside, the car made it into the lot and up to the entrance. Stump and Danville hid behind a small van while JP and Kyle soon wandered through the entrance doors.

Running yet again, Stump followed his suspects into the hotel and watched them get on an elevator. He hurried into the elevator lobby and watched the floor-indicator, which ultimately paused at the sixth floor. His next move was to the registration desk.

"Hello. My name is Kyle Ward," he lied to the young counter clerk. "I'm embarrassed to admit this, but when my friend and I checked in, we both got access keys, but I didn't pay attention to the exact room number. It's on the sixth floor. Could you please look that up for me? Like I said, my name is Kyle Ward."

"Yes sir. That happens quite a bit," she said, tapping away at her computer's keys. "It's 620, sir. Your room is 620."

"Thanks. Can I ask you something else? I'm wondering if my partner paid for a second day like he and I agreed. If not, I'll pay for it myself, right now."

Once again, the young clerk tapped at her keyboard and glanced at her screen. "Yes, it says here he paid for four days."

"Okay, that was nice of him. Thank you."

That last revelation, coupled with the fact that the lotto agency wasn't going to make any immediate payouts, meant Stump and Danville wouldn't have to cling so closely to JP and Kyle. Nonetheless, Stump wanted to keep track of the suspects until the authorities could take over. He pointed across the street. "Let's go back to the pub."

There, he had another chance to call Michael, but got the same result. "I must have really pissed her off for leaving her behind. It's either that or the other thing."

"What other thing, bro?"

Stump hesitated a minute while he contemplated whether he should tell his brother about Michael's history with pain meds and that the marriage was no longer a sure thing. Then his cell buzzed. "It's the London police," he said, glancing at the screen and lifting the phone to his ear. "This is Stump."

"*Hello, is this Mr. Neal Randolph?*" a British voice asked.

"Yes, but I go by Stump."

"*I'm Sergeant Bernard O'Brian of the Metropolitan Police Service. I was told you might know where I can find Julius Crain and Kyle Ward, of the states. Is that true?*"

"Got it handled, sir. They're staying at the Holiday Inn Express for at least a couple more days."

"*Do you know if they're in that hotel right now?*"

"I can guarantee it. We know they travel via Uber so they use the front entrance to come and go. We've had it staked out all morning."

"*Very good. We'd like to talk with you to find out what else you know about them.*"

"Fine with us; we're in a pub across the street from the hotel. I'm wearing a goatee. My brother has a hoodie."

"*We'll be right there. If Crain and Ward come by, stay out of their way so you don't get hurt.*"

"No prob, sir," he said before ending the call and turning to Danville. "Looks like we got 'em, bro. High five."

Less than ten minutes later a shirt-and-tie walked in, waved off the bartender and immediately moved toward Stump and Danville.

"Detective Trent must have called you," Stump said, as the man sat down across from them.

His head bobbed. "That he did. For now, I don't have a lot of time. Tell me the gist of the matter as you perceive it."

Stump took a deep breath. It was always gratifying to be taken seriously. "Sure thing," he said, grabbing his room-temperature beer.

He began his story by explaining El Nino and wrapped

up by saying, "I just didn't believe that double-knock out theory."

O'Brian nodded. "And the other victim was the dead man's wife. Is that right?"

"Yeah," Stump said while two cars, each with official-looking types inside, pulled into the hotel parking lot. One car went around back; the other parked in front, where two dissimilar men piled out. One wore a tie, the other sported jeans and a colorful button-down shirt. They split up, positioning themselves on either side of the front door, obviously pretending they weren't together.

"It looks like the rest of your team has arrived," Stump said.

Sergeant O'Brian rose, excused himself and quickly turned for the door.

"Hey, wait a minute, sir," Stump said to the officer's back. "Don't you want to know what room they're staying in? It's 620."

The man spun a 360, nodded at Stump in mid-spin and hustled out the door.

72

If I had to assess my early days in law enforcement, I would say they were a lot like embarking on a long journey. I never knew when there would be an unexpected surprise or detour. That was part of the challenge, to discover what was around the next curve and deal with it.

When I arrived at the Academy for my initial training, I expected to spend the bulk of my working days wearing blue shirts, cruising around in squad cars and locking up bad guys. But then Dorene and Junior got killed.

On that day, my original pathway collapsed and I was forced to take one of life's unexpected detours. I drifted from being a stoic person who glided through the motions and made sound decisions to somebody overwhelmed by empathy for all victims, especially when families were busted up. Platitudes such as "life is short" became more than mere words to me.

Ultimately, familiar experiences affected me differently than they previously had. In one case, I was called in on a child abuse matter. I'd been to that address before and knew what to expect. Prior to the curve in the road my first instinct would have been to protect the beaten kid by arresting his drunken father in hopes that a a year behind bars would teach bad-daddy a lesson. But after the curve I wondered if a year of family counseling would serve them and society better.

Many of my assessments went that way. Formerly black and white decisions became gray. When an officer's objectivity is clouded like that, it's time to take a side route. But which one?

Fortunately, there were lots of different roads running through a huge organization such as the LAPD. It was on one of those side roads that I discovered I had a gift for undercover work.

Unlike most of the UC officers, who lasted but a few years, I was among the ones who got used to it. Months became years; and those years stretched into a pair of decades. By that time, my son had reached middle school and our daughter, little Brandy, was already in fourth grade.

I still liked working in the UC world. I knew the ropes and could have coasted for another 15 years to retirement, but then another one of those fate-altering curves in the road presented itself. It began in Jack Aladar's office.

I still remember our conversation. It was a week after my former partner, Larry, chased down a car with stolen plates and caught a bullet in the hip for his troubles. He was expected to be back on the job in four months, but that kind of thing gives all officers cause for pause.

When I arrived for my appointment, I traded niceties with Cynthia Koyle's replacement, Jamie Albright, before she announced my arrival.

"Hi, Allen," Jack said cheerfully a moment later. "Take a seat."

I nodded and noticed the room had a lot less clutter than usual. "Are you going to have this place painted?" I wondered out loud.

"Hardly. How's Beck and the kids?"

"They make a formidable team. Whenever there's a family battle over which movie to watch or where to go for dinner, they always gang up on me."

Jack chuckled. "It's good to know that young people still stick up for their moms."

"And vice versa."

"Did Jamie tell you what I wanted to talk about?"

"No. I assumed you had one of those one-of-a-kind assignments for me."

"Well, it's not an assignment this time, but it might be a one-of-a-kind opportunity. I've informed my superiors that I plan to give two weeks' notice in a month or so. I'm retiring."

"Oh, really? I should have guessed this would come up sooner or later, but I've kinda thought of you as one of the fixtures around here."

"It's a little nerve-wracking. We might move to the Midwest, where housing is affordable and the roads aren't packed."

"Don't you have kids and grandkids in LA?"

"They live in Glendale. We want to see them grow up, so we still don't know what we'll do. Anyway, the reason I invited you in here is to encourage you to put in for my job."

And there it was: the proverbial twist in the road. In the old days I would have rejected the idea of working in an office, but my 50th birthday was less than a year off. Gray hair had migrated from my temples upward, and a couple of puffy bags had taken up residence beneath my eyes. A desk job would be safer and a new challenge. "Can I assume there's a promotion and a pay increase?"

"I would think so, but first we have to post the job so others can apply for it, too. You'd have to undergo the same scrutiny as anybody else, but you have a lot of valuable experience, and you could hold down the position for another 10 to 20 years if you want to."

That evening, Beck and I waited until the kids were down for the night before we kicked the idea around. I expressed doubt about whether I'd make a good supervisor. She scoffed and reminded me that I'd slowed down and that there were some extraordinary young men and women in the department who could benefit from my experience.

After that, we just brainstormed it. For every reason we had to turn down the idea, there were two reasons to apply for the position. Finally, we agreed that everybody around there knew me so well that I had as good a chance as anybody. I applied, passed the test and sat through a few interviews.

Two months later, I landed the job and became the next handler.

73

S tump waited for the British sergeant to cross the street, then said, "C'mon, Danville. They're making the bust now."

Since JP and Kyle's room was too far above the ground for them to jump, there were only two ways out: the fire stairs and the front entrance. But if the agents caught JP and Kyle in their room, they would all come out the front way. "This shouldn't take long," Stump said to his half-brother. "Let's hang out by that big tree, near the entrance."

It only took ten minutes. As Stump expected, the officers brought out JP and Kyle in handcuffs.

"We didn't do anything," JP said excitedly to one of the constables.

"Then you don't have anything to worry about."

Then it was Kyle's turn to lie. "You've got the wrong guys."

"Yes, sir. We always hear that."

Seeing an opportunity, Stump tugged on Danville's arm and scooted to a few feet from JP. "Hi, dude, remember me?" Stump asked as he peeled off his 'stache and goatee before pretending to hold a fishing pole. "Hook-up!" he bellowed.

JP scowled as he tried to make sense out of what was happening.

"It looks like my girlfriend should have thrown you two overboard with that other idiot—and left you there."

Danville flipped his hoodie back, removed his sideburns, and took his turn at JP. "Yeah, and thanks for telling me you picked Virgin Airlines. That made it a lot easier for us to follow you guys."

"Okay, gentlemen, that's enough," Sergeant O'Brian said. "I think they get your point."

Stump nodded before getting in one last barb. "For a smart man, you sure have a dumb look on your face."

While several officers escorted JP and Kyle toward the police cars, Stump approached Sergeant O'Brian. "Did you have to read them Miranda rights?"

"We use something similar called the Caution. We told them upstairs."

"Cool. When you interrogate them, you should talk with Kyle first and let us watch the interrogations. We could be real helpful."

"How so?"

"We can instantly refute any lies that they tell, and we can feed you guys some good questions that you wouldn't know to ask."

"Like what?"

"You could ask them where they got the poison that they used to kill Mr. Clayton. If they answer that question, that's as good as a confession."

"What else?"

"I know that Kyle and his girlfriend were at the bank when JP quit his job. You could use that to get Kyle to talk. He may want to protect her. Ask him if he thinks it's fair for her to go to prison when he and JP were the bad guys. He might crack, but JP is too cocky to roll over."

O'Brian paused and rubbed his neck. "I'll tell you what. You can come with us, but if you get in the way just one time, it's all over. Got it?"

"Yes, sir. That's fair. I've done something like this before."

A brief drive later and inside the Metropolitan Police Service Building, Stump and Danville were brought into a small room with a two-way mirror, where they were allowed to observe the interrogation.

Utilizing Stump's tip about Kyle being weaker than JP, the officers brought Kyle in first and placed him in a folding chair, facing the glass.

"What the hell is going on?" Kyle said as two officers seated themselves right in front of him.

"As we said when we detained you, a U.S. judge has issued an arrest warrant regarding two murders."

"We never did anything like that."

"We're told that you allegedly killed a woman who banked where your partner worked and then you both killed her husband on a boat."

"I don't know anything about that."

"Really? As you know, we've been in touch with one of the other people on that same boat. He tells us that you and Mr. Crain were the last ones to see Mr. Clayton alive. Is that true?"

"It's his word against ours."

Stump leaned toward the sergeant and whispered, "The Claytons bought their lottery ticket at the Square in early April. If you ask him if he knows when and where it was purchased, he'll know you're on to him."

Sergeant O'Brian nodded, left the room and spoke with the interrogator for several minutes.

"That's not all you guys have done," the interrogator said after returning to the room. "Locally, you tried to defraud our lottery commission."

"Oh, bullshit. Where are you guys getting your information? From a couple college kids? You can't trust them."

"We know you tried to cash in the winning ticket. You must remember where you bought it. Can you tell me exactly where that ticket was purchased and when?"

"Huh? No. My girlfriend bought it. Get me a phone and I'll have her talk with you."

"Can't do that. Detectives in the States tell us her phone

has been confiscated. Computer, too. People are probably looking through them right now."

"No way. You guys are bluffing just to get me to talk, but we never did anything wrong. There's nothing to say."

At that moment O'Brian's cell rang. He listened closely and waited a couple minutes before returning to the interrogation room. With his cell in hand he spoke for himself. "I'm afraid we've got more bad news for you, Mr. Ward. I've received this picture of your girlfriend making a full statement and signing a confession. Her testimony makes the American case a slam dunk, as you chaps call it."

Finally, like a person who was about to lose a chess game, Kyle was out of moves. He lifted his head and screamed, "Fuck you, Julius Crain!"

On the other side of the mirror, Stump rose and lifted his hand. "High five," he said to Danville. "We did it, bro."

A wide grin stretched across Danville's face. "You're amazing, brother. You know that?"

Back in the interrogation room, the sergeant had one more thing to say to Kyle. "Your Justice Department is making extradition arrangements as we speak. After that, the U.S. Marshalls will be here to take you back to the states. You're going to our cells until then."

74

Sixteen years following my promotion, I woke up one day, saw a greying man in my mirror and realized that I'd gone through more yesterdays than there are pages in a shelf full of novels.

Along the way, Beck aged much slower than I. She could still pass for 45, but we were both seasoned grandparents. Son John and his wife blessed us with two grandkids, a boy and a girl.

"Little" Brandy and her husband topped him. At 27, she had a third child in the oven. Alana would be their first daughter.

With all of those miracles at hand, and my relatively good health, it was my turn to flirt with retirement.

Looking back on all those years, I only had a few regrets. Foremost, I regretted killing a man thirty-five years before. I don't regret my decision to protect the others, but I do regret my making fatherless victims out of his kids. Their kids would have children now. Two generations had never known any of the good qualities that man may have had.

I also permanently crippled a KKK member who attacked a fellow officer at a retreat. Quite honestly, ole Royce is lucky I didn't kill him, but I instantly ended the threat, and that was what I was supposed to do. He'd had to walk with a limp all the rest of his life. Perhaps it served him right, but it didn't make me feel good.

Same goes for the clickity-click man in the public restroom of Hollywood Park. At the time, my back was turned and I didn't know how vulnerable he was. Given the circumstances, my best defense was a quick offense, but the poor man was no match for a determined officer who regularly lifted weights.

I also helped to put some men and women behind bars, a few of them for life. When I first went into police work, that was precisely what I wanted to do, but that was before I really knew that there was no pleasure in breaking up families, even when it had to be done.

In spite of all my failings, I still missed the streets, but it's those same "been there, done that" experiences that gave me the wisdom to be a better supervisor and to know when I had reached the end.

Then I got one of those last-minute calls of desperation from my supervisor. He had one last problem for me to resolve.

In recent years the police, in general, had become the target of some unfair publicity. Some of the officers were accused of profiling, which was basically true, but understandable in a way. Certain communities were known for certain crimes and the perps were usually from those neighborhoods. It only made sense to patrol those areas with an eye out for suspicious behavior. It was good police work when it brought down a bad guy, but it was also unfair to people who got detained for no reason other than that they fit a profile.

The political correctness got to the point that whenever an officer detained somebody it was all going to be on video and if there was any rough talk or arrests, the media would view that video through a ratings' prism and employ words such as police brutality or racism whenever they could.

In nearly every case, juries comprised of citizens of all races and all walks of life vindicated the officers, but the media rarely gave the exoneration part of the story much attention because conflicts always attracted more eyeballs than happy endings.

Regardless, that environment made it more difficult for us to attract enough new recruits. Meanwhile, attrition rates ticked forever onward.

When there weren't enough young folks to replace the departing people, the department grew thin. In short, we had a shortage of officers in patrol and in the undercover groups. Compounding the problem, new troublemakers such as Antifa threatened other citizens and destroyed both private and public property, especially in and around college campuses.

To solve the problem of dwindling personnel, the commander asked me to delay my retirement and establish a small recruitment team, whose job it would be to explore and implement ways we could grow the number of young recruits. By getting more new officers, we could also free up existing officers to move up the ladder. I accepted the assignment.

We developed an email campaign in which we reminded current officers that there were openings in the less traditional departments such as Narcotics, SWAT, Vice and undercover.

In addition, Jamie placed some recruitment ads in national industry magazines and on online websites that might attract some new blood. We also sent officers to any nearby schools that offered criminology courses to announce our job openings.

Finally, we sent out internal emails in which we encouraged our people to inform us of any potential recruits who might appreciate a personal contact about our job opportunities.

In that exercise, I recalled an old friend, who had retired from the department. Sergeant Myles Copper had a son who had solved a handful of crimes beginning when he was in middle school. A sharp young person like that was just who we were looking for.

Naturally, Jamie had Cooper's number.

75

After Kyle's confession, he and JP were cooked like a couple 20-minute eggs. A round of backslaps and a chorus of "attaboys" was well deserved. Sergeant O'Brian of the Metropolitan Police had one of his agents drop Stump and Danville off at a quaint eatery for a late-night dinner of fish and chips.

While waiting for their meal, Stump glanced at the time. "It may be Friday night here," he said to his brother, but its 10:00 on Saturday morning back home. D'you know what that means?"

"Yeah, bro. Your graduation ceremony is just about over."

"Yep. If I'd taken my last tests, I would have my diploma now. My mom would have been proud of that."

"Get real, brother. You were the only person on the planet who figured out who really killed Mr. and Mrs. Clayton. That's a lot more important than a symbolic piece of paper."

"That's what I think, too, but nobody ever called me normal."

"Besides, we both know you'll talk the college into giving you make-up tests, so all you'll really miss is the ceremony."

"I hope so. We gotta get you a second chance too. I couldn't have done this without you." Stump's cell vibrated. "It's Myles. Probably calling to see how the graduation went. Hey, Myles. 'Sup?"

"Hello to you, too. I'm a little confused."

"'Bout what?"

"Katherine and I came all the way out to LA to surprise you and personally congratulate you for your accomplishment. We just sat through the entire service, but they never called your name. What happened?"

Stump sighed. "But you said you guys had other plans and weren't going to come."

"Like I said, we wanted to surprise you. Where are you? Can we meet you somewhere?"

"That isn't going to work for a couple days, Myles. I didn't take my last two finals, so I didn't graduate. I'm in London."

"London? London, England? I don't get it. Why would you work so hard for so long and get right to the finish line and then quit? That's not like you."

"I'm sorry you guys are disappointed, Myles, but I have a good excuse. Danville and I solved a double murder."

"What the hell are you talking about, Stump? You should be here celebrating."

"I would have liked that, Myles, but this was more important and nobody else was going to work it."

For the next five minutes, Stump spoke of the happenings on the boat, how he suspected that the authorities had misclassified the case and how he and Danville had proceeded. "I tried to get the detectives to reopen the case, but their evidence was a lot stronger than mine. It was either follow those guys or take a chance that the murderers would get away. Fortunately, we found their accomplice, who folded and corroborated it all."

Myles paused for a moment, then sighed and chuckled. "I should have known. I'm the only father ever to be both disappointed and proud at the same time—but mostly proud. So, when are you coming back? Katherine and I would like to see you before we go home."

"Our flight leaves in the morning. Considering the time zones, we should be to LA about seven p.m. and Carlsbad a couple hours after that. I could meet you the next day."

"How about lunch at Egg-Zaklee's?"

"That'll work. See you then."

Just then Stump's cell buzzed again. So did his hopes. "Hey, Michael, thank God you finally called. I was worried about you. Are you okay?"

"I'm fine. I just want you to hurry back, so I can spank you for leaving me."

"I didn't leave you, Michael. I wanted you to come with me. Remember?"

"Then you can spank me. The point is, I saw your texts. I'm proud of you and miss you. You deserve a personal reward."

While Stump was extremely happy that Michael was playful and okay, he couldn't ignore the alternating bouts of euphoria and anxiety that seemed to bounce around in Michael's head like a ping-pong ball. "I miss you, too, Michael. I miss you, too."

* * *

The next day, with the Zero Degree Murder in the past and a very long flight behind him, Stump hoped Michael's erratic behavior was over. He dropped off Danville and then hustled to the B&B where she enthusiastically met him at the door. "I'm glad you're home," she said, wrapping her arms around his neck.

"Me, too, Michael. I worry about you when you don't answer your phone."

"Oh, that," she said waving a hand in the air. "I was angry when you wanted to leave so abruptly, but I should have been more understanding. That kind of case always lights your fire."

"We had to stay right on the suspects' tails and the only way we could do that was to take the exact same flight they took."

"Yeah. I get it now. I'll make it up to you later, but for now, tell me about your case. Did JP and Kyle ever recognize you guys?"

Not completely satisfied with her explanation, Stump elected to wait and see how things played out before he shared her happiness. He threw his backpack over his shoulder. "There were a couple close calls, but before I tell you about it, would you mind ordering us some dinner while I clean up?"

"Uber? Sure. How does Italian sound?"

"Anything is okay, just so long as we're together."

"That's what I think, too."

After a quiet, dimly lit lasagna dinner, Michael's easy demeanor and usual sparkly eyes had returned. "I'm really sorry I've been so detached lately," she said. "I've been worrying about Daddy's heart and I don't get much time off to be with him. I shouldn't take out my woes on you."

"I get it," Stump said. "We both have had a lot on our plates lately. It's easy to overlook other people's feelings at times like that—which reminds me, Myles and Katherine want to meet us at Egg-Zaklee's tomorrow for lunch. I know you're tired of that place, but they haven't eaten there for over a year and still like it. After they leave, you and I can go spend some time with your father. He might need some help cleaning up."

"You've always been so thoughtful. That's just one of the reasons I fell in love with you."

Yeah, but sometimes love could be fickle.

76

I contacted my old friend, Myles Cooper, and discovered he was in town for his son's graduation. I was familiar with the young man. He had shown some serious crime solving potential and was the correct age. If he was half the man his father was, I could easily find a spot for him. "We've got a few more openings than we would like," I ultimately said in a conference room, "so we're looking for a few clean young recruits."

Cooper grinned. "Clean? Young? That leaves me out."

"Me, too, but the young ones have computer skills, second languages and new ideas. I understand your son is about to graduate. What is his plan? Any chance he'd like to join the LAPD?"

"I know he's considered it, but I don't think he's made any decisions yet. Eventually he might want to become a detective."

"What about undercover work or the other departments?"

"UC, huh? I don't know if he's ever considered that. Wouldn't it take a couple years just to apply for a position?"

"Ordinarily, but we've had openings in Narcotics, Vice and UC that we haven't been able to fill, and now that this Antifa group has sprung up, we might be able to show a little flexibility."

"Meaning?"

"Considering his accomplishments and his schooling, if he graduates from criminology college, we might be able to substitute his training for a couple months in the squad car. But it would still take 21 months before he'd be eligible to apply for detective or any of these other positions."

"Strange you should mention that, Allen. He was supposed to take his finals last week, but instead he took a sudden trip to London, where he solved a double murder. Now he's trying to make up a test so he can still get his degree. To be perfectly honest, I've always thought he'd make a good detective. He'd probably be good in UC work too, but he's resisted the idea of a uniform."

"Well, that's the only pathway to any of our positions. If I remember right, he's solved several major crimes already, right?"

"More like eight or ten, actually. A handful of murders, a fraud case, a cold case and he sent a serial rapist to prison. That's why I've always encouraged him to become a detective. Can you guarantee him a position after the 21 months?"

"No. I can't *guarantee* it because we're always on the lookout for experienced officers who might like to transfer from other districts and states. People with experience usually get the nod, but to be perfectly blunt, Myles, it would take a stream of those people to fill all the holes we've got, not to mention the new holes when guys like you and me trade our badges for golf clubs and other officers move up the chain."

"I can tell you this. If he comes on board, he is as loyal as they come. He's got good instincts and he's no quitter. I can't tell you how many times he's cut a class or put off his schoolwork to right an injustice of some kind."

"A young man like that would fit in almost anywhere. He'd have the grit to work in patrol, or the problem-solving capability to be a detective, but I also see the potential for undercover work where we could use somebody who is mentally nimble. Do you think he could do that?"

"It's possible. That's right up his alley. He's very clever—

can do pretty much anything he sets his mind to. That's why he's been solving crimes since he was a teenager."

"This sounds like a decent fit to me. We'd start him out just like everybody else. After a couple years, there might be some other options. I'm under the impression that you guys have a small family. Is that correct?"

Cooper grinned. "Yes and no. When he grew up, it was just him and his mother; then she died and he and I teamed up, along with my mother. When he turned 19, he met his biological father, a retired truck driver who lives in Wisconsin. A good man. Xander has a pretty good-sized family. One of Stump's half-brothers is in the same school with Stump, but a couple years behind him."

"Good enough. He doesn't have a wife or kids, does he?"

"No. He's got a nice girlfriend—a former Marine—but from what I've heard lately, they're having a little tension now."

"What about the negatives? He doesn't have a police record or anything like that, does he?"

"Nothing like that, but I'd say he's not a typical suit-and-tie guy and he doesn't get particularly impressive grades, but he's got excellent leadership qualities. I guess that wouldn't matter as much if he were undercover."

"Depends. I like what I'm hearing, Myles. I find that the people who get good grades also follow orders and make good employees, but independent people who don't particularly strive for somebody else's approval accomplish things on their own. That has value, too, especially in the peripheral departments or as a detective."

"That's him, alright. If he could get past the patrol phase, he might do well in any one of several places. We simply never talked about anything other than his becoming a detective. That's what he really wants to do."

"If you don't mind, I'd like to give him a call. I'm meeting with a few other young people soon. I'd like him to join us."

"Sure thing. I've got his number with me. He should be back in town tonight."

77

Just before noon the next morning, ignoring a little jetlag, Stump wandered over to Egg-Zaklee's and sipped a large glass of OJ while he waited for Myles and Katherine. It would have been nice if he could have concentrated on rescheduling his incomplete schoolwork, or his career path or the big crime he and Danville had just solved, but he couldn't get over Michael's recent rollercoaster ride. Down deep, he knew what the problem was, and it forced him to face ugly possibilities such as splitting up.

Half-way through the OJ, he finally saw the friendly faces he'd been waiting for. "Where's Michael?" Myles asked. "I thought she was going to join us."

Stump shrugged. "Her last guests just left and she wanted to clean up before leaving the house. She said she'd be here soon."

"I get that," Katherine said, pulling a wrapped present from within a canvas bag and handing it to Stump. "There's something depressing about returning to a messy house. I hope you like this."

"You guys didn't have to buy me anything," Stump said with a toothy smile. "Especially since I haven't technically graduated yet."

Myles grinned. "Just a technicality."

Stump nodded and slid a classy leathery book from inside the package. *"The Real History of New York City,"* Stump said, wondering if there was any relevance. "This will make a great coffee table book at the B&B."

Katherine pointed at the book. "Inside, there's a ten-day vacation package for two to New York."

"Really?" Stump found the envelope. "I've never been there. What a great idea. The book should have lots of suggestions. Thanks a lot."

"It expires in two years," Myles added. "You have to give it back if you don't graduate though."

"Fair enough. This is really nice of you guys."

While they used up their breakfast time, Stump spoke of his London adventure. "It cost me over $10,000, counting the last-minute round-trip tickets. I plan to ask the police to reimburse me."

"Sounds fair to me," Katherine said. "You basically solved the case for them."

"I wouldn't count on it," Myles said with a smirk on his face. "Those guys operate out of San Diego so it might be different there, but in LA the detectives usually have to get approval in advance for things like that."

"Figures. I'll ask anyway, just in case."

"Maybe the Clayton family will reimburse him," Katherine theorized.

"Speaking of the police," Myles added, "Yesterday, I met with Allen Padget, an old friend at the LAPD. He asked about your plans."

"There she is," Katherine said, pointing to the door where Michael walked in.

"Sorry I couldn't join you people earlier," Michael said, reaching out for Myles and then Katherine, "but I can't stand to have unfinished chores. How are you guys?"

Stump hoped the cheerfulness was not borne of little pills. Within minutes the conversation turned to Michael's father. Stump thumb-pointed out the window. "Michael and

327

I are going to visit him after bit. You guys can come with us if you want to."

"That sounds nice," Myles said, "but we already made plans to go to the beach before long."

* * *

"Are you okay, Daddy?" Michael asked Catts when they arrived. "You're walking more slowly than usual."

Stump had noticed the same thing, but he assumed it was simply a byproduct of aging.

"By the way, your fish has been spoiling my babies, you know," Catts said.

"To tell you the truth," Stump said, "we should have given more of the fish away when we first got home."

"Common mistake. The sooner you eat fish, the better, even if you freeze them. Another few weeks and most of the pusses won't want it—except Tubbs. He'll eat nearly anything."

"That's why he weighs 25 pounds, Daddy. He's as big as a dog."

"Speaking of fishing," Catts said to Stump, "Michael tells me congratulations are in order. Something about solving a murder that took place on your boat."

"Thanks. The police were the biggest challenge. They had some pretty strong evidence, but Michael and I thought some other guys did it."

Michael shook her head. "Don't give me any credit. I didn't notice that those two were acting differently from everybody else. That's all on you."

Stump turned to Catts. "That's because she was busy throwing some idiot overboard because he wouldn't leave her alone."

Catts grinned and pivoted toward Michael. "That's my girl."

"Something else literally *smelled fishy*," Stump added, "One of the perps walked away from his fish at the dock. It just didn't make sense."

"No kidding. I've been on a few of those boats and I've never seen anybody do anything like that."

"Even so, by the time I got to the police, they had already closed the case."

Michael patted Stump's arm. "So, he took his brother across the world and proved them wrong."

"That's when we found out the whole thing was about a lottery ticket that the victims purchased when they were in London."

"That's quite a story," Catts said. "There's no doubt that you're going into the right line of work."

"I'm getting tired," Michael said, rising. "Would you two mind if I go home?"

"You go ahead," Catts said.

"Don't go, Michael," Stump said. "We're enjoying your company. I could make some coffee."

"It's the middle of the afternoon. I don't want coffee."

"What's the matter? Does your wrist hurt again?"

"That and I'm tired."

"Do you want me to come with you?"

"No. And stop trying to make me feel guilty."

"Go ahead, honey.."

"Thank you, Daddy. At least you appreciate my feelings."

Stump waited for Michael to close the door behind her before he rose and then watched out the window while she walked across the street, and past the door to Egg-Zaklee's. As she pulled her cellphone from her purse and punched at the screen, Stump got a horrible sinking feeling.

78

Immediately after Myles and Katherine left town, Stump called the college, got an appointment and informed them why neither he nor Danville had been able to take their finals. As he'd done previous times, he was able to schedule makeup tests for both of them. The next day, he tested for Theories of Deviant Behavior and snagged a solid D+. His test for Advanced Sociology was scheduled for two weeks later, allowing more time to study. Until then, he had more pressing things to worry about. Michael, for instance.

She had canceled all her B&B appointments and essentially lost interest in the day-to-day operations. In addition, her personal grooming and routine housework had slipped. When Stump offered to pay for a cleaning service, Michael refused to allow strangers in her home.

Meanwhile, mood swings, erratic sleeping habits and secretive behavior were always close by. It didn't take a first-rate detective to know what was going on.

Stump recommended that she get professional help but rational words fell on deaf ears. Stump suspected it was only a matter of time until she got worse. Then what? He wondered if he could really leave her behind when she needed him most.

Still, he couldn't spend the rest of his life whiplashing back and forth from gloom to glee. If that train didn't turn around, and soon, he'd have to jump off—and once again he'd be alone, like he was when his mom died and when his first love dumped him and when Grandma Pauline no longer knew who he was. The voids were always agonizing, and it would be like that again.

Afraid to repeat the pain of the past and genuinely concerned for the only woman he'd loved so deeply, he continued to pit his fading hopes against Michael's mood swings and all they represented.

* * *

Somewhere between the black of night and the white of day lay the gray moments in which Stump rotated in and out of sleep. Eventually, his brain delivered him a reminder of a one-on-one meeting scheduled for later that morning with Captain Allen Padget of the LAPD.

But first, like a mother who instinctively checks on her children just to assure they are safe, Stump had an urge to gently foot-tap Michael under the covers. The probe exposed two distinct facts: first, Michael was not in bed; second, her side of the bed was still warm. He lifted his head and saw no light in the restroom.

He listened for noise downstairs and heard instead the ignition of a car just outside. He looked out the window just as Michael drove off. No note was left behind.

He mined his pants for his cell and speed-dialed her. A familiar grayness filled his mind as his call went unanswered. He considered going after her, but she clearly didn't wish to speak with him.

He recalled the previous evening when Michael had wanted to borrow some money. She hadn't done that until recently. Then she became offended when he asked her what it was for.

Now that he thought about it, nearly everything had

gotten weird lately, sex being an obvious example. By this time, they had lived together long enough to have some predictable comfort zones in the bedroom, but Michael had suddenly expanded the margins. On one recent occasion she took over like an insatiable nymphomaniac, but other times she just lumbered through the motions like a bored prostitute might do.

She developed other traits, such as sloppiness and glumness and laughing at unfunny things. Further, she had always been good with her money, but lately some of the tens and twenties had been disappearing from Stump's wallet. There was no doubt who was taking them. Stump didn't particularly care about the money, but down deep he knew what was behind it all.

Temporarily ignoring his misgivings, he took a shower and got dressed. Then he noticed that the book that Myles and Katherine had given him, along with the accompanying vacation package, was gone. What else could be missing?

A quick check of their gun locker confirmed that several guns had disappeared, including one that Stump had received from his grandfather. Saddened, he sighed and tapped at his cell phone.

The third pawnshop he called had both the guns and the envelope with the vacation package. It would take $480 to get it all back.

Another call to her cell went unanswered.

Finally, and just 15 minutes before Stump had to go to his appointment, he heard a car. Out the window Michael rose from the driver's seat and tucked her purse under her arm. Wearing the same clothes she had worn the night before, she lowered her head like a fullback and charged to the front door and into the foyer. "Sorry," she said as Stump moved toward her. "I had a terrible headache and had to get some medication."

"But you've been gone over an hour. You could have left me a note."

"I didn't think about it." Her eyes looked glassy.

"You didn't answer my calls either."

"So what? You're not my mother."

"If I was, I'd point out that your slacks are badly wrinkled and your hair is straight. You never go out like that."

"I told you I had a headache. If you want me to suffer—"

"That's not the issue, Michael. Also, the book and tickets that Myles gave me and some of our guns are gone."

"Maybe the guests stole them. Did you ever think of that? It serves you right for leaving those things lying around."

"It wasn't lying around. I put the book in a drawer."

"People know how to open drawers, you know."

"And other people go to pawn shops, Michael."

She hesitated for a moment. Then, "What's that supposed to mean?"

"You know what it means. Now I gotta pay $480 to get our things back."

"Well, you do whatever you want. I don't have time to argue with you. Now leave me alone."

79

Stump adjusted his new clip-on necktie and took his seat on the left side of the room. As one of eleven recruits who'd been invited to an afternoon meeting of potential LAPD police officers, he was the only male not wearing a sport coat or suit.

Sergeant Meagan Woodward spent the first couple hours discussing the Academy and day-to-day police work. If that had been Stump's only option, he probably wouldn't have gone to the meeting in the first place, but he hung around for the second speaker.

Sergeant Woodward introduced him. "This is Captain Allen Padget, a highly regarded and decorated officer, who will discuss some of the opportunities in the peripheral departments such as Narcotics and Vice. He has worked in that world for nearly 40 years, half in the streets and half in management. He might even share a few wild tales with you." She saluted the esteemed captain as he took the podium. The recruits applauded.

Stump instantly knew why Myles had spoken so highly of his friend. When a person respected lowly recruits enough to dress as if he were on his way to another officer's funeral, he set an example for everybody else around him. Every inch of the man, from the rim of his cap to the pleats in his slacks, reeked of authority. Stump wished he had worn something classier.

The captain carefully laid his hat on the lectern and looked from one recruit to the next. Then, "Before we root around in the weeds of the periphery departments, I want to point out that the officers of the LAPD today stand on the shoulders of those who came before them. There's an unspoken bond of people who would lay down their lives for the man or woman next to them, as well as the citizens they serve. If at any time, you find yourself unwilling to adopt those same principles, you may depart without admonition."

Wow! Mesmerized by this proud man, Stump nodded right along with everybody else.

"To begin with," the captain said, "let me point out that everybody, and I mean everybody, including God himself, has to go through the Academy and gather a minimum of two years of street experience before he or she will be eligible for a detective position or undercover work or any of the other options, such as SWAT. Who knows what SWAT stands for?"

"Special Weapons and Tactics," one of the men in the back said.

"That's correct. SWAT was created in the 1960s under the supervision of Inspector Daryl Gates. In some regards these brave men and women act like a fire department. They put in countless hours of training so that they can instantly deploy specialized or military equipment and end any terrorist-like threat. In 1969, they squelched a dangerous stand-off with the Black Panthers. In 1973, heavily armed left-wing guerrillas known as the Symbionese Liberation Army barricaded themselves in a house and threatened the community. Before it was over, all the radicals were killed while no officers or citizens were injured. I could cite other examples, but you get the drift. I've seen these people work. They are truly special, so it's not easy to get into that elite unit."

Now Stump understood why.

"Regarding some of the other departments, I can best

illustrate what they are like by sharing some personal experiences of my own and of others whom I've known. First, I'd like to tell you of some of my one-of-a-kind assignments. Once in a while, the department has special needs and seeks out the appropriate person for the job."

After several fascinating stories, the captain spoke of his earliest roles. "I spent years infiltrating the KKK and the Nazi party and other dangerous groups. I darn near killed a KKK member back in the '80s. If he's still alive, he's still limping."

"Good," a Latina said, while several others bobbed their heads in agreement.

After that he spoke of some amusing personal experiences in Vice. Stump particularly chuckled about a story of a former officer who kissed a bearded transvestite prostitute to prove he wasn't a policeman.

After sharing a few more personal experiences, the captain took a sip of water. "Are there any questions so far?"

"Yes, sir," an African American man said. "Have you ever had to kill anybody, and if so, what was that like?"

"Affirmative," the captain said. "When I was in patrol an armed man tried to rob a liquor store. My partner and I got the call and had to end the threat; I hated that I left the man's children with no father. Any other comments or questions?"

Stump waved a hand in the air. "I've been listening to your word choices. You never use the word 'cop.' Is that intentional?"

"Yes, sir, it is. I hold too much respect for anybody who'll lay down their lives for others to refer to them in slang terms."

"I have a question," said the woman next to Stump, "about K-9 units. Who trains them? I've always thought that would be interesting."

"You'll never see a stronger bond than that between a trainer and his or her canine. I know a former trainer who was separated from his animal 25 years ago and still mourns the loss. As you would guess, there are very few openings among that group."

A Hispanic male raised a hand. "I'm kinda interested in Narcotics," he said, as a few minor snickers interrupted him. "Oops, not for me, but as a department. Have you been involved in any big drug busts?"

"Yes, sir, but only from a supervision perspective. On one occasion we were part of a multi-jurisdictional, joint task force that intercepted a large drug shipment destined for LA. Upon further investigation we discovered a tunnel in a former KFC in Yuma County, Arizona. It was 22 feet deep and extended 600 feet to a residence on the other side of the border. Anybody else?"

"Yes, sir," another man asked from behind Stump. "What about motorcycle patrol?"

"Those openings are in high demand. You would likely need at least five years' experience to even be considered for an opening. Speaking of motorcycles," he said, smiling for the first time, "how would you like to hear about the only undercover opening that we haven't been able to fill for over 45 years?"

Stump sat up.

"I'm talking about infiltrating the Hell's Angels. These people are anything but angels. They peddle drugs and bombs and dynamite; they commit extortion and they kill people. As much as we'd like to end their reign of terror, there's no easy way to get on the inside of their gang.

"Anybody who expresses interest in joining their group —and they have plenty of candidates—must pay his dues. Their newcomers steal drugs or other things from anybody else including other biker clubs. The profits are turned over to the club. Over time a guy gets 'cred' if he performs his assigned tasks effectively.

"Part of the initiation is to bring in a lady they can pass around for an evening—prostitutes are common for that purpose but condoms are not.

"All along these bikers know there are certain things that undercover officers won't do, like commit violent crimes, so

337

new people are constantly told to rob liquor stores at gun point.

"If by some miracle an officer were to slither his way through that maze, he would want an elusive patch of approval that he can wear on his jacket because it is his ticket to attend meetings and vote on matters of interest.

"As stated, they know how to weed out pretenders. The last night before issuing the elusive patch, they tie the plebe to a tree. Then they bust open a couple kegs of beer and get drunk. When they have to pee, they pee on the plebe."

Several moans erupted from the audience.

"If they still doubt this person's authenticity," the captain proceeded, "they send him away from the main party and allow gang members to take turns performing sodomy on him. None of our fine officers have been willing to endure that kind of treatment, which is why we've never filled the opening."

Wow! If anybody else had told that story, Stump wouldn't have believed it, but he wouldn't dare doubt this particular officer.

80

"**I** bought a real nice ring here about a month ago," Stump said to the elderly jewelry store clerk. "Can I get a refund?"

The man pressed his necktie against his chest. "Is there something wrong with it?"

"No. It's just that our relationship is nearly over and we might have to split up."

"Sorry to hear that. I can give you a full store credit if you take something else, but when we make a custom ring and someone wants their money back, we can only refund 80% of the original price. Assuming the ring is still in pristine condition, we can issue a refund to your credit card or have a check ready within 24 hours. Do you have it with you?"

"I didn't bring it, but it's still like new." Saddened, Stump returned to his car and focused on Michael. He wouldn't ordinarily invade anybody's privacy, but he remembered seeing a set of parents on TV whose daughter died of a drug overdose. They both wept when they said all the signs were there, but they didn't confront their daughter because they didn't want to chase her away. For Stump, the take-away from that interview came from the sobbing mother. "If we had intervened," she said, "we might have saved our daughter's life."

Now Stump found himself in a similar situation because the day before he had observed a portion of a straw in the bathroom trashcan. A closer examination revealed some white powder on one end — seemingly from crushed OxyContin. When Stump confronted Michael, she said it was none of his business and left their home as she'd done other times.

Concerned for her safety, Stump authorized himself to check her Facebook page, her computer history and her email, where he found a couple dozen exchanges with some guy named Sean. Stump recognized the name. A couple years earlier when Stump and Michael were getting serious about their relationship, they both acknowledged having a past. Michael even mentioned somebody named Sean whom she worked for and with whom she'd had a short-term relationship.

If this was the same Sean and given some of the sophomoric code words they used, there was little doubt they were discussing drugs. It was at that point when Stump decided to approach Michael's father about a possible intervention before Michael got worse.

When it came time for that awful meeting, Stump wondered how one would tell a man that the woman they both love may be killing herself with prescription drugs.

"I'm really sorry to tell you this," Stump said as he and Catts sat down to talk, "but it's about Michael."

Catts grinned. "Is she leaving her clothes lying around again? She's always done that, ever since she was little girl."

"No, sir. It's much more serious than that."

Suddenly, Catts's face tightened and he grabbed for his left arm. "Oh no," he uttered past obvious pain as he slouched over the edge of his chair.

Stump rose quickly rushed to place a hand on his elderly friend's shoulder. "Are you okay, Catts? Are you okay?"

Getting no answer, he helped the man to the floor where he might be able to breathe better. "Hang in there, Catts. I'm calling 911 right now."

"9-1-1 operator," the woman said. *"What is your emergency?"*

"I think my friend is having a heart attack. We're at the cat museum in downtown Carlsbad. My name is Neal Randolph."

"Okay, sir. Paramedics are on the way. Until then, I'm going to tell you what to do. Is he lying down on his back?"

"Yes, please hurry."

"Expose his bare chest and place the heel of your hand right between his nipples."

"Ok. Got it."

"Using just the heel of your hand, you're going to press down firmly two inches, for thirty pumps at two pumps per second. I'll pace you. Are you ready?"

"Yes."

"Okay, pump, two, three, four," she said like a drill sergeant while Stump followed her directions to the number 30.

"Now do it again," she said for a second and then a third time. Ultimately, *"...twenty-eight, twenty-nine, thirty. Is he breathing, moving or coughing at all?"*

Stump shot a quick glance to Catt's chest and hands. "His fingers are curling. He's making a fist."

"Let's do it again. Palm between his nipples. Press down two inches. Pump, two, three, four..." Again, Stump did as he was told for two more groups of 30, scanning Catts's finger for any additional action. Then he heard sirens.

"I think I hear paramedics."

"Let's keep going until they take over."

A half-minute later, a gang of experts charged through the front door. One man was at Stump's side in a split second. "I got it now, sir."

Glad to have a pro take over, Stump sighed and backed up.

While the others attended to their duties, Stump called Michael, but she didn't answer. All he could do was leave her a voice message and follow that with an urgent text message.

By that time Catts was receiving fluids and oxygen and had been lifted onto a gurney. Paramedics rushed for the door and Stump followed.

Outside, police cars were flashing their reds and Danville had made his way to the scene.

Stump pointed to the museum and spoke to his brother. "Hold down the place. I'll call you when I know what's happening." He turned to the paramedics who had reached the ambulance. "I'm his son-in-law," he said, simplifying the truth so he could go along and answer any questions they might have.

* * *

A half-hour later, at the museum, the bulk of a street crowd had come and gone. A lone police car still reddened the surroundings while its two officers plus Danville and Yana kept an eye on Catts's building. Suddenly, Danville spotted Michael's SUV arriving across the street. "There she is," he said as she hustled toward them.

"What's going on?" Michael demanded of the officers from some twenty feet away. "Is Daddy okay?"

Danville approached her. "Stump said he left you messages. Your father had a heart attack."

"Oh, my God," she shrieked while mining her purse for her cell and turning it on to scan the messages. "Oh, my God. This is awful." She speed-dialed Stump, who immediately answered.

"*Hello, Michael¬*"

"What's going on, Stump? Is Daddy okay?"

"*I'm not exactly sure, Michael, but you better get here as quickly as you can. Have Danville drive if you need to.*"

Her shaky hands shot to the sides of her head. "Oh, my God. Oh, my God."

81

Stump had seen several corpses before, but he hadn't actually witnessed a death since his mother's passing nine years earlier. For the moment, nothing was official, but when Catts's fingers and fist went limp in the ambulance, it was fairly apparent that they had lost him.

Not willing to give up, the paramedics whisked Catts into the emergency room. Stump found a padded chair in the waiting area and sighed. Thankfully, his elderly friend had never learned that Michael was struggling with drugs.

As Stump sat there, a text message from Danville indicated that he and Michael were on their way.

Stump wondered how Michael would deal with the loss of her father—and how Stump would deal with Michael. He tried to convince himself that Catts's passing wouldn't drive Michael deeper into drugs, but he also knew the term, "pipe dream."

A few minutes later, Stump's teary eyes caught some movement in the doorway. Michael rushed into the room. "Any word?" she asked.

"Not yet," he said, electing not to voice his deeper suspicions.

"We got here as fast as we could, bro," Danville added.

Just then a white-coated man with a clipboard entered the

waiting room. "McFadden?" he asked, looking at Stump and Michael with stoical eyes.

Michael leapt toward the newcomer. "How is he? How's my daddy?"

The man paused a moment. "I'm Doctor Morton. I'm truly sorry, ma'am. We tried everything, but we couldn't save him."

Michael erupted into tears and deep sobs. She pounded Stump's chest with her fists. "You always treated him better than I did. You made me look bad. I hate you."

Stump grabbed her and held her. "No, Michael, you've got it all wrong. He was more proud of you than you'll ever know. I heard him say so many times. He loved you, Michael. Don't take that away from him."

That message seemed to calm her. She put her arms around him. "I lost Daddy, Stump. I lost my daddy."

Stump glanced at the doctor. "Can we see him?"

Several hours later, back home, Michael took a sleeping pill and went to bed without apologizing for attacking Stump.

While she hid from her sorrows, Danville and Stump imagined the days ahead. "What are you going to do about his cats and his building?" Danville asked.

"I'll have to ask Michael, but for now I'll feed them and clean up the boxes."

"I'll help you, bro. What about the B&B customers? Shouldn't you cancel those?"

"Michael already did that for other reasons. I think she'll have to make funeral arrangements too. I guess I'd better call Myles and our father with the news. They liked Catts, too."

"While you're doing that, I can call some shelters and see if they'll take the animals."

"Thanks. You know what's going to be really weird?"

"What's that, bro?"

"The cars in the basement of the museum," Stump said, thinking of the day that Catts said the city made him fill in the alley entrance to the basement garage. At the time, Catts still owned his last six cars, going back to the '50s and they

344

all still ran. Not willing to get rid of any of them, he left them in their respective spots in the subsurface garage and filled in the driveway as required, thereby entombing the vehicles for the rest of his life.

* * *

The next few days, Michael was a hot and hotter basket case; in between sleeping pill-induced naps she asked Stump to handle all the arrangements for the mortuary, the services and the military burial at the cemetery. Stump found himself praying that she'd avoid doing something drastic, like purposely overdosing.

Meanwhile he fed and cleaned up after three dozen cats and moved a handful of the younger ones into new homes, thanks to Danville and Craigslist.

When the day for the services arrived, Michael threatened to stay home. She'd already had three crying episodes that morning. "But you have to go, Michael," Stump said. "Your father deserves to have the person he loved the most in the front row. I'll help you as much as I can."

"Tell them I don't want an open casket. I couldn't take that."

"Of course, Michael. We discussed it. I've already told them that."

In the days following the funeral, Michael slipped into alternating moods. One moment she'd be hysterical, disappointed in herself and filled with guilt; the next moment she'd lash out at Stump because he'd pretended to be nice to her father and made her look bad.

Then she asked Stump a seemingly benign question. "What am I going to do with the museum building?"

"Don't worry about it, Michael. It's not that difficult to unload. I know a commercial real estate broker. He can sell it for us and you won't have to think about it again."

"Oh, my God. I can't believe how callous that sounds."

"I'm sorry if it sounded like that, Michael. I thought that you wanted to get rid of the building."

She sighed. "You're too young to understand how I feel."

"Hold it, Michael. You forget that I lost my mother to a fire and Grandma Pauline to dementia. I know what you're going through. I'm only trying to help you move on."

"That's different. You're a male. You can compartmentalize everything. But this is all that's left of Daddy's life and you talk about it as if it's just a matter of taking out the trash and starting over. I'm not ready to move on. I don't want to 'think about it'!"

* * *

Four days later and alone, Michael ransacked her purse in search of some powdered peace. Not finding what she wanted, she threw the purse on her bed and hustled into the bathroom, where she opened the medicine cabinet and reached for a white-capped bottle. A quick shake revealed it was empty. She threw it at the wall, rushed back into the bedroom for her purse and then her cell phone. A few taps at the screen and a man answered. "*Well, hello to you, old friend. What's up?*"

"Hi Sean. I need some help. Can you still get that *stuff*?"

82

"So what did you think of our meeting last week?" Captain Padget asked Stump. "Are you ready to join the LAPD?"

The day before, Stump had attended Catts's funeral. This was his first chance to think about something else. He tugged at his new sport coat. "I learned a lot. My father had mentioned some of those departments once in a while, but I didn't know about the Black Panthers and their standoff with the police."

"That's why we bring up these things, so you'll know the range of opportunities and appreciate the depth and quality of the people you'll be working with."

"I liked the idea of motorcycles and detectives, but it takes so long to get into those departments I'd sure like to have some assurance that I'd become a detective within a couple years."

"From what I've heard, you have already solved some cases so that's a good start, but we don't make any promises."

"I understand that. As you know, my father was a detective for a long time and he's always told me that I have the aptitude for it."

"I believe him, but there's a lot more to police work than aptitude. How do you feel when you solve a crime?"

A calm washed over Stump. It felt good to talk about something positive for a change. "Exhilarated. I get an adrenalin rush. Part of it has to do with problem solving. But most of it has to do with justice for victims."

"You don't have to be a detective to get that type of feeling. Officers in patrol experience that too—and they're not the only ones. What if I told you that your skill set is perfect for most of these other departments, too? Narcotics and undercover work are good examples. It's all about uncovering information, solving crimes and protecting victims, just like detectives do."

"I never gave those things much thought."

"That's my point, and why we invited you to that meeting. Based on what your father told me and all the people you've helped, I think you'd like patrol a lot more than you realize. After all, every victim has a problem that needs solved."

"I guess that's true."

"Of course, it is. What I'm trying to say is don't underestimate the gratification of patrol. After your first couple years you might like it more than you think. We have officers who wouldn't consider any other departments. At the same time, a lot of our officers end up taking career paths they never imagined in the beginning. I was like that. Something unexpected happened in my personal life and I needed a change. Before I knew it, I found myself infiltrating the KKK. That kind of transformation challenges all of your senses just as much as detective work."

"I have to admit, you know a lot more about it than I do."

"I'm glad we can broaden your perspective a bit. Now let me ask you a question. I understand you were right on the verge of graduating but then you heard about a murder and solved it. Why didn't you call the detectives in that district?"

"I did, but they had some strong conflicting evidence,

so they closed the case prematurely. I couldn't get them to re-open it, so I decided to do my own investigation. I had to go to London, with my brother. I call it the Zero Degree Murder because it temporarily cost me my diploma."

"That's clever. Did you share all this with the college administration?"

"Oh, yes. I even brought them a couple letters: one from the detectives who extradited the bad men, and one from the daughter of the two dead people. She is going to get several million dollars from a lotto ticket, but she was also very grateful to know that her parents didn't kill each other."

"I would expect so. What about the college?"

"They already let me take one make-up test and the other one is soon. But if I have to, I'll register for that one class again. My mother would have wanted me to do that."

The captain nodded. "I've heard about her from your father. She sounds like she was a very fine woman."

"Yes, sir. We may have been poor in some ways, but we were rich in other ways."

"I'm glad you recognize that. Let me ask you something else. Do you have any experience with firearms?"

"Yes, at first with Myles, but also with my biological father, Xander, and mostly with my girlfriend. She was an MP in the Marines. We've gone to shooting ranges quite a bit."

"I heard about her, too. How long have you been going together?"

"A little over two years, but to be perfectly honest with you, it's not working out very well, right now."

"Sorry to hear that."

"I probably shouldn't say anything, but I think she's addicted to pain meds. I've tried to help her, but she gets angry. I don't know how that will work out."

"Things like that can go either way." After glancing at the clock, the captain continued, "I'm going to have to wrap this up. I like the things you've accomplished on your own. That shows good leadership. Assuming you'd pass a very thorough background check, we'd love to have your application—that is, if you're willing to commit 100% to the job."

Stump shook his head. "I have to admit that you've confused me. When I came in here, I was certain I wanted to become a detective, but you've made some good points about patrol officers and those other departments. I'm still considering other ideas like moving to a smaller community or doing something completely different. Once in a while I think about being an advocate for seniors. I seem to get along with them pretty well."

"It's a good thing to have that many options. All I can tell you is this department would love to have you in our ranks."

83

After feeding Catts's remaining houseful of cats, Stump wanted to take a break before cleaning their litter boxes. He crossed the street, walked past Egg-Zaklee's and to the B&B. Inside, it smelled of flowers or a scented candle. A few steps through the foyer and into the living room exposed an unfamiliar, muscular man wearing a button-down shirt and jeans sitting on a couch with Michael.

"This is Sean Fleming," she said succinctly. "He's an old friend."

Stump noticed a refreshing hint of happiness, both in her tone and on her face. "Yeah. I think you've mentioned him before."

Sean rose and moved toward Stump with his hand extended. "I hear you're a future detective. Nice gig if you can get it." The condescension dripped off his tongue.

"I'm weighing my options." Stump turned toward Michael. "Remind me: How did you two meet? Marines?"

Michael and Sean traded glances. "Right after I got discharged, I was looking for a job and a friend told me that Sean had an opening at his microbrewery in Escondido."

"I needed an office manager," Sean said, "but before long, Michael was helping on the floor, too."

Michael smiled for the third or fourth time in a few minutes. "One evening I had to break up a fight."

Sean nodded. "She was good at that, too. We just hit it off."

"I called Sean about Daddy," Michael said.

"That's right. I live in Seattle now. Wasn't doing anything in particular so I thought I'd come down for a few days and cheer up an old friend." Once again, they traded happy looks. Too happy.

What a sham. After days and days of Michael's instability, Stump was supposed to believe that a cowboy rode in from the past and magically transformed her from an angry, weeping wreck into a happy-go-lucky care-free woman. "You don't fool me, Michael. You wouldn't have had this radical of a reversal if it weren't for some help."

"That's why I called Sean. He makes me feel better."

"No way, Michael. Admit it. Your 'old friend' here has brought you some brain-poison. I hope to hell it ain't heroin."

Michael's face tightened. "You think you're smart, but you're not."

"Okay, then. If you're feeling that much better, come help me with your father's cats. We need to clean the litter boxes."

"I can't abandon a friend after inviting him here."

"I call b.s. Sean just said he's going to be here a few days. If he's such a good friend, he can wait for you—or better yet, he can help us. That's what real friends do."

"Hold on there, Stump dude," Sean said. "I'm allergic to pet hair."

"How convenient for you. What about you, Michael? Am I going to get any help from you or not?"

"Maybe tomorrow, Stump. You can handle it until then. Besides, Sean has asked me to go to dinner."

"Just as 'friends,' Stump dude. Just two old friends talking about the past. We'll be back in a couple hours."

"Yeah, right. You guys must think I'm stupid."

Deeply suspicious that Sean was both a source for Michael's drugs and an old bed partner, Stump stomped up the street to the cat museum where he unconsciously cleaned litter boxes and muttered to himself for the better part of an hour.

When done, he went home, took a shower and waited for his girlfriend and her "old friend" to return as promised. Two hours passed and then three. Tormented, he could easily imagine them testing the mattress springs at a nearby hotel. That would end everything.

Finally, well past dark, they returned. Sean walked her to the porch where Stump opened the door and stared without saying a word. Michael and Sean looked at each other like they wanted to kiss, but Sean hugged her instead. "I'm glad you called me."

"Thanks for coming," Michael said as she withdrew from the hug. "You're the only person who knows how I feel."

Bullshit. Stump knew exactly how she felt. He'd lost loved ones too, only he didn't expect drugs or an old lover to heal his heartache.

"I gotta go," Sean said softly to Michael. "I'll call you tomorrow."

Stump held the door for Michael and waited for Sean to turn around before he closed the door. "All right, Michael, who is this guy?"

"None of your business. When you and I first met, we agreed that we each had a past and there was no benefit in grilling each other over the details."

"I watched your eyes, Michael—his too. This wasn't just a couple of friends going out to an innocent dinner. You guys had bedroom eyes."

"I don't have to explain it to you. We're not married, and I never promised you anything."

"Maybe not, but there was implied exclusivity."

"Ha. You may think so, but I sure as hell don't. Now I'm going to go out for a walk."

"That's crazy. If you're going to go off the deep end every time something bad happens to you, Michael, you'll never be stable. You need rehab before it's too late."

"Leave me alone," she snapped, yanking the front door open. "You're the one who's lost control."

While Stump stood there alone, two doors closed simultaneously: One was to the B&B; the other was to their future.

84

Other than when he was a kid, Stump had never spent the night on a couch, nor had he and Michael slept apart after he moved in with her. But all of that changed after Sean Fleming wedged himself between them.

Stump knew from first-hand experience that the people closest to addicts eventually had to choose between enabling the behavior or divorcing themselves from their addicted loved ones.

Stump wasn't about to help finance Michael's habit by lending her money or leaving his things around for her to pawn. But most importantly, he couldn't endure years and tears and fears of self-destruction and feigned contrition.

He had had way too much of that when his mother fought her addiction to alcohol. Either vice could eventually destroy a person, even kill them. Stories abounded of women and men who eventually used up all their resources to buy drugs and then ended up pimping themselves out to get high again.

If Stump couldn't prevent Michael from going down that road, he certainly wasn't going to accompany her.

Rubbing a stiff neck, he rose, walked to the foyer and climbed the stairway to their bedroom. At the landing he could hear Michael's muffled voice. Inside the bedroom he discovered she was behind the closed bathroom door and on the phone. "Okay," she said in a near whisper. "I'll see you then."

A half-hour later, she unceremoniously went for the front door. "I'm going out now. Don't know when I'll be back."

All Stump could do was wipe away the tears that formed in the corners of his eyes.

* * *

Fortunately, or unfortunately for Stump, depending on how he looked at it, he had some other things to think about. For instance, several dozen cats depended on him for their food and well-being. At Catts's place he carried out his routine and watched for Michael and her "friend" to reappear.

Just before noon, he returned to the B&B for a sandwich. Then when throwing a banana peel in the trash he noticed another partial straw. He couldn't help noting the irony: In a time of last straws, the only one Michael had left was made of paper and was used to snort drugs.

Finally, Michael drove up with Sean. "Sean wants me to go to Seattle with him for a few days," she said matter-of-factly.

"Of course, he does, Michael. You're an easy piece of ass to him because you're vulnerable right now. Don't you get that?"

"No way. We go way back. This time is different."

"This time? What do you mean by that?"

She glanced at Sean and back to Stump. "I tried to spare you the details but if you have to know, smart guy, you were correct. Sean and I were very, very close. We fell in love. One night we went to Vegas and got married—"

Sean raised a finger. "But I screwed up. I let another woman, a long-legged bitch who'd been leading me on, drag me away from Michael."

"So we had the marriage annulled."

"Biggest mistake I ever made," Sean said, shaking his head.

Stump slapped the table. "Oh, my God, Michael. You're his 'Plan B.' Can't you see that?"

"You're wrong, Stump. I'm sorry if you can't understand it, but Sean and I have always loved each other."

"I call b.s. You're just in love with his drugs, and he's taking advantage of you. If you can't see that, you're worse off than I thought. You gotta pick one or the other of us, Michael."

"I sure as hell wouldn't pick you. You don't trust me and you made me look bad in front of my father. I'll never forgive you for that. Why don't you just get out of my house before I call the cops?"

Flustered, Stump raised his voice to a near yell. "Suit yourself, Michael. I'm leaving all right and I'm giving you just 24 hours to change your mind. After that, there will be no going back. Got it?"

"Screw you, Stump. Get out. Get out. Get out!"

Stump stomped down the street to Egg-Zaklee's and up one flight to his brother's apartment, where he made arrangements to stay for a while.

Not long thereafter, he lay on Danville's couch, imagining Michael and Sean going into the bedroom. He knew the ritual. She would turn on the table lamp, close the curtains and turn off the overhead light, only this time Stump wasn't part of it.

She had been the greatest lover in his life, but she ripped out part of his heart and there was no way to fix it. If they were to make up, the drama could only get worse, especially if they were to ever have any children. There was only one thing to do: split up and stay that way forever.

He knew exactly what he had to do. First, he had to advise the health department that he was no longer in charge of the cats. Second, he could dull his regrets by focusing on his career. He would do that tomorrow.

Until then he had some weeping to do.

85

That next week the breakup with Michael brought Stump both new thoughts and familiar pain such as when his mother died. Once again it felt like he'd been stabbed in the heart. He couldn't eat. Sorrow gripped his days. Loneliness dominated his nights. He wept about his loss.

In the meantime, to put it all behind him he needed to move forward—into the career phase of his life.

He spoke at length with his brother and both dads. All the options were explored: traditional police departments, forensics and more. Throughout all of that, Myles made the most compelling case.

After a two to three-year apprenticeship in LAPD squad cars—and a ton of annoying paperwork—Stump could eventually snag a detective position and ultimately solve crimes as he always wanted to do. After that, he'd have a lot of respect, a good salary, paid vacations, opportunities for advancement and a retirement plan, much of which he didn't need.

It was all foretold way back in middle school before Stump had known that he had a knack for criminal justice. He'd been wading in that pool ever since.

He made his decision. He called Captain Padget to thank the wise man for his advice and to request a letter of recommendation that he could add to his application to the Academy.

During the call, Captain Padget reaffirmed there would be a criminal and background check. "Assuming there are no problems," he went on, "I can encourage HR to extend an invitation for you to enter the Academy as soon as possible. If all goes well, you'll be in your first class six weeks from now. Someday you just may infiltrate a group like Antifa or become one of our best detectives."

Ever appreciative for the man's support, Stump was grateful to have something positive to think about.

That afternoon, a moving van showed up at the B&B. Several stout men loaded up Michael's things and drove off.

The next morning, Danville said he'd found a shelter that would take all the cats from the museum. Then, a truck showed up and a For Sale sign found its way to the upstairs window of Catts's building. Curious, Stump went outside and looked back to the B&B.

As expected, a For Sale sign flagged that property, too. Michael clearly wanted to sell everything and disappear. Stump bowed his head. He knew he'd never see her again. As he'd done a lot lately, he asked God to look out for her.

Over the next few weeks, Stump got a physical, barely passed his final college test and waited for the LAPD to do their background checks. Then one afternoon when he and Danville were wasting time at the beach, Stump's cell buzzed. A text message from Yana indicated that a letter had come in for Stump. He was accepted into the Police Academy and was to report for his first day in three weeks.

* * *

On the afternoon preceding his first day at the Academy, he dropped by Captain Padget's office. Inside, dusty bookshelves had been emptied and the captain was placing the contents of his desk into a cardboard box.

Surprised, Stump asked the obvious question. "Hi there, Captain. Are you leaving?"

"Oh, hi, Mr. Randolph. Yes. That recruitment project was my final assignment. It's time for this old policeman to do some traveling while his body is still holding up. So, are you excited about joining the department?"

Stump nodded. "I guess so."

"You *guess so*? Usually our recruits are all buzzed up."

"I know. I basically knew it could take a while to become a detective, but I thought it was pretty much guaranteed. But when I heard that I'd have to wear uniforms and work in patrol cars until there was an opening, which could be years, it sounded like a lot of risk."

"I wouldn't worry about it too much. Sometimes, our people make detective right away."

"I know, but it's also possible that more-tenured officers want those same positions. Besides, I've never taken orders from anybody else. I've always acted independently. I've solved crimes, built a doggie park, saved some senior citizens—all without a boss looking over my shoulder. When I had to miss school to solve my problems, I didn't care. Solving the problem was more important than playing somebody else's game."

The captain paused, set his box down and pulled two chairs face to face. "Close the door and sit down. I have something to tell you in confidence."

Intrigued, Stump followed orders.

The captain looked Stump square in the face. "I know the people around here would love to have you, Mr. Randolph, and I know that you'd make a great officer if you put your mind to it, but you've always had apprehensions. If I'm not mistaken, you already have all the money you need. Is that correct?"

"Yes, sir. I have some mutual funds and I developed a commercial building in Carlsbad that generates some rent. Those things bring me all the income I need. It's not a lot of money, but I don't have many bills so it's enough to get by."

"I thought so," the captain said. He leaned toward Stump.

"Since this is my last day and I don't have to worry about much of anything any longer, I'm going to share something with you that I've only said to one other person in my entire career, that is, if you want to hear my opinion."

Of course, Stump did. He shifted in his seat.

86

THREE YEARS LATER

"We're upstairs from the breakfast place," Stump said to his caller. "You'll be here within 15 minutes."

As he disconnected, he heard the outer door open and a moment later his pregnant receptionist stuck her head in his office. "A woman wants to see you. I think it's your old girlfriend."

Stump didn't hear that kind of comment every day. "Send her in."

When the woman walked in, he smiled. "Michael McFadden. How are you?" he said, reaching for a hug. "It's great to see you."

"Hi, Stump. I wasn't sure you'd recognize me."

"Are you kidding? I could never forget you. You're looking good," he said, even though she had aged noticeably since the last time he saw her. "Have a seat."

"I like your mustache," she said as they sat on opposite sides of his desk.

He tugged at the tip. "This one is real."

"I was on the highway and decided to see if Egg-Zaklee's was still in business. I already talked with Yana and James. He told me you'd moved into the upper floors."

"True that. Now we have offices on this level and a couple nice apartments on the top floor. James and Yana live in one apartment with their two kids. Me and Holly—that was her in the reception area—live in the other one. In eight weeks, Sandi Jean Randolph will be born."

Michael smiled. "Congratulations on the baby and the marriage. I know you'll be a good daddy."

"It's a little scary."

"Holly must be really special. Too bad I can't find somebody," she said, holding up a ringless hand.

Stump recalled the ring he'd once bought for that very hand. "You're a good woman, Michael. Somebody will be lucky to marry you."

"I'll keep looking. How did you and Holly meet?"

"Holly and me? A fluke. One day I went to the doctor and she came in with an elderly woman. I found out that she voluntarily provided free rides for their elderly patients who needed it. Since I knew a little bit about helping elderly people, we traded stories and found out we had a lot in common. It went pretty fast from there. What about you, Michael? You seem to be walking with renewed resolve."

She sighed and rolled her eyes. "Finally doing better. I flailed around there for a while. Used drugs and alcohol to hide from my troubles and ultimately blew through half my money. Then I realized Sean was taking advantage of me, just like you said. I checked into a cheap motel and thought about killing myself. I cried and prayed and barely made it through that first night. The next day I got some help and made it through another day, then a few more and here I am."

Stump recalled all those prayers he'd made for Michael, wondered if there was a connection. "I'm glad you pulled through, Michael."

"Thank you. I haven't had any drugs or alcohol for nearly two years and I'm feeling pretty good. I got a job as a manager in an ice cream store. It doesn't pay a lot, but it keeps me out of trouble. That's enough about me. I noticed your sign out on the sidewalk. It says something about serving the community since 1988. What's that all about?"

"Well, that's an interesting story. After you and I split up I almost joined the LAPD. But Myles's friend, Lieutenant Padget, told me I was going into the Academy for the wrong reasons. He said since I didn't need the money, I should just become a private detective where I could work on cases I wanted without all the bureaucracy. The more I thought about it, the more I agreed."

"Makes sense. When we were on that boat, you observed some things that the detectives dismissed."

"Yeah. Since the police weren't helping Danville and me, that made us private investigators, but I didn't even realize it. In fact, when you and I first met, I wanted to find those coins and help my grandmother. The police didn't help with that, either. All of my successful cases went down that same way. I solved crimes that the police weren't working on."

"So, you just started up your own business? Just like that?"

"Not exactly. I went back to the woman I'd spoke with near Cardiff about becoming a PI. Come to find out, they wanted to sell their agency, so I sold some of my mutual funds and bought them out. She was stunned that I had the money, but it was from my trust. Most of her investigators moved here too. Myles said that the lady who gave me the trust money would have liked how it all worked out."

"Sounds like it."

"For the first two years I had to work under the supervision of the other PI's, but that's all over now, so I can work on anything I want. Myles was correct when he said Lieutenant Padget knew his stuff. He was the one who figured out that my personality was better suited to being a 'private' detective than a 'police' detective."

"I'm happy for you, Stump. What kind of cases do you take?"

"There are four other investigators here—three men and one woman. They work on crimes and cheating spouses, insurance claims, missing persons, things like that, but I just stick with crimes that the police department has set aside. A few of them are pro bono, especially when elderly people are involved."

She smiled. "I'm not surprised. You've always liked helping seniors."

"I learn things from them."

She sighed, and then looked him right in the eyes. "I'm sorry I did you wrong, Stump. I'm very ashamed for the way I ended it all. You didn't deserve that."

"Well," he said, shrugging, "You were having a really tough time after your father died. I knew that. It was understandable."

"No, it isn't. Everybody has deaths in their families, but they don't deal with it by taking drugs and being mean to the people who love them. Can you ever forgive me?"

"Absolutely, Michael. You were vulnerable and not thinking clearly. It happens. The important thing is you're doing better now. You said you were driving by. Do you live near here?"

"No. I've got a place east of LA. I was just down here visiting an old friend." She glanced at her cell. "Well, I gotta get going, Stump. It was nice to see you again."

"For me too, Michael. Before you leave let me introduce you to my wife."

On the way out, "Holly," Stump said. "Meet Michael McFadden. I've told you about her before."

Holly rose from behind a receptionist desk. "You sure did. It's so nice to meet the woman who threw a smarty pants out of a boat. I wish all women could do that?"

Michael chuckled. "Well, thanks. I just had more training than most women get. You're a lucky woman, too. To have a nice family, I mean."

"It can be challenging sometimes, but it's worth it. Can we talk you into staying for dinner? It's nothing fancy but—"

"Thanks anyway, but I have to get to work, I just thought I'd stop by and see how everybody was doing."

A couple minutes later, Stump stood at his window looking toward the street when Holly returned to his office. "You know why she was here, don't you?"

"Just to say hi."

"It's more than that. She wanted you back."

He looked back outside. "I don't think so. The last time we spoke I told her I could never—"

"Trust me. She was testing the waters. And I could tell that you still have feelings for her."

"Well, if I lied to you, you would see right through me."

"You got that right, so do you still have feelings for her or not?"

"When you live with somebody a few years, you get awfully close to them and their families. So, I guess I still care about her on some level."

"I'd be ashamed of you if you didn't."

Stump touched his wife's lips. "As it works out, she was just a side road to the woman I'd been looking for all my life: you."

Holly kissed him on the cheek. "Good answer."

Just then another person walked in. "I have a package for Neal Randolph."

"It must be the new sign I bought for outside the door." Stump opened the box and showed the sign to his wife. She read it out loud.

Neal Randolph
Private Detective

ABOUT THE AUTHOR

Like most Americans I liked my career of several decades but I have to admit that I didn't always approach the mornings with wild enthusiasm.

But then, I retired and discovered something I never would have guessed: When the day is mine, I love to get up even earlier. Now I'm the guy who wakes up the rooster. I still work as much as I ever did, only I now work on things that bring me a different form of compensation. Like writing books.

Some have asked me where I get my ideas, but it's no mystery. I had a storied youth with six sisters and a wild family. When I wasn't engulfed in that world, I spent a fair amount of my time wandering the alleys and streets of our neighborhood. A fellow learns a lot from all of those people even before he arrives for his first day of school. If he has the ability to recall the characters and the activities in which they engaged, and blend that with a dash of make-believe, there's a goldmine full of fodder from which to draw his inspiration.

BOOKS BY THIS AUTHOR

NON-FICTION

Instant Experience for Real Estate Agents
(Multiple Award Winner)

Stop Flushing Your Money Down the Drain
(Multiple Award Winner)

FICTION

Three Deadly Twins
(Available on Amazon)

Monday's Revenge
(Available on Amazon)

Grandma's BFF Does Coke
(Available on Amazon)

Zero Degree Murder
(Available on Amazon)

Miranda, In the Wind
(Coming in 2020)

All books available in paperback or ebooks

**Books may be ordered from
Amazon or other online bookstores**

CPSIA information can be obtained
at www.ICGtesting.com
Printed in the USA
LVHW041245290720
661831LV00001B/61